The King of the Fallen

by David Dalglish

BOOKS BY DAVID DALGLISH

THE HALF-ORC SERIES
The Weight of Blood
The Cost of Betrayal
The Death of Promises
The Shadows of Grace
A Sliver of Redemption
The Prison of Angels
The King of the Vile
The King of the Fallen

THE SHADOWDANCE SERIES
Cloak and Spider (novella)
A Dance of Cloaks
A Dance of Blades
A Dance of Mirrors
A Dance of Shadows
A Dance of Ghosts
A Dance of Chaos

THE PALADINS
Night of Wolves
Clash of Faiths
The Old Ways
The Broken Pieces

THE BREAKING WORLD
Dawn of Swords
Wrath of Lions
Blood of Gods

THE SERAPHIM TRILOGY
Skyborn
Fireborn
Shadowborn

THE KEEPERS TRILOGY
Soulkeeper
Ravencaller
Voidbreaker (Jan 2021)

A recap of The King of the Vile for those who need it:

An army of beast-men crossed the Rigon River in hopes of conquering land of their own beyond the infertile and cursed Vile Wedge. They laid siege to the North, whose lord begs for help from the capital city of Mordeina. Help, however, is not immediate in coming, despite Harruq Tun's best efforts in his role as steward to the boy king, Gregory Copernus.

After the collapse of the flying city of Avlimar, and the rebuilding of the golden city of Devlimar, the angels that now rule Mordan are split into two factions. Ahaesarus leads one faction that would remain subservient to human rule, and wishes to help the innocent civilians in the North. Azariah, however, no longer believes sinful humanity should retain control, and would instead fly south to battle the army of King Bram Henley of the southern nation of Ker, who has invaded in an attempt to overthrow angelic rule. While the angels bicker, the Paladin Jessilynn and elven Scoutmaster Dieredon helm a desperate defense of the Castle of the Yellow Rose, but it looks grim. Without help from the angels, there will be no survival.

Meanwhile Azariah brings the people of Mordeina into Devlimar, and upon his golden throne, he declares himself their new king. It does not go as planned. From the crowd emerges an unknown, unimportant farmer named Alric. He gives voice to Ashhur's rage, and orders the angels to fall. And so they fall, their bodies twisted and sapped of color, their wings blackened, their teeth turned to jagged, broken fangs. Azariah himself is anointed with a crown of bone growing from his forehead. Furious, the fallen descend upon all humans within the surrounding miles, slaughtering without mercy in an event known as the Night of Black Wings.

Harruq and his family fight the fallen angels, successfully protecting their friends and family as well as rescuing king Gregory from their clutches. Once outside the city, they reunite with the Paladins Jerico and Lathaar, who have been protecting villages as best they can against the fallen. The reunions continue,

The King of the Fallen

this time with the surprise arrival of the wizard they thought dead, Tarlak Eschaton.

Tarlak, like the rest of Dezrel, had not been having a good time. Having woken up imprisoned by the Council of Mages, he was given a choice by Roand the Flame, the Council's leader: join the organization or be executed. Deciding he liked living, Tarlak obeyed while still working out a plan to escape. Part of that plan involved defeating a mage trainee, Cecil Towerborn, in a duel upon the bridge connecting the two towers. He then froze Cecil's body in secret, and in his final, successful escape plan, projected his soul into the body while his original form was vaporized by one of Roand's contraptions. Now in Cecil's body, he freed the also imprisoned Deathmask, killed Roand, and together they fled back to Mordeina…just in time to discover it conquered by the fallen.

Deathmask remained behind, eager to find Veliana and work to slay Azariah as punishment for Azariah blaming the collapse of the golden city of Avlimar on him and his Ash Guild. Tarlak used his magic to locate Harruq and Aurelia, opened a portal, and rejoined them in a jovial meeting ruined only by the fact that he was still in Cecil's body. Finally reunited at last, the Eschaton Mercenaries debated a future plan for the people of Mordan, but their only conclusion was that things were, to put it mildly, royally fucked.

To consolidate his rule, Azariah takes his fallen south, to the retreating army of King Bram. Bram is slain, though his wife Loreina survives to rebuild Ker's defenses. Amid the army of Ker lurk Paladins of Karak, and they are all too eager to join forces with the fallen king if it leads to a newfound spiritual awakening across Mordan – one where Karak is treated equal, if not superior, to the god Ashhur.

Meanwhile Ahaesarus and his angels still loyal to Ashhur arrive too late to the Castle of the Yellow Rose. All but Dieredon and Jessilynn are dead. Taking Darius's sword for his own, Ahaesarus forces the beast-men into servitude, declaring himself their king. They will aid him in defeating Azariah, and in return, he will grant them a land of their own. So begins the third Gods' War, waged between the King of the Vile and the King of the

Fallen. But the story doesn't start there. It starts far to the south, at Ashhur's Sanctuary tucked into the Elethan Mountains…

Prologue

The great halls of Mordeina's castle surrounded Bernard Ulath. Corpses hung from the rafters. Blood covered the myriad paintings. The beautiful mosaic carpet had been burned away to reveal cold, gray stone.

Bernard walked among the dead, and his faith withered. This shouldn't be. He had fought this fight before. He touched the living dead chained to the walls, his fingertips banishing the foul necrotic magic that give them life. They shattered into dust, but there were just so many, and ahead loomed the throne room.

"Choose another," Bernard said. "Please, a younger man. A stronger man. Have I not sacrificed enough?"

The throne room's doors were closed. A dozen men and women hung naked above it. Chains looped about their wrists and forearms to keep them upright. They were dead, but still they writhed and wailed.

There will be death.

Ashhur's words, but why? What did they mean? And why did Ashhur yearn so deeply for Bernard to speak them?

"I can't," he said, not even certain what he refused, only knowing that the burden was far more than he could bear.

He clapped his hands together, banishing the hanging bodies to dust. He would listen to no more of their wailing. With them silenced, he pushed open the doors. Melorak stood waiting before the throne. The pale imitation of Karak's Prophet spread his arms wide as if in greeting. His robes were deep black, his visage a slowly shifting combination of a thousand different faces.

There will be bloodshed.

"Welcome back," Melorak said. "It's been so long, priest."

"I killed you," Bernard said. "You exist only in the fires of the Abyss."

"That's the trick about Dezrel. Dead things have a habit of not staying dead."

The entire castle shook as if the foundation of the world was furious.

But it won't be in my name.

"Not in *your* name?" Melorak asked, somehow hearing the voice as well. His maggot-filled grin spread wide. "Then who carries the guilt? Who suffers the blame, priest? It can't be me. It can't be my god. After all...we lost. You defeated us. You won."

The stone cracked. The walls of the castle crumbled. Bernard grabbed Melorak's wrist and flooded his rotten form with the power of his faith, just as he had five years ago. It burned away the body. It banished his necrotic soul. It did nothing to cease the breaking of the world.

One final word blasted apart the castle, the surrounding city, and all the rest of the nightmare that haunted Bernard. One word ended the dream, bringing him back to the waking world.

FALL!

Bernard sat up in bed and grumbled. The night was still deep, but he doubted he could fall back asleep if he tried. For a week straight he'd endured that exact same dream, and always it ended with that final cry to *fall*. It wasn't the first time someone had heard that foreboding pronouncement. Every priest within the Sanctuary had heard the words, the denial of death and bloodshed, and the final cry. Every syllable had seemed to shake the stone walls of their home. What exactly it meant, the priests debated fervently, each idea more frightening than the last. So far, they had no answers, only theories.

"We could send someone to Mordeina to ask the angels," one of his fellow priests had suggested. "Azariah might know what such a pronouncement means."

None had dared go, for they all shared the same deep-seeded fear: what if Azariah had been the target of Ashhur's rage? The command to fall echoed the fate of Avlimar, which led many to wonder if it had collapsed at Ashhur's hand and not the hands of an interloper, as was first believed.

Bernard slid his feet into his slippers, doing his best to dismiss such thoughts. The night was cold, so he wrapped a thin blanket about himself as he exited his room. Sometimes the Sanctuary felt claustrophobic, and this was one of those times. He walked the quiet halls, remembering a time not so long ago when younger priests in training would be scrubbing the stones, replacing candles, and preparing the next morning's meal. Now there were no new trainees, no new young class striving to replace the men and women walking the original path.

What need was there of priests and priestesses, whose prayers Ashhur did not answer, when the sky above was marked by the flight of angels?

The stone hallway was silent. He passed flickering candles and approached the front door. Bernard removed the metal bar locking it shut, followed by the wood block across the center. The door was a recent addition, and not just by the ancient Sanctuary's standards. Qurrah Tun had broken the first, and then its replacement had been claimed by fire during the second Gods' War.

"Not exactly better days," Bernard chuckled. "But certainly more interesting ones."

He'd not been there for either of those events, given his station in Mordeina at the time, but the Sanctuary's previous head priest, Keziel, had been eager to regale him with the tale when Bernard settled into the Sanctuary some five years ago. Old age had claimed the man's lungs only two years prior.

A foul burn settled into Bernard's throat as he exited the holy building. There had been a time he could have prayed over the dying priest's chest and cleaned away the illness clogging his lungs and denying him air. That power had faded from him, and from all of Ashhur's priests, after the war god's death and Ashhur's apparent turning of his gaze from Dezrel so he might rest with his beloved Celestia.

What need was there of his prayers, he thought again bitterly, when Ashhur's angels guarded the skies?

The forest had recovered nicely from the blaze that had claimed much of the surrounding woodland. He walked along the forest edge, enjoying the sound of the leaves rustling in the breeze while observing the beauty of the night sky. A long walk was his preferred method for soothing restless dreams, had been ever since he was a young man.

Tonight, though, there would be no relief, for an angel approached from the north. Bernard crossed his arms and waited, unsure of why he was suddenly so nervous. He held no reason...no reason, but for the dreams, and the phantom cry to fall.

The angel neared, closer and closer, yet his wings remained dark. A trick of the moonlight, Bernard prayed. Far better than the unknown alternatives. He resumed his walk back to the Sanctuary's entrance, keeping just beyond the trees to ensure the angel would notice him during his approach.

The angel descended from the sky, confirming all of Bernard's fears.

"What fate has befallen your children?" Bernard whispered. This was no trick of the moonlight. The angel's skin was ashen, his feathers withered and black, his robes dull instead of white and lustrous. His armor, once a vibrant gold, now looked twisted and crafted with bone and tar. Bernard clenched his hands into fists. In his mind, he felt the presence of a power that had been gone for him for five long years. That it would awaken now, of all times...

"Who flies before me?" Bernard called out. "You bear not the red wings of Thulos's war demons, yet neither do you bear the white of Ashhur."

"A friend, if one is still willing to listen to reason and accept offered wisdom," the angel replied. He lowered to hover a half-dozen feet above Bernard's head. A spear was strapped to his back, its edge jagged and stained with dried blood.

"I would not judge you by appearances alone, but I fear Ashhur's grace may no longer be with you, angel. What wisdom might you offer me?"

The angel's calm smile flickered momentarily. In the brief drop of the facade, Bernard saw a seething ugliness, a rage that defied reason.

"My name is Raegar, and I bring the wisdom of one who has walked the verdant lands of eternity. I bring the wisdom of a soldier who fought at the vanguard of the oldest war. Karak and Ashhur, brothers once, brothers still. They were enemies in a time forgotten to all but us, and we seek an understanding that would join their beliefs and desires to recreate the land of Paradise. Would you listen, priest, or are you beholden to old ways that now descend into irrelevance?"

The King of the Fallen

Bernard felt a stirring inside his chest, familiar as the dawn, once comforting, now terrifying. He dared not dwell on it. His hands shook. The faintest shimmer, like captured moonlight, glinted in the corners of his vision.

"What might you tell me that I would not dismiss outright?" he asked. He stared up at this being, once a beautiful creation, now stolen of all that had once been beautiful or noble. "I watched Karak burn the world. I witnessed the destruction unleashed by the horde of undead created by his prophet. If you would speak to me of peace with Karak, then I will hear none of it. Be gone from here, angel, and take your heresy with you."

The burning in his chest grew. A presence settled over his shoulders like unseen, comforting hands. If this angel noticed, he did not speak of it.

"Old men and women hiding in a mountain at the end of the world," said Raegar. "I should not be surprised you are too set in your ways to listen. I will spare you the lessons, if you are content to remain absent from our reborn Paradise, but only if you cooperate. I seek the boy king, and I have reason to believe he might be hidden here at Ashhur's Sanctuary. Is he with you, priest? Do you hide him within your walls?"

The angel had been stripped of Ashhur's presence, and now he hunted the rightful heir to the throne of Mordan? Bernard did not know what transpired in Mordeina, but he feared the absolute worst. He met Raegar's gaze and let the weight of his every single year upon Dezrel carry in his voice.

"Whether he is here or not, I will not answer you. My god has cast you aside. We faithful heard his words throughout all of Dezrel. It has pervaded our dreams. It has haunted our waking steps. The command was clear, and I see it in your withered wings. Fall, Ashhur demanded of you, and I see it true before me. You may fly through the air, but your souls crawl through the muck. Begone from here, angel. I fear not your reprisal, nor your wisdom."

Raegar removed the spear from his back and flipped it so its point aimed downward.

"I will search your halls for the boy king," he said. "And if I have to do it over your corpses, then so be it."

Bernard could never hope to defeat the angel through physical means, yet he did not attempt to flee. Instead, he stood perfectly still, the burning in his chest fully consuming him with such power that there was no room for disbelief. His prayers would no longer go unanswered. Ashhur had returned to him, and it was his familiar voice that whispered in his ears.

My eyes are open, and I am ready. If there must be war, let there be war. I stand with my faithful.

There had been a time when his god's presence had comforted him, but not like this. Not when the words he spoke were the embodiment of rage. Bernard lifted his hands; shimmering wisps of light sparked off his fingertips.

"Now they open," he said, and he looked up to the fallen angel. "But at what cost?"

Raegar dove with his spear leading, moonlight shining off its jagged tip. From within the center of Bernard's raised palms rolled a blinding shield of purest light. The spear's metal tip shattered on impact. The twisted bone shaft cracked and split down the middle. The fallen's momentum ceased, and he hovered in mid-air, paralyzed by light, clutching his ruined weapon. Amid it all flowed a deep, distant song, like a choir singing a single stubborn note.

"I faced the culmination of Karak's rotten faith," Bernard said, the shield of light slowly pulsing in rhythm with his heart. "I stood against the Prophet. I broke the corpse of Melorak and denied his hold over his undead dragon. But you, you wretched angel? You are but a pale shadow. I will hear nothing of your wisdom. My ears are closed to your lies."

The shield rolled outward, brighter, stronger. Swirling lines throughout it sparkled like lightning, enveloping his foe's body with a sudden, booming cry. Bernard watched with stoic silence, though inwardly he trembled. This power he felt...it was far beyond anything he had wielded in the second Gods' War. This awakened magic, this new fury, was terrifying in its intensity. The fallen angel's body, already ashen and withered, crumpled away like so much banished dust. Not a shred of it remained that was not blown apart upon the wind.

Bernard lowered his hands, ending the prayer. With the fallen angel's death, and the darkness that followed the banishment of his shield, the priest dropped to his knees and wept.

"Must you ask this of me?" he begged the cold night air. "Must you ask this of *us?* We held no need of your magic, if only we believed your kind gaze still fell upon us. Instead you give us this. Your faithful have fallen. Your angels cry out for slaughter."

Bernard wept for Dezrel. He wept for her children. And yes, shameful as he felt to admit it, he wept for himself.

When his tears were fully shed, he returned inside. He packed what belongings he could carry into a rucksack and bid goodbye to the rest of the priests. When pressed for an explanation, he told them only of what he had seen, and of the curse that had befallen Ashhur's chosen. As for his own path, he remained silent. To even speak it risked breaking the trance that had overcome him. By the time the sun rose, he was already on the road east, the Sanctuary a fading mirage of stone towers carved into the base of the Elethan mountains.

Bernard settled for the night alongside the northern edge of the Corinth River, which he'd been following eastward for the past few days. Nothing outwardly told him to stop there, but he could not have continued even if he wanted. A presence lingered in that empty stretch of grass, heavier than any stone. He set his pack down, and after only a quick search, found the remnants of a campfire.

"You were here, weren't you?" he whispered.

Creating a fire with a snap of one's fingers was a wizard's trick. Thankfully Bernard had a small wooden tinderbox, and after a few minutes of scrounging up twigs and dry grass, he used the flint to light a new campfire. He tended it carefully, content to stare into the growing flames as the sun set and the night came.

"Who were you?" he asked the silence. "Was it a blessing Ashhur granted you, or a curse?"

He had expected no answer from the night, but it gave him one nonetheless. The stars shifted in the sky above. A man emerged from the mud and filth of the nearby river. His clothes shimmered with a ghostly light. Bernard stared at the phantom, overwhelmed with pity and shame. This man, he appeared so plain, his hands calloused, his skin tanned from long hours in the sun. His dark hair was long, disheveled, and matted to his face from a frantic swim across the Corinth.

"If I must," this unknown ghost of a man said as he staggered over the riverbank. "Ashhur help me, if I must."

"Must you?" Bernard asked the ancient memory walking across grass that did not bend at its touch. "Forgive me, stranger. Forgive me, if you are still alive to offer that forgiveness."

These dreams he endured were not the first to haunt his nights with prophetic power. Months prior, the nightmares had begun. He had walked through streets of crystal and gold, surrounded on all sides by a teeming mass of people. It was the earthbound city of the angels, Devlimar, that he knew from his previous visit. This dreamlike version had been different, though. The way the light sparkled off the crystal felt drained, hollow. The gold shone with no luster. The people around him weren't joyous or uplifted, but terrified.

In that dream, Bernard had pushed through to the front of a crowd. A great throne awaited him, resting atop a dais wrapped in red silk. From the sky descended a shadowed man, his eyes white portals, his shoulders hunched, his wings ragged and black. He sat upon the throne, and as his body hunched upon it with a heavy burden, a silver crown had formed about his head. Upon witnessing that crown, Bernard had cried out, and the nightmare trembled, so close to breaking yet refusing to release him. Not yet. The image was not yet finished.

The red dais melted like ice beneath a summer sun. The silk turned to blood. The golden throne became one of bone. This shadowed man lifted a jagged scepter. The ground rumbled and the crystal buildings collapsed into shards. As the sun and moon danced backwards in the sky, Bernard had stepped before this wretched king and lifted his arms to the heavens. He had drawn in a breath, and from his chest boomed out a single word of condemnation.

He never remembered the word. He never remembered the destruction that followed. Bernard had always awakened, soaked with sweat and sobbing uncontrollably. For weeks, he had endured that nightmare. For weeks, he had told himself he was merely getting old and struggling with memories of war. Gods had sundered his homeland, and he had lost so many beloved friends and family, why wouldn't he still bear the mental scars? Dreams, he insisted. No one else at the Sanctuary endured anything similar. Meaningless dreams.

Except...

Bernard watched this phantom stranger lurch north. There was no question his direction. Devlimar. The city of the angels.

One night a few weeks past, Bernard had awoken from the dream and staggered to the side of his bed. He'd clutched his hands together in prayer and given in to his shame. He pleaded for Ashhur to spare him. He begged for an end to the dreams, and that the cup be passed to another. He had fought his war. He had endured the wrath of Karak's followers. Let him die peacefully within the Sanctuary. Let the struggles of the road, and the condemnation of prophets, be given to another man. Never before had he felt so weak, so ashamed of himself, but the task felt too grand for his weary shoulders to bear.

And so Ashhur had done exactly that.

"I'm sorry," Bernard said, and he fell to his knees and bowed his head as the stranger faded into the night. "I'm so sorry. The path you walked was mine. Forgive my cowardice. Forgive my fear."

When the dreams had stopped, and quiet days resumed, Bernard had told himself those dreams had meant nothing. They were lingering guilt, delusions, or a future never meant to be. And then all of Ashhur's faithful had heard those words, felt their every syllable deep in their bones. Then came the new dreams. Then came the fallen angels, the shadows of their black wings falling upon the Sanctuary.

"I don't know who you were," Bernard whispered to the dirt. "I don't know why you were chosen above all others, but I do know why you were chosen over *me*. You were brave when I was not. You were willing to act when I sought to hide. You cried out against the rot while I closed my eyes and prayed it was only an illusion. For what strength I have left, I promise to make amends. I feel the rage, blessed stranger. Soon Ashhur's betrayers shall feel it, too."

All too easy to make promises after the mistake was made and the damage done, but Bernard could not change the past. He could only determine his future.

The campfire before him dwindled, the stars shifted again, and he felt the heavy weight pass as the moment ended. The night was quiet, and without memory or magic. He removed his bedroll, laid it out beside the fire, and succumbed to a fitful sleep, one blessedly lacking in dreams.

When he awoke that next morning, Bernard scattered the ashes of the fire, drank the last of his water, and began his trek north. Into Paradise. Into the land of fallen angels.

1

Azariah slowly paced the circle of stones lying atop the bare floor. The angel had twisted this room at the very top of a tower for this very purpose. He'd had his undead rip up the carpet and haul out every piece of furniture to make space for rows and rows of bookshelves to line the walls. High above the wretched human city, Azariah would turn it into a place of wisdom and power. A place of magic.

"Thirteen stones," he whispered, taking in each and every stone with satisfaction. Blue-silver runes were carved into their tops. "Thirteen stones, thirteen runes, thirteen words of power. You had many faults, Celestia, but the structure of your magic was inspired."

The angel had to relearn much about the nature of arcane magic. Over the centuries, he'd grown to view it as confused and inelegant compared to divine magic, the flowing nature of the prayers required to draw power from Karak and Ashhur. The verbal components twisted the tongue, forcing spidery phrases and guttural barks tangled amidst one another. Now, was he starting to appreciate their construction again, as he had the first time the gods had clashed.

Pulling in power from Celestia's Weave was a complicated and dangerous prospect. Everything required an exact understanding, and the long phrases and syllables were all meant to convey an extreme amount of knowledge and control in a very short time. Simplicity, Azariah remembered, did not always mean best.

A knock at the door broke his concentration. Azariah didn't need to ask who was there. He'd carved a simple scrying spell into the deep wood, allowing him immediate knowledge. With each passing moment his connection to the Weave grew, filling in the absence of divine power Ashhur had once granted him.

Thinking of his once-beloved deity set a frown to the fallen angel's face. He pushed the thought aside and opened the door to greet Judarius, his newly appointed Executor.

"I pray this matter is urgent," Judarius said. He stood at the top of the spiraling stairs that wound their way around the outside of the tower before halting at the chamber door. His gray wings were folded behind him, his face covered but for two eye slits in an obsidian mask that matched the black hue of his platemail. He'd commissioned it from one of Mordeina's smiths shortly after they'd been cursed. The sight of gold seemed too painful a reminder of what they'd once been, before Ashhur's great betrayal. Azariah knew part of it was also to hide Judarius's newly changed face. The wounds were too fresh. Hopefully in time, the rest of his brethren would learn to accept their new physical nature.

"I need you to wait here for my return," Azariah explained as he stepped away from the door. "If I do not, you must assume command of the city before any confusion or chaos may result."

Judarius ducked low, his wings folding even tighter to fit through the doorway. The room was more than large enough, given humanity's tendency to exhibit wealth by sheer size of occupied space, but doorways were still designed for mortals instead of their heavenly kind.

"I don't need to be told how to keep order," Judarius said. He frowned at the circle of stones. "And what spell are you attempting that puts your life in such danger?"

Azariah suppressed a smile. Though the interior of his lips had hardened and calloused significantly, the spreading of his flesh across his sharp teeth still risked drawing blood.

"It is not the spell that puts me in danger, but where I go. My intent is not to stay long, but complications may arise, especially if the veil is still weak and torn."

"Veil?" asked Judarius. "Speak plainly. Where are you going?"

Azariah turned to the thirteen stones, each one a little beacon in his mind.

"To where it all began."

He raised his arms, extended his palms to the ceiling, and began whispering the words. They were simple and short but needed to be repeated multiple times to build up the energy required to create a portal. He could summon a weaker one without need of runes and extensive preparation, but that would only take him so many miles. To open a portal all the way to the other side of the continent was a far greater feat.

Upon the thirteenth repetition, he shouted the final syllable while thrusting his arms downward. The glowing light of the runes leapt from the stones and into a tiny blue tear in space hovering in their center. It grew larger, larger, and then ripped open entirely to create a passageway to Veldaren's long-abandoned throne room.

Excitement swelled in the pit of Azariah's stomach. He'd debated traveling there many times since Thulos's death, but he'd never wished to be absent from Mordan for so long, not during those formative years, and certainly not now with Ahaesarus and the Godslayer attempting to destroy all he'd accomplished and bring the world back into chaos. But as his magic grew, so too did his bravery.

My mind has been locked to my wings and the divine magics for too many centuries, he thought, stepping into the portal. *I must begin embracing the new. And the old.*

The sensation that struck his mind was of striding through a door. On one side was the cold dark stone of his tower; on the other was the grand hall that had been the throne room of dozens of kings since the first day of humanity's creation. Azariah's mind recoiled against the sudden change, along with the heavy, distorted sensation of traversing great distances in a blink. Effects of traveling via portal, the fallen angel knew. He closed his eyes and endured until they passed.

The vertigo ceased. He stood to his full height, stretched his wings, and looked about the ruins. The curtains and carpet were burned to ash. The doors leading to side halls were broken on their hinges. What had been fine portraits of former kings were now twisted bare frames hanging from exposed nails. The throne itself was missing, and Azariah wondered what the occupying orcs had done with it. Only one part matched the pristine glory Azariah remembered, and that was the great painting on the wall behind the throne.

No fire, blade, or magic had succeeded in tarnishing its color. It portrayed the brother gods, Karak and Ashhur, stepping from a grand portal into a land of plenty, marked by green fields and tall mountains shining gold in the sun. The goddess greeted them in her human form of pale skin, solid black eyes, and dark hair wrapping about her waist on its way to her ankles. Her pointed star, representing her divine form, pierced the blue sky above like a second sun. Azariah approached the painting, his footfalls echoing like thunder in the silent hall.

"We followed you," Azariah whispered to the brother gods. Memories of a time before humans, before Dezrel, flitted like fireflies inside his mind. "When the war god destroyed our homes, you offered us escape. We came with you to Dezrel. We came with a promise of a better world. When you gave life to humanity under Celestia's gaze, and named us their Wardens, we were honored. Let these frail little children know nothing of disease and death, you each decreed. Let them learn from the words of the divine. You would walk among them, let them hear your words, and teach them a way that meant hard work. They harvesting fields cyclical in their life and death, living in little villages knowing only friendship and peace."

Azariah put his hand against Ashhur's painted hand, the colorless gray of his skin a stark contrast to the vibrant bronze of the deity's. Tears flowed from his eyes, and they itched upon his skin until he wiped them away.

"We raised them to have no need of sin," he said. "We did all we could, and yet humanity would never have it. Their failures spread. Their imperfection took hold. Each of you succumbed to it, I understand now. It was never Ashhur the glorious good and Karak the sinful evil. You were two brothers who, in their desire to perfect their children, adopted their children's imperfections without ever realizing it."

He struck a fist against the painting.

"We were their Wardens, meant to protect humanity from all dangers, but how do you protect humanity from itself? How do you root out that deep need to destroy oneself? It's in them all, each and every one. I feel it like a thousand thorns jabbing into my mind! This ravenous hunger for sin. This inability to accept peace, and love, to think of others beyond the importance of oneself. No wonder it broke you. No wonder you warred, confused and conflicted as to how your perfect creations broke so thoroughly within a perfectly crafted world."

Azariah took in a shuddering breath. With each day in charge of the remnants of humanity he took on a greater understanding of that ancient war. As a Warden, it'd seemed so simple. He was the warrior for the side of righteousness. Karak was his foe, and therefore his servants were to be defeated. If only the world could remain so simple, but its children viewed things in such a naïve way, not the wise.

"Perhaps you hate us now," he said to the portrait of Ashhur. "Perhaps you consider us a betrayal to your beliefs…but know we will ever strive for what you started, only we will do it with our eyes open to the faults and failures of humanity."

Azariah turned his back to the three deities. The swirling blue portal he'd created remained hovering in the air, the image of Judarius on the other side worryingly thin and faded. Silently, he berated himself. He'd allowed his emotions to distract from his purpose. If the spell broke due to his incompetence, it'd be a very, very long flight back home to Devlimar.

A loud clang broke the silence, followed by shouts. Azariah listened for the source. Down one of the side passages, it sounded like the slamming of another door. As for the voices themselves, they were deep and guttural, speaking a language of which he possessed only passing knowledge.

"Celestia's cursed are playing house in Karak's once grand castle," the fallen angel said, and shook his head as he laughed. "It seems both brother gods suffer humiliation and defeat. Perhaps you escape the cursed visage we now bear, Karak, but you are humbled all the same."

His chatter seemed to alert his sudden guests. Clanging steel rang out, along with a boisterous cry. Azariah crossed his arms, amused by the orcs' lack of concern. And why should they show concern? Veldaren was theirs, and barring a few stubborn pockets of resistance, so was the entire eastern half of Dezrel.

"Welcome," Azariah said as two half-naked orcs barged into the room. They looked decidedly drunk. One held an ax in both hands while the other wielded a sword in one and a giant tankard in the other. A foul brown substance sloshed across the floor when the orc pointed the tankard at him and shouted in the human tongue.

"What the shit're you?"

Azariah spread his pale wings to their fullest extent, ran his fingers across the horns growing from his skull that created his ever-painful crown. He smiled, paying no heed to the little trickle of blood it sent down his teeth and across his tongue. The fear cutting through their drunken stupor was far too amusing.

"I am your guest," he said. "Will you not offer me a drink?"

The two howled, either not understanding or not feeling particularly generous. They raised their weapons and charged. No caution. No guarded approach. Just a mad run to overwhelm him with strength and steel. It was almost worth another laugh.

Azariah pulled his wings tight against him and stayed grounded, deciding he should at least keep things fair. He outstretched his right hand, fingers curling into a specific shape to convey the rune needed to command the energy he pulled from Celestia's Weave. Words passed over his tongue, feeling more and more natural with each attempt. Fire grew in his palm, a blazing seed held above his skin with little red streaks of electricity. With but a thought it flew toward the orcs, striking the stone just before their feet.

Flame exploded in all directions in a perfectly controlled ring. It washed over both orcs, blackening huge swathes of their gray skin and knocking the closer of the two off his feet. The other howled in pain and fury but continued to charge. Commendable, really, the willpower to endure. A swift death without pain, Azariah decided. That is what such concentration deserved.

The orc crossed the distance, sword raised high and ready to cleave the fallen from shoulder to hip. Azariah waited, his muscles tense. The moment the orc swung, he shifted to one side, his left wing beating to push him back another foot. The sword cut the air, missing by inches.

The King of the Fallen

Azariah's hand shot out, grabbing the orc by his meaty neck. The orc looked baffled as he pulled his sword back for another swing. Another spell enacted, and the power flowed out Azariah's fingers with a satisfying surge. Electricity poured into the orc's throat, traveling throughout his body. His muscles tightened. His jaw clenched shut and his eyes exploded. Another jolt, stronger, fiercer, scorching the hapless thing's mind.

The orc's body collapsed. His sword clanged against the stone, released from its owner's limp hand.

"Demon," the other orc spat as he struggled to his feet. The left side of his face was horribly charred, along with much of his upper body. Blood more oozed than bled from sections of his exposed muscles and ribs.

"No, not demon," Azariah said, thinking of the red-winged servants of Thulos. "We resemble something else on this broken little world."

He whispered the words of another spell, one he had yet to try. Purple sparks swirled around his fingers, materializing into an invisible hand clutching the orc and lifting him a foot above the ground. The orc shrieked in pain from the pressure on his scorched flesh. Azariah stepped closer, soaking in every detail. The pallid color of the orc's skin. The unhealthy hanging of his ears. His twisted teeth, seemingly angled and sharpened to cause as much pain to the orc as any potential prey. Revolting, absolutely revolting.

"You were beautiful once," Azariah said. "As were we. Elf and angel. Orc and fallen. To think you are what Ashhur would have us become."

Azariah slammed both his wrists together and bathed him in fire. He blackened and peeled away every inch of the cursed flesh, reducing it to bones and ash that collapsed to the floor in a scattered mess.

"It seems a theme of this world," Azariah said. He crossed the hall, the interlopers already gone from his mind. "The loved becoming the cursed and despised. The elves, cursed into these ugly gray orcs. Your angels, ordered to fall. But there was another who was before us, first in many ways upon Dezrel."

His footfalls released heavy echoes. A smile stretched his lips when he spotted the artifact he sought, lying forgotten in the far corner of the room.

"Do you hate him still?" Azariah said, kneeling beside the small, seemingly innocuous book. Seeing it still there, unharmed and intact, flooded him with relief. "I wonder that myself. For centuries I thought I knew, but now I fear the First Man was also the first to understood the true impossibility of our task."

Through the spells, the orcs, and the fire, the journal had survived. When the war god's forces set foot upon Dezrel, it'd been discarded and forgotten, its purpose served. The knowledge remained, once blasphemous and hated, but now…

Now Azariah held the worn journal of Jacob Eveningstar, First Man granted life by the brother gods, the one who betrayed Ashhur and took the name Velixar. Azariah flipped through the pages, examining its tight scrawl. Passages of spells stood out to him among the notes. There were so many. Attempts to understand madness, to break down a mind and rebuild it in different ways. As if Velixar could rebuild humanity in a manner that would remove their impulsive need to sin. Azariah discovered spells to control the undead, manipulating them in ways the angel was only beginning to understand. Passages on Celestia and her strange, absent role in guiding history through the occasional intervention of her Daughters of Balance.

One spell in particular stood out most, the spine of the journal sorely bent to naturally lead one to its location. Bits of ash licked the page, but to the fallen angel's great relief, they did not obscure the words.

"You opened a door to a world of war and destruction." Azariah stroked the page with reverence. "But there are other worlds. Better worlds."

He closed the book and tucked it underneath his arm. His portal was growing weaker by the second. He could read and memorize later, in the comfort of his tower chamber. Quickening his steps, he stepped through, enduring the terrible wave of nausea and vertigo. It assaulted him much stronger now than during the first trip, and he fell to one knee, simultaneously gagging and coughing once he exited. Judarius hurried to his side, his clumsy

The King of the Fallen

steps scattering the thirteen stones and closing the portal with a loud hiss of air.

"Was your mission a success?" his brother asked.

In answer, Azariah held aloft the book.

"It is time we dream a far grander dream," he said. "For if Dezrel is our prison, I have obtained the key."

2

Tarlak frowned at his reflection in the creek, squinting as if doing so might smooth the faint ripples across its surface.

"Does this look like the right color to you?" he asked, beckoning Harruq closer. "More red? Less red? Or maybe the yellow tint isn't quite proper. Of course, I'm not pure and total red. I'd look like Jerico if I was."

Harruq stared at him, his confused gaze enough to tell Tarlak that his friend had no idea what he was talking about.

"How do you not know the color of your own hair?" the half-orc asked.

"Because I've spent the majority of my life with it on my head and not in front of my face," Tarlak snapped. "Speaking of face, I'm still worried about my nose. Is it too pointy? I think it's too pointy."

Harruq rolled his eyes and refused to comment. Tarlak had spent the past day constantly tweaking his features with the polymorph spell he'd crafted during his time imprisoned within the Council towers. Though his body might have belonged to Cecil Towerborn, Tarlak was determined to shape and change every single bloody part of it back into the glorious red-haired wizard he had once been. The problem was, nothing ever felt or looked quite right. Sure, to everyone else he looked like his old self, but the feeling was always there, like a particularly bothersome itch.

"I don't get why you're so determined to look exactly like your old self," Harruq said. "If you're willing to change your nose and eyes and face and hair, why not try to improve it? Make yourself even more handsome or something?"

Tarlak lifted an eyebrow. "Are you saying it is possible for me to be *more* handsome than I already am?"

"Forget it," Harruq said, waving his hands in surrender. "Pretend I didn't ask."

"But you did. I heard you. And I won't forget this horrible betrayal of friendship and character."

His friend already had his back to him, returning to the village they'd camped at for the night. The half-orc lifted his right hand, forming an obscene gesture.

"Love you too, Tar," Harruq shouted over his shoulder. "And hurry up. The paladins are waiting."

Tarlak returned to staring at the creek. On second thought, maybe his nose wasn't too pointy after all. But then why was he so convinced it was off?

You know why.

Tarlak sighed. Enough fiddling with his facial features. There were matters of slightly more importance to attend. First and foremost, saying goodbye to the two paladins. He splashed the surface of the water with his palm to distort his reflection and then hurried across the field.

While the hundreds of refugees from the Night of Black Wings had gathered in the village's streets and homes, his surviving Eschaton camped just to the south, hoping for some measure of privacy as they planned out their actions for the next few weeks. Tarlak approached with arms crossed over his chest to keep his fingers from fidgeting. He'd developed a bad fidgeting habit since escaping the Council, much to his displeasure. Yet another thing to reinforce the notion that his stolen body was not his own. Which it wasn't. But that was beside the point.

Jerico and Lathaar waited side by side, with the little King Gregory between them. The boy had his arms wrapped around Jerico's leg. He looked thoroughly worried. Harruq sat with his wife, bouncing a happy Aullienna on his knee. Waiting nearby were three more paladins, the younger students Tarlak didn't recognize and whose names he had not bothered to learn.

"I see the whole gang is here," Tarlak said when he strolled up. "Well, save for Qurrah and Tessanna. Did they go off to cause more mischief?"

He winced inwardly at the anger that his own lighthearted jest caused him.

"They're down by the river," Harruq told him with a frown. "Staring at the stars or something."

"Auntie Tess doesn't like goodbyes," Aubrienna added.

"Ah, yes," said Tarlak. "But not the rest of you. Did you say your own tearful goodbyes already?"

"Already done while you were doing...whatever it was you were doing at the creek," Jerico said.

"Important facial reconstruction."

"Sure," Lathaar said. "We'll accept that. So how close can you get us to the Citadel?"

"It depends," Tarlak said. "I should be able to cross a good fifty miles or so for you, if I push myself. Or you could wait a day for me to do the required rune carving to make a more powerful portal. With that, I can put you right on your Citadel's doorstep."

The two stared at him blankly.

"Why didn't you start on that last night when we decided to escort Aullienna and Gregory there?" Lathaar asked.

Tarlak shrugged. "Because I didn't think to start on it until you just asked. Sorry. Been a little preoccupied, what with remaking a stolen body after escaping from certain death at the Council towers. I'm going to point out Aurelia over there is equally as capable of this as yours truly."

"Enough, enough," Jerico said, cutting him off. "Ashhur help us, you whine more than a child. We have no time to wait for you to prepare a stronger portal, so send us as far as you can."

"Safely," Lathaar added.

Tarlak shook his head, put his back to them, and began moving his arms in a circle.

"Shave a little piece of your faith in Ashhur off to spare for me, would you?" he said. "I've only helped save the world."

"You're right, Jerico," Lathaar chuckled. "He *does* whine more like a child when you really start paying attention."

Tarlak yanked his arms downward, ripping a blue portal into existence with a loud hissing intake of air.

"Be glad I'm fond of you two," he said with a glare. "Otherwise this portal would send you high, high above the Gihon River."

Tarlak realized Gregory was watching him with wide eyes and immediately brightened. He smiled at the boy while dropping to one knee. A twirl of his hand and a little silver coin appeared between his thumb and forefinger. He offered it to the little king.

"This coin here is incredibly good luck," he said. "I've never once had a bad thing happen to me in my entire life while carrying it. Times are tough though, so…do you think you can hold this for me, Gregory? Keep it nice and protected?"

Gregory snatched the coin and held it against his chest.

"I will," he said with the seriousness of a man accepting a lifelong quest.

"Excellent. I'll sleep much better at night knowing you're guarding over it."

Tarlak stepped away and nodded at each of the paladins.

"Stay safe, all right?" he said. "And keep our little king here safe, too."

"Ashhur watch over you," Lathaar said. He clapped Tarlak across the shoulder. "And do not worry about us. Of all the places on Dezrel, the Citadel is the safest and most holy place to Ashhur. Azariah and his fallen angels won't stand a chance if they try to break inside."

Except the original Citadel had been destroyed and the paladins within wiped out years ago. Tarlak decided that might be a bad point to bring up. It might spoil the goodbyes.

Harruq lifted Aubrienna into his arms as he stood, and together he and Aurelia whispered their parting words. Lathaar, meanwhile, took little Gregory by the hand.

"It's nothing scary," he told the lad as they approached the portal. "Just a single step, that's all."

Gregory said nothing, only nodded. Tarlak admired his courage. For how young he was, his behavior should have been similar to others of his age, at least by Tarlak's understanding: whiny, annoying, and often a brat. Poor kid. Like many in Dezrel, he was about to grow up infinitely faster than the previous generations.

Lathaar and Gregory hopped into the portal on the count of three. Tarlak felt a twinge in his forehead, similar to a headache, as more power flowed out of him and into the spell to keep the portal open. The three paladin trainees were next, each bowing in respect before entering. After that was Aubrienna, who proudly declared she would enter on her own. Harruq and Aurelia kissed their daughter's cheek, then stood hand in hand, watching the elven girl sprint through the portal. Jerico, the last to enter, hesitated.

"I know I'm supposed to be the hopeful one," Jerico said. His tone had changed. More worried. Almost embarrassed with its seriousness. "But I can't stay blind to the obvious. Azariah's angels will come to the Citadel eventually."

"It's still safer than roaming the countryside with us," Tarlak said. "He'll at least be in a defensible position."

"That's not what I'm trying to tell you," Jerico said. He glanced at Harruq and Aurelia. "We're one of Ashhur's last few loyal bastions, and Azariah's twisted mind won't leave us be. He'll want to convert us or destroy us. Of that, I'm certain. We'll be a tough nut to crack, and given all the other threats to his rule, I'm praying he decides to save us for last."

Tarlak made a face. "I sense a 'but' here, and one you expect me to solve."

Jerico chuckled. "But if Azariah realizes the boy isn't with the rest of the Mordeina refugees, he'll begin wondering where else he might be, and it won't take him long to focus on us. There is no escape from the Rebuilt Citadel. No secret tunnels, no hidden waterways. Should he besiege us, it will only be a matter of time, which means you can't let him do so. You *must* convince that fallen bastard that Gregory is still here with you."

"Oh, sure, give me all the difficult and likely magic-involving tasks," Tarlak said.

Jerico thudded a hand into Tarlak's breast.

"Hey, I'm going to join my friend and pupils in a stand against the fallen that will likely cost all of us our lives," he said. "Not everyone gets the easy tasks."

"Well, I guess much is required of those who know what they're doing," Tarlak said, smiling. "Don't worry. I already have a plan in mind to keep Azariah's attention locked on us."

"I couldn't ask for more." The paladin looked to the portal. "If the fallen lay siege to the Citadel, I will assume it means your efforts here failed. We won't expect rescue, and we won't let the children be taken. I do not want to imagine the life they might lead in Azariah's hands."

"We understand," Aurelia said, even though saying the words clearly pained her.

"Don't lose your hope yet," Harruq said. He grinned as if he could force his cheer to become infectious. "We've endured worse."

"That seems our rallying cry these days," Jerico said, brushing aside his red hair and turning to the portal. "We've endured worse. We've succeeded against far more dire odds. I'm not sure what hope I find in knowing how terrible and bloody all our lives have been. I'd rather be reminded there's a world worth saving that isn't so preoccupied with murdering one another."

Tarlak remained silent. Let the paladin have his moment of quiet doubt. On the other side of that portal he'd be teacher and instructor to the paladins under his tutelage. There'd be no chance to show the cracks in his armor there. Harruq stepped up, and he put a hand on the paladin's shoulder. Jerico patted it once, accepting the quiet confidence, and then strode through the portal amidst a crackle of energy. Tarlak immediately closed it, returning the field to silence. The wizard crossed his arms and frowned.

"Well, shit," he said. "That was depressing."

The world most often is.

"I don't like it any better than you do," Harruq said. "You're sure you can keep Azariah fooled with your illusions?"

"If he scries for Gregory, or even Aubrienna, he'll see them at our sides," Tarlak said. "Trust me, I don't make mistakes, not when the lives of those kids are on the line. They'll be safe at the Citadel, or at the least a whole lot safer than marching alongside us to war. Keep your focus on the fallen, and on killing a whole bunch of them with your shiny black swords."

Aurelia slid her hand into Harruq's and leaned her smaller frame against him.

"And we do trust you," she said. "Please do not mistake our worry as doubt over your abilities. There is nothing rational in fear."

"Nor is there anything irrational about worrying what that psycho angel in charge of Mordeina might do," Tarlak said. "Trust me, no offense taken. Now that this matter is settled, there's an even larger one at hand. Where do we go from here?"

Since the Night of Black Wings, the survivors had relied on Harruq to guide them. Not a surprise, given that he was the storied Godslayer that had saved Dezrel from Thulos's reign. Harruq, on the other hand, hated every second of it and deferred to Tarlak and Aurelia as often as possible.

"There really only seems like two options," the half-orc said. "North or south, and I'm not a fan of either."

"South takes us to Ker, who has shown no love for the angels," Aurelia said.

"A long trip," Tarlak said. "And one that will take us through the land of several recently deceased lords."

"Which means their replacements should aid us," Harruq tried arguing.

Tarlak shrugged, not necessarily buying that logic. Loyalty to the boy king would go far, as would disgust at the thousands killed during the Night of Black Wings. On the other hand, if the lords felt that they faced a single choice between annihilation and bending the knee to Azariah, well...it wasn't hard to blame any who decided it better to keep their subjects alive. Not that it'd make things all that much more palpable should they be betrayed.

"On the bright side," Tarlak muttered, "If we *are* betrayed, then it'll end this whole rebellion thing before we put too much effort into it."

Good job, a voice echoed in his mind. *Brilliant reasoning.*

Harruq crossed his arms and stared at the empty space where the portal had just been. It was as if he were trying to see through it, to where Aubrienna now traveled.

"The other option is that we curve northeast," he said. "We skirt Mordeina and link up with Ahaesarus and the angels he took into the northern lands."

"Assuming Ahaesarus didn't suffer the same fate as the rest," Tarlak said.

"A big assumption, I know," the half-orc admitted. "But we won't win this war without the angels, I think we can all agree on that."

"Why not go for both options?" Tarlak suggested. "Take all who can fight north. Those who can't, we send them south. Ker is a land free of angels, after all. The people's path would also take them near the Sanctuary, and I believe the priests there would offer people aid."

"We were at war with Ker before Azariah performed his coup," Aurelia said. "Are you sure safety can be found there?"

Harruq threw his hands into the air. "Where exactly *is* safe in this world?"

Good point.

"Good point."

Tarlak winced as if stung. Harruq noticed, and his frustration melted into concern.

"Hey, are you all right?" he asked. "If you're stretching yourself too thin, it's fine if you…"

"I'm fine," Tarlak snapped, immediately regretting his tone. "Seriously, Harruq, I'm…I'm all good. It was a rough few weeks trapped in the tower, that's all."

Neither Harruq nor Aurelia looked convinced, but they thankfully honored Tarlak's unspoken request for privacy.

"Just don't push yourself too hard, all right?" Aurelia said. "We'll need you at your best if we're to have any hope for victory."

Tarlak waved her off, having no desire to argue, not with the elf, and not with himself. The thought of wandering through the noisy, chaotic mess of people, tents, and homes made him physically ill, so instead he returned to the stream. He could use some rest. Some silent meditation, that was all he needed.

Taking in a deep breath, Tarlak slumped beside the muddy edge of the water with his legs crossed beneath him. He set his hands on his knees, closed his eyes, and pretended all the worries of the world were, far, far away.

But they're not far away, Tarlak. You know that, don't you?

Rage built inside Tarlak's chest. No, no, no. He wasn't hearing that. He wasn't feeling that.

"You're just my imagination," he muttered. "A tired, overactive imagination, that's all."

Denial is only going to make this worse. That, and have me enjoy this so much more than I already am.

"You're...not...real!" Tarlak screamed. His fists beat against his knees. His teeth gritted in frustration. He opened his eyes, and when he looked at his reflection he did not see long red hair and lightly tanned skin. Instead he saw Cecil Towerborn smirking up at him from the water's surface.

You stole my body, Cecil's voice spoke within his mind. *And I want it back.*

3

Deathmask knelt atop the roof and glared at the crumbled building on the opposite side of the street. Hopefully Veliana would be waiting for him inside that dilapidated mess. A longshot for sure. He was about to go through a lot of headaches for nothing if she wasn't. The night was dark, the moon and stars locked away by thick clouds, but there would be no safety here, no secrecy. The fallen bastard Azariah had made sure of that.

"Every corner," he said, shaking his head. "Every single goddamn corner."

Deathmask had fought necromancers and followers of Karak who made the dead arise at their command. The difference this time was that they weren't forced to hide their arts in the dark. The dead weren't just an army, they were now the fallen angel's eyes and ears.

From street corner to street corner stood a rotted husk of a man or woman. They did not move. They did not sleep. They merely turned their heads from side to side. Watching. Listening.

"Is this how you'll create Paradise?" Deathmask muttered. "Under the belief that humanity won't sin if they believe they're always being watched?" Purple fire bathed Deathmask's right hand. "For being a thousand years old, you're really fucking naïve, Azariah."

He stood, his cloak folding around him. He kept his burning hand outstretched, his gaze locked on the undead watcher beneath. A single gesture sent a concentrated ball of fire out like a shot, colliding with the undead's skull. The bone shattered instantly, the necrotic energy trapped within released. Deathmask spun, sending a second orb toward another watcher farther down the street. He couldn't see that one quite as well, but its collapse confirmed his aim was true.

Deathmask put a hand on the rooftop edge and vaulted into the air. A snap of his fingers enacted a simple spell that lessened his weight. He glided down to the street, settling softly before the splintered remains of a heavy wooden door. The broken and burnt building was a tavern Deathmask had never frequented during the five years since he'd rebuilt his Ash Guild following the war god's defeat. It was for that exact reason he'd chosen it as a meeting place for him and his trusted second in command should things ever go to shit. And by god, how they had gone to shit.

"I'm home," he said softly as he ducked through the door. Wood creaked beneath his boots. Many floorboards were already broken. The clouded sky above was easily visible through the collapsed ceiling. Deathmask lifted his burning hand, letting a soft purple hue shine across the charred walls, the broken furniture, and the veritable pit of broken glass bottles near the room's center.

Silence greeted his welcome. Deathmask tapped his foot and waited. Killing two of the undead watchers would certainly alert Azariah something was amiss, though hopefully he'd killed both before either had seen him on the rooftop. The question was, how long could he wait before a squad of fallen angels arrived to investigate?

"Was I really gone so long?" he wondered aloud. "Surely you didn't think me dead?"

That was a much better reason for her absence than her having died during the chaos that had befallen the capital. But that possibility was preposterous. Together they'd survived Veldaren's destruction. What was one more pillaged city among friends?

Except they hadn't been together. He'd been taken to the Council of Mages, to be tortured and burned by their twisted master, Roand the...

A sharp blade pressed against the base of his skull.

"Move and I kill you," a blessedly familiar voice spoke.

"Vel," he said, a smile spreading unseen behind his gray mask. "I knew you'd survive the…"

"Shut up, don't move, and prove it's you." The blade pushed harder, piercing his skin. Deathmask winced, his initial instinct to turn immediately halted.

Deathmask frowned, wondering what in the world had spooked Veliana so.

"I dyed my right eye red to match yours, the Worm gave you your scar, and while hiding from the Darkhand in a mausoleum I spent far too many hours making corpses dance for my own amusement. Now may I turn and greet my beloved Veliana?"

The blade pulled away. Breathing a tiny sigh of relief, he spun and smiled at his long-time companion. Veliana wore the uniform of their reformed Ash Guild, dark trousers and shirt hidden beneath a long gray cloak. Her good eye twinkled, her other eye milky and white mixed with a faint blur of blood. A smile spread across her beautiful face.

"I almost killed you when you called me 'beloved'. How uncharacteristically emotional of you."

"I've had some bad days. Once we're somewhere safe I'll tell you all about them."

"There is no safe place left in this gods-forsaken city." Veliana pulled a similar gray mask up from around her neck to hide the lower half of her face. "Follow me, and I'll take you to the next closest thing. Once we're there you can tell me how in the Abyss you're still alive."

She led him out of the busted tavern and across the street, scaling the wall to the roof with ease. Deathmask was hardly so nimble, but a quick snap of his fingers and gesture from his other hand levitated him high enough to grab the roof's edge. Veliana helped him up, and together they raced along the rooftops in the black night.

"It's almost like being in Veldaren again," he said as they leapt from rooftop to rooftop. "Eyes everywhere on the ground, the rooftops our only solace."

Veliana paused at a ledge, lying flat on her stomach while peering her head down. Deathmask squatted beside her, trusting her instincts far more than his own.

"Except there's eyes in the sky as well," Veliana said. "And the eyes on the ground don't even blink."

She pointed to one of the many undead watchers. This one appeared to have been female, a tattered dress hanging from one intact sleeve. Ragged black hair frayed past her shoulders, slowly scraping along her exposed spine as her head traveled left to right.

"I've seen them," Deathmask whispered. "Azariah's little pets, I assume?"

"Correct. If you're spotted it won't take long before one of the fallen appears. Same goes for if you kill one. I've done some tests, and they're listening, too, but not very well."

"Is that a surprise? Their ears have rotted off."

"And most don't have eyeballs, either. I don't know how the magic works, but it does, which is all that matters. Have you seen the patrols?" Veliana shivered. "A dozen of those things marching in a group. They'll open doors, peer through windows, creepy as shit. Azariah's not been in charge long but it's already miserable to live here. You can't even sleep without thinking you'll wake up to a pair of dead eyes looking you over."

Deathmask noticed Veliana was watching the sky as much as she was the ground.

"What are they looking for?" he asked.

"Not now," she whispered, and held a finger to her lips to silence him. She flung her cloak across her body and gestured for him to do the same. Deathmask dropped to his stomach, obscuring himself as best he could. He twisted his head so he faced Veliana, who had shifted onto her side so she could watch the sky.

"They're always up there," she whispered. "Just waiting for an excuse to punish us sinful humans."

Deathmask couldn't help but chuckle. "You act as if that's different than before."

She did not share his cheer.

"Except this time they'll do it with swords instead of words."

Deathmask joined her in looking upward. It didn't take him long to spot the pair of black wings circling overhead. The feathers were darker than the night itself, the sight sending a cold trickle of sweat down Deathmask's neck. He told himself he wasn't afraid of any fallen angel, and he'd already bested one with Tarlak's help when they first returned to Mordeina…but the image awakened something primitive inside him. A sensation Deathmask had rarely felt his entire life: that of being hunted. Of being the prey instead of the predator.

"He has to be at least a thousand feet up," he whispered. "Can he really see us?"

"Their eyes are like hawks. Sadly, when Ashhur yanked everything beautiful out of them, he didn't take their eyesight."

"Ashhur is hardly known for acting rationally. It's all about the big gestures with him."

The circling wings drifted to the south, hovering over the closest neighborhood.

"Hang the big gestures," Veliana said, rising to her feet. "For once I'd love for Karak and Ashhur to make the world a *quieter* place when throwing their tantrums. Now, do you see the female watcher over by the corner?"

"I do."

"Blast its head off when it's looking the other way, then get ready to run."

Deathmask readied another spell, this time choosing a far less flashy one. Now that he realized how many eyes were watching from above, he felt foolish for striking down the earlier two with bright purple flame. Words of magic floated off his lips, guided toward the rotted cavity that was the creature's chest. A living being would feel the heat growing within them, resisting the magic or simply moving aside so the energy dispersed harmlessly through the air. The undead watcher held no such instincts. The magic pooled, a swirling inferno of fire encaged with ribs and rotted flesh. It didn't take long, just a single subdued flare to transform the body to ash and bone collapsing upon the road.

Veliana leapt off the rooftop and hit the ground running. Upon crossing the street, she immediately spun and sprinted back, to Deathmask's confusion. She didn't slow at all, leaping straight through an open window of the home they'd hid atop. Deathmask hung from the edge and then dropped, wincing at the jolt to his knees.

"Vel?" he asked, glancing through the window.

His companion stood atop a rotted corpse, her daggers twirling in her hands. She kicked its severed skull underneath the empty bed.

"Azariah's getting clever," she said. "This is bad. This very bad."

Her eyes widened, and that warning was all he needed. Deathmask dove aside, biting down a curse as a massive spear smashed through the cobbles where he'd stood. Power flared across his fingertips in the form of crackling purple lightning. He glared at the sky, and the pair of descending forms with black wings.

"There's two," he told Veliana. "Do we run or fight?"

His companion crawled out the window.

"Fight, then run," she said. "I'll keep them off you as best I can."

Deathmask doubted she could do any real damage to the two enormous forms crashing toward them. He dashed for the opposite side of the street, keeping his head lifted to track their descent. Veliana tumbled away as one landed beside the spear, the fallen's beefy hand yanking it out of the earth with ease. The other halted above the street's center with a great gust of air, his black wings spread wide. The bone-white of their armor seemed to let off a pale glow across the fallen angels' ashen skin.

"Submit for trial," said the spear-holder. His focus was solely on Veliana, who stood just outside the reach of his spear. "Azariah may show mercy if you cooperate."

"There will be no trial," the other said, readying his shield and pointing his sword. Its hilt had once been magnificent gold, but now it appeared carved from a hip bone, the blade jagged and cracked. "It's him. The destroyer of Avlimar."

Deathmask grinned behind his gray face-cloth. "It's nice to know I'm famous."

He slammed his wrists together, releasing a great burst of energy in a swirling beam of crackling violet lightning that screamed straight for the hovering fallen. The angel raised his shield, wings pounding as his body braced for impact. Deathmask knew it should have slammed the bone-metal apart and ripped through the fallen. The fallen bellowed, energy swirling across his shield, licking at his ashen skin, and burning a deep groove into the cracking center. When it ended, he cast his shield aside and gripped his sword with both hands.

Apparently, there was much Deathmask needed to relearn.

The King of the Fallen

Attempting to dodge or flee would only get him killed. He remained on the offensive, his hands a blur of motion. The angel dropped to the ground for a heartbeat before kicking off with both legs and a mighty beat of his wings. Deathmask slammed his hands together. The fallen's lunge carried him straight into an invisible wave of rolling force. The sound of metal scraping against stone filled the quiet night. The fallen's lunge turned sideways; his left hand kept hold on the hilt of his sword even as the rest of his body slammed into the magical wave. The bones of his face and hand snapped, and Deathmask allowed himself a moment of pleasure at the sight of his pain.

The sword dropped from the fallen's hand, but still he charged. Deathmask started a spell, only to abandon it when instinct told him he wouldn't have time to finish. A fist smashed the right side of his face, confirming his theory. The gray cloth fell from his face, trailed by reddened saliva. Deathmask rolled with the punch and reached out blindly. The moment his fingers brushed skin, he spat out the necessary word with a bloody tongue.

"Hemorrhage."

The skin he touched exploded outward in a gush of blood and opened veins. The tear spread from neck to shoulder, the spray covering all of Deathmask's arm. The fallen angel rocked backward, his eyes widening at the influx of pain. Deathmask stepped closer, his crimson hand searching for another hold. Black wings folded before him, then swung outward. Deathmask held in a scream as the wings' sharp, brittle edges scraped across his skin and tore holes into his clothing. H reflexively turned away, an act he immediately regretted. The next blow hit him completely unprepared, a vicious elbow to the base of his neck.

"Not...very nice," he moaned, sprawled out on his stomach. Deep throbbing aches spread all along his spine. Through blurred vision, he saw the angel's feet before him. Good enough. He hooked his fingers into the necessary shape and then flailed his hand outward. Blood flicked from his fingertips and splattered across both the angel's legs. After a single moment of silence, the blood he'd thrown erupted into black flame.

His foe rewarded his efforts with a flaming boot to the face. Deathmask's nose crunched in, his already blurred vision now swimming in wild circles. He rolled away from the fallen, a feat easily accomplished given how the kick had lifted half his body off the ground. His addled mind ran through ideas, each one quickly dismissed. He didn't have time, and the fallen showed no sign of slowing from the pain and blood loss.

An admirable trait, really. One he'd admire if they weren't trying to kill him.

"I could use some help, Vel!" he screamed as he pulled up to his feet and put his back against the door to a quiet home. He glared at the approaching fallen, black light swelling in the center of his palms.

"I'm *busy*," Veliana shouted back at him. She vaulted over the head of her own foe, his black wings flaring upward, barely missing her flesh. Her violet-glowing daggers dug into those wings as she twirled with her arms extended. The daggers cleanly sliced through brittle feathers and thin, hollow bones alike. The angel let loose with a horrific scream when the upper third of his wings crumbled.

"Doing better than I am," Deathmask muttered. He felt his energy draining, yet still kept a spell prepared for an attack. His foe hunkered down, wings curled around his body, his right arm clutched awkwardly to his chest. The fire on his legs had died out, exposing charred flesh and hints of bone across his shins and his now-bootless feet. Deathmask hoped he'd charge recklessly, but instead the angel backed up a few steps and picked up his sword with his good hand.

"Your evil knows no bounds," the fallen said. His neck twitched and flinched, blood flowing from the wicked gash across his throat. "I fear to send you to the Abyss. Karak might praise you instead of torturing you as you deserve."

"How about you go visit him instead, and I stay alive to torment your deranged king?" Deathmask asked, trying to keep his bravado up while keeping watch on Veliana from the corner of his eye. Her attacks were relentless, her shimmering daggers hammering against her opponent's spear. If only Deathmask could survive until she took him down…

A gust of wind was all that warned him that his opponent had lunged suddenly. The sword came screaming in for his chest from the angel's fully extended arm. Deathmask dropped to his knees, his head tilting against his left shoulder. The sword cut a gash across his right cheek before driving deep into the wood of the door behind him.

The fallen attempted to yank the weapon free, and that was all the time Deathmask needed. His hands pushed forward, the shimmering magic in his palms releasing several thick bolts of shadow, their tails flickering white with stars. One slammed the fallen's chest, the other his stomach. They hit with the force of sledgehammers; the sound of snapping ribs filled the night air. The fallen let out a gasp. His stomach retched and his upper body heaved. Deathmask slid out from under the sword, balancing on unsteady legs. He grabbed the beaten angel around the throat.

"Tell whichever god takes you that I said hello," he growled. "*Hemorrhage.*"

The flesh beneath his hand ruptured, warm blood blasting across his already soaked clothes. The fallen's body went limp, and when Deathmask released his grip on his throat, he dropped to the street with a dull thud and rustle of feathers.

Deathmask turned back to Veliana. In the time it had taken him to dispatch his opponent, his longtime companion had lost her advantage. Veliana was now on the defensive, dodging and weaving as the fallen's spear pierced the air mere inches from her flesh. Deathmask didn't know what had turned the tide, but the blood pooling across her left arm seemed a likely reason.

"We've got no time for this." Deathmask spared a glance to the sky, saw distant outlines of black wings approaching. They'd barely handled two of the bastards. A squad of any size would be their end. He conjured slithering shadows in his hands while Veliana continued to dodge, awaiting the right moment. The angel always followed, keeping close, refusing to allow her a moment to breathe…

Veliana dropped to the ground, the butt of the spear whirling above her head. *There.* The opening he needed. A bolt of shadow crossed the street, striking the fallen square in the face. His forehead caved in from the force, instantly dropping him to his knees. Veliana hopped back to her feet and stared at the kneeling angel, her shoulders rising and falling with rapid breaths.

"And I thought you'd be the one saving me," Deathmask said, striding toward her. His pale humor vanished upon seeing just how deep the cut went into her shoulder. "Shit. Vel, are you…"

"I'm fine," she interrupted. "More coming. Move."

Veliana started moving, dexterously wrapping her cloak around and across her shoulder and arm into a makeshift sling while she ran. Deathmask followed, expecting her to head down one of the alleys, but instead she advanced on the home she'd initially approached before spotting the undead watcher lurking in the window. There seemed nothing unique about the squat little building, other than perhaps how dilapidated its walls were compared to its neighbors. And also the fact it was only a hundred feet away from a pair of angel corpses. Veliana kicked the door open and barged in.

"Won't they search this place when they find their dead brethren?" Deathmask asked, trailing her through the empty living room. By the copious amounts of dust and cobwebs, he assumed no one had lived here for several years.

"For starters, we're not hiding here. Second, you're not the only one who knows a bit of magic."

They exited at the rear of the home, entering the cramped space between it and the building's neighbor. Veliana leaned over a barren stretch of wall and snapped her fingers. The wall blurred, the illusion fading to reveal a set of wooden slats. She pulled the slats aside to uncover stone steps leading down into a cellar.

"Get in there," she said.

The small room was cramped, and nearly pitch-black after Veliana resealed the entrance, but Deathmask could at least solve one of those problems. He snapped his fingers, forming a little purple fire at the end of his forefinger. It hovered a moment, then settled down to the floor between himself and Veliana. It wasn't much, but it was something. Veliana slumped against the wall and removed her mask. Without having to watch for fallen in the sky and undead watchers along the streets, she seemed to relax. He tried to smile despite the ache of the gash across his cheek.

"Your face," she said, her eyes widening.

He touched the cut, realizing his face was bare without the cloth.

"It's nothing," he said. "It'll scar, but what's one scar among many?"

"No," she said. "The...the burns. Did they do that to you at the Council towers?"

Deathmask closed his eyes in thought. Reliving any of his time there was an unwelcome proposition, but Vel deserved that effort.

"Roand the Flame considered himself an artist when it came to torturing people with fire spells," he said. "My face was his canvas while I was imprisoned there. If it makes you feel any better, we killed him with his own magic instruments before we left."

"It doesn't."

He quietly laughed through his pain. "Well, it made *me* feel better." He let his head thud against the wall. "What was it like, Vel? When the angels fell?"

Her turn to fall silent for a moment.

"Azariah had called thousands of people to Devlimar for a proclamation," she finally said. "He dressed it up with flowery words, but in essence, he declared himself king while dissolving all courts, nobility, and law. Ashhur's law, that was all that'd matter, and execution awaited all who broke it." She shook her head. "But only after you repented, of course. Azariah wanted to make sure you had a nice clean soul before he cut off your fucking head."

"I'm not really surprised. It sounds like the inevitable result of Azariah's constant struggle to keep humans from acting like humans. I take it this proclamation didn't go over well?"

"You could say that." Veliana bit at her lip. "But while we were all murmuring to each other this man stepped out from the crowd. Looked a bit like a farmer, or maybe a well-off beggar. I don't know who he was. I'm not sure if anyone did. But he started shouting at Azariah and his angels, calling them out for their hypocrisy. And then he commanded they fall."

She laughed, painfully bitter even for her.

"And so they did. You've seen the results. It hit them all at once, and by their screaming, I'd say the transformation hurt like the Abyss. They went mad afterwards. If you weren't one of them, you were a target for their swords and spears. It was awful, Death. I've seen my share of slaughter, but this… People call it the Night of Black Wings. That's that kindest way to describe the butchery. Our guild dissolved that night. Surprise, surprise, no one wants to steal or trade in pilfered goods for a few extra coins when the fallen king has undead eyes on every corner and the punishment for the smallest of crimes is execution. I've been hiding out ever since, trying to survive while I waited for you to return."

"What if I hadn't returned?"

Veliana stared into the little purple fire dancing between them.

"Truth be told? I'd have fled this walled off *Paradise* of Azariah's and gone south to Ker. It won't be long before the black wings conquer its skies, too, but at least I might have a few years of peace before all of Dezrel turns to shit."

Deathmask wasn't much for comforting gestures, but he sensed the enormous strain she had been carrying on her shoulders since his capture. He put a hand on her ankle and squeezed it tightly, to her non-reaction.

"I wouldn't have blamed you for a heartbeat," he said. "But I'm here now, and if you're with me, I have a far better idea."

She brushed his hand away. "Oh please, do tell."

He wiggled his fingers at the flame. It spread in size, brightening as its shape twisted, changing into the fallen king's face, hovering between them like a haunted mask.

"That shit-weasel Azariah handed me over as a present to the Council," he said. "In return, I'm going to rip his head off his thrice-damned shoulders. How's that for a plan?"

"I'm in," she said. "But only on one condition."

"Name it."

Veliana scattered his fire with a wave of her hand, plunging them back into darkness.

"When he's dead, I get to be the one to toss his head off the wall for all his insane angels to see."

Deathmask laughed, yet again reminded of how much he'd missed his precious second-in-command.

"Deal."

4

Jessilynn awoke to an aching back and throbbing pain in her fingers. Her eyes fluttered open, the morning light adding an unwelcome edge to the headache pounding the back of her skull. *No, not morning light,* she thought as she pushed herself up. *Late afternoon. I slept too long.*

The young paladin rose to her feet and grabbed an edge of the wall to balance herself. She'd slept on the outer ramparts of the Castle of the Yellow Rose, preferring the rough, flat stone and cold wind to any room or clearing within the castle proper. Too many had died in there. The carpets, the furniture, the beds: they all stank of blood.

Not that it was much better outside. Jessilynn glanced over the broken walls and was surprised to see the many vile creatures still digging at the dirt. Ahaesarus had arrived with his angels the night before, and after slaying their leader, Manfeaster, he'd ordered the creatures to bury the bodies of all they'd killed. It'd been a slow and thoroughly unpleasant process. While being up high helped alleviate the reek of decay, it did little to diminish the constant sounds that assaulted her ears. All the scratching, snarling, and howling that accompanied the beast-men doing their work.

Jessilynn looked for Dieredon but saw no sign of him, nor did she catch glimpse of his white-winged horse, Sonowin. The elf would be around eventually, and likely upset with her for sleeping so ridiculously late. Best to worry about that when he appeared. For now, she wished to speak with Ahaesarus. Given her troubles, he seemed the perfect person to offer a solution.

"Assuming he'll even talk to me," she muttered. Pieces of the previous night flashed through her mind, unbidden and unwelcome. The angels had arrived too late to save anyone from the beast-man army that ravaged the castle and killed Arthur Hemman, its Lord. When Ahaesarus had landed she'd struck his chest and demanded answers for their abandonment. It was hardly the respect a centuries-old angel of Ashhur deserved. Now that he'd declared himself King of the Vile, he might have even less time to worry about the crumbling faith of a young paladin.

Still, better to try than to mope atop the ramparts avoiding bad smells. Jessilynn strapped on pieces of her leather armor, then ran her hands through her hair in a vain attempt to wrangle it into the approximate shape of 'down' instead of 'out and everywhere'. Done, she slung her bow and quiver over her shoulder and turned for the stairs.

Jessilynn paused, realizing she'd not offered a prayer to Ashhur upon waking. It used to be second nature to her, even if only a single sentence or two with her eyes closed. That she had forgotten, and even worse, held little desire to do so upon remembering, was a worrisome scrape across her mind.

"I'm sorry, Ashhur," she whispered. Her hand brushed her bowstring, her swollen fingers still raw from the night before. "Just…give me some time, all right?"

Ahaesarus had positioned himself and his angels around the main castle entrance, forcing Jessilynn to trot through the scattered armies of the vile. The nearest was a tribe of the bird-men, and they glared at her as their sharp claws raked the earth. A dozen fresh graves were beside them, and nearby, a pile of seven bodies waited their turn. One of the bird-men whistled at her, an unpleasantly coarse noise. She flinched despite herself. Part of her wanted to apologize, the other part of her aghast at the very notion. Of course they'd hate her, for how many of their kin had died to her glowing arrows? But they'd also slaughtered thousands of innocents. The few she killed were nothing by comparison.

"Focus on your work," she said. "Those you murdered deserve their proper resting place."

"Waste of good food," one of the bird-men grumbled. His feathers were black from head to toe, and he had dark eyes to match. The human language was awkward on his tongue.

"Angels says they innocent," remarked another. "Guilty. Not guilty. Their blood tastes the same."

"Don't you dare," Jessilynn said. She reached for her bow, immediately earning contrition from the beasts. They thought she still possessed her god-blessed arrows. For a moment, she'd thought so as well, and the remembrance hurt deeply.

"We only speak truth," the black-feathered one said. "Girl wouldn't harm us for speaking truth?"

"The wolves are the ones eating," said another. "They eat before burying, like dogs, they are. Just want to bury the bones."

"Right," said black-feather. "You punish us for speaking of what others do? Punish them! Punish the rotten wolves."

Jessilynn released her bow.

"Just...get back to work." She shook her head and hurried away. The smell was already getting to her. The stench of blood was thick in the air, coupled with a sour tinge of rot. Jessilynn weaved through the camps, giving them each a wide berth. When she passed a cluster of twenty wolf-men, their bodies so tightly packed together she could not see the graves they dug, she fought down an urge to confirm the bird-men's accusation.

Even the interior of the castle was not free of the smell. Reaching it meant ascending a small hill, and the grass was bathed in the blood of hundreds both man and beast, many cut down by her arrows. More had died inside the castle itself, and though the angels had cleared out the bodies, the sourness of death would linger for years to come.

Jessilynn pushed the memories away. She'd spent the previous night reliving each and every moment, from the brutal kills, to the dying soldiers, to the screams of the dying as the vile creatures descended upon them like prey. Only when the sun had cracked the horizon had she finally slipped into a restless sleep.

Two angels stood halfway up the hill, and they asked Jessilynn to wait.

"I wish to speak with Ahaesarus," she said, feeling strangely timid. "Is that all right?"

"Of course it is, child," said the golden-haired one on the left. "But our leader currently speaks with another."

Jessilynn tried not to be upset with them calling her a child. They'd dwelt in the Golden Eternity since Karak and Ashhur left the mortal realm. Of course she'd be a child to them.

"Then do you know where Dieredon went? I haven't seen him since I awoke."

The pair looked oddly amused.

"That is who Ahaesarus speaks with. They are discussing a great many things."

"All the more reason I should be present." She stepped between them, hesitating to see if they would try to stop her. They did not. "So I'm free to enter?"

"You are a Paladin of Ashhur," said the golden-haired angel. "One of the last of the faithful. We will bar you from nowhere, and no one."

"Good."

Jessilynn stormed through the broken front gates of the castle and hurried down the halls. She did her best to ignore the claw marks across the carpet and paintings, to pretend the splashes of blood were not there. Less than a day ago she'd assured Lord Arthur Hemman in his meeting chamber he could trust Ashhur to save them from the beasts' wrath. Now he was a corpse in an unmarked grave, if not in one of the awful creature's bellies. Jessilynn guessed, correctly, that Ahaesarus and Dieredon would be in that same chamber.

"Why would the Dezren elves refuse to give us aid?" Ahaesarus said as she stepped into the room. The angel towered over the grand, detailed map of northern Mordan, his wings curling around the wooden edges. His golden hair flowed down past his neck. His jaw was square, his face handsome, his muscles bulging. He looked less like a human and more a being carved from stone. A statue of physical perfection. A much smaller but no less imposing Dieredon stood opposite him, his arms crossed over his chest and his wicked-looking bow slung across his back.

"Because they are under no obligation to do so," Dieredon said. He glanced over his shoulder and acknowledged Jessilynn with a nod. "They have been chased across both sides of the rivers by human armies. They have watched the second Gods' War tear apart the entire eastern half of Dezrel and leave behind an abyssal hole filled with their cursed orcish brethren."

"They, always they," Ahaesarus said. "Do you not count yourself among their number?"

Dieredon shook his head, his smile a mixture of sadness and amusement.

"I speak what the majority of my people will believe," he said. "Know that my own thoughts are decidedly different."

Ahaesarus realized Jessilynn was there, standing awkwardly in the door, and he gestured for her to come closer.

"Welcome, Jessilynn," the angel said. His frustration melted away into a charming smile. "Your opinion would be most welcome in our discussion." He nodded to Dieredon. "For now, the elf is explaining to me why his Dezren elves won't join us in striking down Azariah's blasphemous rule."

"Tell me, since when have elves cared for the blasphemy of Karak or Ashhur?" Dieredon asked. "Has Azariah declared himself their ruler? Has he proclaimed elves obligated to follow the teachings of Ashhur? What threat does he possess to them, their lives, their customs, or their Goddess?"

Each question erased an increasingly larger portion of Ahaesarus's smile.

"The Dezren would be so selfish they will ignore the suffering of others so long as they themselves go unaffected?" he asked.

"Consider it a trait we've learned well from humans," Dieredon said, a bite edging into his words. "I dare say the human kingdoms have perfected the art."

Ahaesarus raised his hands in surrender. "Forgive me. My frustration leads too often to anger. If not the elves, then what allies are left to us?"

"You have the creatures of the vile," Jessilynn said. "Are they not enough?"

In answer, the angel gestured to the wood-carved map that lay atop the table between them.

"Azariah's numbers are twice ours, and he commands what is left of Mordeina's forces. Perhaps it is enough, but we must find out what is happening to Ker's invasion force. I pray they are a worthy ally, or at worst a useful distraction for us as we prepare our own army. As for the vile, their purpose will be soon revealed. With their deaths they will cleanse the sins of their lives, a valuable tool for retaking my city."

Jessilynn felt uncomfortable listening to the divine being discuss the lives of others so flippantly. Such talk was certainly common among lords and kings, but she expected...better from the angel. A demeanor different from all who came before. The thought of Ahaesarus becoming like mortal men terrified her.

"You promised the creatures a land of their own," Dieredon said. He kept his tone guarded, but Jessilynn could tell he also sensed the change in the angel.

"You would accuse me of lying?" Ahaesarus asked. His wings fluttered as if he were trying to remain calm. "My word is true, always and forever. These creatures gave their lives to tear down these walls and rip the life away from those cowering in fear within. If they would die for such a pale blessing, then let them face those same risks for a goal worthy of blood and sacrifice. The survivors shall have their land, as well as our guidance. Perhaps in time they will not be known as the vile, but as friend."

He pulled the enormous greatsword off his back and laid it over the map with a heavy thud. It was the weapon of the deceased paladin, Darius, former servant of Karak who turned to Ashhur near the end of his life. His visage had appeared to Jessilynn when her situation was most dire, and she stared at the weapon with fondness.

"I have seen what may be accomplished when the greatest among you gives everything for the lives of others," he said. "From the bravest and strongest to the vilest creatures of a forgotten war, all will be held to such high standards. Anything less will see victory slip from our fingers."

Jessilynn felt much of her nerves ease. Now this was the being Jerico and Lathaar had told stories about while they sat around the late-night campfires in the shadow of the rebuilt Citadel. Life had returned to those brilliant green eyes, his posture straightened, his entire demeanor commanded respect and authority. Perhaps the angels had fallen victim to politics and infighting, perhaps they had arrived far too late to save hundreds from the jaws of the vile, but that was in the past. War had come, and Ahaesarus was ready to lead.

"I'm sorry if it seemed we doubted you," Jessilynn said when it was clear Dieredon would offer no such concession. "You've done so much for us already. You deserve better than that."

"Indeed," the elf said, his tone the exact opposite of agreement. "So that settles it, then. We make way for the Castle of Caves. Spread word to your angels. I'll leave it to you to decide how best to organize and order about these...creatures you call an army."

Dieredon spun and exited the room without offering the slightest bow of respect. Jessilynn almost followed, but she'd sought out the angel for a reason.

"Ahaesarus," she said, her hands crossing behind her. She struggled for the correct words. "There's something I want to talk to you about..."

About what, though? About the vanishing of the god-blessed arrows that had helped her defend so many? Should she confess her lack of faith in Ashhur's protection after witnessing the absolute slaughter the night before? Or should she reveal her insidious, wiggling doubt that her desire to regain Ashhur's blessing was only a desire for her powerful arrows to return, and nothing to do with worry for her own soul?

Ahaesarus drummed his fingers across the hilt of Darius's greatsword, his eyes lost on the intricate details carved into the map.

"About what?" he asked without looking up.

A million things to ask, and zero words to properly convey the questions. Jessilynn shook her head and dropped her eyes to the floor.

"Never mind," she said. "It can wait. There's too much to do before nightfall."

Jessilynn left, and was hardly surprised to find Dieredon waiting for her outside the castle doors.

"You expect too much from these angels," he said. "Their own god has abandoned them, and for good reason. They are not infallible. Our role is to question their decisions and demand better, not to make them feel good about themselves."

Jessilynn had not the heart to argue. She brushed past him but halted when he latched onto her wrist.

"I have no desire to lecture you on matters of faith," he said. "But before the siege ever started, I warned you that this was a hopeless endeavor. You prayed for a miracle, and one did not arrive. Now is not the time to lay blame on others. My wisdom said all would die. Your faith said beyond all odds, we'd succeed. Consider this a lesson for the next time we find ourselves in a similar predicament."

His words stung deep. Tears blossomed in her eyes, and she was too exhausted to fight them off. Before the battle she'd insisted they stay, and Dieredon had called her a light in a very dark world. Why betray those comments now?

"You said you were honored to stay at my side and fight," she said, yanking her hand free. "I guess your sense of honor does not last beyond a single night."

Jessilynn stormed away before he could reply, glad to put her back to the elf. Must they argue, blame, and debate while the stench of the dead filled her nose and soured her tongue? Couldn't they just let her grieve, if only for a moment? The thoughts were emotional and tired and selfish, but she didn't care. She'd sworn her life to Ashhur, and since leaving the Citadel with Dieredon, she'd had her face scarred, her faith mocked, her body bruised and broken, and been forced to witness the deaths of hundreds. Couldn't she be human for a few hours?

With nowhere else to go, Jessilynn hurried through the ranks of the vile creatures toward her sleeping spot atop the wall. Angels flew overhead and landed among the scattered groups of beast-men, no doubt relaying orders from Ahaesarus. Most groups Jessilynn passed looked finished with the burials, except for one.

She stopped at where the bird-men had mocked her and threatened to eat the dead. Their stack of corpses to bury remained at seven. Two open graves showed bloodied bodies covered with only a small smattering of dirt. As for the bird-men themselves, she saw no sign of them. Jessilynn pulled her bow off her shoulder, telling herself not to worry. The vile creatures were disdainful of all authority. It didn't mean anything.

She waved at one of the angels flying overhead until she gained his attention.

"Yes?" the dark-haired angel asked as he floated down to a hover just above her head. "Is something the matter?"

"The group that was here," she said, pointing to the corpses. "Have they been ordered to move elsewhere?"

The angel frowned.

"I don't believe so, certainly not with their punishment yet to be completed."

"Search the rest of the castle grounds," she said. "I'm sure they've only joined up with one of the other groups."

Jessilynn knew it wasn't so even as she suggested it. The angel's wings pounded the air, vaulting him upward. She watched him scan for several minutes, his circling growing more and more erratic as time passed. Jessilynn climbed the stairs to the wall when it was clear he'd find nothing. The sun was setting, its orange haze on the horizon painful to the eye. She squinted, thinking she saw a distant speck descending a hill that might have been the cluster of bird-men, but her eyes were not those of an elf, and she could not be certain. Of course, there was someone who *did* possess keen elven eyesight...

Dieredon was with Sonowin at the castle stables when she found him. The elf had a brush in hand, and he methodically massaged the winged horse's side so that he never missed a single inch. Jessilynn knew the activity calmed him, and she felt a spiteful bit of pleasure in the thought that Dieredon was just as upset about their argument as she was. She felt a brush of air against her back, and a second later, Ahaesarus landed behind her.

"I see I have become popular," Dieredon said, patting Sonowin's side. "Is something the matter?"

"About forty of the bird-men have fled the grounds." Ahaesarus glanced at Jessilynn. "I'd like you to track them before they escape."

"Escape?" Dieredon asked. "I thought they were your soldiers, yet now it seems they are your prisoners."

"They bent their knee and accepted me as their king," Ahaesarus said. "They have sworn their lives in return for a home, and I will not have them betraying their promise. Will you aid us or not?"

The elf sighed. "I do this, but not for you. Those forty pose a danger to the innocents you're sworn to protect. Better them under your thumb than running loose in human lands." He whispered something into Sonowin's snow-white ear, eliciting a loud snort from the horse. "I know. I'm not a fan of them, either."

Sonowin trotted out of the stable. Dieredon hopped onto the horse's bare back and gestured for Jessilynn to join him. She vaulted up behind him, wrapping her arms around Dieredon's waist.

"How would you like for me to signal you?" Dieredon asked.

"You will have no need of signaling," Ahaesarus said. "I will be flying alongside you, as will my faithful."

Dieredon shrugged. "So be it."

He patted Sonowin twice on the neck. Her wings spread wide, their span tremendous to behold. The horse sprinted forward, two beats of her wings lifting them skyward. Jessilynn watched the castle recede behind her, clusters of wolf- and hyena- and bird-men lit orange across their fur and feathers by the setting sun. A large part of her wished she might never see it again.

Dieredon guided Sonowin low, his eyes scanning the ground along the outer edge of the castle walls. They looped for another pass, and this time he spotted something among the blood and debris that she could not. Sonowin's path curled southwest, then straightened out. Ahaesarus followed several hundred feet behind, at the head of a group of seven angels. Sonowin guided them over rolling hills and thin, scattered forests. Jessilynn had learned much about tracking from the elf, but they zipped over the grass far too quickly for her to make sense of anything. Dieredon obviously could, however, for within minutes they crested another hill to find the bird-men racing ahead. They saw Sonowin and immediately bunched together in preparation for arrows that did not come.

Dieredon slowed to a hover, letting Ahaesarus catch up.

"Land with me," the angel said. "I would speak with them."

"As you wish," Dieredon said. "They're your prisoners."

The barb did not go unnoticed. Ahaesarus folded his wings and dropped. Dieredon led Sonowin on a more gentle, roundabout dive. As the roar of the wind softened, he leaned back toward Jessilynn.

"Ready your bow. I do not know what Ahaesarus plans, but I doubt he will easily convince these creatures to return."

Dieredon leapt off Sonowin's back before the horse's hooves touched grass, landing lightly on his feet with his bow drawn and an arrow nocked. Jessilynn lacked such grace, and she waited for Sonowin to halt before she slid off the winged horse's back and touched ground. She drew her own bow, and together she and Dieredon flanked Ahaesarus, who towered before the group of bird-men. There was no confusing the vicious, angry cries emanating from deep within their throats.

"Like thieves in the night you flee my command," the angel said, silencing them all with the sheer volume of his booming voice. A shiver ran through Jessilynn when she imagined such anger directed her way. "Have you forgotten your vow? For I have not forgotten your many sins."

"Death or servitude," the leader among them shouted, Jessilynn recognizing the black-feathered bird-man with even blacker eyes. "That is no vow. That is prison."

"You would speak to me of death?" the angel asked. He hoisted Darius's blade off his back and held it above his head. "Manfeaster wielded this blade as he led your attack that slaughtered hundreds. Death is what you deserve, you vile creatures, but Ashhur desires even the most wretched to elevate themselves above their sins. You deserve death, yet I offer you a land for your own. Is that truly such a prison?"

Jessilynn thought the offer better than the bird-men deserved, but apparently they did not share that belief.

"Your land is a lie," black-feather said.

"I do not lie."

"You need not lie!" He squawked three times in succession, a painfully high-pitched cry to show his disgust. His clawed fingers pointed at the six other angels remaining in the air with weapons drawn. "We will never have that land. We will be dead. We will fight, and die, long before all your pretty white wings are stained with blood. Better we return to the home we fled than die for nothing."

It was a powerful accusation, and not without merit. Jessilynn had shared similar thoughts with Ahaesarus earlier that day. But where Ahaesarus had convinced her with his sincerity, the angel used a far different tactic with the bird-men.

"There will be no returning home," he roared. "The vile wedge is gone to you. Your vows are made, and I do not release you from them. The first Gods' War created you, and now that we walk in the shadow of the Third, you will fulfill your purpose. Fight for your new land, or die here on a nameless hill."

"Then you make us choose between death and death," black-feather shrieked. "If we must choose, we choose the one with honor. The one where we fight for ourselves."

Ahaesarus's voice dropped to a sudden, dangerous growl.

"I offer you your only chance for honor. Kneel, now, or reject it."

Jessilynn prayed for peace. She prayed for at least a pause in the bloodshed.

"Death over slavery," the bird-man shrieked, and the rest took up that cry.

Ahaesarus gave no order. He never said a word. One beat of his wings, and he tore into the center of their group. Darius's sword slashed through their numbers, hacking off limbs and rending flesh. The other angels dove in unison, their spears and swords tearing into their foes in an explosion of feathers. Dieredon and Jessilynn each drew an arrow, but there was no reason to fire. The slaughter was finished in an instant. The meager creatures never bore a chance.

The six other angels flew away when the killing was complete. Ahaesarus turned to face Jessilynn and Dieredon while cleaning blood off his blade. Jessilynn stared at him, shivers running through her to see Darius's sword wielded so casually. Her arrow remained nocked, the string pulled taut.

"It is a cruel world we walk upon," Ahaesarus said as he sheathed the sword upon his back. "But we do as we must."

"This will continue," Dieredon argued. "Angel, I ask that you reconsider your idea in using these creatures in your war. They have a strong sense of honor and loyalty, but it will never be to you. Send them back across the Rigon River, or kill them on the field of battle they created. They feasted on the slain. Do not dishonor their victims by pretending they might somehow redeem such a vile act through forced servitude in your holy war."

"And do you agree?" Ahaesarus asked, turning to Jessilynn. She could read nothing in the angel's tired green eyes, and she hated having to give an answer. She remembered her time imprisoned by Manfeaster and Moonslayer. They were terrifying beasts, but they also lived a desolate existence. The sons of Redclaw had united the various creatures with a promise of a better life. Could she truly blame them for that desire?

"I don't know," she said, and slowly released the tension of her bow. "Everything I think I know seems wrong."

Ahaesarus nodded but said nothing. He spread his wings wide and took to the air, leaving the forty dead bird-men behind to rot on the hillside. Jessilynn closed her eyes and fought back a wave of exhaustion and sorrow. Any desire to speak with the angel about her lack of faith died.

Despite looking right at her, Ahaesarus never once noticed her arrow lacked the light of their god.

5

Bernard's daily walks had carried him westward over the past few weeks, where he hoped to eventually traverse the more well-marked and well-traveled road that led from the Bloodbrick Crossing at the border to Ker all the way to the front gates of the capital city of Mordeina. He had expected to travel the many miles alone, but it seemed Ashhur had other plans.

"An army?" he wondered aloud when he first saw the many cook-fires filling the northern sky with smoke. "And if so, whose?"

He kept to the road nonetheless, praying his status as a priest of Ashhur would keep him safe no matter the allegiance of the army, be it from Ker, Mordan, or the angels themselves. As he crossed another half-mile, he saw it was no army at all. Instead he saw dozens of children and elderly riding wagons, while at the forefront marched hundreds of younger men and women. All of them carried their belongings on their backs in leather packs or tied blankets and cloth. The sight was a sadly familiar one for Dezrel—refugees fleeing yet another ruined city.

"Hail," Bernard called out to the beleaguered men and women who passed him by. If there was a leader among them, he saw no sign of it, nor did many seem to care for his presence. "Is there room for a priest among your number?"

"Room for everyone," a middle-aged woman said as she strolled on by. "So long as you're willing to walk."

The fallen were north, but the people fled south. For Bernard, it wasn't much choice. He turned about and followed, traveling in the very heart of the several hundred men and women. He listened to their tales, those with the strength to tell them. He heard of Azariah declaring himself as king and first-hand accounts of the visions Ashhur had shown him of the angels' fall in dreams weeks prior. He remained silent as those with him took their turn to describe the Night of Black Wings, and the chaos that followed. Slaughter without hesitation. Murder without reason. It was the rage of the heavens unleashed on an unsuspecting, defenseless populace, and it broke Bernard's heart with every new telling. Not a soul there was spared. Everyone knew a friend or family member who died at the blade of a fallen angel.

"Such punishment feels inadequate to the crimes," Bernard said at one point when being told of the faded skin, black wings, and crown of bone that Azariah had been inflicted with.

"What crimes did we commit?" a man beside him had asked.

That the people considered the curse cast upon the fallen as punishment to *them*, and not upon the angels, was telling enough. Bernard never spoke of it again, nor did he answer those who sought enlightenment on Ashhur's reasoning. Truth be told, he did not have one.

Their travels done for the day, the people started setting up their camps, Bernard scoped out the ramshackle village that would be their camping spot. No doubt it had once thrived off travelers between Mordan and Ker, but it had been destroyed years ago by Thulos's army and never recovered. People crammed into the hollowed out buildings, preferring dilapidated shelters to open sky. Someone brought Bernard a stool, and the priest graciously accepted. He set the stool in the center of the village, sat by his lonesome, closed his eyes, and asked Ashhur for his blessing.

"Bring me those in need," he said. "I care not how heavy or light their burden. Bring me them all."

Bernard was not prepared for just how many came to him, no matter their destitute state. It reminded him of the first days of the Second Gods' War, when the refugees of Neldar and Omn arrived at Mordeina. People had packed into the various churches while the priests had prayed incessantly for days to cure the myriad aches, fevers, and broken bones. Even if he had not been told of the angels' fall, he'd have been able to piece much of it together. The many wounds, the inflamed flesh and cuts that desperately needed cleaning, all told a grim story.

Hours later, Bernard could barely lift his head or keep his eyes open. Despite several dozen people still patiently waiting, he bid the helpers who had joined him in setting up the line to dismiss those gathered.

"Tomorrow," he said. "I will do what I can on the morrow, but for now, I must sleep."

As tired as he felt, he knew it miraculous he had healed so many. Such feats should have been beyond him, but there was no doubting the influx of strength and power granted to him by Ashhur since leaving the Sanctuary. As he lay his head on a pillow graciously given to him by one of the refugees, he closed his eyes and tried to sleep within the bedroom of one of the few intact homes, an honor given to him for his hours of work.

Sleep, however, was not yet coming.

My enemies await, whispered Ashhur's voice within his mind. *You fled your duty once before. Do you now echo your previous shame?*

"And if I do?" Bernard whispered back into the night.

My gift is not granted freely. Overcome your weakness. Stand tall before those who would harm Dezrel.

"I seek not to fight your enemies, my lord. Consider it weakness if you must, but I would aid your people all that I can."

Then why do you travel south? Will you not aid my people?

"Your people travel south," Bernard answered.

The Fallen rule to the north.

"Are they your people? Or are they your enemies?"

He received no answer, nor did he wish for one. He merely wished to sleep.

⌖

Bernard learned more of the state of Mordan as he walked among her people.

The refugees had started out as survivors fleeing from Mordeina during what was known as the Night of Black Wings. Their numbers had split come morning, those armed and able to fight staying with the Godslayer and his friends. The rest traveled south, fleeing for the presumed safety of Ker. Only one fighting man had come with them, sent to lead and organize as they traveled: a very grumpy and unhappy knight, Sir Wess Langton. Bernard was introduced to him early that next day.

"Captain of the guard," the knight muttered after their introduction. "Captain of the guard for all of Mordeina, safekeeping thousands upon thousands of civilians, and what does that half-orc bastard order me to do? Wet-nurse a bunch of refugees."

Bernard liked Sir Wess, but he confessed a predilection toward such military personalities. He was fond of these stern men and women committed to order, rank, and commands. His fondness was certainly selfish, for such people understood the nature of Ashhur's relationship toward humanity in similar roles, of a higher authority giving orders to those below. It made his own position easier, even if it meant sometimes correcting the oversimplification of matters during post-sermon discussions.

"The Godslayer put in your hands the most vulnerable and helpless, for you to guide and protect," Bernard said in response. "There is real honor in that."

Sir Wess frowned deep enough to scrunch his white mustache between his lip and nose. "Perhaps there is. But I still wish I could have stabbed a few more of those damned angels prior to heading south."

"I pray you do not get your wish, good sir. We still have many miles to cross before we reach Ker."

Their group was large enough that news of their approach arrived in towns long before the convoy itself did. Many more people joined in the procession, for even if their homes had been miraculously spared the trauma and death of the Night of Black Wings, they were not willing to risk living in the land that Azariah had renamed Paradise. Those who joined gave to others whatever belongings they could not carry themselves. Even some of those who stubbornly remained behind often donated what they could. Others sold food, blankets, and wagons, at reasonable prices. When the destitute and desperate arrived at your doorstep numbering in the thousands, even the most ruthless of barterers realized angering the mob was asking for everything to be taken, with nothing offered in return.

After a week of travel, the group arrived at the Bloodbrick Crossing. As Bernard had feared, crossing the Corinth River into the land of Ker would be no simple task. News had reached the refugees of King Bram's defeat at the hands of the fallen, so as expected, the surviving army was camped along the riverbank, manning the blockade that had been erected over the course of the escalating tensions between Mordan and Ker. Instead of approaching the bridge, Sir Wess ordered the people to halt half an hour out from the crossing. The tired and impatient people reluctantly obeyed. Bernard prayed over the sickest and most hurting of the lot until someone came to fetch him for a meeting.

"Is something the matter?" Bernard asked upon his arrival. A dozen or so men and women gathered together at the forefront of the refugees. Sir Wess was there, of course, while the others were but faces among many. From their clothes, he could tell they came from wealth and prestige.

"We must choose someone to speak for us when we attempt to cross into Ker," Sir Wess said.

Bernard glanced about the group.

"And you want it to be me," he said.

"We have no lands, no titles, and no wealth," Sir Wess reluctantly admitted. "Even my rank as a knight is meaningless at this point, for it's not as if I have a home or lands to return to after all this. Humble as you may pretend to be, you're still a powerful priest of Ashhur."

Bernard bit his tongue, rankled at the accusation that his humility was a ruse. "Ker has rarely shown much love for Ashhur, even less since the arrival of the angels," he argued.

"It's still more status than any of us hold," said another. "Please, speak for us. We fear no one else here will be listened to."

As much as he hated the responsibility, giving voice to the voiceless was one of the explicitly demanded rolls of a priest of Ashhur.

Ten minutes later, Bernard crossed the muddy ground between the refugees and the bridge, his hands raised in peace. The soldiers lining the Bloodbrick shouted for him to halt.

"I speak for those who lack the voice to do so for themselves," he said, figuring it couldn't hurt to add a bit of flowery language to his request. "Who among you may entreat with me?"

"I guess I can," said one of the soldiers. "What is it you want? We've orders to let no one cross. Don't matter if you're priest, prince, or pauper."

"Surely simple orders did not anticipate refugees of such numbers, nor their pressing need," Bernard said. He set foot onto the bridge, glad to have firm stone beneath him instead of muddy earth. "Who is in charge here? Might I speak with them and plead my case?"

Several soldiers exchanged quick words.

"I'll tell the Commander he has a guest," one finally said. "Though heaven knows if he'll have the time."

"I am a patient man," Bernard said. "If he is busy, I shall wait until he is ready."

Bernard sat on the stone, set his hands atop his knees, and wordlessly hummed a hymn to pass the time. Life as a priest had granted him a tremendous reservoir of patience, and it wasn't like he had anywhere else to be. As the hours passed, the soldiers nearby grew increasingly uncomfortable with his presence in the center of the Bloodbrick. Despite someone having gone to inform their commander of his request, it seemed no one would be coming to address his concerns. The idea was almost laughable. Did whoever was in charge think the teeming mass of refugees would magically vanish into thin air if they were simply ignored?

"You can wait with your people, and we'll come for you when the Commander is ready," a soldier finally said.

"I'm fine here."

"Then at least stop with the damn humming. You've been at it for hours."

"Hours, has it?" Bernard said. "I didn't notice. You're right, though. Time will pass swifter with an actual song."

He sang, knowing full well his voice was not the most pleasant to the ear. After another twenty minutes, one of the soldiers stormed off. When he returned, an older man decked head to toe in chainmail arrived. He carried a gleaming shield on his left arm bearing the crest of the Bram family, that of a screeching eagle.

"Are you the old priest harassing my men?" the newcomer asked.

"I merely sing hymns in worship of my god, Ashhur," Bernard said.

The King of the Fallen

"I'll take that as a yes. I am Commander Lurik. Follow me."

They crossed the bridge, passing between uneven rows of wooden spikes and piled barricades of stone. Bernard glared at the defenses. None of it would matter to winged angels flying overhead. Were they so frightened of the refugees? Or did they anticipate a human army chasing after them?

An extravagant tent marked the Commander's abode. By the level of furnishings, it seemed the man planned to be here for some time. By Ashhur, he'd somehow hauled over an entire dining room set for himself, as well as a bed propped atop flat stones so its supports did not sink into the ground. Such a sight colored his opinion of Lurik. His uniform was pristine, his chainmail polished to a blinding sheen. In lieu of a helmet he wore a foppish hat with three bright red feathers. Perhaps at one point he had been handsome, but age had taken its toll, helped none by the heavy scars across his forehead and cheeks. No doubt he had seen many a battle during the seconds Gods' War.

"No thank you," he told Lurik when offered a drink of what appeared to be lukewarm tea in an iron kettle atop the table. He did take a seat, though, for after humming and singing atop the bridge for so long it felt nice to sit down in a proper chair. "I have no need of pleasantries. All I seek is an answer for the people's predicament."

"If you seek an answer, then I shall keep it simple and give you one," Lurik said. "Your people cannot cross."

"Cannot, or will not?" Bernard pressed.

"Do not needle me as if winning an argument will grant your people passage. Ker suffers, and it is by Mordan's hands. King Bram's invasion cost us dearly. Hands that should have been tending crops instead wielded swords in a foolish invasion to the north. Crops rot in their fields, and I fear the coming winter."

"I fear it, too," Bernard said, careful to keep his mildly pleasant smile locked in place upon his face. "Though I suspect for different reasons. Will you hold the barricade even as the snows fall? Will you deny us entrance while you watch us freeze and starve?"

Lurik crossed his arms amid a rattle of chainmail. "We speak of treaties, politics, and the difficulty facing entire nations. Do not try to guilt me over a few assorted rabble."

"Does the Queen share your opinion?"

"I will not speak for the Queen Loreina, nor pretend to know her opinion on this matter beyond what orders she has given me. But since she left me in charge of the defenses, let me tell you *my* opinion, priest."

"Please do," Bernard said. It was becoming harder and harder to maintain that pleasant façade.

The Commander leaned on the table to shrink the distance between them. His voice lowered. His animosity deepened.

"You, and all those people with you, worshiped Ashhur's angels. You let them rule you, and you condemned us for refusing to kneel in servitude just like you. So as far as I'm concerned, it is *your* problem, not ours. *You* deal with the consequences."

Bernard drummed his fingers atop the table. He did not flinch before such ugliness. Lurik might try to appear intimidating, and to many he likely was, with his armor and scars and the sword strapped to his side. But Bernard had walked hallways lined with the living dead. He had confronted the vicious priest Melorak, and aided in banishing a dragon of pure darkness. This old Commander was but a stubborn child compared to them.

"I care not for your opinion," he said. "So instead I seek the opinion of she who rules above you. Where is Queen Loreina? Let her decide if her nation can support a few hungry and tired people fleeing for safety."

"The Queen rides south, to muster what additional troops we can afford in preparation for the war your mad angels will certainly bring us," Lurik said.

"I presume she will bring those soldiers here to help defend the river?"

The realization that he'd said more than he intended dawned on Lurik's face. He shrugged and said, "Possibly."

Even though it was obvious to them both she indeed would.

The King of the Fallen

"Then we shall wait for her return," Bernard said. "And we shall see if her opinion matches your own."

The Commander smirked. "Angels of Mordan slew her husband. You hold out hope for a miracle."

Bernard wearily rose to his feet. He dreaded returning to camp, and the painful conversations that would follow as he informed the refugees of their denied entrance.

"Has no one told you?" he said bitterly. "We come from the land of miracles."

6

Azariah slowly circled the room, checking each and every rune carved into the thirteen stones for the slightest imperfection. The night was deep, and nine lanterns hung equidistant about the walls to add to the faint starlight shining through the windowed ceiling.

"Yet another of your portals," Judarius said. "You seem to have adopted strange hobbies over the past weeks. Is this the effect elven magic has on a person's mind? I would greatly prefer you focus on building an army to chase the people fleeing south to Ker. At the least, we need confirmation from many lords that they are loyal to us and not the missing boy king."

Azariah held back a smirk. Here, at the very top of the reformed castle tower of Mordeina, he would replicate a feat performed only by a daughter of balance. To call it a mere hobby was insulting, if one knew the actual extent of the efforts and skill required. Which Judarius certainly did not. Azariah's Executor was ever-much a being of strength and swords.

"This is no mere portal," Azariah said upon finishing yet another inspection. He wasn't satisfied, but he doubted he would ever be. Delving into such realms of power would always carry a risk. "This is so much more. As for the lords, they will bend the knee. They hold no choice in the matter, so why concern myself with their actions?"

Judarius grunted and crossed his arms. His armor rattled.

"I take it this is yet another trick or fascination you've plucked from the prophet's journal?"

In answer, Azariah withdrew Velixar's spellbook from his robe pocket and flipped it to his chosen page.

"Not a trick, my dear brother. Nor mere fascination. At last I am ready to save us from Dezrel's madness."

For centuries, the pair had watched over Dezrel from high above. Azariah knew his brother better than perhaps any being alive. The subtle shift in his arms? The slight rise of an eyebrow? He could read those like he read the prophet's neat handwriting. Something disturbed his Executor, even though he tried to hide it.

"And how will you accomplish that?" he asked.

In answer, Azariah gestured to the faintly visible stars high above, their twinkling muted by the thick glass that was the tower chamber's ceiling.

"For every star, there is a world," he said. "Each crafted in worship by the god or goddess granted dominion over it. Thulos conquered several worlds, yes, but he was a bird pecking away at grains of sand as if he might one day conquer the ocean. There are thousands more, vibrant and beautiful, with mysteries we cannot begin to fathom. They need not be barred to us. I know the words. The door is no longer locked, for I hold the key."

Judarius stepped closer, and for perhaps the first time in Azariah's entire existence, he did not know his brother's thoughts.

"You would have us flee?" he asked softly.

"If you must put it so improperly, yes, we will flee."

His brother shifted his weight back and forth on his heels. Angry, Azariah realized. Furious, even. Had he erred in revealing these deeply held truths so soon? Was his brother not yet ready for these brutal realities?

"We are the masters of this world," Judarius said, the volume of his voice steadily increasing, until by the end he was shouting. "We are the guardians of these wretched humans and their eternal souls. You would flee that responsibility like a coward? You would deny our sacrifices? We died for these people, Azariah. We fought their wars, and now we fight for their hereafter. How can you think to turn our backs on our god?"

"Because he is not our god!" Azariah shouted.

Judarius staggered as if Azariah had punched him in the neck.

"You would, here at the end of all things, deny our merciful god?" he asked.

Azariah flared his wings to either side and stood to his full height. He may not compare in size and strength to Judarius, but he still felt taller, larger, a more complete presence than any other being alive.

"Ashhur is not our god, and neither is Karak. Neither of them is whole. Neither of them is complete. We are imprisoned here, my brother. Forced to live under the inane laws and beliefs of a god who split his very being in a horrid, failed experiment. Thulos, Karak, Ashhur, all the countless others who have been slain...they never should have been separated from Kaurthulos. They are unfulfilled imperfections. They are the broken shards of a statue insisting each was the original work of art. And so long as Celestia refuses to let one slay the other, they will always remain apart. It will drive them mad, Judarius. It *has* driven them mad. Does all of Dezrel's history not prove my words true?"

Judarius had Azariah by the throat before he could react. The mighty hand closed about his neck and lifted him off the ground. The world blurred, and Azariah cried out as his brother slammed his back against a wall, pinning him there. Judarius's pale eyes burned with fire. Blood dripped from his mouth as he bared his jagged teeth.

"Our fallen brethren hail you as our leader and King," he said. "And yet you would speak to me such heresy?"

Judarius's fingers loosened so he might speak.

"Is it heresy?" Azariah asked. "Look at our flesh, brother. What delusion do you labor under to believe Ashhur holds love for our kind? I would acknowledge the truth before us. My words and laws honor the Ashhur who walked Dezrel in the original days of creation. So too do I honor Karak as he was prior to being cast into the Abyss and made lord of murderers and thieves. I honor all the broken pieces of Kaurthulos, for he is the only divine being worthy of our worship. But that being will not return, perhaps not until the stars are swallowed by the eternal space beyond."

Judarius's fingers tightened. Azariah endured the pain. Magic gathered in his fingertips, fire and lightning that he could unleash at a moment's notice. He did not fear for his life. He only feared that when he finally escaped this insane land, his brother would not follow.

"You mock my faith and make light of our sacred task," Judarius said. "I have ever performed my duty to Ashhur. I have ever been loyal to my god's desires."

The King of the Fallen

"Ashhur's command was to *fall*," Azariah argued. "His only desire for us now is to suffer and die. Will you honor that wish, too? Or will you finally see it as the true betrayal that it is?"

He prayed his brother understood, even as the first crackle of lightning sparked off his palms and into the wall he was pressed against. He did not wish to explore the unknown alone, but neither would he allow his life to be taken in Ashhur's name. His god had asked everything of him, even his own life once, and Azariah had given it. No more. He would give Karak and Ashhur nothing but the faith and loyalty their initial incarnations deserved, when Paradise was still an achievable reality.

Judarius glared, and within his mind an unspoken battle raged. It ended as suddenly as it began.

"Do as you wish," he said, and released Azariah's neck. "I shall watch this experiment of yours, and say nothing of it to the others."

It wasn't quite a promise to accompany him, but Azariah felt confident that when the time came, and the decision must be made, his brother would make the right call. He smoothed out his robes and let the excitement of the task soothe his bruised ego. No matter how well he understood Judarius's frustrations, it was still insulting to have him raise his hand in violence against him. Even if he planned to abdicate his throne, he was still King, and would be until the portal tore open before him.

"Be quiet and observe," he said, doing his best to push away all those distracting thoughts. "This will take tremendous effort, and I cannot afford to fail."

He stood before the circle of stones, the spellbook resting on a wooden lectern so he might read with his hands free. In many ways, the principle was the same as opening the portal to Veldaren. What changed was the sense of distance, shifting to a scale that was difficult for mortal minds to comprehend. But that distance was irrelevant when ripped apart by magic. He could do this. Others had done so before, after all. Still, he looked over the words in Velixar's spellbook and rehearsed them a dozen more times while building up the nerve.

"Can you truly open a link between worlds?" Judarius asked, watching from beside the door to the tower, having positioned himself there to avoid getting in the way. "It took the might of Qurrah, Tessanna, and Velixar to open the last one. I question whether you possess the power of a daughter of balance, let alone those three combined."

"That was a portal meant to draw in armies," Azariah said. "Not escape a chosen few."

No more stalling. No more dwelling upon the miserable land of Dezrel. Azariah lifted his arms, called upon every shred of his divine power, and read aloud the words. The spell was over fifty lines long, Velixar's handwriting even tighter than normal to ensure it all fit on one page. At the start, it seemed his nerves were undeserving. The words flowed easily despite the difficulty of pronunciation and variance in pitch. It was just a spell, the fallen told himself, once everything was boiled down to its barest essence. Just a spell like any other spell.

The slightest tear split the air before him, wriggling like a hair lodged in his retina, and then the true cost of the spell struck him. The needed power ripped forth from his chest with savage fury. He gasped as his mind threatened to turn white. Every single part of his essence flowed out of him like a broken dam. The portal, it needed so much more than he felt he could give. The strain, it was unbearable.

No, his mind screamed. He would endure. He would survive. He was stronger than Tessanna, stronger than the wretched half-orc betrayer. His vision faded, the colors turning into a strange mixture of reds, purples, and yellows. Yet despite the distortion, the spellbook blazed upon the lectern as if wreathed in flame. Wind howled, flickering out the candles and swirling in a great funnel that scattered books and rattled Judarius's armor.

He should have done this in Veldaren, he realized far too late. He should have done this where the wall of the world was at its thinnest. He should have enlisted the aid of other angels who had begun learning magic alongside him. His pride...his arrogance...

Azariah was doomed.

There was no stopping the spell. The words bellowed out of him with no need for the spellbook's guidance. The storm

The King of the Fallen

grew, blasting apart bookshelves, scattering papers, and making a mockery of the stone walls. The floor rumbled beneath him, as if the portal would bring the entire tower crashing down with its unleashed fury.

"Brother!" Judarius cried, his voice sounding distant. "You must stop this! Halt it now, before we perish!"

But Azariah couldn't halt it. Nothing could. His mind flailed as if pulled by wild horses. Pride had convinced him of his inevitable success, but that pride shattered beneath fear and helplessness. Azariah tried to say goodbye to his brother, to say anything other than scream. He failed.

"Damn it all, I said enough!" Judarius screamed. With an arm up to protect his face from the blinding light of the uneven portal, he barreled straight into Azariah with his shoulder. The impact sent Azariah flying, shock ending the flow of words from his tongue.

Yet it was not the end. His momentum sent him tumbling into the incomplete portal. A sensation like blunt razors scraped across every inch of his skin. He felt himself falling, falling, and then all the world turned black.

This was not death, for Azariah had experienced its sting before. The cosmos swirled about him, colors slowly growing amid the empty. A cloud of violet. A crimson wisp of smoke. Below him, perhaps hundreds of miles, perhaps only a single foot, he saw a stretch of grass disconnected from all realities. Fifteen blades growing from a little patch of dirt, an island of color amidst a yawning black abyss. He was not in water, yet he floated in place, somewhere within the deep depths of nothing.

Where am I?

The moment he thought those words, color exploded about him, the black canvas painted by an invisible brush greater than the hand of a god. His confusion was given material form, and he saw himself, not once, not twice, but a thousand versions standing in a small patch of light enveloped by darkness. They surrounded him on all sides, like frozen drops of rain amid a downpour.

And then he understood, and the knowledge terrified him.

Azariah was lost amid the Weave, the very essence of magic that composed Celestia, and perhaps many other gods and goddesses throughout the countless worlds of the stars. His physical body, assuming he still occupied his physical body, was in a realm he'd not dared enter even during his time in the Golden Eternity.

At the remembrance of the Golden Eternity, the world about him changed again. He saw verdant hills beneath a crystalline sky. He felt the peaceful calm of the land, then the horror of it being stripped from him. In his sudden torment, the sky turned red. Blood fell like rain upon the grasslands, which shriveled black and died. It was a warning to the reality of this place, of how thought itself could be made manifest. The words spoken on the material plane of existence merely tapped into this power, giving form to the formless to create fire or summon lightning with a flick of a wrist.

Azariah? his brother's voice echoed across the void. He was still nearby, in the castle tower, calling out to him. *Can you hear me?*

Hear? asked a crystalline, feminine voice. It shimmered through the expanse. Its every word made the colors vibrate and dance. The fire and destruction of the Golden Eternity faded away, to be replaced with a rainbow of infinite length that curled and looped into eternity. *Nothing shall make the closed mind hear.*

Azariah's fear heightened tenfold. There could only be one entity speaking to him now. The divine creator of the Weave. The elven goddess, Celestia. This must be her domain, and it must be her voice. Would she cast him aside? Destroy him with a thought, as she most certainly could in this floating expanse of magic and chaos?

"Closed?" he called out to the unseen goddess. "Closed, though I see clearly the purpose of all the gods? Blind, for peeling back the false layers of dogma to see your true nature?"

The rainbow tightened about him, its colors bleeding so that the green and blues were bathed with red and orange.

The King of the Fallen

Who are you? No god. No prophet. Fallen one, wretched being, clinging to hate and lusting for violence. I mock you. I deny you. My lover has turned his back to you, and now I behold why.

The surrounding rainbow of colors rippled, long streaks of it burning with sudden fire. The goddess' rage and contempt were shaping the Weave. Azariah felt heat on his skin, shocked at how fiercely it burned.

"I am a king!" he screamed to the infinite. Flames sparked, danced, and died across his robe. "No living being bears my wisdom, my power, or my righteous purpose. Who else alive deserves to sit upon a throne? Who would you put above my knowledge? My claim must be honored, goddess. It must be treasured. Do not deny me my crown!"

Crown? purred that mysterious voice. *Here is your crown. Every crown. In every realm.*

Darkness consumed the rainbow of color. Heat died, becoming cold frost that swirled unseen through the black. In the distance, he heard a sound like breaking glass, and it marked a sudden bloom of light. An image appeared before Azariah, that of his own reflection. He gazed upon it with such clarity that his mind ached. The reflection split, first once, then twice, then a thousand times, until a seemingly infinite array of reflections filled the space before him once more. He witnessed them like little mirrors, images of himself, locked in a moment of time.

In some he knelt. Others he crawled. In some he bled from a wound in his neck, another from a gash in his side. Sometimes he stood outside the Mordeina castle, other times in the room with his failed portal.

In all of them, he died. In all of them, the Godslayer, Harruq Tun, killed him.

"Let me out!" he screamed. His voice felt so meager and pathetic in this magical space. The Weave, it mocked him, his fate, his purported 'destiny'. A million times over, the half-orc stood over his body, Salvation and Condemnation dripping with his divine blood. What did it matter if he escaped the Weave, the reflections seemed to ask. Why live, if that fate ultimately awaited him?

But this was a realm of magic, *the* realm of magic, which meant it still followed rules. The words flowed from his tongue, and he focused on a specific location. It couldn't be far, after all. Part of him was certain he had never left the tower. The magical incantation for a portal finished, he lifted his arms and screamed out the final words. The darkness parted, and in clear blue light he saw his own body lying unconscious on the floor. Judarius knelt over him, cradling him in his arms.

Azariah didn't think. He didn't hesitate. He leapt straight on through, felt himself rising, felt his limbs growing cold and his face warm with sudden fever...

"Azariah? Azariah, my brother, please say something."

He pulled himself free of Judarius's arms, gulping in air as if he'd been drowning. Sweat clung to his neck and face. Where the portal had meant to be in the room was now a deep crack cut into the stone floor. Nothing else remained of the great magic storm but for the mess of scattered shelves and papers.

"You're alive," Judarius said. "The magic, I thought it took you from me."

"I saw," Azariah said, ignoring his brother's concerns. His sanity felt so close to breaking, so very close. "I saw, I saw, I saw..."

"Saw what?" a baffled Judarius asked.

"My deaths," he said. "Every death. Every murder. One hand, all at one hand."

"What are you rambling about? I don't understand."

But Azariah understood. There was no possible misinterpretation. A thousand lifetimes. A thousand outcomes, yet his doom had been singular. It was a cruel jest, but perhaps it might serve a purpose. He spoke his lone hope, gave voice to the words so that he would remember them as his vision darkened and he felt himself slipping away into a much-needed slumber.

So long as the Godslayer lived, he himself would not. There was no alternative.

"Harruq Tun must die."

7

Deathmask quietly slipped into the flow of people heading east, Veliana at his heels. Curiosity kept him moving despite the risk of traveling in broad daylight. Fallen angels had circled overhead for the past ten minutes, demanding attendance for some balefully important event, and they guided people toward a common destination with short barks and points. Deathmask and Veliana traveled without mask or guise, lest they inadvertently draw attention to themselves.

What maniacal nonsense have the fallen cooked up this time? Deathmask wondered.

The gathering was in an ancient open-air theater, its curved space surrounded with wood walls and sporting low, flat benches of stained pine. The stone stage, if Deathmask remembered correctly, had been built by Ashhur himself all those hundreds of years ago when he still walked the land. To enter the theater through either of its two enormous doorways, they had to pass through lines of undead watchers standing perfectly still. Once through that rotten barricade, Deathmask found himself blessed with the sight of three fallen waiting on the center stage, that number swelling to six as time passed and the streams of people trickled in.

Deathmask and Veliana positioned themselves at the farthest edges of the crowd in case they were recognized and needed a hasty escape. The few people nearby gave them only cursory glances, their attention locked on the theater stage. Constant murmurs soaked the crowd, only slightly diminishing when the center angel on the stage stepped forward to begin whatever ceremony was to take place. His armor was smooth and finely polished, yet instead of reflecting sunlight off it in a blinding radiance, it seemed to soak it all in, appearing shadowed and gray even in the bright light.

"People of Mordeina," bellowed the angel. "I am Ezekai, loyal servant and friend of your King, Azariah the Wise and Just. Today marks a momentous occasion, for I come before you to deliver a new way to rest your tired feet, a new truth for your burdened hearts, and a new salvation for this broken land we call Dezrel."

Ezekai paused, letting his words sink in.

"I shall not be making this revelation alone," he continued. "For we shall not be *enacting* this new order alone. To aid me in this, I present to you Paladin Umber of the Stronghold."

A fresh wave of murmurs marked the arrival of the Dark Paladins of Karak from behind the stage. There was no mistaking the six of them, men and women covered from head to toe in painted platemail. The unholy Lion was carved into their breastplates, and its roaring visage marked the faces of their shields and the hilts of their swords. To see them walk so proudly amid the fallen, angels who had so recently fought on the side of Ashhur and laid waste to entire armies of Karak, unnerved even the normally stone-hearted Deathmask.

"Have the angels turned to Karak since Ashhur cursed them?" Veliana whispered. She was hardly the only one with that thought, based on the whispers that washed through the forcibly assembled crowd.

"No," he replied in an equally low voice. "Something about that feels...off. I suspect we shall soon have our explanation."

"Do not burden yourself with confusion," Ezekai shouted. "Answers will come, and our priests will be lecturing every third hour throughout the city to help educate you to the new ways. But for now, we shall grace you all with the honor of being the first to hear the new Three Laws that shall guide not just those here within Mordeina, but all those living in the perfected lands of Paradise."

"Oh, I can't wait to hear these brilliant laws," Deathmask grumbled.

"And then promptly break them," Veliana added.

Ezekai removed a small scroll from his belt and dramatically unfurled it. He stood to his full height, his black wings fanning outward to make him seem that much taller and grander. His voice boomed across the theater. His right hand held the scroll, while his left lifted high above his head and pointed a lone finger.

"The First Law: worship Ashhur for his grace and forgiveness, and as messenger for the kindness you are to show others."

"What nonsense is this?" Veliana whispered. "They suffer Ashhur's curse yet still claim to serve him?"

Deathmask held a finger her direction to shush her. It wasn't that he disagreed, only that he wished to hear the remainder of the laws.

The fallen angel retreated a step, and the man Deathmask presumed to be Umber spread his arms and addressed the people as if they were his beloved children, a sight that filled Deathmask's stomach with an unhealthy amount of bile. He was a younger man, his face a mixture of freckles and scars. Even more striking were the twin lions tattooed on either side of his neck.

"The Second Law," shouted Umber. "Worship Karak for his judgment and wisdom, and as a model for the firm hand you need to reach perfection."

"Oh, piss on all of this," Veliana seethed as the crowd susurrated in mutual surprise. She seemed incapable of keeping her thoughts to herself despite Deathmask's insistence. "They're working together. Karak's paladins and Ashhur's former angels, preaching inglorious harmony."

Umber stepped back, and the angel fluttered forward.

"Last, but equally vital," Ezekai announced. He held three fingers above him. "The Third Law: worship Azariah and his angels for their ceaseless guidance, for they shall lead you to Paradise."

There it was. Azariah had put a crown on his head, and now he demanded the people elevate him to a status equal to Karak and Ashhur. That level of arrogance astounded even Deathmask, but he doubted the fallen angel saw it that way. Those in power had a supernatural ability to be blind to their own faults and failures.

Both Umber and Ezekai addressed the crowd next, and they did so with drawn and raised swords.

"Kneel!" they shouted in unison. "Bow your heads in prayer."

The wave started at the front. Men, women, and children dropped to their knees and bowed their heads to offer the demanded worship. Deathmask glanced at Veliana, and they shared an unspoken agreement. She slipped a mask over her face. He dipped a hand into his pocket and scattered ash into a frozen whirlwind about his head. This was stupid, so incredibly stupid. The two of them could not take on six fallen angels and six dark paladins simultaneously, let alone the rows of undead that awaited outside the theater. Yet they would not bow. They would not pray falsely. Besides, they were in a theater. Why not give the people a show?

Deathmask ran two of his fingers across the dagger in his left hand, drawing blood. He focused upon it, channeling power through a mental incantation. By the time all in the crowd bowed, only Deathmask and Veliana remained standing with their weapons drawn and their faces hidden. The sight of them was a bolt of energy through frightened masses. Both Umber and Ezekai started for a brief moment before readying their blades.

"No," Deathmask said, a tweak of magic ensuring his calmly spoken words echoed throughout the theater. "We will not kneel."

He flicked his fingers toward the stage. The scarlet drops of blood flew over the crowd, shimmering red with magic. One of the dark paladins beside Umber dove in the way, sensing a threat even if none were yet visible. The blood drops splashed across his crossed arms, as well as his chest and waist. Deathmask snapped his fingers.

The paladin's instincts were indeed correct. The blood exploded into dark fire. The sound of wrenching steel filled the theater, accompanied by a pained wail that was magnified by the theater's acoustics. The paladin collapsed, his body rent in half. The fire continued to burn as if the blood were suddenly gallons of oil. Though the stone stage itself could not catch fire, the same could not be said for its luxurious crimson cloth covering. The kneeling crowd reacted instantly to the sight of smoke and fire by stampeding toward the exits.

"Time to go," Deathmask said cheerfully, but Veliana was way ahead of him. He sprinted after her, barely keeping ahead of the frightened mob. He stepped outside to find her slamming into the wave of undead watchers that formed a neat, orderly line near the entrance. Her daggers shimmered with violet fire, adding power to each and every cut. Two quick thrusts tore apart the face of the nearest undead, and a sudden rotation on the ball of her foot sent her heel cracking into the neck of a second. His spine snapped, dropping him.

"No time to play," Deathmask said, and slammed his wrists together. A bolt of shadow burst forth, flying across the space to smash the chest of a third. Though the shadow appeared to be thick, malleable darkness, it bore the weight and impact of stone. The dead man's armor crunched inward, then broke as the bolt pushed all the way through and out his back. His bones collapsed, his rotted flesh sloughing off as the magic holding him together faded.

More undead soldiers rushed to face them, but by now hundreds of people had swarmed out the exits. Against that tide, the few dozen undead were but a hiccup. Any that tried to halt the people were quickly shoved aside, and those that fell were trampled underfoot. Veliana took lead, Deathmask right behind her. He feared no dark paladin, not with a fleeing crowd between them. The angels in the sky, on the other hand...

"This way!" Veliana shouted, and before he realized what was happening, she'd grabbed his arm and pulled. Together they stumbled into the nearest alley, the upper half of which was a crisscross of drying clothes hanging from ropes tied between the buildings. Deathmask resisted his friend's urge to continue, and he ripped his sleeve free of her grasp to spin about. His hands danced in the air, preparing. Anticipating.

An angel swooped into the alleyway at full speed, wings tucked against his sides like a diving hawk seeking prey and his entire body turned sideways to fit into the cramped space. Even prepared, Deathmask nearly faltered when faced with such speed. He clenched his hands into fists, releasing his prepared magic. Spikes composed of an inky dark substance swirling with foul magic tore from the walls on either side of the alley. They slammed together, but while they should have enclosed the angel completely, they only succeeded in severing his upper half from his lower. The wait and legs that remained became fast-moving projectiles of steel and gore that tore through the clotheslines, and it was only Veliana's firm grasp that pulled Deathmask out of the way of the carnage. Even then, he did not escape completely. A boot clipped his forehead on the way down, adding a dizzying spin before he collapsed onto his stomach.

"Fuck me," he muttered. The world spun and his stomach debated whether or not to empty itself.

"Hardly the time or place," Veliana said. She was already lifting him up and forcing his legs to move. "For now, we need to get the Abyss out of here."

Even with his injury, it didn't take much for them to vanish from the rest of the patrolling angels. After years of dealing with the guilds of Veldaren, hiding in alleys from fallen angels was almost leisurely by comparison.

"I'm getting pretty sick of this particular cellar," Veliana muttered as she led the way inside. Once they'd shaken their pursuers, they'd shifted their direction to their current hiding location of choice, the dim basement where she'd brought him when he returned to Mordeina.

"I know I've promised to kill them before," Deathmask said, slamming the door shut and enveloping them in darkness. A quick snap of his fingers, a whispered cantrip, and magical flame sparkled from his palm. He gently pushed it forward, floating the flame to the center of the cramped space so it could cast its violet glow across the entire cellar. "But this time I swear I will *really* make sure they die a hundred horrid and painful deaths. I don't care if they say they follow Karak or Ashhur. Dead. I'm going to make them dead."

He gingerly touched his forehead. An enormous welt had already sprouted from where he'd been clipped by the fallen angel's boot. Given the intensity of his headache, he wouldn't be surprised if it'd cracked the bone.

"I never considered you someone who cared about another person's worship," Veliana said.

"As far as I'm concerned, both gods are responsible for destroying the world," Deathmask said. "So in my humble opinion, fuck them all. Fuck Ashhur. Fuck Karak. By the Abyss, even fuck Celestia for putting up with those two brats in the first place. If she'd known any better, she would have stomped us humans out the moment we crawled from the mud and muck."

Veliana settled into one of the cellar's corners, shifting aside some wet pieces of broken wood so she might have someplace moderately dry to sit.

"If that's what you think, why are you so upset about any sort of agreement between Ashhur and Karak?" she asked. "Even if it's just fake, like theirs obviously is? No one believes Ashhur guides the angels he so clearly cursed. No one's praying to Karak out of loyalty or sincerity. It's all fear and control to get what Azariah wants. Does it matter what form that fear and control takes?"

Deathmask snapped his fingers so the cloud of ash obscuring his features dropped to the floor in a gray poof. "You sound so very much like me five years ago. I'm flattered."

"And you're avoiding the question."

That he was, without even realizing it. He squirmed a bit, his back uncomfortably pressed into a shelf filled with jarred vegetables of unknown age. Talking about religion was one of his least favorite activities. Rarely did he give the time or energy to consider what any of the gods might want, beyond how they may try to stifle him in an adversarial role. Yet with Mordan effectively ruled by angels, there hadn't been much choice in the matter over the past five years, and now Azariah had come along and thrown yet another jug of oil onto an already out-of-control fire.

But Veliana wasn't wrong. The idea of what Azariah proposed, and the faith he seemed determined to create, did bother him to no end. The intensity of it surprised even him. So what was it?

"I suppose it's because I've always felt humanity can be better," he said. "For all our faults and failures, there is the potential we accomplish something meaningful during our dismal little lives. And for a lot of people, the gods help them do that. They give them the incentive they need to actually give a damn about others, as sad as that sounds. Yet too often the priests and servants of those gods dress up the requirements. They saddle good deeds with required tithes. They give cowardly outs to those with guilty consciences. Don't step out your front door and help others, just hide at home and offer Ashhur your intercessory prayer instead. That's good enough, isn't it?"

"Be better," Veliana said. "You truly think humanity can be better? That all this shit we find ourselves in isn't our own fault?"

Deathmask had been so focused on his own ramblings and rants he hadn't realized how emotional his dear friend had become. She crouched in the corner, her jaw clenched so tight she resembled a beast baring her fangs. Her right hand rested upon her face, fingers tracing the scar carved into her flesh many years ago by a bastard known simply as Worm.

"Perhaps," he said. "Or perhaps I am talking out of my ass. You've seen the absolute worst of us, Vel. And the gods know I've used the weak impulses of others to turn a profit for myself. Maybe we're all damned and rotten, but I won't let Azariah get away with this wretched compromise of his. If the divine hold any meaning to humanity, it should be to inspire hope. It should lift up those who need it, and who seek it. Not kill. Not destroy." He laughed. "Leave the killing and destroying to the twisted bastards like us. At least we don't pretend our actions are divine."

Veliana pulled her hand away from her scar. Her gaze turned unfocused as she receded into her memories.

"I had a friend once," she said. "Perhaps 'friend' is too strong a word, but we trained together for a few years. Her name was Zusa, a member of a particular cult of Karak that forced its women to cover up every shred of exposed skin in some sort of atonement for supposed sins. It took such a long time for her to grow comfortable showing her face, even to me. It took even longer for her to break from the guilt they saddled her with. She was so skilled, so beautiful, and yet all she'd been told throughout her life was to hide herself in shame and was convinced that her value was found only in servitude to Karak."

Veliana stood, clutching the hilts of her sheathed daggers as if she needed something to grasp lest she lose control. The rage, the disgust, was beyond anything Deathmask had seen in her before. It impressed and frightened him in equal measure.

"Azariah would wrap the entire world in cloth," she said. "He would crush every instinct for joy, uniqueness, or discovery in the name of a so-called Paradise. Every man, woman, and child will be saddled with so much guilt and told the only way, the only path to salvation, is through blind obedience. I will not have it. I don't give a shit about the divine. I don't care if they can help humanity, or hurt us. Save our souls, or burn them in the fires of the Abyss? Piss on either. I refuse to let Azariah turn the entire world Faceless. His name, Karak's, Ashhur's, it doesn't matter whose. We won't be bound. We won't be imprisoned for a Paradise that is nothing more than a joyless graveyard of bones."

"I applaud your enthusiasm," Deathmask said. "But we are a mere two against an entire city of undead, a host of fallen angels, and dark paladins of Karak. What, exactly, do you propose we do to prevent Dezrel from sliding into such an accursed fate?"

She drew her daggers and flipped the handles twice before pointing their edges his way.

"We kill, and then kill some more," she said. "I do believe you promised to roll Azariah's head down the steps of the castle, did you not?"

Deathmask laughed. "That I did."

"And have you abandoned that plan?"

He leaned against the shelf, closed his eyes, and grinned. By the gods, he did not deserve a friend so fierce, so wonderful.

"Not at all," he said. "And should I ever consider it, I expect you to keep me on the proper path to much-needed revenge. Oh, and before this horrid headache makes me forget: add Ezekai and Umber to the list of those whose heads I need to roll."

8

Jerico stepped into the small room of the Citadel, finely furnished with a padded feather-mattress, a slender standing mirror, and a chestnut wardrobe. When planning the rebuilding, the room had been meant to serve visiting dignitaries. Jerico found it doubtful the haggard-looking farmer sitting on the edge of the bed was what the angels had in mind.

Lathaar waited for him inside, still in the casual white undershirt and faded brown trousers he'd woken up wearing that morning. His swords, however, were nearby, and Jerico worried at how his friend kept nervously tapping his fingers upon their sheaths.

"I was told we had an injured guest," Jerico said, throwing the farmer a wide grin. "Yet you seem far from injured."

"It's nothing, sir," the farmer said. He looked in his late thirties, his skin deeply tanned and his clothes permanently stained from sweat. His voice carried the heavy drawl common to those in the western portions of Omn, before the majority of its populace had crossed the river during the second Gods' War to settle throughout the nation of Ker. "Just a bit of a bleeding foot from the walk. I stepped wrong on a branch near the river, that's all."

"I prayed over it already," Lathaar said as he stood. "No reason in letting our good man here suffer while we waited for you to arrive."

Jerico exchanged a look with his fellow paladin. The shadow that fell across Lathaar's eyes was all he needed to know that this visitor brought nothing but ill tidings.

That bad? he silently mouthed.

Maybe worse, Lathaar mouthed back.

"Well, the two of us are here," Jerico said cheerfully. He grabbed one of the two ornate chairs set on either side of a tiny window-table and sat down. "Care to share what brought you to our Citadel?"

"It's them orcs," the farmer said. "Sorry, I should retreat things back a bit. My name is Jenava, from Selma village. We're eighty miles south of here. Have you heard of us?"

The King of the Fallen

"Of course we have," Jerico said. "Before the Citadel fell, we used to travel the river to Selma every fall for cider brewed from your apples."

The farmer smiled, his nerves easing at pleasant memories from a time before the second Gods' War reshaped Dezrel.

"Yeah, them were the days," he said. "My pa used to say our village owed our existence to the Citadel's hungry students. Then it fell, and well, we made due. The war spared us, what with us being so far north up the river from the bridges. But something stirred up the orcs living in Omn. A group of ten crossed the Rigon on a boat and demanded a tithe."

Jerico shot Lathaar a look, and his fellow paladin shrugged. So far as either of them knew, orcs were more known for smashing, grabbing, and pillaging whatever they desired than expecting something so formal as a tithe.

"A tithe?" he asked, unable to hide his incredulity.

"A goddamn tithe," Jenava said. "Like they have some nation or king."

"What did your village do?" Jerico prodded.

"We gave it to them. Ten armed orcs, eager for a fight? We gave what food we could spare, and plenty more we couldn't, until nothing more fit in their boat. After that they said they'd be visiting other towns along the river, but come a week, they'd be back for more. That's why I'm here. I'm asking for help. If we give any more, we'll starve in the coming winter, But if you'd seen the look in their eyes, you'd know that telling them that ain't an option. We'll be dead either way."

Jerico rose from his chair and patted the worried farmer on the shoulder.

"Don't worry," he said. "Nothing bad will happen to your village. Now if you don't mind, I need to speak with my friend here."

Jerico and Lathaar exited the room, shut the door, and descended several steps of the winding staircase so they might go unheard.

"The orcs picked an Abyss of a good time to start stirring up trouble," Jerico grumbled.

"King Antonil feared they might set up a true kingdom when he marched east," Lathaar said. "There might be truth to it. But what do we do?"

Jerico furrowed his brow. "What do we do? We go help them. I didn't think this was in question."

"A small group of farmers," Lathaar said. He dropped the volume of his voice by half. "We're in the middle of a war. Villages are displaced all the time. We could send Jenava on his way, with a message for anyone living alongside the Rigon to flee deeper into Ker."

"You don't want to help them?"

"Of course I want to help," Lathaar said, punching the brick wall behind him. "The idea of doing nothing makes me want to vomit, but what of Aubrienna and Gregory? They've been entrusted to our care. Would you leave them behind? Gamble their safety with our students? We're relying on Tarlak's cleverness to keep their existence here a secret, but he's not infallible, and Azariah is no fool. At any moment that self-proclaimed king might arrive at our Citadel with his fallen angels. Is this truly worth the risk?"

Jerico tried to view things from a rational point of view, but could see no alternative that made things any less clear. Yes, he had promised his friends to keep the two children safe. He had also sworn his entire life to protecting the innocent. To place Aubrienna on a pedestal above others simply due to friendship, or to declare Gregory more important than dozens of others due to his station at birth, directly contradicted his most deeply-held beliefs. All people were sacred. All were worthy of life, love, and happiness.

"We help those in need," Jerico said. "That hasn't changed. That must never change. I'll go. It will only be a few days at most. You'll still be here, and with our students to aid you."

"And if a host of fallen arrive?" Lathaar asked. "Do you believe that will be enough?"

Jerico cracked a bitter smile. "Do you believe it'd be enough even if I were there with you?"

They both knew the answer. Lathaar looked away and slowly shook his head. Satisfied, Jerico continued: "If Azariah comes for us, our fate will not be in our hands, but in Ashhur's. That hasn't changed, either. I'm going to Selma. My mind is made up, so if you plan to keep me here, you better find your swords and go in my place."

❖

Jerico and Jenava sailed south along the Rigon in one of the Citadel's many boats instead of the derelict raft the farmer had arrived on. Jenava was clearly at home with a paddle, to which Jerico was happy take advantage of. The hours passed peacefully, Jenava guiding the boat through the center of the wide river and singing songs that had been passed down through generations. Based on calculations made prior to leaving, they would cross the distance between the Citadel and Selma in a little under two days, which meant beating the orcs there by a day. Their boat stopped for nothing, and when either needed a break from rowing, they let the current lazily carry them.

"It's a shame we don't have one of those summoning lights the bigger villages got," Jenava said on their second day on the river, as the two of them ate from the basket of food Jerico had brought. The basket even contained a sealed jar of cider that most certainly came from Selma, a fact that gave Jerico mild amusement.

"For the angels?" Jerico asked. Over the five years since Thulos's defeat, the angels had passed about magical devices that could shine great lights into the sky, meant to catch the attention of distant angels to bring them flying in to solve whatever dilemma or danger befell the people.

"Yeah, it would have spared us all this trip," Jenava said. "Surely one or two angels would have cleaned up those orcs nicely."

Jenava didn't know, Jerico realized. So far from the capital, the little village was likely weeks, if not months, from rumors carried by travelers reaching the eastern edges of Ker. At least it meant they had been spared the fallen's initial rage, they had wantonly slaughtered any human with the poor fortune of living near the capital.

"The angels would bring you no safety or comfort," Jerico said. "Events have turned...ill, in Mordeina."

Over the next half hour, he explained the events to the quiet farmer. He told them of Avlimar's collapse, the rebuilding of Devlimar, and Azariah's eventual declaration of himself as king over humanity. Then came Ashhur's condemnation, the horrendous Night of Black Wings, and the ensuing massacre of innocents. Jenava's face darkened with the news, but he didn't seem surprised.

"My pa told me of bad dreams he'd been having," Jenava said. "Some of the older folks mentioned the same. Truth be told, we were nervous about calling for any angel to help us. That's why we went north, to your Citadel, instead of south to Gendram to use their holy torch. Too many were fearful that Ashhur had abandoned us. Sounds like it was true."

"Ashhur has not abandoned you," Jerico said, much more defensively than he intended. "Am I not on my way to protect your friends and family?"

"*You* are," Jenava said. He took up the oar and began paddling as he talked. He seemed unable or unwilling to meet Jerico's gaze. "But you ain't Ashhur."

"Does a king not defend his borders by sending his solders? Or does it count only if he wields a sword at every border skirmish?"

Jenava scratched at the scraggly brown beard growing along the sides of his face.

"Maybe it's just my upbringing, but we folk along the Rigon teach our children that the fault of a deed belongs to the hand that done it. After the war ended, we were told Ashhur left us his angels to protect us, and to praise Ashhur for that gift. Now those angels want to kill us. How come Ashhur gets none of that blame? I see you trying to have it both ways, paladin, and my mind don't like it none."

Now it was Jerico's turn to look at the muddy water instead of Jenava's brown eyes.

"You speak more truth than I'd like to hear," he said softly. "I have seen enough of war and destruction to know that sometimes the quiet mouth issuing the order carries far more blame than the thousands enacting out that deed in their name."

The King of the Fallen

"Is that Selma?" Jerico asked as the thatched-roof homes appeared beyond the riverbank. It was a charming little place, one Jerico vaguely remembered from his days as a young student. Several docks marked the edge of the village, plus an enormous barn for storage just far enough from the water's edge to keep it safe should the spring rains bring a flood. The homes themselves were a quarter-mile farther back on a winding dirt road. From within that collection rose thick plumes of black smoke.

"Aye, that's home," Jenava said. He slammed the oar into the water with panicked strength. "And it's burning."

"We have another day before the orcs said they'd return," Jerico said, trying to maintain hope.

"That's thinking orcs count the days and weeks the same as us. For both our sakes, grab the other oar and get to paddling. Your shield might already be needed!"

Jerico was all too happy to help, and ten minutes later their boat struck the docks. Jenava was the first out, tying the boat with the speed of a man who had crafted the necessary knots a hundred times before. Given the weight of his shield and platemail, Jerico waited until the boat was safely secured to step off. The well-worn boards groaned beneath his feet.

"Damn it, I was hoping it was just some foolhardy bonfire for cooking," Jenava said, pointing to another boat tied to the docks. It was larger than the others nearby, painted with white and red stripes along its edges. "But that one ain't one of ours."

Jerico put a hand on the farmer's shoulder.

"Pray to Ashhur for your family's safety," he said. "And then run with me."

Jerico had managed far greater distances during the Gods' War, though he was keenly reminded by muscles sore from two days on a cramped boat that he had been a much younger man at the time. His armor rattled as he ran, his eyes locked on the smoke. He wasn't too late, he told himself. He wouldn't stumble upon some horrific sight. Dezrel had enough suffering to last it a lifetime. It needn't spread so far, nor taunt him with it now.

Boisterous cries mixed with fearful shouts and crying filled the air. Jerico readied his mace and shield as the first of the homes he and Jenava neared, and he slid off the path so he might hide behind it and observe.

Jenava slid in beside him. "Anyone hurt?"

Jerico observed the village's crowded communal yard. It seemed the entire village had been rounded up and set before a roaring bonfire. From what he could tell, the fire was built of a rushed collection of the villagers' belongings, be it clothes, tools, or furniture. The orcs, ten in number as Jenava had promised, formed a loose perimeter around them. Their armor was a chaotic assortment of chain and plate worn by soldiers from all four kingdoms across Dezrel, be it Neldar, Omn, Ker, or Mordan. No doubt the orcs had scavenged the armor from conquered city vaults, or looted the many battlefields scattered throughout the east. Their weapons were sharp and well-cared for, a fact that hardly surprised Jerico. The orcs had suffered life in the barren and crowded Vile Wedge. They knew how to fight, how to scavenge, and how to maintain what little resources they possessed.

As for Jenava's question, Jerico saw a single body lying very still near the bonfire.

"Only one death so far," Jerico said upon leaning back behind the house.

"Food!" one of the orcs shouted at the top of his lungs. "All we asked for was food! Not gold, not trinkets, just a tithe of food. Was that so wrong? No killing. We had no plans of killing. We be nice like that, but no, a tithe of food is just too damn much for you sorry lot!"

The crying, most of it from children, heightened in volume.

"Too much!" other orcs joined in.

"Yeah, just too much!"

"And so it looks like we gotta teach you some lessons," the first orc resumed. "No food for us? Then nothing that ain't food for you. That's fair, right? You go on and keep that food we know you got hidden. You keep it, and you see if it's worth it when we come a-knocking next year!"

The mockery obviously set Jenava's blood to boiling, because his cheeks bloomed a bright red and his breathing quickened. Only Jerico's firm hand kept the farmer from dashing around the corner to join the others in the village center.

"Calm yourself," Jerico said. "You're not even armed, and they carry weapons and armor scavenged from armies."

The farmer's jaw clenched so tight it looked like his teeth might crack.

"Fine," he said. "Then what will you do?"

Jerico tightened his grip on Bonebreaker and shifted his shield into a more comfortable angle on his arm.

"Save your village," he said with a mischievous grin. "Isn't that why I'm here?"

After one last prayer to Ashhur, Jerico stepped around the home and casually sauntered toward the village center, Bonebreaker swinging playfully in a circle as he twirled it by its leather strap.

"Hey, hey, hey now," Jerico said, and he grinned as if he had stumbled upon Dezrel's wildest party. "What's this I hear about taking tithes?"

The orcs turned his way with bulging eyes and hanging mouths. They certainly acted as if they recognized a paladin of Ashhur, but they also seemed baffled by his presence, his cockiness, and his very appearance. Jerico relied on all three.

"Get on home now, all of you," he told the villagers. "There's business to be handled."

"St...stay where you are!" the largest of the orcs shouted.

"I said go home, now go," Jerico said, louder and with the slightest hint of impatience. "Don't make me say it thrice."

The people of Selma scattered without further instruction. The attention of all ten orcs locked upon him, and while they were clearly frustrated with the sudden dispersal of the crowd, they dared not look away. Not when a shimmering light blazed across the surface of his shield, the very sight of it setting their eyes to water and their stomachs to knot.

"Who are you?" the leader asked. Unlike the other nine, he wore a long red cloak that, if Jerico's guess were correct, had once been fancy draperies of some mansion or castle. "You these people's king?"

"King?" Jerico asked, his stance always shifting so that he could observe the entire clearing. With the crowd still in the process of departing, the orcs would be able to close in on all sides of him. Jerico's heart picked up in anticipation of battle. "No king. Just their protector."

Ten to one, fully surrounded, without the benefit of surprise? The orcs didn't have a chance.

Jerico dashed to the nearest with his shield leading. The orc had but a moment to lift his sword, thinking to block, but then holy light flared from the shield's metal surface. It didn't just blind. The orc rocked backward as if punched, and that was before the shield made contact. Bones shattered across his face and chest from the impact.

Twirling Bonebreaker above his head, Jerico sent it crashing back down upon another orc seeking to attack while he was distracted. The mace caved in his skull as if it were glass. He kicked the body away and spun again, knowing the easy part of the battle was over. He'd caught them overconfident and unaware, but now they roared with unleashed rage and came barreling in.

Instinct and training took over, all of it flowing with an innate sense of warning and guidance from Ashhur. He blocked an ax swing, smashed in a kneecap, and then chose a random direction and sprinted with his shield leading. The holy light smashed away his foes, giving him a momentary reprieve. He took advantage of it, Bonebreaker always in motion. Another orc fell, every bone in his ribs pulverized. A second tried to overwhelm him with a massive overhead smash of his sword. Jerico met it with his shield, and he grit his teeth and endured the sudden shock to his arm. A tremendous flash of light accompanied the impact. The metal of the sword cracked down the middle and then split in half. Jerico retaliated before the orc realized he was defenseless. One swing took off his jaw. The second split his head like a watermelon.

"That it?" he cried to keep them riled. "That all you bastards' have for me?"

Again they tried to bury him, again he shifted and turned amid their numbers. Not quite the dancer that the Watcher had once been, but still never giving them a free strike at his back.

The King of the Fallen

Always turning, always swinging so they could not go on the offensive, or paid dearly if they tried. The flanged edges of his mace tore into exposed muscle. The light of his shield sent jolting pain up their limbs with every blocked blow. Another exchange of hits, and two more orcs fell at his feet. The rest, save one, broke for the boat. Jerico ignored the ones who fled, for the red-draped leader stalked toward him with a tremendous sword wielded in both his hands.

"I'm gonna roast you over a fire and make soup of your guts," he said.

"Better than you have tried and failed. Killing me, that is. I don't think anyone's tried to eat me yet. Actually wait, there were those wolf-men of the North…"

The orc howled with fury. He relied on strength over skill, and against any other opponent it might have worked. Jerico braced his legs and intercepted the wide swing with his shield. He would not be moved. He would not be broken. He let his anger keep him rooted, let his faith keep his shield strong. The orc's weapon exploded into shards, and as the metal splinters filled the air, Jerico pressed forward like a charging bull. His shield struck the orc in the chest. There came a momentary gasp of silence, and then power rolled through his body, ruining the aggressor. The orc collapsed, bones a mess, his innards jelly.

"A whole nation to yourselves, and still you come to pillage," Jerico said, shaking his head. "You have no one but yourselves to blame."

He clipped Bonebreaker to his waist and slid his shield onto his back. He saw Jenava come running and offered him a wide grin, only to have it returned with a look of absolute fear.

"You need to run," the farmer shouted.

Jerico gestured to the many bodies. "What? Why? They're all dead."

"Not the orcs." He pointed to the sky. "*Them.*"

Jerico followed the direction of his finger. They were still distant, but there was no question that three sets of black wings flew in from the west. Jerico's heart sank.

"Such wonderful timing, as always."

"What do we do?" Jenava asked.

"Pretend you killed them yourselves." The farmer looked at Jerico like he was insane. "Well, do you have any better ideas?"

Jenava grimaced. "We'll do our best."

Jerico sprinted toward the nearest house, all the while muttering at his miserable luck. He dove through the door just before the fallen landed, and he quietly laughed with the grim humor that had kept him going throughout the years.

"This isn't fair. Couldn't you have at least shown up to help with the orcs first?"

9

"I have the worst luck," Jerico muttered, backing against the wall adjacent to the window. "At this point I think it's provable beyond a doubt, really."

There was no reason to fight the three angels on his own, not if they left the farmers alone. If any of them survived, they might tell Azariah of his presence. The fallen king was clever enough he might wonder why Jerico was back at the Citadel instead of fighting with Harruq and the others. But Jerico kept his mace and shield ready, just in case. After that initial Night of Black Wings, the fallen had seemed to gather control of themselves. Even the most savage bloodlust could be glutted after such a slaughter. Could they be coming to help with the orcs? It was possible, but Jerico's instincts said otherwise.

"Gather around," one of the three fallen cried after the trio had landed in the center of the village. "I am Bathala, and I would speak with all members of this village."

First orcs, now fallen angels. It was enough to make Jerico feel bad for the people here. He carefully peered around the window's edge to watch the events unfold.

"What transpired here?" Bathala asked once the villagers had gathered.

"Orcs crossed the river," Jenava hurried to answer before others might. "But we fought 'em off, didn't we?"

The three fallen glanced about at the bodies. Even a cursory glance put such a story in doubt.

"With what weapons?"

A very good question, one Jenava obviously had no answer for. They possessed mostly farming instruments, maybe some knives and hammers that could make do in a pinch. To deal the colossal damage Jerico had done with Bonebreaker?

"With whatever we got our hands on," Jenava answered. "When your lives are on the line, you do what you must. A hoe might till soil better than muscle, but it can still pack a wallop when swung right."

A few others around him nodded and murmured in agreement. It was a weak excuse, but it seemed enough for the fallen. From what Jerico could tell, the gray-skinned monsters seemed only vaguely interested in the orc bodies bleeding out around them. It was a distraction from their true purpose, which their leader unrolled a single scroll to address.

"Next time do not fear to call to us for aid," Bathala said. "We are still your guardians, even if our appearance and purpose has...shifted due to Ashhur's callousness."

Shifted. Jerico smirked. Yes, that was indeed one way to put their black wings, ashen skin, and jagged teeth. Just a mere shift toward the monstrous and away from the beauty they once possessed.

"We come bearing news from Mordeina," the fallen continued. "We come with wisdom, and guidance, for the people of Dezrel to cherish within their hearts in this new age that our world finds itself in after Thulos's defeat. In my hands is the wisdom of Azariah the Wise and Just, King of the Angels, Lord of Devlimar, and the guiding hand leading humanity to its divine purpose."

Jerico clenched his jaw and had to order himself to keep still. He'd been told that Azariah had declared himself king of Mordan, but this was his first time hearing such claims with his own ears. It galled him to his core.

"King of the angels?" someone in the crowd asked. "Didn't think the angels had no king."

Bathala extended a bloody smile the man's way. "We change, just as Dezrel changes. There are no kingdoms of man, not anymore. Mordan and Ker will be merged, and all of humanity ruled under a single nation. Paradise, children of the brother gods. Your nation is Paradise, just as it was when Karak and Ashhur first walked the lands of Dezrel in the only time of peace your race has truly known."

More worried murmurs.

"What of King Bram?" Jenava asked. "What of Queen Loreina? Have our lieges handed over Ker's lands to your rule?"

"King Bram Henley is dead," Bathala said, clearly displeased with the question. "As for Queen Loreina, it is only a matter of time. Humanity has ever been a stubborn child when it comes to accepting what is in their best nature, but we believe that wisdom shall prevail."

That gave Jerico a bit of hope. If Ker could withstand the fallen's conquest, there might be hope for an alliance. That, of course, involved Ahaesarus and Queen Loreina overcoming their own differences. Not guaranteed, but more likely as the fallen grew greedier and eyed conquest of all human lands.

Bathala lifted his scroll, clearly eager to bring matters back to his proclamation.

"We have tried granting rules and laws to govern your sinful nature," he said, resuming his rehearsed speech. "But Azariah has seen the folly of this method. Instead we shall hand down three key rules for humanity to follow. The Three Laws, they shall be known. Simple guidance that all may understand upon hearing, and learn over the course of a lifetime how to better honor and perform these truths. They are divine in nature, and obedience is vital. If you are to survive through these harsh days and reach the sunlit future, you will keep them close to your hearts at all times."

Jerico slammed a fist against his thigh to keep himself from moving. Azariah would toss aside all of Ashhur's teachings, and for what? Three little rules he'd crafted on his own? What arrogant, prideful nonsense was this? His initial fury only grew as he listened to Bathala read the Three Laws with such pompousness, as if he expected the people to weep with amazement from merely hearing them.

"The First Law: worship Ashhur for his grace and forgiveness, and as messenger for the kindness you are to show others. The Second Law: worship Karak for his judgment and wisdom, and as model for the firm hand you need to reach perfection. The Third Law: worship Azariah and his angels for their ceaseless guidance, for they shall lead you to Paradise."

Nothing, no other combination of words in all existence, could have come from Bathala's lips and angered Jerico more.

"How dare you?" he whispered. "How...*dare* you?"

It was maddening enough to hear Ashhur and Karak equated to one another on equal terms, as if Karak's faithful hadn't torched half the world in their mad quest to free their god. Worse was hearing Azariah elevate himself in equal terms to the two gods, and demand similar worship. Even Karak held better claim to humanity's heart. Azariah never crafted humanity from the dust and clay. He did not grant the divine gift of a soul into a mortal vessel. Damn it, the angels were meant to be humanity's *protectors*. To abandon that role and demand prayer and worship...

"What you ask, it can't be right," an older man said. He pushed himself to the front of the crowd. "I've worshiped Ashhur all my life. To pray to Karak? To pray to Azariah like a god? That's a sin, angel. It's a sin, and by the look of your wings, you've done some sinning yourself. Ashhur ain't with you, is he? Not if the nightmares we share are true."

The three fallen spread their wings. Bathala drew his sword.

"Hold your tongue," he seethed.

The fury in the fallen's every movement was overwhelming. The way the black wings shivered reminded Jerico of an angered rattlesnake's tail.

"Forgive an old man," was the man's response, for he clearly realized his life hung by a thread. He bowed his head and kept his eyes to the dirt. "I merely ask so I might understand."

It might have been good enough to spare his life, but it did not soothe the indignation that boiled over all three of the fallen.

"You speak as if you are still equal to us in privilege," Bathala raged. "You address me as if I am not your divinely appointed superior. This ignorance will not stand, people of Selma. Your sinfulness, your wretchedness, shall abide no longer. The Three Laws are not guidelines for you to ignore. They are not warm words to allow you to sleep well at night. They should inspire fear. You should hold them in your hands like nails, and clutch them tightly no matter how much they make you bleed."

He swung his sword in a wide arc.

"All of you, on your knees. You shall pray. Pray to Ashhur for forgiveness. Pray to Karak for mercy come the time for judgment. Last, pray to Azariah. Pray that the angel king will lead your sinful kind to Paradise. Hold in your hearts a yearning to become better creatures, better humans, and that dream may become truth."

It started as a few, but the few became the whole village as men, women, and children dropped to their knees and bowed their heads. The fallen had their weapons drawn, and they towered over the populace with faded armor and black wings. None could resist, so better to feign prayer and mouth a few empty words. Jerico knew it was wise to let them leave. There was no reason to risk his life, nor the lives of the villagers. But the words burned his ears. The demand filled his chest with bile. Wise or not, safe or not, he refused to cower while the fallen forced people to kneel in worship. He carried his mace and shield for a reason, and this was it.

"I know you're not with them," Jerico prayed at the door to the home. "But please, stay with me."

He stepped out from the home. Light shimmered off his shield, and it seemed to grow with Jerico's fury as he called out to the fallen.

"Three Laws!" he shouted. "Three betrayals!"

The fallen startled at his presence, and all three soared several feet into the air.

"What deception is this?" Bathala asked.

"Deception?" Jerico roared. "You demand people kneel and worship with a blade against their throats, and yet you prattle to *me* about deception?"

The fallen were far more terrifying villains to face than orcs. Worse, if they fled, he could do nothing to chase. He had to keep them furious. He had to bait them into Bonebreaker's reach. Given the disgust he saw on their ashen faces, he did not think that would be too difficult. They were trying, though, clinging to a veneer of respectability and honor that matched nothing of their wretched forms.

"We know you, paladin," Bathala said. "Jerico of the Citadel, great champion of our god. We need not spill blood this day, if you are willing to listen to reason. We bear wisdom, and ask only that you accompany us into this new age."

"Wisdom," Jerico said, grinning through clench teethed. "Tell me, what is your wisdom?"

"The brother gods were once one!" the fallen angel shouted as if he spoke some great revelation Jerico hadn't known since his earliest days in training. "And in the earliest of times, when Dezrel knew peace and prosperity, the gods ruled over all as true kings, directly handing out their laws and verdicts. They worked together as a force for Paradise, un-beholden to kings, queens, or mortal lordlings. We shall return to that time. We shall have humanity ruled directly through the Golden Eternity's wisest, the closest replication to the divinity we yet possess."

"You mean Azariah," Jerico spat.

"King Azariah," Bathala said, rising higher into the air. "Wisest among us, and chosen by Ashhur himself to be the leader of his religion before his banishment into the eternal realms by the elven goddess. Would you claim yourself wiser than he? Do you believe your few meager decades of mortal existence can compare to the centuries he has experienced? We witnessed humanity climb from the dirt. We watched your kingdoms rise and fall from our golden perch. We suffer, and endure this curse of our mortal flesh, all for your benefit. We shall drag humanity, *all* of humanity, into the light of eternity so that none must suffer the punishment of Karak's darkness. Let the purifying flames bear no purpose. Let sin be extinguished so the brothers may be rejoined. This is the path of the righteous. This is the way of the divinely chosen."

Jerico's skin crawled. He had fought these fallen before, but not heard them proclaim their 'wisdom'. He thought somehow Karak's influence had warped them, but this was something far deeper. This was a rot that went all the way down to the root, and Karak was not to blame. Not even Azariah could have done this on his own. Had he been blind to the symptoms? Had they all not seen the potential dangers of a Mordan ruled by angels?

"You say your way is righteous," Jerico said. He stood tall and lifted his shield. "You say you understand the truth of the gods. I say you are liars and cowards. I say you have elevated yourselves above those you were meant to serve, and have confused pride and arrogance for loyalty. Come, prove to me your supposed *truth,* you bastards. I'm right here, and I say you're full of shit."

The two other fallen looked to their leader. Bathala clutched his sword in both hands and pressed its bone hilt to his lips.

"Not all are capable of seeing wisdom in this life," he said. "May you find it in the hereafter."

The fallen to his right rotated mid-air and then dove, black wings fluttering, sword leading. Jerico braced his legs and flexed the muscles of his arms. He had stood against gods. These broken angels would mean nothing. The sword struck his shield, the impact jarring all the way up to his elbow, but the shield held firm. Next came the fallen's body itself, his momentum carrying him onward. Light swelled across his shield's surface, and within that holy power Jerico felt Ashhur's rage. His feet skidded, his heels dug grooves into the soft earth. A primal, wordless cry roared from deep within his chest. He would not be moved. His foe's bones broke. The twisted sword shattered.

With one last flare of light, the fallen collapsed into the earthen groove Jerico's feet had carved, dead.

"Wisdom," Jerico shouted to the remaining two. "Here is your wisdom. It lies bloody in an open grave."

The fallen dove in unison, swords out and hungry. As their black wings spiraled, Jerico braced himself. He feared he couldn't take them on simultaneously, not with raw strength against strength, but what other choice did he have? He couldn't outmaneuver them, not with their wings. He had to endure, he had to be the stone that would not break. Ashhur's anger washed over him, and he prayed that would be enough.

For a moment there was a strange calm. The fallen's movements were slow and calculated. They did not attempt to collide, only flash past him while swinging their weapons. His mace parried one, his shield blocked the other. Jerico spun on his heels, forced to track the constant shifts in direction as they looped back up and around for another pass. Another hit on his shield, hard enough to leave his arm numb. He dropped to one knee to duck underneath a swing, and though he tried to clip the fallen with Bonebreaker, he missed by mere inches.

Up and around, coming in for another pass. They would wear him down, using their constant plummets from the sky to add strength to their attacks so they would never tire. He had to bring them low and keep them low. Had to surprise them.

"Were you watching at Veldaren?" he asked, turning his head to the side when another swipe clanged off the center of his shield. "Do you remember the siege of Mordeina?"

The two fallen joined for a singular attack, Bathala hovering slightly above his partner as they dove with swords leading. A tired grin crossed Jerico's face.

"I guess not." He lifted his shield to greet them, a single word screaming off his tongue. "*Elholad!*"

A glowing replica of his shield flashed off its surface and grew, becoming a wall of light. The fallen angels slammed into it, their pained screams cut short as they ricocheted off to either side. Feathers scattered. Their bodies rolled, and the thin bones of their wings snapped.

Jerico gave them no quarter. Before the nearest could even rise to his feet, Bonebreaker came smashing down, caving in his chest. He turned, his mace twirling in his hand, and faced Bathala.

"Wisdom," Jerico said. "I'm still waiting to see it."

Bathala's wings curled together behind his back. One remained at an awkward tilt from the broken bones. There was no hiding the pain on the fallen's face, and that pain seemed to amplify the rage he had attempted to deny with his constant vomit of 'wisdom' and 'understanding'.

"You are wretched!" he screamed. "You are sinful and stubborn and deserve the fire Karak would bathe you in!"

"I thought you wanted to spare me Karak's fire."

Bathala cut the air with his sword. "I would see all of Dezrel bathed in Karak's cleansing fire if it brought this world peace. Your imperfections are monumental. Your failures are legion. To have your kind among us in the eternal lands is an insult too far. If Ashhur is not wise enough to see it, then let Karak be the one strong enough to speak that truth."

There it is, Jerico thought as he approached the angel with Bonebreaker slowly rotating in his hand. *Their true face. Even now, you whisper into their ears, don't you, Karak?*

Yet again, Karak had poisoned what was once beautiful. Yet again, Ashhur's followers would bleed to make it right.

"Remember his words," Jerico shouted, ignoring the fallen. The villagers of Selma were watching their battle. They heard those words. Let the contempt and mockery burn into them a lesson far deeper than any lecture of Ashhur could achieve. "Remember his disgust, and remember who stood at your side."

"Enough!" Bathala screamed. He sprinted across the dirt, moving with inhuman speed despite his injuries. Jerico batted his shield side to side, batting aside the blows. He read the movements of the fallen's arms to predict the attacks and positioned himself accordingly every time. Seconds slipped past, heartbeat by heartbeat, as Bathala failed to wear Jerico down beneath his onslaught. Yet every block burned into the fallen's hands with the light of his shield. Every hit robbed a bit of strength Bathala no longer could spare.

Finally, Jerico let his shield lead the way and took the offensive. He slammed it into Bathala's sword, smashing it away like a child's toy. Holy light washed over the fallen's ashen skin. With the inevitability of mountains, the unstoppable nature of rivers, Jerico bore down on the fallen angel. When he finally swung Bonebreaker, it was for the kill. Its magic activated, and when it hit Bathala's exposed left side, it blasted apart his rib cage, continued inward, and snapped his spine in half. The fallen's body collapsed, his death-cry a raspy, furious protest against the failing of his internal organs.

With Bathala's death, the village fell silent. Jerico stood in its vacant community center among a field of bodies. His shoulders lifted and fell with labored breaths. The eyes of the villagers were upon him, and though they were grateful, he could feel a hint of fear at the power he wielded. He looked to the corpses of both orcs and fallen angels. Another reminder that his purpose on Dezrel involved far more killing than preaching. Necessary it may be, but it still put a vice about his heart. The Gods' Wars were supposed to be over. When they rebuilt the Citadel, Jerico had envisioned a future of teaching, of lectures and leading through example. Not more death. Not more killing.

"Do not bury them," he said as he clipped his mace to his belt. "Give them to the river."

He slung his shield over his shoulder and began his trek north. Jenava rushed to his side while the rest of the villagers slowly emerged from hiding within their homes.

"Where will you go?" Jenava asked.

"Where else?" he said, doing his best to put the words of the fallen out of mind, and away from his heart. "Home."

10

"Who is he again?" Jessilynn asked. She stood beside Dieredon at the front of Ahaesarus's army. A thin river known as Deer Crossing quietly flowed at their feet, separating them from the Knothills controlled by the Lord of the Castle of Caves.

"A war hero," the elf said.

"Which war?"

Dieredon winced. "The Gods' War. Decorating and cheering on those who fought my people has fallen out of fashion over the past five years. Lord Eston's soldiers defended Mordeina during its first siege, and he was one of the few minor lords to refuse surrender when Melorak took control."

"So they've fought armies of the gods before," Jessilynn said. "Will they do so again?"

The elf glanced over his shoulder at the thousands of beast-men impatiently waiting at the Crossing.

"Some holy army this is."

"It's not much of an army on the other side, either."

Lord Samuel Eston rode atop a horse on the opposite side of the wide but shallow river. Green banners marked by a red rose in the center fluttered from seven tall poles carried by young men. Jessilynn knew the yellow rose was the mark of the Hemman family, but after Lord Sebastian's death years prior, and the subsequent Gods' War, the family had lost control over the lands. This new lord had apparently been a knight of some renown, and accepted King Antonil's appointment during the first few chaotic years following the start of his reign. An additional dozen mounted soldiers flanked his sides, and they too wore tabards decorated in green and marked by a red rose. Stretching out behind him were another five hundred or so armed soldiers. They lined the edge of the river, the bank of which bore spikes pointed toward the water. Not many, only a few dozen, which implied the defenses had been hastily constructed.

Though the water was shallow enough to wade through, and Ahaesarus's angels themselves could fly overhead, they had stopped at the river upon sighting the forces. A trio of men floated across on a log platform to greet them. The platform scraped along the bank, guided by the poles of two soldiers.

"Lord Eston is happy to speak with your leaders," an older man with a graying beard said. He gestured to the tightly wrapped and nailed logs of the platform. "This is for any who don't bear wings, so long as they are elf, human, or angel."

Ahaesarus, standing to Jessilynn's left, crossed his arms and glared at the messenger.

"Is my army not welcome throughout the North?" he asked.

"Human, elf, and angel," the older man said. "They are my orders, and they will not change on repeating."

Ahaesarus glanced Jessilynn's way. She had to steel herself to prevent from flinching.

"Very well," he said. "I shall honor our guest to the very letter. A human, an elf, and an angel. Dieredon, Jessilynn, would you accompany me across?"

There was no denying such a request, and so Jessilynn found herself on the opposite side of Deer Crossing, kneeling before Lord Samuel Eston on his horse. He looked like a man of battle, though his gray beard hid a bit of fat and wrinkles around his neck, and his chainmail was layered over a stomach that had drank more wine than water in recent years. Still, his face bore several scars, including one along above his eye that kept the eyebrow bald, as well as portions of his hair as it snaked upward to the crown of his skull. That he had lived through what appeared to be a truly vicious cut was impressive.

"Greetings, angel of Ashhur," Samuel said. "It is good to see not all of your kind have become the monsters that now rule Mordeina."

Though he said nothing and kept his expression passive, Jessilynn caught the little flutter of the angel's wings to mark his dismay.

"Is there a place we might speak?" Ahaesarus asked, his baritone voice smoother than silk. "Somewhere we may plan and make promises?"

"I am not one for secret handshakes and whispered agreements, angel," Samuel said. He projected his voice so all around him might hear. "And I thought angels of Ashhur would believe the same. Am I wrong? Or are you at risk of suffering the same punishment that befell your brethren in Mordeina?"

From the corner of her eye, Jessilynn saw Dieredon reach for his bow. For one brief moment she thought the elf was insane, that he would try to put an arrow through Samuel for the insult. It was only when she followed his gaze that she realized he was watching Ahaesarus's every move. The tension, already unbearable, intensified around her so that she suddenly found it difficult to breathe.

"Given the tragedy that befell Mordan, what you call the Night of Black Wings, I will forgive any fears over the loyalty and safety my angels and I present," he said. It sounded like every word was tremendously difficulty to lift off his tongue. "But we march toward Mordeina, and aim to bring low those whom our god has cursed. With the Yellow Rose broken, we thought to come to the Castle of Caves, and from within its safety, plot out the future of our war."

"And I would gladly accept your white wings among my halls," Samuel said. "But the Knothills shall not suffer the clawed feet of the beast-men. Those beasts over there? They stay there, on the eastern side of the river."

Ahaesarus took a step back, appearing surprised at such a refusal.

"Those beasts are working to make amends for the slaughter and violence they have unleashed upon human lands," he said. "And they do so by serving under my command."

"I do not care who they serve. Deer Crossing marks the outer edge of lands entrusted to my care. No beast-men of the Vile Wedge shall set foot upon it. I will not entreat with their kind, nor risk the safety of my people to those…monsters."

"And I give you no choice?" Ahaesarus asked softly. "If I demand that you grant all my army succor in the Castle of Caves?"

That the lord did not quiver before such cold rage impressed Jessilynn to no end.

"Then you shall have to kill the five hundred I would pledge to your aid instead. I doubt you can suffer a single unnecessary casualty if you are to retake Mordeina from the mad angel. Is your pride…" He shook his head and then pointed to the beast-men on the opposite side of the river. "No, is *their* pride worth that, angel? Think wisely. You know their place. Accept what help I can offer. Five hundred trained soldiers, given to you in aid instead of sent to Mordeina as the King of the Fallen has demanded. Do not be a fool."

Ahaesarus's voice dropped.

"You would refuse your king?" he asked softly, but even a soft word by him traveled throughout the lines of soldiers gathered in waiting.

"I serve King Gregory Copernus," Lord Eston said. "Is he with you, angel? If so, then bring him before me, and if he gives the order, I shall let your beasts cross. Not before then."

Ahaesarus was a terrible liar, that much was clear. He looked ready to rip Samuel's head off his shoulders, and that anger and frustration was evident in every single word he spoke. It made a mockery of his attempted diplomacy as he boomed out a statement meant to be heard by the gathered armies of both sides.

"I am ever grateful for the aid given, Lord Eston. I accept the offered soldiers, and look forward to leading them into battle against those who would threaten the safety and prosperity of Mordan."

The return trip over Deer Crossing was a cold and quiet affair. The moment they stepped off the raft, Ahaesarus spread his wings and bellowed orders for the army to prepare for marching. Meanwhile, behind them, the five hundred soldiers granted by Lord Eston started wading through the hip-deep water with their swords and shields raised above their heads. Jessilynn remained still, quietly working over a question she wanted to ask. Dieredon noticed, and he leaned closer to her.

"Trouble lingers, and I will let you speak it in private," he whispered. He then bowed low to her and Ahaesarus and trudged back toward the Sonowin, who nibbled grass farther back from the riverbank. Jessilynn would have preferred he stayed. She didn't like feeling so alone and overwhelmed by the powerful angel.

"Is something the matter?" Ahaesarus asked, finally noticing that she had remained at his side. He furrowed his brow, as if he knew something was amiss with her but was uncertain of its cause. Jessilynn decided to just come straight out and say it instead of beating around the bush.

"You didn't tell him what you're planning," she said. "Lord Eston refuses to acknowledge the beast-men in any way. Do you think he will allow them a nation of their own that borders his?"

"He will allow what I command."

"Or you have no intention of commanding it in the first place."

Ahaesarus often carried himself with an air of calm authority. He walked, and talked, how she would imagine a true king would behave on Dezrel. That seriousness took on a dark edge when he loomed over her. It was not mercy or compassion she now expected from him, but an angered king's judgment.

"Would you call me a liar, little paladin?"

"I would call you King of the Vile," she said. She cast her arm to the beast-men army already preparing to march. "Behold your subjects. To what fate do you lead them? To what nation? To what graves?"

Ahaesarus crossed his arms, and the hardening of his features frightened her more than any wolf-man fang. Before he might answer, another angel flew down to join them, racing in with such reckless speed Jessilynn briefly feared they were under attack. The angel was overwhelmed with excitement, and he clapped his hands excitedly, oblivious to Ahaesarus' frown.

"Wonderful news," the angel said. "We have made contact at last."

"With who?" Jessilynn asked. The angel scout turned her way and beamed a smile.

"The survivors."

"That's right, put your whole arm into it," Harruq said. "Come on, soldier, thrust like you want to kill me with that sword, not tickle me a little. No evil angel is gonna care if you poke his skin like a mosquito."

His training partner, a short man absolutely packed with muscle, repeatedly thrust his longsword at Harruq's midsection. He was putting in a good effort, and would actually kill a regular foe, but Harruq knew he needed to stretch his body to the absolute limit to overcome his limited stature. Plus, regular foes were not what they'd face on the battlefield, but Azariah's cursed angels. They fought in a clear field amongst dozens who sparring after their midday meal, getting a bit of frustration and training in prior to resuming their tedious, exhausting march across the countryside.

"I'm better than a damn mosquito," his foe shouted.

"You sure? Swatting you away is easy enough, you could have fooled me."

His training halted the moment he saw wings fly overhead. Panic was his first reaction, but the approaching wings weren't black, but feather-white, like a swan or dove. Harruq let out a loud whoop that was quickly shared by dozens around him. Ahaesarus's angels...they were still alive!

"No rest, not for you all," he told the other soldiers as he sheathed Salvation and Condemnation. "But methinks I got a meeting to be at."

Aurelia met him halfway across the clearing. She looked beautiful as ever with the soft wind teasing her hair and the edges of her dress.

"Good news, I hope?" he asked.

"It's not bad news, at least," she answered.

"I'll take it."

She slipped her hand in his, and together they approached Tarlak's tent on the far side of the camp, pitched underneath the shade of a lone oak tree. The angel scout departed before they arrived. Tarlak had sprawled a map of Mordan out atop a grand oak table that he, inexplicably and most certainly through magic, kept transporting around everywhere they went. While Tess was absent, Qurrah stood off to the side, content to listen in on the planning even if he didn't contribute. It looked like neither he nor Tarlak had said a word to each other as they waited.

Harruq wished they could get along, but it was a fool's hope. Even if Harruq could forgive Qurrah for Aullienna, nothing forced Tarlak to forgive for Delysia's murder. At least they weren't trying to kill each other, Harruq thought grimly.

"So, what do we got?" he asked, putting a grand smile on his face to pretend he didn't see the awkward glares between the two waiting spellcasters.

"Ahaesarus's army is here," Tarlak said. He pointed to the thin river snaking southward from Deer Lake. "Just at the entrance to the Knothills. According to the angel's scouts, Azariah is sitting tight and waiting for soldiers to come in from the various lords scattered about the south."

"The North refuses Azariah's rule?" Aurelia asked.

"It's more that there's not much *left* to rule after the beast-men crushed the wall of towers and slaughtered the survivors at the Castle of the Yellow Rose." Tarlak winced. "Gods, what a sorrow state of affairs. Regardless, enemy soldiers are to our south. As for us, Ahaesarus is northwest. So that makes our path clear. We skirt the eastern edge of Mordeina, staying as far away from that nightmare capital as we can, while making our way toward the Yellow Rose. Ahaesarus will fly westward, and if his scout's estimation of time is correct, we'll meet halfway between Mordeina and the ruined castle."

"Finally linking up our forces," Harruq said, and he smiled as he crossed his arms over his chest. "Does he have any ideas of what to do then?"

"Ahaesarus isn't thinking with subtlety or tact," Qurrah answered before Tarlak could. "He wants to take a straight line to Mordeina and lay the city under siege."

"Do we have the numbers to pull that off?" Harruq asked incredulously.

"Does it matter?" Tarlak asked. He snatched the map and rolled it closed. "We've got a destination, so we'll march toward it and hope for the best. Maybe if we're lucky, that bastard will come out and face us instead of waiting like a coward. He's ruled as king for far too long. Time to break his crown."

11

The Queen would not meet with him. Her army had arrived in a great flourish of trumpets and drums. So much of it had been pompous nonsense, for the gathered number paled when compared to the invasion force that had so recently tried, and failed, to overthrow the angels' rule over Mordan. For three days, Bernard had approached the Bloodbrick and requested a meeting. For three days, he was denied.

On the fourth, black wings marked the northern sky.

"You see them, do you not?" Bernard shouted to the soldiers that stopped him halfway across the bridge, at the exact point where it was officially considered part of Ker. "We have no weapons. We lack all means to defend ourselves. Grant us passage, or at least grant me an audience with your Queen!"

"I'll go check with her," one soldier relented, though he seemed much more worried about the approaching fallen than Bernard's wrath.

Ashhur grant me patience, Bernard thought as he waited. Perhaps he considered himself a patient man, but lives were on the line. Those fallen angels most certainly came with death in mind. The refugees had fled their nearby encampment, and they crowded just outside the entrance to the Bloodbrick, still holding out hope that Bernard might secure timely passage.

Bernard thought that if his request were granted, he'd be brought back to the same tent as Commander Lurik, but that was not the case. Soldiers kept him in place, and it was the Queen herself who came to greet him, flanked by a squad of six knights. The Queen was radiant as ever, traces of youth still on her dimpled face, but her auburn eyes carried the tired wisdom of multiple wars. Her long brown hair was tightly braided, woven with silver lace, and then wrapped about her neck. Bernard had never met her, only heard the occasional story. She was brilliant and ruthless – the absolute worst personality to deal with when trying to procure aid for the refugees.

"Thank you for this honor," Bernard said with a bow. Given all the people depending on him, he had to behave perfectly

The King of the Fallen

in this encounter. "The refugees of Mordan have elected me to speak for them. Forgive me if I do so in haste, for black wings approach."

"A priest of Ashhur, frightened by angels of Ashhur?" Loreina asked, her tone pleasant but her words biting. "Forgive me for my confusion, priest."

Bernard shook his head. "Those who chase us are condemned by Ashhur. He has cast them down, cursed their bodies, and declared them unworthy of his love. In response, they rage against those they were meant to protect. They hate us, and slaughter us. Please, Queen Loreina, grant us succor in Ker's arms. Allow us safe passage. Whatever demands you make of us, they shall be met. Whatever work is required, we shall perform. I speak for a frightened, desperate people. No task shall be too great if it grants us freedom from those black wings."

A trumpet sounded before the Queen could answer. Fallen angels filled the sky above the refugees, just outside reach of any arrows from the soldiers lining the riverbank. One of them flew closer, and he bellowed out a message for all to hear.

"Citizens of Paradise!" shouted the fallen angel. "I am Phanuel, obedient servant of King Azariah the Wise and Just. I come offering mercy. Whatever escape you think to find in Ker, it will elude you. Your souls are tarnished, but there is still time for things to be made right. Like frightened children you fled, but we are forgiving parents. Return with us to Mordeina. Come hear the words of your king. Adopt his wisdom in your heart, and together we shall recreate Paradise."

Bernard turned back to the queen, hoping that such a proclamation would finally convince her of their dire need. Loreina stared at the sky, much of the color drained from her face.

"Do you hear it?" she asked softly. "That fanaticism? It was always there. We heard it in every speech and every sermon. We saw it in every white feather that conquered the skies. It brought you comfort, once. It has always brought us fear."

"Perhaps we were blind, but we see now, and we are equally afraid," Bernard said, fighting off his panic. "Will you not extend us mercy?"

"You made your bed," she said. "Now lie in it."

"They will kill us, Queen Loreina. This offer is but a demand for slavery and torment. Please, I beg of you, grant us passage."

She pointed to Phanuel high up in the sky.

"Mordan is the land of angels," she said. "You asked them to rule over you, so let them rule. I shall watch over my people. You watch over yours. Good day, priest."

Bernard swallowed down what felt like an iron rod lodged into his throat.

"So be it," he whispered.

He left the Bloodbrick. Within moments he was surrounded on all sides by refugees demanding answers. He walked for a few moments still, his mind racing, before he stopped to address the growing crowd.

"No entrance," Bernard told those who gathered to hear word of the queen's decision. "I'm sorry. Even now, we are denied."

Twenty fallen angels, that was it. Compared to the hundreds of armed soldiers protecting the border, they were no threat. No challenge. Yet the queen still refused entry for the refugees. Even knowing the consequences, she would not relent. There was no possible way to interpret the message her decision sent. It was better these people were dead than living in her lands.

It seemed in mere moments the entire crowd knew of the queen's decree. Panic spread faster than an autumn wild fire. People rushed toward the bridge, but were easily held back by the barricades and the wall of shields. Both crowd and soldiers grew violent, and Bernard heard shoving and the rattle of armor. He dared not turn to look. Time was not on his side.

"What shall be your answer?" Phanuel demanded of the Mordan refugees. "Ker is a land of sin, and will not accept those who have lived among the angels' light. Come home. It is not too late to bend the knee. It is not too late to return to Paradise."

Paradise. The name sickened him. While not his favorite topic, Bernard had given sermons over the almost mystical kingdom of Paradise that had once existed (as a priest for over forty years, he'd given sermons over almost *every* topic imaginable). When Karak and Ashhur agreed to divide the world, the portion of the continent west of the Rigon had been named Paradise, and Ashhur himself had walked the lands, overseeing the steadily growing human civilization. It was a nation that knew no hunger, no sickness, no war.

Many idolized that existence, but Bernard had not. Children, he had called the people living there in that time during his sermon. Denied all responsibility for their own lives, and separated from half the world living in Karak's nation of Neldar. It was natural to yearn for that ease of life. One could not stumble on a path if one refused to take a single step. But it meant a faith weak and brittle. It meant a conviction as strong as a flower petal.

Azariah wanted brittle people. The fallen angel sought a populace beaten, broken, and humiliated. His Three Laws existed only so he could prop himself up as the salvation for the hardships he himself inflicted. He would be the savior for the sins he alone defined.

"Paradise," Bernard said, stepping out from the frightened crowd surging toward the Bloodbrick. "Ashhur spare us from any such Paradise."

Alone, he walked to confront the threat to his people. In what felt like an age past, he had watched Harruq Tun go to do the same. The half-orc had knelt before a coming tide of evil, ready to give up his life in symbolic atonement for his sins that led to that evil's arrival upon Dezrel in the first place. The sky had split, and angels had come to humanity's aid in arguably the defining moment of their entire world. Nothing had ever been the same. Now the priest stared at those same angels, wielding spears and swords to threaten the lives they had been sent to save.

"High Priest Bernard Ulath," Phanuel said once the distance between them closed, and they could address one another without shouting. "Do you come to speak for the refugees?"

"I do not," he said.

The fallen leader frowned. "Then you speak for yourself?"

"No. Not myself." He closed his eyes and felt something stirring in his heart. "I speak for the father."

The twenty fallen reacted as if he had threatened them. They drew their swords and lifted their spears. Their group spread out to surround him, ensuring danger lurked on all sides from the sky above. Bernard hardly gave them a thought. He felt tremendous power gathering deep inside his chest. He felt a presence he had known only fleetingly throughout his life, and he heard words that carried such weight it constricted his throat and burdened his heart.

I give you my power, Ashhur's voice thundered inside his skull. *I give you a sword to craft with your rage. Wield it as you were destined, my child.*

"Your child," Bernard whispered. He stared up at Phanuel as light began to shimmer across the priest's hands, face, and robes, as if beneath his flesh and mortal garb he were a burning sun. "Tell me, Ashhur, what shall this child do with this power?"

Have I not always sought the safety of my children? Have I not always sought their joy through grace and mercy? Slay those who would deny that to my beloved. Bring my fury to bear on the ruiners of life and light.

"As you wish, my god."

He lifted his arms, and the sensation overwhelming him was unlike any he had experienced in his life. He felt no fear, no doubt. The sky itself swirled, and storm clouds blossomed where there had once been clear blue sky. No power, no previous prayer, compared to this presence. Ashhur was with him. The spears and swords of the fallen meant nothing, absolutely nothing. They could not pierce his skin blazing with light. They could not cut a shield woven from the very fabric of the divine. A few even tried, but the spears shattered to dust not even halfway toward reaching Bernard's body.

Yet amid this faith he did not feel peace. This was not the comfort he envisioned throughout his youth when he prayed for his god to embrace him. The priest clenched his hands into fists. He felt raw, unbridled rage. Soon, the world would feel it, too.

"We are all your children," he said, and he turned to face the Bloodbrick. His words shook the land. "So let my children pass."

Bernard dropped his hand, and in doing so, dropped the thunder of the heavens upon Queen Loreina. It manifested in a gleaming bolt of lightning as wide as the Bloodbrick, its length reaching the very heavens. The meager barricades blasted apart like twigs. Soldiers collapsed, charred within their armor. The queen herself was the focal point, and he need not see her body to know she was obliterated to ash and bone. A tremendous *boom* followed, so deep the ground rattled and a long crack split through the center of the Bloodbrick.

With the Queen dead, and the defenses on the Bloodbrick destroyed, the remaining forces were shocked into inaction. The Mordan refugees flooded across the bridge, seeming just as shocked and frightened by the display as those from Ker. Bernard turned away from them. He had to hold out hope that the better parts of humanity would win, and the people would be given homes. Perhaps, in the chaos after the queen's death, they would not. It was out of Bernard's hands. He could only pray for the best.

The priest lifted his arms in prayer. The fallen bristled, fearing another tremendous display of holy magic. They need not be so afraid. Ashhur's anger and disappointment swept about him. The granted power faded. No, not faded. Revoked. Bernard looked up at the fallen, and seeing their mixture of betrayal and confusion only confirmed to him he had made the right choice.

"Your time is coming," he told them. "But it won't be by my hands. Flee home, fallen ones. Await your reckoning."

A few of the fallen discussed with one another, but there was little hope for them to stop the refugees. With the people rushing across the bridge, they were safely amid the army, whose size still vastly outnumbered the fallen. The people of Mordan were beyond their reach, at least for now.

"Reckoning?" asked Phanuel, and he threw his spear. Its aim was not perfect. The sharpened point tore through Bernard's robe and cut a gash into his side before burying into the dirt. Blood poured forth. Bernard let loose a fierce shock of pain.

"I'm sorry, Ashhur," he said as he dropped to his knees. Another spear sliced through the air, and unlike the first, its aim was true. It plunged into his stomach and exploded out his back. His vision turned white from the pain, and he gasped with lungs that were suddenly filled with blood instead of air. His hands clutched the shaft out of instinct. He lacked any strength to remove it. "This is where I belong."

Phanuel landed before him. His armor was bleached bone, his skin sickly gray. His dark hair was tied into a long ponytail that hung down to his waist. At one point it might have borne a healthy luster, but now it seemed permanently stained with flecks of blood.

"Perhaps we will meet again," the fallen leader said as he took hold of the spear lodged in Bernard's chest. "In the lands of eternity, when mortal years have come and gone and the fruits of our labors have been made manifest. Let us see who Ashhur greets with open arms when Paradise is made righteous, and her people free from sin."

"Faith through bloodshed," Bernard said, forcing out the words despite the tremendous pain. A dying smile lit his face. "Karak would be proud."

Those words stung exactly as he had hoped.

"Damn you," Phanuel said. "Damn you, and damn your people."

He ripped out the spear, twirled it above him, and then slammed the sharpened tip straight into Bernard's forehead. The last thing he saw was the fury in the eyes of an angel, and then the gates of the Golden Eternity opened, and he heard the sound of bells.

12

"And you are certain he has not been harmed?" Azariah asked as he and Ezekai flew over Mordeina, the city a gray blur beneath them in the morning fog.

"I'm capable of following orders," Ezekai responded gruffly. "Though I wonder if you should wait for a greater offense."

"All offenses against the divine are great enough to deserve reciprocation." He hid a grimace. "And after the humiliation during the reveal of the Three Laws, we must doubly make amends."

Their destination neared, a wide crossroads in the southern portion of the city. Undead soldiers formed an outer ring surrounding the people who'd been forced into attendance. A tall signpost marked the crossroad's center. Two fallen stood guard over a young man tied to the base of the post. He had been stripped naked, as requested by Azariah when he'd been informed of the man's capture. Azariah looped twice overhead and then landed atop the post so all would be forced to look up at his presence.

"Kneel before your King!" Ezekai bellowed. The crowd of hundreds quickly dropped to the ground in supplication. That it had to be demanded irked Azariah, but what was he to expect from such rebellious people? If humanity learned easily, and obeyed promptly, then the angels would never have appeared on Dezrel in the first place.

"Children of Paradise!" Azariah shouted. "Lift your eyes to the heavens. Lift your eyes to me. I would have you listen. I would have you learn."

It seemed every other day brought a new teaching moment for the ignorant humans, but Azariah was determined to remain stubbornly hopeful. Perfection would not be easily reached, especially not when starting with so flawed a base as an entire race of beings created by a fractured Ashhur and Karak.

Speaking of flawed, he turned his attention to the man tied to the post. He had the scrawny yet muscular look of a feral cat. His long red hair was matted to the sides of his face; blood leaked from a cut across his forehead. More blood dripped from his split lip, glistening in his short beard.

"Fuck him and fuck his *I'll have you learn* bullshit!" the man shouted. "That asshole doesn't deserve to lick the balls of a—"

Ezekai's fist ended the insult before he could finish. Azariah crossed his arms, holding back a sigh. This man was trying to stir the fallen king's emotions, but his endeavor was futile. Insults and crude language would never upset Azariah. A man's inability to lead a life worthy of the eternal soul granted to him, on the other hand, did. Such a waste of a divine gift.

"Tell me, children, what is the new First Law your king has decreed?" Azariah asked the crowd. The answers came uneven but mostly in unison.

"Worship Ashhur for his grace and forgiveness, and as messenger for the kindness you are to show others."

"Kindness?" the bound man spat through blood-caked teeth. He laughed as if losing his sanity. "Kindness!"

Azariah hopped from the top of the pole, wings fluttering as he glided to a stand before his prisoner.

"Children, what is the Second Law?" he asked, his back to them.

"Worship Karak for his judgment and wisdom, and as a model for the firm hand you need to reach perfection."

A grim smile crossed the prisoner's face. This was the law the man had broken, and they both knew it.

"What is your name, child?" Azariah asked.

"Lazu. And I ain't no child, just like you ain't no king."

This was hardly the first time Azariah had heard this sentiment, but it was one that needed to be eradicated. Humans clung to their old structures with a desperate strength. It was one of the reasons he wished to see Gregory Copernus hung from the city gates. There would be no human kings or princes, not for the rest of eternity. Azariah was king, and he would not age, nor relinquish his rule until the gods and goddess acknowledged his works. The children of Paradise needed to learn and accept this. Doubly so given the trials that might soon follow, with Ahaesarus's gathered army making its way toward the city.

"Shall you tell the people your crime, Lazu, or shall I?"

The man sagged forward as if he wished to whisper to Azariah a secret. The ropes holding him groaned at the strain.

"You want them all to know?" he asked. "You want them to hear why you've stripped me naked, beaten me bloody, and tied me to a post to be mocked and laughed at? Fine. You hear me, you cowards sitting there doing nothing? You hear me? My crime, my unforgivable *crime*, was to curse Karak's name when demanded I pray those three damn laws. Fuck Karak, I said, and now I'm tied. And I'll say it again. Fuck Karak. *Fuck Karak*, fuck the fucking prick so fucking har – "

Another fist shut him up. The crowd grumbled. As Ezekai had mentioned, it was a rather paltry crime given humanity's great breadth of sins and vices. But these were the Three Laws, the new guiding principles for Paradise. To disregard them so callously, and to a fallen's face no less, could not be allowed. If this was what the man said publicly, what did he say privately to his friends and family? The health of a crop starts deep in the soil where the sun does not always shine, after all.

"The brother gods, working in necessary and blessed union, created all of humanity from the clay of the Rigon," Azariah said, addressing the crowd as much as he did Lazu. "You would curse the name of your creator? You would deny him his rightfully deserved prayer?"

Lazu spat out another glob of blood. His grin widened, and he lunged against his restraints.

"Have you lost your damn minds? You *fought* Karak's army. How could you force us to pray to that bastard?"

Now *this* was a much more serious problem. Azariah saw one of the fallen nearby flinch as if he'd been struck. All of the angels were former Wardens who had served Ashhur in the original days of Paradise, and upon being gifted wings in the Golden Eternity, they had returned to Dezrel hundreds of years later to protect Mordeina from an army led by Karak's infamous prophet, Velixar. But Velixar had not been alone...

"We fought against an army from another world!" Azariah shouted. "We fought the war demons of Thulos, to whom Karak's treacherous prophet had sworn allegiance in his thirst for power. Just as we now fight Ahaesarus and his rogue band, who would seek to keep you locked in sin, forever begging to Ashhur, and Ashhur alone, for mercy and forgiveness. Dezrel is a world split, my children! It is split down the middle by the Rigon, it is split into two great kingdoms, with two brother gods. Reunion must come. Atonement must be made. These divisions, they must end, and the wisdom of *both* gods must be acknowledged, lest we wander lost in the wilderness for centuries to come."

Azariah reached out to Ezekai, who drew his sword and offered the hilt. Taking the blade, Azariah aimed its sharpened point directly at Lazu's throat.

"Three Laws," he said. "Offer Ashhur your love for his grace and forgiveness for your multitudinous sins."

Lazu stared at him for a long while, a simple mind debating simple concepts.

"Aye, Ashhur, thanks for all you've done," he said.

Azariah pressed the tip closer.

"Offer Karak your thanks for his judgment and guidance in maintaining order amid chaos."

Again, the bound man debated.

"All right," he said at last. "Thank you, Karak, for showing us all how great your judgment is."

There were ten layers of sarcasm across each syllable, but Azariah would allow it...for now. All that was left was the third and final law.

"Offer me your thanks. Let me hear your gratitude to your king for guiding your soul to Paradise."

This time there was no hesitation. Lazu reared back, grinned, and spat an enormous blob of blood and saliva directly onto Azariah's face.

"Piss off, angel!" he screamed. "Long live Gregory! Long live the boy king!"

Azariah wiped off the filth, clenched his teeth hard enough to crack them, and then cut Lazu's head from his shoulders. He received no satisfaction as the head rolled across the street. His only emotion was of a deep desire to burn the entirety of Dezrel to the ground and declare himself King of Ash. It was a frustrated, childish reaction, and thankfully it passed quickly.

"Burn the body," he told Ezekai as he handed the fallen back his blade. He turned to the crowd, which was still locked into a tight circle due to the undead soldiers. Controlling the undead had gotten ever easier, so much so that now he sometimes forgot about their presence. With a thought he had them scatter back to their patrols.

"Go," he told the crowd. "And remember what you saw. The Three Laws must be given their due."

Azariah flew to his tower for a welcome reprieve from the sinful rabble. His frustrations were bubbling over, helped none by the recent reports of Mordan refugees successfully escaping into Ker. Every day, it seemed, his plans to save humanity slipped further and further into the realms of the impossible. A break from it all was what he desperately needed, but instead of finding solitude in his tower, he discovered a waiting guest.

"Tarlak Eschaton?" he asked, his entire body freezing in place at the shock of seeing the yellow-garbed wizard standing in the center of his private sanctum. The wizard looked up from staring at the ground and smiled. He was obviously struggling for some reason, with his hands trembling and sweat coating his brow.

"No, not...not only," he said, a statement that made no sense. Fire swelled inside Azariah's palm as he prepared a spell, but he paused when Tarlak's image flickered. Parts of his robe turned translucent.

A projection, Azariah realized. If it was Tarlak, it wasn't him in the flesh.

"Not only?" the fallen asked. "Do you not come before me alone?"

"Alone?" The wizard took a single, unsteady step forward. His knee wobbled. "Not alone. Never alone. He stole *me* from me, angel. He stole me. Stole my body. I want to make him pay."

"Stop spouting nonsense," Azariah said. "Why are you here?"

Tarlak laughed so hard he doubled over and clutched his fists together. It was as if he were being stabbed from within.

David Dalglish

"I'm here...I'm here because I can be," he said. He looked up, madness and rage sparkling in those tear-filled eyes. "Because I know something he doesn't want me to know."

Something bizarre was happening here, but damned if Azariah could figure it out. His behavior was too erratic, too strange to be an act. The founder of the Eschaton Mercenaries obviously suffered under some strange malady or distress, but what? What did he mean, not alone? And how in the Abyss did the wizard survive his time at the Council of Mages in the first place? Azariah had believed the troublesome man dealt with and out of the picture. Yet again humanity failed him, and in its most skilled, over-specialized act: killing someone.

"Whatever this farce us, I want no part of it," Azariah said. "Take your games and leave, wizard, before you try my patience. Besides...you look unwell."

Tarlak jammed his fingers into the sides of his skull with such force it looked like he was trying to claw out his own brain.

"NO!" he shrieked. "I won't lose – I won't lose control. Not yet. Not until you listen. Gregory, Aubrienna, I know where they are. I know where they're hidden. Tarlak, he couldn't hide it, not from me, not this place where *I* live."

Another seeming bit of nonsense from a wizard that looked to have lost his mind. Azariah kept wondering what the catch was. Did the wizard hope to confuse him? Perhaps lead him astray as part of some ploy?

"The boy king and the Godslayer's daughter both travel at his side," Azariah said. "I've seen it with my scrying magic."

"The images you see are lies," Tarlak said. "Meant to fool you. Don't...don't look for them. Look to the rebuilt Citadel. You'll see them there. Hiding. Cowering. Praying you don't notice." He suddenly stood up perfectly straight, and looked around as if bewildered. His voice changed slightly, adopting a softer tone. "Where...?"

The scream that tore out of him was bone-chilling. Azariah retreated a step and prepared fire on his fingertips. If this wasn't a trick, then something was deeply wrong with the man. The wizard crumpled to his knees and tore at his hair, his scream stretching on and on until at last he had no air left in his lungs.

The King of the Fallen

The scream seemed to have purged him momentarily of his confusion, and he staggered back to his feet with a most devious grin.

"I have to go," Tarlak said. "Can't let him know. Surprise. It won't be fun if...if it isn't a surprise. Don't disappoint me, angel."

As suddenly as he appeared, the wizard flickered away into nothing. Azariah stared at the space the image had occupied, his mind racing. He'd always assumed Harruq and his gang would keep the two children alongside them. Where else might they be safer in all of Dezrel? But if there was a place they'd believe the two sheltered from harm, it would be in the care of Ashhur's paladins. The fallen shrugged. What was the harm in checking? Scrying spells were far from the most taxing of arcane magics.

Azariah retrieved a chair from beside a bookshelf and set it in the center of the room. Once seated, he closed his eyes, lifted his hands, and began the necessary words of magic. His mind drifted, pulled toward its destination through sheer focus. He imagined the rebuilt Citadel in his mind's eye, and so he witnessed it as it was in the real world. For a brief moment he felt resistance, and his inner sight dimmed while simultaneously flooding over with a deep fog. The rebuilt Citadel had been warded against scrying magic, but Azariah himself had overseen the construction. He knew exactly how those worked, and how to bypass them with a simple thought.

His sight cleared, and he witnessed the Citadel once more in the warm daylight. Azariah hovered beyond like a bird in flight, and with a mental command he soared inside through one of the windows. He zipped and twirled, racing up and down steps, checking rooms, caring not for the young paladins who lingered about.

His first discovery was the paladin Lathaar, whom Azariah had believed still marched alongside Harruq and Aurelia. If someone so powerful had retreated to the Citadel...

Sure enough, two floors down, he found them. Aubrienna and Gregory bounced atop one of the beds, laughing as they alternating shouting out numbers.

"Five!" shouted Aubrienna.

"Six!" shouted Gregory, and he flung a pillow her way.

Azariah opened his eyes, banishing the image.

"Seven," he whispered. He hurried to the tower door, flung it open, and addressed the fallen stationed there.

"Fetch me Ezekai," he commanded. His smile spread ear to ear. "Our army must prepare for flight. We have a king to capture."

◈

Tarlak stumbled across the grass. Where...where was he? One moment, he'd been in his tent. The next, he swore he stood in some strange hollow tower surrounded by windows and bookshelves. But that couldn't be right. He was in a field now, a stubby plot of land fenced in by the family of farmers who lived nearby. It wasn't tent fabric or tower stone above him, but a clear blue sky.

You're cracking, Tarlak, the damn ever-present voice of Cecil mocked. *And I'm slipping through those cracks.*

"Like shit you are," he muttered. "You're not even real."

He paused to grab one of the thick fenceposts. Sweat soaked his body. It felt like he'd run a mile, based on how his heart hammered in his chest. The first pangs of panic simmered in his mind, and he fought them down. He had to focus on the task at hand. First off, where was he? He looked around, truly taking in his surroundings. There, not far to his left, was the human army. Their campfires dotted the sky with smoke.

"See, not so hard to get your bearings, is it?" Tarlak asked aloud. He tried very, very hard not to wonder why he was a good ten-minute walk away from the camp. He was stressed, that's all, stressed and perhaps sleepwalking.

You'll believe anything if it means not believing in me.

"I'd sell my soul to Karak and Ashhur both if it meant sparing me from your smug, idiot voice," he muttered. A bad habit, talking to himself, but what else was he to do? Ignoring Cecil Towerborn's voice had proven ineffective. Pretending it wasn't there didn't work, either. What options were left? If he was going to work out a solution, he first needed to understand the problem. What exactly was Cecil? A lingering shadow within the mind? A delusion made up over guilt of using the body?

Stealing the body, Cecil shouted within his skull. **Stealing** it. *Don't mince words, you damn coward.*

Vertigo overwhelmed Tarlak, and before he knew it he was on his knees. Screaming, he realized. He was screaming. He didn't remember starting. He didn't feel like stopping, either.

"Get out of my head," he hollered to the sky. "Get out, get out, get out!"

Something rolled him onto his back. No, not something. Someone. Himself. His hands and legs were thrashing of their own accord.

Or *his* accord...

"No!" Tarlak shrieked. He clamored back to his feet despite the world shifting beneath him as if he were in the midst of an earthquake. "No, gods damn it, not like this. Not to you!"

He ran as if wolves nipped at his heels. He ran as if fires swirled around his every step. Laughter chased him, far more terrifying than any wolf or fire. At first his destination was the army encampment, but it soon became an act solely about itself. Running, because he chose to run. His arms and legs, moving as he demanded of them. This body, this stubborn collection of meat and bone, would follow his commands even if it killed him.

He ran and ran until the world around him blurred. His heart pounded with such force that he felt the veins in his neck pulse. His lungs burned. Every shred of his energy flowed into his legs, yet it didn't matter. He couldn't outrun the laughter, the one thing in all the world he needed to escape. How does one outrun their own mind? How did one escape the bone cage attached to their shoulders?

Time lost meaning. It might have been minutes, it might have been hours, but his run halted as if he'd slammed into a stone wall. Tarlak staggered backward, completely unaware of his surroundings. He thought he'd hit the ground, but didn't. Arms held him. Very big, very strong half-orc arms.

"Tar?" Harruq asked. They were still in the field he'd 'awoken' in. "Hey, are you all right?"

Tarlak glanced to the grass. He'd been running in a small circle for long enough to carve a groove into the earth with his boots.

"No," Tarlak said, finally giving in and laughed along with the phantom Cecil. "No, Harruq, I very much don't think I am."

13

"You know, you're starting to make me a little nervous," Tarlak said as everyone gathered around.

"You collapsed in a field after running in circles for hours," Aurelia said. "We're all worried."

"*You're* worried?" Tarlak pulled on the ropes that tied him down to the chair they'd borrowed from one of the nearby farmers. They'd positioned him behind a barn, so rest of the army, which was currently pitching tents, digging trenches, and preparing campfires, couldn't see him. "I haven't been tied down like this since one very experimental trip to Mordeina's more colorful parts, and it wasn't an incident I'd like to repeat."

"Do you ever cease joking?" Qurrah muttered, giving Tarlak a sour look as he bent over one of the nine stones he'd set up in a circle around the chair.

"I'm as serious as often as you are jovial, Qurrah. It's how we counter-balance one another."

"Then may the heavens forgive me for being any part of that balance."

Tarlak tried to remain calm. He'd gone through far worse, hadn't he? Sure, it was weird that Qurrah restrained him and didn't bother to explain the process he planned to enact, but that was just Qurrah being Qurrah...wasn't it? The ropes were to keep him still if he endured another seizure. Nothing nefarious. Nothing weird.

Harruq and Aurelia stood nearby, both watching with concern on their faces. Qurrah scrawled and carved on the runes, while Tessanna relaxed on a blanket just beyond the stones, humming softly to herself, her gaze locked on the clouds that rolled across the sky. Tarlak envied her calm indifference.

I envy her peace of mind, Cecil's voice grumbled in his head. *But don't worry. I'll have that soon enough.*

You'd have to be goddamn insane to envy her *mind,* Tarlak thought with grim amusement. He bit his tongue, hoping the lingering presence of Cecil felt the pain as keenly as he himself did.

At least it momentarily shut him up, allowing him to hear Harruq and Qurrah talking.

"I'd appreciate if you'd share what you knew," Harruq said. "You're scaring Tarlak half to death."

Qurrah stood upright and stretched. "An apt punishment for frightening all of us. But if it will make all of you feel better, that is the last of the stones, which means I am ready to explain the situation."

"Good, explain away," Tarlak said. "But I don't see what's so difficult to explain, nor why it involves me being tied to a chair. I killed Cecil Towerborn, froze his corpse to keep it from rotting, and then projected my consciousness into it right as Roand the Flame used one of his personal contraptions disintegrate me. I'm guessing the body...I don't know, *remembers* a bit of its former owner and I need some time to acclimate to it? Nothing to worry about, right?"

"Wrong," Qurrah said. He paced around the circle, snapping his fingers above each stone in turn. Violet runes shimmered to life, one after another, and the sight of their pulsing power put a deeply-seeded fear into Tarlak's gut.

"Wrong not to worry?" Tarlak said, trying to laugh the half-orc's concern off.

"Wrong in your understanding of the premise," Qurrah said. He finished the circle and joined Harruq and Aurelia in standing before him. The frailer half-orc's brown eyes seemed to see right through Tarlak's face and deep into his mind. To call it 'unnerving' was putting it mildly. "You've been hearing voices, haven't you? Perhaps seeing Cecil lurking about?"

Tarlak cleared his throat. He'd not told Qurrah any of that upon awaking, only given a cursory explanation of his momentary confusions of identity.

Yes, Tarlak, tell them. Tell them I'm with you at all times.

"Perhaps," Tarlak said. "He...he keeps insisting I stole his body."

"To be blunt, it's because you did. As for your flawed premise, you did indeed freeze his body, but I suspect you froze it too well. Cecil never died. You plunged your soul into a living, occupied body, Tarlak. That you've maintained control as long as you have is astounding."

"What? That's...that's insane." He glanced between Qurrah and Tessanna. "You two! You're both skilled at this sort of thing, the mastery of souls and death and other creepy shit. Just...yank his soul out of me. You can do that, right?"

"You're intertwined," Tessanna said, rolling from her back onto her stomach so she could rest her chin on her hands and peer at him curiously. "Like roots of two trees locked together in one plot of land."

"We yank out Cecil, we yank you out as well," Qurrah said. "Which means you need to be disentangled first."

The violet runes on the stones flared brighter when the half-orc lifted his arms. The magic pulsing over them was intense enough that Tarlak felt it like a heat on his skin. His hands shook, and he found himself stammering.

"Why surprise me? Why—why—wait, what are planning? Why was I not warned?"

"He hears everything you hear, sees everything you see," Qurrah said. "Forgive me, wizard, but to warn you would mean warning *him*. Two souls cannot occupy a single body, not without tearing each other apart. You'll need to be stronger than him. Your mental will is far superior, of that I am certain, but this is his body, and his advantageous battlefield. Give him no quarter."

Sparkling purple light collected on Qurrah's pale hands. Tarlak struggled against the ropes, suddenly overcome with a fear far beyond any normal threat. He would rather face a thousand armies with magic leaping off his palms. He'd rather stare down an angry, returned Thulos. Anything was better than sitting here helpless. Anything was better than the mystery Qurrah presented.

"Good luck, Tarlak Eschaton," the half-orc said. He lifted his hand for one last snap of his fingers. "Oh, and be forewarned...this will likely be very, very strange."

⚜

The snap boomed like a roll of thunder from the grandest storm ever recorded in the history of Dezrel. It shook Tarlak's bones and rattled his teeth. Qurrah's visage shattered, fading to dust as the blue sky turned black. The rest of those gathered were lost behind a gray fog that swarmed in from all sides. The chair vanished, and Tarlak found himself standing atop a field of smoke. It was a dream of some sorts, but unlike any dream he had experienced. There was a clarity to his senses that defied the vague looseness of a dream. He saw so clearly the individual curls of the mist. He felt a cold wind on his skin. When he looked to the sky, seeing darkness without stars or a moon, the vertigo threatened to twist his stomach and overwhelm his mind with a sensation of falling upwards.

"Oh, oh, this is delicious," said a disturbingly familiar voice that echoed from everywhere. "You're here. You're actually *here*."

Tarlak spun in place. The fog withdrew, yet it revealed only a strange, barren stone for him to stand upon. No speaker, not yet, but he knew Cecil was lurking somewhere nearby.

"Of course I am," Tarlak said. "Nowhere else I'd rather be but in my own mind. It's nice and cozy compared to the rest of the absurd world out there."

"*Your* mind?"

Tarlak stopped. There he was. Cecil Towerborn stood mere feet away, arms crossed over his chest. He still wore his red apprentice robes, and his hair was shaped in the plain bowl cut inflicted upon those still in training. His smug grin was worthy of a thousand slaps. Just seeing it reminded Tarlak why he'd tried to make the man's life miserable every single waking second he had spent recovering within the Council towers.

"Nice robes," Tarlak said. "Even in a post-death existence, with your soul locked in stasis, it seems you're still stuck as an apprentice."

Cecil flinched as if shot by an arrow. "At least they aren't piss yellow."

Tarlak gestured to his multi-layered wizard robes containing over a dozen hidden pockets and pouches.

"I like to think it's the color of the sun. Warm and inviting, like a pleasant beacon to all, one might say."

"But haven't you noticed? There's no sun here."

The fog blasted outward with sudden intensity, and Tarlak's vertigo was replaced by an overwhelming fear of the open space. Forever, he thought. The distance went on forever, in all directions, a gray ground sprawling out to infinity, never to touch a horizon marked with a pitch-black sky lacking stars, moon, or a sun.

He felt small. He felt like he might fall upward, only for the world to spin on its head and slam him right back down. Nothing about this made sense, and yet it assaulted him with shocking, painful clarity. His legs wobbled, and despite his stubborn pride, he dropped to one knee.

Stare at your hands, he decided, and focused on his clenched fists. *They're real. Ignore the rest. This is all illusion and make-believe. You're trying to comprehend things far beyond the mortal realm.*

"Brutal, isn't it?" Cecil said, the smugness in his voice intensifying. "Looking about this expanse and realizing just how insignificant and helpless you are. That's how I felt when I first awoke after our duel. This crippling helplessness."

Cecil grabbed Tarlak by his chin and forced him to meet the gaze of his sky-blue eyes.

"That's why you managed control so easily at first," he said. "That's why you thought you had won. I needed time. I needed familiarity, and understanding, but I have that now, you bastard. This is *my* body. *My* mind. *I want it back.*"

"Your body?" Tarlak said, fighting off an instinctual desire to look away. His stomach churned. "But you weren't using it. Not very well, at least."

Cecil's mouth twitched, a brief flash of teeth revealing the seething rage that lived underneath his mockery. "Your body? So strange. I remember it so well."

Tarlak felt himself falling into Cecil's mind. The world shifted, the ground warping to match a blossoming memory. The dark sky became a world viewed from a cosmic set of eyes. Cecil was but a child, years ago abandoned at the Council steps by parents he never met. He was crying.

"I can do it," he was telling himself, scanning the words of a simple cantrip. Over and over he recited them, hour after hour, while doing everything he could to forget the teasing of his classmates. "I know I can do it, I know it!"

His frustration slipped into Tarlak's own conscious mind. He felt the feverish yearning to surpass his fellow students, crippled by a need to prove himself their better, to turn their mocking jests back on them.

The memories shifted, one after another, but in so many ways they were all the same. Cecil giving his everything, and it never being enough. He felt jealousy for friends who left apprenticeship to become permanent residents of the Masters' tower. He heard the laughs, the questions whispered just loud enough to reach his ears, wondering why he didn't simply resign as a mage and accept his limitations. Tarlak crumpled beneath the emotions, falling to his knees within a world of memory.

Get it together, he told himself. *His memories are not yours. These emotions are...not...yours.*

"I've never understood," Cecil said. His every word was a mocking lash on Tarlak's strained mind. "Why yellow? It was always the first thing that anyone discussed in the rare times when conversation within the towers turned your way. Was it to stand out? Make yourself memorable? Or did you steal the robes from someone, just like you stole my body from me?"

Tarlak witnessed their climactic duel atop the bridge connecting the two towers, only now from the opposite perspective. The vertigo of it—seeing himself being defeated by himself—threatened to crush his identity completely. Just who was he? This shame, he didn't remember it. Were these feelings of inferiority actually his?

Cecil lorded over him, laughing, somehow taking joy in his own failures, solely because he could now use them as a weapon. The attacks were savage and unrestrained, like a charging horde of soldiers without any discipline. For that's what this was, a war of memories. Tiny pieces of the divine *self* squabbling over the impermanent flesh of the body. The strength of conviction mattered. The overwhelming force of a belief in belonging, in needing to continue, to remain in the land of Dezrel.

And in that competition, Tarlak refused to entertain the possibility of losing. He stared down at himself, at his yellow robes, and remembered who he was.

The King of the Fallen

"You think, for even a moment, that you can challenge me?" he said. The sky roiled, and the memories shifted. Tarlak slowly rose to his feet. "You think your meager life can compare? You think your petty, cowardly crawl toward power withstands the light of mine when I have risked my life to save others?"

Tarlak countered his opponent with memories of his own. Cecil's time studying magic crumbled, replaced with the stench of blood and intestines. Together they walked through a war-torn battlefield, demons in red armor soaring through the skies as humanity's frantic defenders fell. The view shifted, became morning, and they stood on the walls of Mordeina and watched the sky split above a kneeling half-orc praying alone in the field.

"When I lived?" Tarlak exclaimed.

Laughter filled the air, so full of life it made a mockery of Cecil's bitter memories. Tarlak sat at a table in his tower, Harruq and Aurelia bickering at one end and taking out it on each other by throwing the steamed corn Tarlak had so carefully prepared. Delysia ducked and ran for cover, Brug cursed a storm, and Haern calmly deflected any occasionally errant kernels with his knife while reaching for a steaming slice of bread.

"When I loved?"

Taking his sister into his arms for the first time since escaping his Karak-worshipping teacher, Madral. Clapping Brug on the shoulder after successfully defending Veldaren from burning to the ground due to the Darkhand's madness. Bouncing little Aullienna on his knee as they sat beside the warm fire of his tower.

"When I lost?"

The infinite sky became a storm, and rumbling through it like thunder were his darkest memories. Kneeling over Brug in a cursed corner of the king's forest. Clutching Delysia's lifeless body, the word 'Tun' carved into her forehead. Haern, Aullienna, Antonil... so many beloved, now reduced to mere memories. There was power in the trauma, the shaping of a life from misery that Cecil could never understand in his sequestered, insular existence in the Council's towers. Tarlak lashed him with the pain, but not just the pain.

Every single moment he had carried on afterwards. Every spell he cast, every jovial word he spoke despite his heart breaking. When he stood tall while all the world seemed ready to die. He let that conviction burn through Cecil's arrogance and self-pity. In the great tapestry that was his life, this feud with Cecil was nothing, an annoyance, a bothersome set of hiccups. He had dueled a daughter of balance. He had warred against a god. What was a sheltered, spoiled brat compared to them?

Tarlak grabbed Cecil by the scruff of his shirt and yanked him close. He grinned like a madman, a savage thrill coursing through him. The surrounding world-scape trembled with remembrance.

"Why yellow?" Tarlak asked. "I've told no one, but we're intimate now, aren't we? We're the best of friends. We're closer than lovers. You want to know, then know, Cecil. Know exactly why you will never win. Take a look. Live the memories as I lived them."

Together they shifted into one another, no different than when Cecil had commanded the memories. Time lost meaning and they again fell into the past, to when Tarlak returned home to Veldaren, having slain Madral for his role in destroying Ashhur's Citadel. His every belonging was stuffed into a small sack he carried over one shoulder. His sister lived in a pitiful little home, a far cry from the mansion they had once occupied before their father gave away his wealth to join the priesthood. He knocked on the door, and his beloved sister emerged, looking radiant in the white and gold robes of an acolyte of Ashhur.

"You're home!" she'd cried, and wrapped her arms about him. She was so small yet so strong, and it made him feel like he was the younger. Time shifted as Delysia invited him inside. They shared tea, Tarlak unpacked his things, and soon they sat beside one another in front of a warm fire.

"How did father die?" Tarlak asked, finally comfortable enough to brave the subject. He'd heard only rumors when it happened, what little information he obtained coming filtered through his teacher's careful, biased tongue. Tarlak's obligations had kept him away, even when his every desire had been to flee home and comfort his sister.

"Preaching," Delysia said. "I was...I was there when it happened. He was condemning the thief guilds. They knew he was dangerous, so they killed him. I don't even know who did it, just someone with a knife and a quick hand. They sought my death as well, but the tale of my survival is a bit of a long one. Let us save that telling for another time."

Tarlak accepted her decision to withhold, instead ruminating on his father's death.

"He should have known," he said. "This world would never accept the change he wanted."

"Of course he knew it would not accept," Delysia said. "Of course he knew this hurting world would lash out. Do you think I don't know it, too? Do you think we never hear the snickers or feel the glares of the guilty?" She stared into her cup of tea. It was an image Tarlak had never forgotten. She was so burdened by heartache from the reopened wound, yet her determination never wavered. Her faith was stronger than whatever torment life might throw at her.

"Father felt the world could be better, so he acted on that belief. He gave away his fortune, his time, and eventually his life. The day he first put on Ashhur's robes, I remember he was..." She sniffled and wiped away a few stubborn tears. "He was so proud. He came running into my room like a child, so eager to let me see them. I was so young then, so foolish. I told him he looked like he was wearing a dress. 'They mean something,' he told me when he was done laughing. 'Even to those who don't believe, they'll know it took time and dedication to obtain them. And if that little bit helps, then I'll wear them, and wear them with pride....even if it makes me look like I'm wearing a dress.'"

Tarlak remembered looking upon his sister, who now wore the robes of a priestess, having followed in their father's footsteps in a far better manner than he with his spells.

"He was a good man," Tarlak said. "A great man, even. But I dare say the outfit still looks better on you."

The memory shifted, guided by Tarlak's overwhelming presence. He carried Cecil even further into the past, to a singular event inexorably linked to that previous memory. Tarlak sat at a desk in a candle-light library, one of Madral's many books spread open before him.

"There is power in color," his cruel master lectured. "Symbolism can change minds before a single word is spoken. Red is blood, anger, and fury. It can be used to convey dedication, and willingness to both protect and destroy. Black encompasses all; it is the overwhelming certainty of Karak, the fearlessness of the night. Blue is the sky and the ocean, and it will inspire hope as well as loyalty. Green is most often associated with the elves, forests, and nature. There's a humility to the color that is not possessed by those who wear a purple sash or crimson dress."

Tarlak leafed through the pages. During his entire apprenticeship, he had said nothing of his faith in Ashhur, or the pendant of the Golden Mountain his father had given to him in secret on the day Tarlak had been accepted for tutoring. The memories had remained, though, slowly shifting and molding as he learned. After scanning the symbols and explanations of the book, he settled on a single page.

"What of yellow?" he asked.

There was no hiding Madral's disdain.

"Yellow is the color most closely associated with Ashhur and his followers. His priests line their robes with it. His paladins gild their weapons and the edges of their armor, for they serve the Golden Mountain. Ashhur's morality is the apotheosis of everything we wizards strive for. We seek knowledge, not limitations. We need not dress up selfish choices with words like mercy or forgiveness. The fate of others is irrelevant to the mastery of our own destinies."

Madral slammed the book shut.

"I assure you, Tarlak, you will never, ever see a wizard of any worth wearing such a hideous color."

Tarlak put his hands atop that closed book, no longer a child, and no longer staring up at a master that had secretly worshiped Karak and helped bring the original Citadel tumbling to the ground. Cecil stood where Madral had been, and they were no different to him now. Bitter, angry men, clawing for power solely because they craved its hollow, false comfort. He did not fear them. He pitied them.

The King of the Fallen

"I have always known who I am," Tarlak told the trembling image of an infinite soul. "And I have always known who I wanted to be. No matter who has doubted me, who has mocked me, or who has tried to stop me, I have succeeded. I'll succeed in this too, Cecil. Mourn your foul luck if you wish. Complain to Karak how unfair your fate. Maybe he will give you the pity I will not. I excise you like a splinter. I banish you like a thief. Be gone like a disease burned away by fever. I've got shit to do, Cecil, and a world to make better."

Cecil was so small now, not in age or size but in his presence, so thin he approached translucent, so ephemeral he might be smoke from a snuffed campfire. Tarlak put a hand on the man's chest and pushed, scattering him like the petals of a dandelion.

"I am the wizard in yellow, and I want you gone."

Tarlak's eyes snapped open. He drew in a long, singular gasp of air, as if his lungs had remained empty for millennia. Sparkling ethereal diamonds, like a shower of starlight, burst out his throat when he exhaled. Qurrah stood before him, haloed by the light Tarlak had breathed out. The half-orc grinned with devilish glee, his hands curling upwards.

"Finally," he said, and crooked his fingers. The dust, the scattered essence of a soul, flung heavenward. Tarlak did not watch it go. He held no desire to witness the final disappearance of what had been Cecil Towerborn. He'd seen enough of him to last ten lifetimes.

"So...is that it?" Harruq asked. "You back, Tar? Are you...you?"

Qurrah certainly seemed to believe so, for he was busy undoing the knots tying Tarlak to his chair. Instead of answering, Tarlak took his freed right hand, dipped it into one of the pockets of his robes, and withdrew a long white handkerchief.

"The idea of casting a spell sounds horrible right now," he mumbled, vaguely aware he sounded heavily intoxicated. "Can you fill this with ice, Aurry?"

Aurelia took the handkerchief without a word, summoned a small collection of smooth ice shards with a quick waggle of her fingers, and then tied the handkerchief shut to seal it in.

"Thanks," Tarlak said. He leaned back in the chair and set the ice against his forehead. He could tell the others were still worried or curious, but he couldn't care less. He had done it. He was free.

"And yes, it's me, just me," he said as he closed his eyes and let the ice do its work. "Now please, forgive me if I pass out for a few days. By Ashhur almighty, I have one Abyss of a headache."

14

Lathaar watched the black wings gather from a window on the second floor of the Citadel.

"Damn it, Jerico," he muttered. "You just had to go out and be a hero, didn't you?"

He patted his sheathed swords. They might be without his dear friend's shield, but they had his blades, and they had the great walls of the dark tower. It would be enough. It *had* to be enough.

The door to his room barged open. Lathaar shot a look over his shoulder to find the oldest of his students, Samar, standing in the doorway. Fear tainted his jade eyes.

"We don't know what to..." Samar began, then gathered himself. "What are your orders?"

"Ready your armor and weapons. And have everyone meet me on the ground floor."

"And the children?"

Years of training allowed his face to remain perfectly passive. "Keep them in their room, and hang blankets over the windows. They mustn't see what happens next."

Samar left. Lathaar stared at the door, the weight of dozens of lives settling upon his shoulders as he calmly strapped on his platemail. His whole life, he had endured such a burden. For years he'd thought himself the last surviving paladin of Ashhur, until he met Jerico. He'd stood against Karak's forces, the undead of the prophet Velixar, even waged war on the demons of Thulos. From the ashes and rubble, he'd rebuilt the Citadel. Every step of his life was a struggle. His entire past was a trail of blood and tears.

When he finished dressing, Lathaar took one last look out the window. The fallen angels surrounded the tower, and though their weapons were drawn, they made no move to attack. They wanted to talk, as expected. Azariah hovered at their forefront. Lathaar knew the angel well enough to anticipate his next move. Azariah believed himself so wise, so noble. Lathaar prayed that before the day was done, he'd be able to show the angel just how wretched he truly was.

"Are you with me still?" Lathaar whispered to his god. He turned his back to the window. "Because we sure could use you right now."

He descended to the first floor, which was built explicitly for battle. The entry door was narrow, yet the space immediately beyond was wide and curving. Barging into the Citadel would mean charging into a concave of defenders. The problem was, those defenders were young and inexperienced. Only a few, such as Samar, Mal, and Elrath, had tasted battle. And even then, they'd known only capture and torture.

A handful of students lingered in the wide room, overturning a pair of tables to use as barricades. Lathaar nodded to them, then gestured for one, the tall, dark-haired Mal, to come closer.

"Shut the door behind me," he said.

"You're going out there?" Mal asked, eyes bulging.

"Only to talk, not to fight. As insane as it sounds, I expect Azariah to try to do this honorably. If I can, I'll stall for time."

"What good will time do us?" asked Elrath, stepping up beside him. The second-oldest student in the Citadel was a shorter man, but stocky with muscle and skilled with the use of a blade. His dark hair was pulled back from his face in a stubby ponytail. "No one is coming to rescue us. No one will save us. We're on our own."

Lathaar grabbed him by the front of his shirt and yanked him close.

"Dozens of fallen angels are here, as well as Azariah himself," Lathaar said, his voice an angry whisper. "And if they're *here*, then they're not causing trouble *elsewhere*. Our fate may not change with an extra day, but how many innocents flee to Ker even as we speak? An extra day may mean life and death for them, so that's why I'm going out there. All we do, we do for others. Never forget that. Now go put on your damn armor."

Elrath's face blushed a deep red. "Yes sir."

Lathaar didn't watch him leave. Couldn't focus on that now. Over the years, when times were quiet and the tower halls dark, Jerico and Lathaar had discussed their students' lack of faith. It had worried and perplexed them both with equal measure. How could one lack faith in Ashhur when his angels watched over the land, and the god had saved them from Thulos's annihilation? Now he felt that same worry, only a thousand times worse. Those angels, who were meant to inspire faith, now surrounded the tower, their skin ashen, their wings black and foreboding. What did it matter if they were saved from Thulos if they then must bend the knee to Azariah's crown of bone?

They'll stand strong with you, Lathaar thought. *Hold faith in them.*

"Remember, shut and locked," he told Mal, then stepped out to speak with the king of the fallen.

The angels had landed. Lathaar put their numbers at nearly one hundred, forming a ring about the Citadel with their wings barely touching one another. Their brittle feathers bristled despite no wind blowing. Lathaar could feel their revulsion. Had they been corrupted so quickly that the mere sight of a paladin of Ashhur sickened them? Their angry eyes stared at him, their gazes like pinpricks on his skin. Pretending not to notice or care, he walked with his head held high until he was several dozen feet from the Citadel door and then lifted his arms. The silence weighed heavily upon him. The angels only glared.

Azariah stepped up to him and pulled back his lips into a grin, exposing his jagged, bloodstained teeth.

"I would greet you, but you are no longer welcome guests to the Citadel," Lathaar said. "For this is a house of Ashhur, and Ashhur no longer calls you his beloved."

"Beloved," Azariah said. "Is that what you are, Lathaar? Beloved of Ashhur? Why is that?"

"Because I kept the faith even amid the hardships."

"Is that what you believe? Ashhur's loyalty was because of your faith?" The angel king shook his head. "You were an excellent murderer, Lathaar. A soldier who killed all that Ashhur deemed worthy of death."

"Do not belittle my love and faith."

Azariah stepped closer and his raised his voice for all to hear.

"Tell me, Lathaar, were you gifted the greatest signs of love and faith during moments of teaching and mercy, or on the battlefield?"

They both knew the answer. It was true that Lathaar's blade of pure light, the Elholad, was not an instrument of mercy, but that felt like such an over-simplification, a bastardization of Lathaar's responsibilities.

Realization struck him, and the comparison that he now saw felt like ice to his veins. The way Azariah mocked him, and belittled his faith…it was just like speaking with Velixar.

"I am not here to argue matters of faith with one of Ashhur's fallen," Lathaar said. "Why are you here, angel?"

"You know why I am here. The children. Hand them over to me if you wish for you and your students to live."

Lathaar did his best to act as if he were confused, if not annoyed, while inside his chest his heart kicked into double time.

"What are you talking about?"

Azariah didn't look the slightest bit convinced. "The boy king, and the Godslayer's daughter. They're both here. Hand them over, willingly, and I will show you mercy. I hold faith that, given time and meditation, you will reach the same realizations regarding Ashhur's incomplete wisdom. I would give you a chance to observe the changes to Dezrel I will bring. But if you force me to assault these walls, I will spare not a soul. My mercy is not that deep."

Lathaar bit down a curse. Tarlak was supposed to have been using his magic to convince Azariah the children were with their army and not here. The wizard had failed somehow, that or Azariah's magic was stronger than they believed. Whatever the reason, this was the worst possible outcome. If Azariah had come solely aiming to convert the Citadel's students, then he could have stalled for time. The angels might have only quarantined the Citadel to keep them out of the current conflict, which also would have been just fine with him. But if Azariah knew the children were there…

"We won't hand them over," Lathaar said. "We'll fight you to our last breath. You'll be attacking one of the most holy sites of Ashhur's faithful, in a building made for war. You will lose many of your fallen, Azariah, numbers you will never replace. You are already king. What does it matter if Gregory lives? Do you truly think the nobles will need him as an excuse to rebel against your tyranny?"

He never could have predicted the rage that flooded through Azariah's entire being. He snarled, baring his jagged teeth. Black feathers fluttered loose from his shivering wings.

"It is not the boy's position I care for," he said. "It is the use I have planned for them that matters."

Lathaar felt a wretched, bitter taste settle across the back of his tongue.

"Hostages," he said. "You need hostages."

"The Godslayer and his elven wife will never raise hands against me if I hold a dagger to Aubrienna's throat. Now enough of this banter, paladin. You know my terms. Hand the children over, or watch as I bleed the life out of your every student. You will die last, that I promise you, both you and Jerico. Now make your choice."

The angel thought Jerico was with them. Lathaar wondered if that was for the best, or if it merely showed how confident the angels were in their attack. They believed that if Jerico was at his side, they could still win? Nothing could move his friend when his shield was high and his faith strong.

"I will speak with my friends," Lathaar said. Even if it were only minutes, he would buy what time he could. "But I wouldn't hold my breath."

Lathaar returned to the Citadel. Its thick door creaked open as he approached. He stepped inside to find all his students gathered together, their weapons readied and their bodies protected with chainmail. None had been outfitted with platemail yet. Too young. Too inexperienced. They fell into a fearful silence at his arrival.

"Well?" Mal asked. "What do they want?"

"They want the children," Lathaar said. "If we hand them over, Azariah claims he'll spare our lives."

"So...what do we do?" Samar asked.

It took Lathaar a long moment to realize the question was serious. He looked at the young man and shook his head. His resolve hardened. A lifetime of war settled over his mind.

"What do we do?" he echoed. "We do what we must. We do what I have always done throughout my life. We draw our swords, we ready our shields, and we stand before the storm. We cry our voices to Ashhur and demand the strength we need from our beloved god."

"They'll kill us," Samar said. It wasn't a question. It was a statement of fact.

"They might," Lathaar said softly. He looked about the room, meeting the eyes of his students. He would be strong for them if he must. Let them see his ardent belief. And in them, he saw the future. He saw hope.

"I have risked my life for others, and every time I drew my sword, I knew it might be my last. Not once have I regretted it. I will fight for others on this dark world. I will bleed and die so others might live, might know joy and peace. You may not feel it, you may not believe it yet, but that same strength resides in you. This world, it is a world of miracles, is it not? Have we not seen it again and again? I have seen the sky split open. I have spoken with gods. I have seen life given to the dead, and I have held strong when all the world would call me doomed. Azariah believes us doomed yet again, but do you know what I say? Raise your weapons. Sing praise in your hearts. We will stand. Do you hear me, my students? We. Will. Stand."

Raise their weapons they did. The blue-white light of Ashhur shone off naked steel, a reflection of their faith, yet it was so faint. These young men were nervous, terrified. Lathaar wished he could give them his confidence, his years of experience, but that went counter to the very hope of a land of angels had once promised. Such brutal lives were meant to no longer be necessary. Yet in the end, as always, the darkness came. Lathaar drew his swords and let their gleam shine upon them all.

"Until the end," he said to a dead silent room.

Lathaar returned to the door and pulled it open. Daylight shone upon him. He looked to the ring of fallen angels. Once their protectors, now their foes.

"We have your answer!" he shouted to them. They readied their weapons. Ashhur's warning cried deep in Lathaar's mind, but he only smiled.

"We will not surrender!" he bellowed at the top of his lungs. "We will—"

A sharp pain pierced his side. His muscles locked up, and his neck arched from the constriction. It made no sense. His back. The pain came from his back. His legs went weak, when he felt a tugging sensation. The world pitched unevenly, and he dropped to his knees. Blood poured down his side. Hardly a new sensation, but it shocked him nonetheless. He'd been stabbed. Though he should be angry, he felt only surprise and bewilderment. He slowly turned his head.

Samar stood with bloody sword in hand. He looked like a frightened ghost.

"Why?" Lathaar croaked. Even saying that much was suddenly difficult.

None spoke. The other students were pale-faced and wide-eyed. Even the fallen angels watched with their mouths hanging open. An army of angels, and a Citadel of students, and yet Lathaar bled out in what seemed the quietest place in all of Dezrel.

And in that dead silence, the first sound to pierce through to torment his ears was Azariah's uncontrollable laughter.

"What the fuck?" one of the students shouted. Lathaar couldn't make out who. His hearing was starting to grow fuzzy.

"Do you want us all to die?" Samar asked. "There's what, forty of us? And we should all throw our lives away for two damn kids? It doesn't matter what we do. They'll kill us, all of us. Now go get them, or I will."

Still none moved. Samar swore and bounded up the stairs. Lathaar collapsed onto his stomach, his platemail feeling impossibly heavy.

Keep calm, he thought. *Keep...calm...*

He still had his prayers. He still had Ashhur's healing magic. If he could recover, he could rally the students and prevent this grand betrayal. Surely Samar was alone in his cowardice.

Wasn't he?

Lathaar's hand settled over the wound, and he whispered words a prayer. He demanded his god mend the flesh and sew muscle back together as if it were never torn. Light shone across his fingers. A soft ringing of distant bells calmed his mind. Already his pain started to fade.

Samar returned down the steps dragging Gregory and Aubrienna each by the hand. Upon seeing Lathaar, his eyes spread wide and he shouted out a curse.

"Stop!" he screamed, releasing the children to re-draw his sword. Lathaar lifted his other hand in a meager protest. Samar ran, legs fueled by panic, arms strengthened by fear.

Down came the blade.

The sharp pain was marked by the screaming of the children. Lathaar gasped and rolled away from him, momentum carrying him out the Citadel and onto the pale grass. He lay there, jaw clenched tightly shut as he pressed his hand against his neck.

It wasn't a clean cut. Though Samar likely meant to open his throat, the blade had missed his bronchial tube. Based on the blood poured against his hand, it didn't matter. Lathaar pushed with every ounce of pressure his muscles could manage, trying to stem the flow. Another healing prayer floated through his groggy mind, but he couldn't speak the words. He tried to tell himself it was because of his injuries, because moving his lips induced incredibly agony. It was a lie.

Lathaar looked to his students and his heart broke in a way it never had in all his life.

"We won't do this," someone shouted.

"It's too late now," countered someone else. Weapons clanged together. Fighting? Who was fighting? He couldn't see. Whoever it was, it ended quickly.

"Then get out," Samar said. "Go with them."

Lathaar lifted his head so he might see their identities. Elrath and Mal were the only ones to exit the tower in protest. They stood defiant, shoulders back and heads held high. Samar walked ahead of them, dragging Gregory and Aubrienna by the wrist.

"We won't go along with this," Elrath told the angels. "We'd rather die."

The King of the Fallen

"Die?" Azariah asked. The angel strode toward the Citadel, so close now that Lathaar could have smelled him if not for the overpowering odor of blood that filled his nose. "I made a promise. Your lives for the children, and I will not break that promise." The bastard knelt down beside Lathaar. His sickly image blocked the sun, casting a shadow over his already fading vision. "Besides, your suffering is great enough. What more might I add? Only one person dies, and I will not be the one who killed him."

Lathaar wished he had a biting remark to offer. Jerico might have known a good one.

The fallen angel's wings spread wide as he wrapped his arms around a crying Aubrienna. Another lifted up Gregory. Samar quickly turned and fled back into the Citadel. Its reinforced door slammed shut with a rattle of wood and metal. No last remarks, no goodbyes. The fallen king took the skies, his horde of angels with him.

Elrath and Mal, knelt over him, and he heard them faintly praying through their growing exhaustion and tears. Would that he could comfort them.

Lathaar's vision turned dark as the world rapidly departed him. He thought he'd feel more regret, more anguish, but his dying mind thought only of a promise made so very long ago.

"Mira," Lathaar whispered. "Are you still waiting?"

The answer awaited his final breath. He closed his eyes, released his hand from his neck, and gave in.

15

Jerico awoke that morning with a sense of dread he could not shake, so he started north long before dawn. It seemed every few minutes he sent another prayer to Ashhur, begging for the safety of his friends.

"We've survived so much," he muttered to as dawn slipped into day. "We'll survive this too, won't we? With you at our sides?"

He patted the shield on his back, but its sturdy heft was no comfort, not this day.

Not long after midday he saw three men approaching from up ahead. As he closed the distance, he realized that two of the men were carrying the third between them, his arms draped over their shoulders. Dread told a thousand stories, but Jerico denied them all. He would not give in to wild thoughts when these three figures were still so far away.

But that didn't mean he couldn't jog instead of walk. When he saw the way the third figure hung limp in the arms of the other two, the jog turned to a sprint. His fear disappeared, replaced by a vast emptiness. Jerico didn't want to think at all. He didn't want to believe.

"Elrath?" he called when he was close enough to make out their features. "Mal? What…what happened?"

The man they carried was Lathaar, stripped of his armor, down to a simple pair of bloodstained underclothes. He was still. So very still. The two young apprentices came to a halt before him, gasping for breath after carrying such dead weight.

"Jerico," said Elrath. His blue eyes, normally the beautiful color of the sky, were a vicious red. "I…we…"

Neither had words. Jerico's sprint plummeted even deeper. His jaw hung open and trembled. His heart halted in his chest. So much blood covered his friend's body. Too much.

Jerico's knees gave out, and he slumped before them. His vision blurred from a sudden swell of tears. "No," he whispered. "No, no, no, it can't be, it can't. We've survived so much, so goddamn much."

He cast his shield and mace to the dirt and lunged back to his feet. He took Lathaar's body from the two youngsters, embracing the corpse of his old friend as he wept. A thousand memories swept through him, of fighting side by side, of rebuilding the Citadel, of that joyous moment when they'd met at the Sanctuary and realized that they were not alone in the cruel world of Dezrel.

But Jerico felt so very alone now, and he choked down his screams so he would not break completely before his two students. He clutched a corpse, not a man. He wept for the loss, and then he buried his emotions beneath a wave of rage.

Elrath and Mal remained silent through it all, their gazes cast to the dirt to give him a semblance of privacy.

"What happened?" Jerico asked once he had composed himself. "Tell me everything."

And so they did. Jerico listened, and he realized that first wave of rage he felt was but a prelude to fury. It burned like fire throughout his veins. He listened to the story of betrayal, of Samar's fatal backstabbing, and of his students handing over Gregory and Aubrienna to spare their own lives.

"We wanted to bury him," Elrath said when they were finished. "But it didn't feel right to hold a funeral or pyre without you."

"And we didn't want the others to watch," Mal added. "They don't deserve to be there. They don't get to mourn him after what they did."

Jerico gently laid Lathaar's body on the grass.

"Bury him here," he said. "In the soft soil beside the river. We deserve a grave in the wilderness, the both of us. It's where we lived our lives. It's the world we walked when the Citadel first fell."

"Won't you help us?" asked Mal.

Jerico slid his shield over his back and clipped Bonebreaker to his hip.

"No," he said. "I'm going to the Citadel we built. As for you two, follow the river once you finish with the burial. Skirt wide around the Council of Mages, and continue south. Until you reach the ocean, if you must. Make yourself a home in Haven.

Live what life you can, in the world the fallen angels would leave us."

"What will you do?" Elrath asked, dread hanging heavy on his every syllable.

Jerico sighed. "Truly? I don't know."

He knelt over Lathaar's corpse, kissed his forehead, and whispered his final goodbye.

"We are embers of light from a dying fire, but you burned brightly, my friend."

✣

The grasslands passed in a haze of anguish and subdued rage. Jerico's heart could not burn so brightly and for so long, not when he had several more miles to cross before he reached the Citadel. He barely saw the grass where he walked. His mind drifted through memories, trying to cling to the pleasant ones but often failing.

"How many friends must I say goodbye to?" Jerico asked the silence. Sandra, his first love; that loss had hurt him most, but there were others. Darius, the former paladin of Karak. Haern, a tortured young man with a kind heart and a brutal childhood. Delysia, who had shown only kindness to a world that sought cruelty. The cranky blacksmith, Brug. The villagers of Durham, whom he'd failed to protect despite preaching daily to them of Ashhur's mercy and grace. His mind rubbed raw at the death. Velixar's army of the dead. Thulos's war demons. The destruction of Veldaren. The siege at Mordeina.

Through it all, he'd stood shoulder to shoulder with Lathaar, two bastions of Ashhur holding the line against the evils of the land that would see the innocent suffer. They'd fought demons, beast-men, undead, and fallen angels. None had brought them low.

Until a blade to the back.

At last he saw the Citadel looming in the distance. Jerico paused a moment to stare at what had been, until that morning, his proudest accomplishment.

"I can't keep doing this," he softly whispered. "I can't keep bleeding for you, Ashhur. One day I will have no blood left to give."

The King of the Fallen

But it wasn't yet that day. He continued on, veering away from the river and settling onto the worn path that lead to the Citadel's entrance. He buried his sorrow with his every step, imagining each footfall casting a handful of dirt atop Lathaar's corpse. Elrath and Mal would bury him, pray over him, and honor him well. Jerico would do the same, only he would do it here, at the Citadel.

No one came out to greet him when he stopped before the entrance. To his left lay Lathaar's armor and swords, stripped off and cast aside so the two students could bear the weight of his body. He stared at the now-useless mound of steel and leather, letting the grim sight stir the rage that had momentarily faded beneath his sorrow. A twinkle caught his eye, a hint of gold amid the trampled grass. Jerico knelt down, brushed aside some dirt, and lifted his prize: the lucky coin Tarlak had given young Gregory when they first parted. Jerico clutched the coin in his fist hard enough to hurt, then slid it into his pocket. When he stood and turned his attention to the Citadel, he saw frightened faces peering at him from the windows.

"Come forth!" he shouted.

None dared move. Was it fear? Disrespect? He shook his head, not caring. They would not hide in the Citadel, not from him. His lips curled into a snarl.

"*Come forth!*" It was a command with power like the stories of old. The faces vanished from the windows. Moments later, the doors to the Citadel opened, and the first of his students flitted out onto the grass. They surrounded him in a semi-circle, not a one capable of meeting his gaze when he glared their way.

That they came armed did not go unnoticed.

Samar was the last to arrive, and he pushed to the front of the group and stood with his arms crossed and his jaw clenched. He looked ready to argue, almost eager for it. Jerico stared at the sword sheathed at his hip. He imagined that blade plunging into Lathaar's back, just beneath the lower edge of his breastplate. He shook his head to banish the thought, and it seemed Samar took it as a sign to plead his case.

"I saved all our lives," Samar started. "If not for—"

"Bite your tongue," Jerico said, silencing the young man with a glare. "I will not hear a word from your lips. No lies. No truths. No excuses, no reasons, and no arguments."

Jerico pulled the shield off his back and settled it over his left arm. The blue-white glow of his faith shimmered across its surface. He turned so all might see it. Despite everything, it still shone brightly. It still burned with holy light. Once finished, he unclipped Bonebreaker from his belt and pointed its flanged edges toward Samar.

"Draw your sword," he told him.

"What?"

"Draw your sword," Jerico repeated. "I would see its light."

"Is that how you'll judge me?" Samar argued.

"Not me," Jerico said. "I am not here for judgment. That is Ashhur's place, not mine. I come with a different purpose, now show me your blade."

Samar drew his sword, and he held it before him in a combat stance. Sunlight glinted off its naked blade. No glow shone from its surface. Jerico clenched his jaw, his teeth grinding together as he fought off a fresh wave of tears.

"How did I fail you all so terribly?"

He moved faster than Samar could react. A single blow from his mace ripped Samar's jaw from his face and snapped the bones of his neck. The young man collapsed in a heap. The surrounding students cried out.

"The rest of you," Jerico said with a leaden tongue. "Show me your faith."

The ringing sound of metal filled his ears. Dull, naked steel. No light. No glow. The only color he saw was the red that painted his vision. A rage so deep it terrified him.

"Is this the faith I have fostered?" he asked. "Cast me into Karak's fire if this is the sum of my work."

He thrust his shield forward. Its after-image leaped forth, brilliant in its glow and growing larger as it progressed. It struck down those it touched, knocking them to the ground as if it were a solid stone wall. The students erupted in panic, these young men he'd trained, and those who remained standing lashed out at him

The King of the Fallen

with their weapons. Jerico shifted his shield from side to side, his mace parrying what his shield could not block. The attacks were scattered, disorganized. He'd like to think he taught them better than that. Results said otherwise.

A sword clattered off his pauldron. Another dented the plate on his leg. Jerico blocked the blows, and he saw the pained looks in the eyes of any who made contact with his shield. The holy light stung them. Ashhur's grace, it would burn them, blind them.

"Damn my failure," Jerico whispered.

He stopped defending and went on the offensive. Bonebreaker shattered through his students' meager defenses. Swing after swing, limbs were crunched. Pained screams and frightened cries filled the air. Jerico didn't see or hear them, not really. His training took over as his mind retreated deep inside. With each death, he felt a piece of himself wither.

Guilt warred with fury each time he brought a body low. He thought righteousness would fuel him. He thought it would blunt the trauma, justify the slaughter. Lathaar's betrayal, the handing over of the children they were to protect…was there forgiveness for such crimes?

But there was. Jerico had preached it a thousand times before. He deflected the swipe of an ax off his shield and caved the young man's head in with Bonebreaker. No forgiveness for him, though. None for the number of dead and dying at his feet. Jerico was screaming now, a mindless pain that infected his entire soul. Another life. Another. Another.

They were fleeing now, scattering in all directions. Jerico collapsed to his knees, for he had not the spirit to chase. Every beat of his heart felt like a punch to his chest. His face was soaked with tears he didn't remember shedding. Blood and gore covered his armor and weapons. The stench of the dead overwhelmed him.

Beyond tired, beyond broken, Jerico looked to the Citadel he and Lathaar had rebuilt, and upon it he saw Ashhur's face.

"Is this it?" he softly asked. "Is this our legacy?"

The ground shook in answer. The foundation of the Citadel broke, and with a terrible roar of stone and earth, the building began to collapse. Jerico bowed his head and stared at the shadow tipping toward him. He would not run. Everything here, the dead, the fleeing, the bodies and the betrayals, he would let it settle upon him, bury him if it must.

A long, snaking crack split the building in twain. The two halves fell to either side of him, as if ripped apart by enormous hands, and then slammed deep into the ground, leaving him unscathed. Dirt churned. Dust and smoke flooded his vision, for which Jerico was thankful. He did not wish to see the fleeing bodies crushed beneath the rubble. He didn't need to see more death. The deafening noise of the tower's fall slowly receded into a painstaking silence broken only by the distant sound of the flowing Rigon River.

And in that silence, Jerico wept. He finally allowed himself to feel the full horror of it all. He shed his tears at the foot of the Citadel, the weight of his decisions crashing down like so much worthless brick. He had walked in darkness before, but never before had he felt so alone. Even when Thulos had marched upon Mordeina, Jerico had believed in a brighter future. He'd believed, with the confidence of a much younger man, that his strength alone could save the world. Now his salvation carried death on black wings, and Ashhur felt so very far away.

Yet even now, Jerico would not remain motionless in his sorrows. He'd spent his time in the Vile Wedge in self-imposed exile. He'd had his moment away from the world, and its sins and hardships. Never again. He rose to his feet, mind raw, heart bleeding, and looked to his mace, Bonebreaker. When he visited the Citadel after its first collapse, he'd found the weapon lost amid the rubble. It'd belonged to a paladin named Jaegar who'd given his life defending their home from an undead army. The first Citadel, brought low by Karak. Now Jerico stood before the second, broken by Ashhur's own hands.

"Again and again we suffer this dance," Jerico whispered. "We build, and we break. We stand before an army of hatred and death, and upon claiming victory, we find only another army. Will there be no reprieve? Must it all end in rubble?"

Jerico flung Bonebreaker to the grass. Perhaps, in a distant future, a good man or woman would find the enchanted weapon. Perhaps it would give them the hope and strength they needed. It would not be his. Not anymore.

Lathaar's discarded belongings had escaped the building's collapse. Jerico lifted his friend's longsword and withdrew it from its sheath to check its edge. Still sharp. Jerico wasn't trained to use a sword beyond rudimentary lessons, but that was fine. His shield was his true weapon, as it had always been since his earliest days in the Citadel. He buckled Lathaar's sword to his waist, set his shield across his back, and looked once more to the rubble.

Angels had helped rebuild the Citadel after Thulos's defeat, a symbolic construction to mark Ashhur's return to Dezrel. Jerico wished he had a proper eulogy to give the building now that it lay in ruins, but he had nothing witty to say, no wisdom to give, and no audience to hear it.

"We tried," he told the silent air. "If only it were enough."

Jerico trudged west. The miles were many, but he would walk until he reached Mordeina, the city of fallen angels. The world was not kind. It was not just. Nonetheless, he prayed that before his own life reached its end, he would bathe Lathaar's sword in Azariah's blood.

16

"I thought they'd never leave," Deathmask said. He peered to his left, where Veliana perched beside him atop Mordeina's western wall.

Fallen angels flew overhead by the hundreds, a sight reminiscent of a stirred flock of ravens departing a field. They soared above the combined might of the newly-crowned Paradise. On the ground, making up nearly two-thirds of the army, were the undead soldiers enslaved to Azariah's whims. They marched along the well-worn road in perfectly even rows, ten by ten. Which made adding up their numbers fairly easy. Five thousand undead, obedient little soldiers ready to punch, bite, and claw at whatever enemy they were commanded to kill. After them followed the collected living soldiers of the lords and ladies that had slowly arrived in answer to the fallen king's summons. Half the number of the undead, they were still an impressive sight, with hundreds of men clad in shining chainmail. Behind them marched three companies of archers, each carrying longbows across their backs.

"It's hard to imagine Ahaesarus having anywhere near the numbers needed to survive against such an army," Veliana said. They were far enough to the south of the western exit that they need not fear being spotted by the soaring fallen angels, but Deathmask had wrapped the both of them in magical shadows just in case. The last thing he wanted to do was take an unnecessary risk right when things were getting interesting.

"Rumors claim Ahaesarus has enslaved the beast-men that were rampaging across the north," Deathmask said. "That alone gives him a sizable killing force. Tarlak is with them, I'm sure, and I suspect so is the Godslayer and his wife. How many undead soldiers do they alone count for?"

"Though from what you've told me, Azariah possesses aid from the Council of Mages. I'd still prefer Azariah's army over Ahaesarus's."

Deathmask tracked the sky at the mention of Azariah. So far he'd not seen the fallen king lead his army out, which seemed odd. What could be so pressing that would make him linger

The King of the Fallen

behind? Thousands of men and women had gathered along walls and on rooftops to watch the army leave. Was this not the display of power the angel was so fond of?

Veliana tugged his sleeve and pointed toward the castle. From the grounds beside the tower flew a lone angel. When the soaring form grew closer, Deathmask noticed the ornate robes. There was no mistaking it, that was Azariah, now heading toward his army...but what had he been up to?

Azariah flew into the great cloud of black wings and feathers. Though they were too high to know for sure, it looked like he was having a discussion with several of his fellows. After a few minutes, Azariah pointed back toward the castle. A trio of fallen abandoned flight with the rest of the army and flew back toward the castle. For a moment Deathmask thought they were to remain behind to rule in Azariah's absence, but then they veered off from the castle to land in the grounds just to its south.

"Curious," Deathmask said, rubbing his mangled chin. "What could be so important that our fallen king would work on it to the very last minute?"

"You think something is amiss, don't you?" Veliana asked.

He winked at her. "Care to go find out?"

❈

Deathmask and Veliana approached the castle, openly walking the streets for the first time in what felt like ages now that the legion of undead watchers had left for war. Plenty of people stared at them as they passed, but none dared intrude. Deathmask figured a few human soldiers would remain behind to keep order in the city, but he doubted anyone would be foolish enough to summon them. If there was anyone more frightening in the city of Mordeina than the fallen angels, it was him and Veliana.

Once they neared the castle, Deathmask shifted off the main road, trying to visualize where the trio of fallen had descended. It was not so hard to figure out. Beside the grand outer walls of the castle were the royal gardens. The three angels stood at its entrance, talking amongst themselves. Deathmask darted behind the nearest home the second he saw them, gesturing for Veliana to do the same.

"They look upset," Veliana whispered, peering over his shoulder. The road led directly to the garden entrance, which was marked by a gigantic stone archway with the family name 'Baedan' embossed along its highest point.

"Wouldn't you be?" he whispered back. "Ever since the Night of Black Wings they've been slobbering for the chance to kill their brethren. Now the war resumes, and these three are stuck at home guarding...well, we're not sure yet what they're guarding but I doubt it is as appealing as murdering Ashhur's angels."

Veliana drew her daggers. "An interesting idea. Let's go find out for ourselves."

His comrade led the way, sprinting around the corner as fast as her legs could carry her. Surprise was their best weapon, and the three fallen were so deeply absorbed in their own conversation that they didn't realize the danger they were in.

Veliana crossed the span in a heartbeat and lunged at the nearest angel with both daggers leading. Violet flame surrounded the blades, enhanced by Vel's minor skill in magic. Deathmask raised his arms, words of a spell rambling off his tongue. When the three fallen turned, he dropped his arms, wrapping all three angels in an orb of pure darkness.

Blinded and confused, they were defenseless against Veliana's attack. She dove straight into the orb. Deathmask lost sight of her when she vanished into the spherical darkness. He heard the sound of metal striking metal, heard a pained cry, and then out the other side Veliana emerged, blood dripping from her naked daggers.

Two angels flew skyward out from the orb, rendering it no longer useful. Deathmask banished it with a flick of his fingers. Its disappearance revealed the third angel lying dead on the ground, his throat and face hacked to bits.

Get down here, Deathmask thought as the two fallen attempted to fly beyond reach of spell and blade. He hooked his fingers into the necessary shapes. Matching hands made of pure shadow formed upon the two nearby rooftops. The hands lunged upward like those of a giant. Each of their six fingers slammed together, clapping about an angel between them. Deathmask laughed. Easy as killing a fly. Though unlike a fly, the angel shrieked at the horrid pain, still alive as he fell, the hollow bones of his wings snapped.

Anger replaced caution for the third fallen. He looped around, his sword gripped tightly in both hands. Veliana returned to Deathmask's side, standing guard before him while he readied another spell.

"I can't slow him," she said.

"Then get out of his way."

The fallen angel barreled toward them in a dive, his speed rivaling that of a hawk or eagle. He weaved slightly side to side, attempting to dodge any potential projectiles. Deathmask hurled nothing at him; he kept his spell readied, the dark magic swirling about his right hand. The angel would have to pull up right before contact, or he'd splatter himself upon the street.

Deathmask's legs tensed, and right before impact he dove left while Veliana dove right. The fallen angel sliced through the air, his sword missing Deathmask's shoulder by the width of a hair.

Momentum carried the angel forward, but he arced his back and curled his wings, looping himself up and around to greatly reduce his speed. The move also positioned him right above Deathmask. It was exactly the maneuver he'd anticipated. Deathmask dropped to his back, his hands his extended, his mouth locked into a grin.

"Predictable."

A tremendous bolt of shadow shot from his palm. It intercepted the descending angel, cracking into his chest with the force of a boulder. He let out a ragged shriek when his armor crunched inward and the shredded metal pierced his skin. His trajectory shifted, and the moment he landed unevenly on his feet, Veliana was upon him. Two quick thrusts with her dagger pierced his heart, dropping him.

"Nicely done," Deathmask said, pushing himself back to his feet. He wiped at the dust and dirt clinging to his robe. "Though perhaps wait for me to open with a spell next time before rushing after our foes?"

"And give away my approach?" She wiped blood off her daggers and slid them into their sheaths. "You have magic that can hit far in the air. I don't."

"Fair enough." He chuckled and walked to the garden entrance, then spun about. With a low bow, he swept his arm toward the opening.

"After you, milady."

They entered the gardens, which of course were overly extravagant, meant to impress upon visitors the wealth of the kingdom. Statues of two dozen kings and queens were cut from marble to flank the initial pathway, their haughty eyes judging who entered the garden proper. They passed through a second archway, four cherubic angels wielding bows standing atop it to keep guard. At one point, the sight might have been cute or disarming. Nowadays it just felt grotesque.

"There's something familiar about this place," Deathmask said as he walked a stone pathway through hedges that grew all the way up to his shoulders.

"It's the royal gardens," Veliana said. "Of course it's familiar. I'm sure we've been here before. Likely for some social nonsense while re-establishing the Ash Guild. It's been a long five years."

He shook his head. No, that was too simple an explanation. Something else tugged at his mind, a remembrance of something from years ago. When they first arrived at Mordeina...

"Azariah flew with nearly every fallen angel at his disposal," he said, his eyes sweeping the area. Most of the flowers were wilting from the chill that heralded winter's arrival in the coming months. Lattice partitioned the grounds into dozens of walkways, the white-painted wood covered with vines. Stone benches and stools filled each passage, positioned so it seemed there were a near limitless stretch of private areas to converse, or for the brave, perform more intimate acts during parties and events.

"So why leave a few behind to guard an insignificant garden?" Veliana asked.

"Exactly."

Though he chose no specific path, it seemed all stone walkways inevitably led to the stone fountain in the center of the garden. Deathmask paused before it. Carved as decoration was a leaping deer positioned above an open oyster. Water flowed all around it, and when Deathmask checked, he found little glowing orbs, enchanted to ensure the water continued to flow from some unseen reservoir. He wondered if Aurelia or Tarlak might be responsible for that little bit of craftwork.

What was key, though, was how new it felt compared to the rest of the garden. Why was this fountain so novel? And again, why would Azariah have positioned guards to protect its entrance? Azariah was hardly sentimental toward gardens...

"Death, here," Veliana called. She was on the opposite side of the fountain, and kneeling over one of the pathway steps. When he joined her, he saw a rune carved into the stone.

"Do you know what it is for?" she asked.

Deathmask frowned. It was magical, that much was obvious, but he didn't recognize its origin. It didn't feel quite right on its own, and by itself the squiggly marks meant nothing. However, now he knew what he was looking for, he paced the other pathways. Sure enough, he found several more runes, all chiseled into the surface of the stone. By the fifth, Deathmask realized why the symbols meant nothing to him. Each rune was a piece of one grander symbol.

Deathmask returned to the runes he'd already discovered, piecing their shapes together in his mind.

"A lion," he said after analyzing the eighth, this one cut into a stone and hidden underneath a bush. "Karak's lion. But why?"

Each rune was positioned equidistant from that center fountain. Its importance was key, but why? Its newness called to him. As if the old had been recently destroyed, and this deer been its replacement. Everywhere he looked he found more runes, painstakingly cut into stone. Pieces of the Lion, but this wouldn't summon Karak, nor open a gate to his Abyss...

Realization struck him. Deathmask had not seen its creation all those years ago, nor had Veliana, but they had seen the results. His lips stretched into a wide grin.

"Rakkar," he whispered, quietly enough not even Veliana could hear him. "You damn foolish angel. Are you so desperate and shallow you would reach to your inferiors for ideas?"

"What is it?" Veliana asked, trudging over from locating the ninth of these mysterious runes.

Deathmask brushed his cheek with his fingertips, the lightest touch for the darkest memory. Though Roand the Flame had artfully scarred his face, as had Tarlak under the mad wizard's guidance, there had been another man who wielded fire against him and had managed to leave a set of scars. A delusional priest who had declared himself Melorak, Karak made flesh.

He gestured around him. "This garden,, these runes. Azariah is setting things in place in case he loses his upcoming battle against Ahaesarus. If he retreats to Mordeina, this will be his backup plan. It is from here he will summon his final defense of a city he so desperately wishes to rule." He pointed to the fountain. "And it'll spring to life right here, in the same place as the old. It's almost ambitious enough to leave me impressed."

Veliana crossed her arms and glared at him. "You're being purposefully vague."

"I know. Now hand me your dagger."

"Why?" she asked, her left eyebrow arced to the top of her forehead.

Deathmask's grin spread ear to ear. "Because I have some carving to do. When Azariah attempts to use these runes and this garden for his magnificent display, I'm going to steal it, ruin it, and then laugh my goddamn ass off. Trust me, Vel. This is going to be glorious."

17

The excitement that spread throughout the army was palpable. Aurelia couldn't deny feeling it herself. She marched alongside her husband, as ever near the front of the teeming mass. The hills steadily flattened as the terrain shifted closer to the grasslands of Mordeina. To head directly toward the capital after fleeing it mere weeks before was almost hard to believe, but multiple scouts from Ahaesarus's army had been coordinating with theirs, which hopefully would lead to an eventual meeting of forces. Rumor had it they would officially link up tomorrow.

"It's gonna be so damn nice," Harruq said. Sweat trickled from his forehead as he marched. Winter might have been approaching, but it hadn't arrived yet, and her husband's armor wasn't ideal for travel.

"What will?" she asked.

"Letting someone else be in charge."

Aurelia brushed her fingers across his neck, whispering faint words of magic. Frost wafted off her fingers, blue mist curled about his head. He shivered from the cold, then blew a kiss her way.

"Thanks," he said, his face losing a little bit of redness.

They stopped to rest at midday, though none appeared eager to linger, unlike previous days. Aurelia crafted a trio of chairs out of lumps of earth for Harruq, Tarlak, and herself to sit in, positioned a few hundred feet away from the rest of the army. Sitting back, she watched all those soldiers filling their own bellies, some wearing expectant grins on their faces.

She prayed their optimism wasn't unfounded. From what they'd learned, Ahaesarus had approximately four hundred angels flying under his command, along with six thousand beast-men he'd forcibly conscripted. The how or why remained elusive, since none of the scouts were willing to reveal more information than the fact that the beast-men were fierce fighters and could be trusted to obey.

Obey. Aurelia's stomach twisted, and it had nothing to do with the bland biscuits she forced herself to eat. She knew the beast-men had crossed the Gihon River on a mission of conquest. Ahaesarus had taken one-third of his angels to the Castle of the Yellow Rose to oppose them, and that act had spared them the curse Ashhur inflicted upon Azariah and the rest of their kind. Preliminary reports suggested that rescue had come far too late, however. Hundreds of innocents, slain. If that were the case, why did the beast-men travel with the angels? Were they prisoners? Slaves? Or was Ahaesarus willing to overlook their slaughter if they fought in his name?

"Looks like we've got another messenger," Harruq said. He pointed to a distant pair of white wings. "Coming in every few hours now. Bet even Ahaesarus is excited to see us."

"I'll signal him over," Tarlak said, having already finished his meal. He stood, clapped his hands together, and then lifted them skyward. A bolt of flame shot from his fingertips, showering multi-colored sparks every direction. It was a far less dangerous, and much more showy, spell than one he might use in battle. The angelic scout noticed and veered toward them.

"We go days without any word, and now you bug us every other hour," Tarlak said once the angel landed. "I suppose all or nothing is just how it goes with you angels."

"I wish I had more time to share in jests," the angel said. He was slender for their kind, with brown eyes and extremely dark hair. Aurelia did not recognize him, but as usual, he recognized them, the heroes of the Eschaton. "Ahaesarus sent me with a warning. The army of Devlimar finally marches, and there is no doubt to their destination."

"About time," Harruq said, punching his fists together. "That bastard finally tired of hiding out behind his golden walls?"

The angel dipped his head. "It seems he has. I wished to inform you of this in case we inadequately gauged their movements. By flight alone they could harry you before we meet, but it seems they lag behind to accompany their human and undead forces. Even so, we shall patrol the airspace between us as an additional measure of safety. Ensure your forces are ready, and do not anticipate any rest when they meet up with our army. The deciding battle approaches."

And with that, he departed. Tarlak scratched at his goatee as he watched him fly.

"Not much we can do to protect ourselves from the fallen that we aren't already doing," he said. "A night raid by some advanced fliers is within the realm of possibility, though. We'll make sure we camp close together, maybe post a few more guards than usual. Qurrah and Tess both seem like night people, so maybe we can get them to nap a bit and do some patrols themselves."

"I'll go spread the word," Harruq said. He stretched sore muscles and groaned. "Gods damn it all, I am so tired of marching."

Aurelia poked him in the stomach. "Did all that time in Mordeina as the king's helper turn you soft?"

"If anyone turned me soft, Aurry, it's you."

"Really now?" She shot him a wink. "I thought I caused quite the opposite reaction."

"Pack it up, the both of you," Tarlak snorted. "We've still got dozens of miles to cross."

◈

Knowing there was potential for an ambush led the army to more carefully decide on where they might camp for the night, even though it cost them a potential hour of two of marching, Aurelia insisted they set up just inside the dense forest whose eastern edge they'd skirted for several miles.

"Setting up camp in the woodland is a complete pain," Harruq said when she proposed the idea. "And no one likes sleeping on roots and underbrush."

"The forest has a spring for water," Aurelia had insisted. "And we camp just at the boundary. If the fallen attack, we can retreat beneath the branches and remove their flight advantage."

"Better here than the open fields," Tarlak agreed, ending the discussion. The army settled down, beginning the laborious process of starting cook fires, pitching tents, and raking aside whatever rocks and twigs might interfere with a decent night's sleep. Aurelia had often broken the ground with her magic to summon a stream, but thankfully the location of the spring removed that need. Exhaustion clung to her like spiderwebs. She told herself it was only nerves for the coming battle that filled her stomach with a nameless dread.

That dread only magnified tenfold when a trio of black wings marked the eastern sky.

"Well isn't today an exciting day," Harruq grumbled. He and Aurelia had been watching the sunset when murmurs of the fallen angels' approach reached their ears.

"It's not an attack," Aurelia said. "What then? A parley?"

"We'll soon find out."

They joined Tarlak, Qurrah, and Tessanna atop a gentle hill overlooking the camp. Several dozen soldiers formed a ring about them, more a show of support than any real strength. Aurelia knew that with four spellcasters, they could easily obliterate a mere three fallen should they try anything foolish. Head high and hands sparkling with magic, she watched the trio land a respectful distance away, slightly below them on the hill. Aurelia recognized the middle fallen, a muscle-bound angel with a sword nearly as big as he was. He dipped his head in respect, a gesture that surprised her.

"I wish to speak with the Godslayer," Ezekai said.

Harruq stepped forward. "Well, I'm here. Speak away."

"Alone," Ezekai said, and crossed his arms. "It concerns a truce...and your daughter."

Aurelia's lingering dread magnified into horror that tightened her stomach into knots and looped iron chains about her throat. Harruq glanced her way, the question obvious on his face.

"Leave us be," Aurelia shouted to the soldiers surrounding them. "We must speak matters of politics."

The others reluctantly scattered until it was only the five members of the Eschaton that remained before the fallen. Aurelia took her husband's hand in hers and she squeezed, trying in vain to hold back the panic threatening to overwhelm her. Their daughter? Why would Azariah wish to speak of Aubrienna?

"Not quite alone, but this is as close as it's going to get," Harruq said. "Now you best explain yourself before I ask all my very talented and magically gifted friends to turn your body into seven kinds of mush."

Ezekai smirked. It was profoundly ugly. "I would not recommend doing so, half-orc. Not if you wish to spare the life of Aubrienna Tun."

"Aubby's safe with us," Aurelia lied. "Your threats mean nothing."

"No more games and illusions," the angel said with a shake of his head. "I come with terms. They are fair, and just, and I strongly suggest you accept them." Aurelia's fingernails dug into her husband's palm. It couldn't be. Her fears were exaggerated. Her mind was leaping to the worst conclusion. That's all.

"Then spit them out," Qurrah said, his own patience wearing thin. "Best we hear and turn them down now so we may slaughter one another on the battlefield without hesitation."

"But we won't meet on the battlefield," Ezekai said, clearly enjoying himself. "At least, the Godslayer won't. Our forces have captured Aubrienna Tun and Gregory Copernus. The moment the Godslayer sets foot on any battlefield, or raises his swords against the armies of Paradise, we shall have the both of them executed."

The world stopped being real. Aurelia felt herself leave her own body. This couldn't be happening. Her little girl...in the hands of those monsters...

"Give them back," Harruq said. His voice was deep and frighteningly calm. That voice, that tone, she heard so very rarely. Her husband wasn't just contemplating murder. He was imagining it with glee.

"We will, if you cooperate. There is a particular copse of trees several miles from here. Come nightfall, use your scrying magic to find myself there. When you do, you will also find them. We shall make a trade. In exchange for the lives of those two children, we demand the life of Harruq Godslayer Tun."

Fire burst from Aurelia's free hand. Shadows swirled around Tessanna's. Harruq lacked magic, but he had his swords, and he pulled out of Aurelia's grip so he might draw them. He said nothing, only bared his teeth and struggled to keep himself from charging.

Ezekai didn't so much as flinch. "Why such fury? It is one life for two. Did I not promise a fair exchange?"

"Leave," Harruq growled. "Now."

"So be it," Ezekai said, casually shrugging. "Bear in mind, this offer is only good for tonight. Should you fail to make an appearance, then our terms change. The moment *any* of you five make an appearance in battle, we shall immediately execute both children. Consider this a kindness, Eschaton. We know the leverage we wield. We could have demanded far more."

"I said leave!"

The three fallen spread their wings and lifted several feet into the air.

"You want the boy king and your daughter?" Ezekai shouted. "Then offer yourself up for them. Those are the terms. We'll await you tonight. For once, half-orc, make the right decision."

The trio turned to leave. For a brief moment, Aurelia thought Qurrah would strike them out of the sky with fire and shadow. For a brief moment, Aurelia contemplated doing the same.

"What in Ashhur's name is going on?" Harruq asked once they were gone. He jammed his swords into their sheaths and looked ready to erupt. "Is he lying? Tell me he's fucking lying."

"It's a bold lie if true," Qurrah said.

"And one I intend to find out for myself," Aurelia said. She closed her eyes, her hands dancing as she cast divination magic. She focused all her mind on her beloved daughter, but though she felt her presence sweep across Dezrel, she saw nothing. Changing tactics, she searched for Gregory instead. Yet again, it was like searching for a shadow in the depth of night.

Ger eyes fluttered open. "Protected against scrying."

"Then let's try something else," Tarlak said. He closed his eyes in turn. "When the children go missing, the first person to check in with is the babysitter."

His frown deepened, his skin paled. Whatever fragile remnants of hope Aurelia felt quickly died.

"I can't find Lathaar," he said softly. "But I found Jerico. He's miles north of the Citadel. Give me a moment while I open a portal for him."

The King of the Fallen

Aurelia leaned against her husband, waiting for Tarlak to tear open the fabric of reality. Harruq's arms wrapped about her, and she tried to let his touch calm her. It helped, but only a little. In her chest churned a maelstrom of fear, sickness, and rage. She had lost one daughter already. How dare Dezrel threaten to take a second from her?

"It'll be all right," Harruq whispered.

"We don't know that."

"Then we'll make it right."

The portal opened, and after a moment's hesitation, Jerico stepped out from its swirling blue surface. He glanced about the five of them, and his dour expression hardened.

"You know, don't you?" he asked.

That was it. That was all it took. Aurelia's tears slid down her face. Qurrah swore and turned away.

"I'll murder them," Tessanna whispered. "I swear, I will murder them all."

Tessanna stormed away, and though Aurelia thought Qurrah would follow, he remained behind. She turned back to Jerico, who stared at the ground, exhausted, broken, and ashamed. Aurelia wanted to ask questions, to demand an explanation, but she couldn't speak a word.

"What happened, Jerico?" Tarlak asked, the only one of them seemingly able to keep it together. The paladin let out a long sigh, clenched his hands into fists, stared at the grass.

"Lathaar is dead," he said. "And the Citadel fallen."

It was every bit her worst fear. Aurelia closed her eyes and fought against the emotions. She had to focus. Had to think. The life of her daughter most certainly depended on it.

"Please," she said, forcing out the words. "Tell us everything that happened."

They all listened in silence as Jerico told the tale of the fallen angels' arrival, the betrayal of the students, and the collapse of the tower at Ashhur's hands. He minced no words, not even when describing the slaughter of his students, committed by his own hands.

"I've been marching north ever since," he said. "Hoping to reach Mordeina in time to kill the bastard. I suppose I should thank you for sparing me the miles. I guess all that matters now is, what do we do?"

"What do we do?" Harruq said. "There isn't much choice, is there? I go, and I accept their terms."

"You can't," Qurrah snapped.

"I will. *I must.*"

Aurelia held onto her husband's arm, trying to make sense of her feelings. Harruq and Aubrienna were her world. To sacrifice one for the other was too horrific to imagine. But it wasn't a choice, not really. The life of a parent for the life of a child? Of course Harruq would accept such a trade. Aurelia would have as well, had it been asked of her.

"We could try to attack instead," Tarlak suggested. "After all, we've got a shit-ton of magic at our disposal."

"They'll kill the children the moment anything appears out of the ordinary," Aurelia said. "And it's possible they won't bring the children to the meeting until Harruq makes an appearance. We are not the only ones with access to portal magic, remember."

Tarlak threw up his hands. "Then what do we do? Just give up? Let them win? Sacrifice Harruq all for...for whatever sick game Azariah is playing?"

"Yes!" Harruq bellowed. "I'm not risking Aubby's life, you hear me? She's my girl, my little girl, and if I have to die, then I'll die. Got it? All of you? You got that?"

Tarlak muttered and turned away. Harruq pulled away from Aurelia, though his hand lingered in her arm. She knew it was an attempt at affection as he fought the rage overwhelming him.

"I need some time to calm down and think," he said before storming off. Aurelia watched him go, unable to make herself follow. Dimly, she realized this might be the last few moments she had left to spend with him. That realization only paralyzed her more.

"Come on, Jerico," Tarlak said after a long, awkward pause. "Let's get you a tent and some good cooked food. I doubt you've had much of either on your trek."

The King of the Fallen

That left only Qurrah and Aurelia standing atop the hill. She thought he would exit next and leave her the privacy she craved, but instead he approached her like one would a frightened deer. Slowly. Cautiously. He said nothing until he was close enough to take her hands in his. It was a surprising act of tenderness from a man who showed such a side so rarely.

"Aubrienna means much to me," he said in his gravelly voice. "And she means the entire world to Tess. For your daughter to lose her father is a cruelty I will never let her endure. I swear it."

Aurelia gently slipped her hands out of his. There was something about the look in his eyes that gave her pause.

"You have a plan," she said. It wasn't a question.

"Indeed, I do." He glanced over his shoulder, in the direction his brother had stormed off. "A desperate one, perhaps, but in such a grim hour, can we hope for anything other than desperation?"

"We can hope for peace," she said. Her stress and fear threatened to free another wave of tears, but she held firm and kept her tone flat. "We can hope for joy, and laughter, and a world that isn't so damn cruel and broken as this one."

Qurrah smiled, and despite all their anger and sorrow, it appeared genuine. "But a broken world is the only world we have. So we must not hope, but instead act. Forgive me, Aurelia. I helped break this world. If you would allow me, I shall do what I can to make this right."

18

"There will be death," Azariah whispered, echoing the words that haunted his every fitful attempt at slumber. "There will be bloodshed. But it won't be in my name."

The condemnation of his god, granted through the tongue of a humble, nameless vagabond. Azariah looked about the cluster of pines, where his fallen brethren hid. If the bloodshed would not be in Ashhur's name, then whose name did it belong to? Who deserved the blame?

"Must it be me?" Azariah asked the night. He lifted a hand to the stars and imagined his curled gray fingers clutching those twinkling orbs and crushing them until they turned to dust. It was a guilt he was willing to carry. Even Ashhur's condemnation would not be enough to dissuade him from the path laid out before him. All of Dezrel needed this. Did the sins of her people not already prove that? Karak and Ashhur, two split pieces of a whole. Thulos had hoped to slay them both so he might be the lone inheritor of divine power, but Thulos was dead. All that remained now were the two brother gods. If their beliefs could be unified, if the brothers could be made whole in a way they had not been since humanity was molded from clay, the potential for Dezrel was unlimited.

Azariah smiled despite the jut of bone slicing across his lips and drawing blood. It was a glorious future to imagine, but to bring those revelations to the broken land of Dezrel meant surviving to accomplish them, and the glimpse of the future that Celestia's Weave had granted him made it all too clear what would happen if the Godslayer lived.

He was not proud of what he must do, but it was necessary. It was needed. When compared to the fates of hundreds of thousands of souls, what did another meager body of flesh matter? What did *any* body of flesh matter? He glanced over his shoulder, to where Aubrienna and Gregory were each held in the arms of a fallen. The children wisely kept quiet, with only the occasional whimper. Each of them possessed remarkable strength for their age. They would be great leaders, if given time and circumstance to grow. Perhaps, once Paradise was settled over with peace, Azariah could begin molding their minds...

A swirling blue portal ripped open at the entrance to the cluster of trees. The other fallen readied their swords, but Azariah merely lowered his hand and removed the smile from his face. The increasingly familiar touch of magic sparked from his fingertips. Celestia's magic, wielded by the hand of a Warden of humanity seeking to unify the brother gods. How could anyone deny that he was Dezrel's true, perfect hero?

But Ashhur's faithful were far too blind to see it, and Azariah saw that same unseeing rage in the eyes of the paladin that stepped out from the portal.

"Not the man I expected this night," Azariah said wryly. "You've crossed many miles since I left the Citadel."

Jerico crossed his arms and glared at the gathered angels. "The magic of portals. I'm here to ensure you keep your word."

"With what? Your shield?" His bleeding grin returned. "Or the sword of your slain brother in faith?"

Jerico's hands clenched into fists, but he kept them crossed over his chest. If his glare could kill, Azariah would be ten feet underground already.

"Ashhur's grace will ensure even your lies will mean nothing to my ears," he said. "So give me your word that you will honor this deal. No one else will step through that portal until I am satisfied."

Azariah gestured a command to the two fallen holding the children. In response, each drew a knife from their sides and held the sharp blades against soft, slender necks.

"If you seek my word, then have it," Azariah said. "If Harruq comes before me and forfeits his life, I will hand over both Gregory and Aubrienna. No harm shall befall them, nor shall I attempt to keep them in my custody. With the Godslayer dead, my reign will be assured."

He paused a moment to let Jerico mull over his words. Paladins of Ashhur carried an innate sense to determine truth from lie, and Azariah had spoken with absolute honesty. His survival was all that mattered. With Harruq dead, his victory was assured. Once it was clear Jerico understood this, Azariah stepped closer, and he sank a hard edge into his voice.

"But if Harruq does not come before me tonight, then I will ensure he regrets that decision for the rest of his days. I will brutalize these children in ways that will leave them scarred but breathing. I will employ magic and blade. I will humiliate and traumatize their little minds, and as they suffer, I will sing sweet words in their ears at how it was Harruq's fault for being a coward. I will tell Aubrienna her beloved father left her to suffer. I will tell Gregory his cherished hero was selfish and afraid. Every night, every day, I will break them with that truth."

Both children began crying. Azariah stepped closer to the red-haired paladin, lifting his shoulders in a playful shrug.

"Tell me, paladin, have I yet spoken a lie?"

"You haven't, you sick bastard," Jerico said. For one brief moment, Azariah thought he might draw his sword and attack. Though it might complicate the night's transfer, Azariah almost hoped for it. People like Jerico had outlived their usefulness. They were brutes meant to fight and kill for a society that did not desire wisdom. Once Azariah changed the very nature of the world, and peace overcame sinfulness, then the war-like paladins would be forgettable relics. They would be useful in stories, and stories only. Reality held no need for their stubborn inflexibility.

"Then go, and tell them what you have heard."

Jerico shot him one last glare before stepping back into the swirling portal. Azariah slowly drew in a deep breath and let it out. Excitement tingled through his limbs. This was it. The moment of freedom. One final confrontation, settled not by muscles and skill with a blade but with ruthless cunning and a willingness to do what must be done. Needed steps, he told himself. One of many needed steps to haul Dezrel out of its eternal war of brother gods and into something akin to Paradise.

"It is not too late to change our minds," Ezekai said. With Judarius remaining behind to lead the armies of Paradise, Ezekai was the highest in rank to accompany them on this rendezvous. The fallen lingered at Azariah's side, his hands clutching the hilt of his sword as if they were nailed together.

"Tell me, why now should I waiver?" he asked.

The King of the Fallen

The other angel would not meet his gaze. "Two hostages, the boy king and the elven daughter, could keep more than the Godslayer off the battlefield. Other members of the Eschaton, for instance. I fear we give up too much to receive far too little."

Lightning crackled across the portal's surface. Azariah shook his head. Memories of his foretold death hovered at the edges of his vision at all times.

"No," he said. "This one death is all we need."

Harruq and Aurelia Tun stepped through, followed by the paladin. Upon seeing Aubrienna, Harruq took a single jolting step forward before Aurelia caught his wrist and held him firm.

"You fucking wretch," Harruq said, his voice seething with hatred, but he remained at Aurelia's side. "I'm here, now let the children go."

"So you might attempt to kill me once they are safely away? No, Godslayer, we will not be playing that game." Azariah lifted his hand, and so too lifted the knives of the fallen holding the two children. "Give me the slightest hint of betrayal and they shall die while you watch. If I see one inch of naked steel, one sparkle of magic on that elf's fingertips, their blood stains the grass. Behave, and the deal we struck shall stand. Do we understand one another?"

"He's telling the truth," Jerico said.

"I know he is," Harruq muttered. "He's enjoying himself too much to be lying."

A pleasurable shudder worked its way through Azariah's black wings. Before him were three of the most powerful beings alive in all of Dezrel, and yet all three stood broken before him. He'd worked hard to remain humble over the years after the second Gods' War ended. Now that he had abandoned such pointless endeavors, now that he had stopped trying to deny the inherit superiority of his people, it felt incredible to be treated like the king he was always meant to be. One of Ashhur's many mistakes had been to declare his angels, the former Wardens of humanity who had tasted the divine, be mere servants of the sinful, imperfect humans once again.

This was better. This was proper.

"Come forth, Harruq. Stand before me and offer your head."

The half-orc glanced to his wife. "It's all right. Fear no regrets. I chose this, remember?"

Aurelia wrapped her arms about him, and she buried her face against his neck, whispering something Azariah could not hear. When they separated, Harruq unbuckled the sheaths holding Salvation and Condemnation and handed them over to Jerico.

"I'm sure you can think of someone who could use these," Harruq said with a crooked grin.

"I've a few in mind." Jerico flicked his gaze toward Azariah. "And if the world is kind, the next body they pierce will be a certain angel king."

"A kind world," Harruq said. He laughed softly as he crossed the empty stretch of grass and approached Azariah. "That'll be the day."

Azariah stared at this half-breed being that had slain countless foes. Orcs, elves, undead, demons, fallen angels, even a god had fallen to his blades. Yet all his accomplishments were through the combined might of others. Celestia's orcish curse melded with that of a faithful elf. Velixar's swords and armor. Ashhur's blessings to fight as his avatar against Thulos's forces. It seemed all of Dezrel had conspired to create a perfect killing machine.

And that killing machine would be undone by the love he felt for his daughter.

"Stand still," Azariah said, closing his eyes and summoning strands of magic from Celestia's Weave.

"What betrayal is this?" Jerico asked.

"No betrayal," Azariah said. "An assurance you perform no betrayal yourselves."

He stretched out his hands, and invisible waves of magic washed over Harruq. The spell was simple in nature but powerful in purpose: no illusion would endure its touch. This Harruq before him would be the real Harruq, real flesh, real bone, and not some trick of magic and light. Azariah held his breath, fully expecting to discover this was a replacement, some hapless soldier selected to be the half-orc's sacrificial replacement. Instead, the magic passed, and Harruq remained unchanged.

"Satisfied?" he asked, his left eyebrow crooking upward. "Now let my daughter go, damn it."

"Not yet," Azariah said. "Not until the deed is done."

He looked to Ezekai, standing protectively nearby, and outstretched his hand. The angel drew a jagged blade and offered him the hilt. Azariah took it and swung the weight casually about. The air whistled from the sharpened blade's passage.

"I have thought often of your legacy," Azariah said, settling the tip against Harruq's throat. "Of how it deserves to end. Now prostrate yourself."

"I will not die kneeling," Harruq said.

"You would deny me?"

"You would change the terms of our deal? My life for theirs. Nothing says I give it while pleading, begging, or worshiping you on my knees."

Both children cried out as the fallen angels holding them pressed their knives hard enough against their skin to draw blood.

"Refusal puts the children at risk," Azariah said. Aurelia spoke up before her rattled husband might answer.

Aurelia scowled through the tears in her eyes and pointed a sparking finger his way. "The only thing keeping me from tearing this entire clearing apart with my magic is knowing it will cost me the life of my daughter," she declared. "But if you were to convince me her life is already forfeit..."

Despite his warning, the elf let a brief flash of fire wash over her palms and. Azariah's pride cried out at the insult, but he swallowed it down. There was no reason to endanger what was already in place. Numbers were drastically on his side, but the elf's magic was legendary. Victory was the purpose of this night, not mutual self-destruction.

"So be it," he said. He glanced over his shoulder, to the fallen holding Aubrienna. The little elf girl was softly crying. "Open your eyes," he told her. "There is something you must witness."

Harruq took a step closer, his eyes widening.

"You bastard."

"You will watch!" Azariah screamed to Aubrienna, his temper finally out of control. "You will witness the fate of those who remain forever locked in the past. You will learn from it, child. You will learn." He pressed the sword harder against Harruq's throat, and he met the fierce gaze of those brown eyes. "You will learn that no matter how many great and noble deeds you accomplish in your life, you are promised nothing, not even your next breath. A million victories mean nothing if you insult gods and kings. It only leads to despair."

Harruq lifted his chin, pushing his own throat into the blade. Blood dribbled down his neck.

"The life I go to next is not the one I deserve," he said, his voice surprisingly soft and thoughtful. "But of my life, and my many sins, I know this here and now is the one act which atones for it all."

There was a certainty to his words that unnerved Azariah, an unwavering faith that reminded him of that wretched nameless farmer who had stepped from the crowd to demand the angels to fall.

"On the day I die, both gods will throw open their gates and beg for the privilege of my soul gracing their presence," Azariah said. "Go to whichever god will take you, Harruq Tun, and await my celebrated return."

Azariah sliced open the half-orc's throat. Blood gushed across them both, its shade of crimson the only color that shone with any sort of vibrancy to Azariah's cursed eyes. It was beautiful. So beautiful. Harruq wobbled, and despite his insistence otherwise, he slumped to his knees. Aurelia quietly sobbed; the two children wailed.

Harruq fought against blood and mortal injury to stand. His legs betrayed him, and he dropped onto his back. He spoke with a croaking voice as his hands clutched at his neck. Blood poured across his gray fingers.

"But a moment," he said. "I leave...but a moment..."
He fell still.

A wave of pleasure shivered through Azariah's limbs and shook feathers from his wings. He nodded to the fallen, and they released Gregory and Aubrienna. The children sprinted past the lifeless corpse. Aurelia knelt and opened her arms. Aubrienna slammed into her mother, who wrapped her in a desperate embrace and held onto her for dear life. Jerico accepted Gregory into his free hand, the other still holding Harruq's twin swords.

The air chilled, and a strange silence overcame the clearing. The only noise was the howl of the wind blowing through the portal and the intermixed crying of the children.

Jerico exited first. The portal crackled with power. Aurelia stood, her daughter's face buried in her breast. Her walnut-colored eyes could not convey the true depth of her anger, but they did a damn admirable job.

"I will kill you, angel," she said. "I swear it on the souls of every single man and woman you've slaughtered."

"You are welcome to try," Azariah said. "But I have witnessed the many threads of fate, and only the Godslayer possessed that right."

"Is that so?" she said, and despite her sorrow, despite her rage, she flashed him a grin that promised pain. "We shall see."

She departed through the portal. A sharp hiss of air marked its closing. The song of cicadas invaded the quiet, the only sound until Ezekai clapped his hands and joined Azariah's side.

"A fine trade, all things considered," the fallen said. "Without the half-orc to bolster their ranks, Ahaesarus's army will suffer greatly against our legions, whereas neither child shall hold any sway over the battlefield. Their spellcasters remain the biggest worry now, and I suspect Jerico will stay with them to protect from our aerial attacks rather than join the melee. That leaves the ground forces wanting for heroes."

Azariah nodded absently, his gaze never leaving the half-orc's corpse. It was only after a long pause that he realized Ezekai had offered him his hand to retake his sword.

"Shall I bury the body, or burn it?" Ezekai asked upon wiping clean his blade.

"Leave it."

Ezekai didn't question. He spread his wings, shouted an order, and together the collective fallen took to the air to rejoin the distant camped army. Only Azariah remained behind, transfixed by the corpse. Even when the cicadas and owls were his only company, he could not shake a deep, primal feeling of there being something amiss.

We shall see.

"There is no honor among sinful mortals," he said, as if voicing justification for his doubts would make them valid. He knelt beside the body, which had already begun to stink, and pulled out Velixar's spellbook from the satchel he'd sewn to his robes, so he might keep it with him at all times. It didn't take long to find his desired spell, for he'd committed much of the book to memory. The amount of knowledge the First Man had accrued in his centuries of life was incredible, and not all of it was focused on the necromantic arts. This, however, was very much Velixar's specialty. After mentally rehearsing the words several times, Azariah placed his hands upon Harruq's temples and closed his eyes.

I must know, he thought before beginning the words of the spell. The ancient language flowed off his tongue. The power pulled from inside him, now a familiar strain after so much practice. Harruq was dead, and his soul already departed, but within the meat and organs lurked memories, and Azariah would see them. He would relive them.

It felt like falling, a great plunge face first into the half-orc's forehead. His senses shifted, altered, the life of another taking over so he lived it, breathed it, and acted it as if it were all his own.

19

"No!" Harruq shouted.

He and Qurrah lurked on the outside of the camp. The half-orc's outburst was loud enough that distant soldiers glanced their direction. Qurrah turned his back to them, pretending he and his brother were completely isolated instead of standing there in plain sight of most anyone.

"No, you won't," Harruq said defiantly. "I won't allow it. This isn't up for debate."

Qurrah sighed. "You're right. It's *not* up for debate, but also not for the reason you believe."

"She's my daughter."

"I know."

"My responsibility."

"I know."

His brother let out a long sigh and looked all about, as if seeking some foreign help for an argument he was already doomed to lose.

"And you're still going to do this, aren't you?"

Qurrah settled a hand on his brother's shoulder. To most, Harruq was a monster of a man, but to Qurrah he was still the stubborn frightened child from their days on the streets of Veldaren. He might be taller and stronger, but not to his eyes. Not to his presence.

"After everything I have done?" he said. "After what I have cost everyone? You know I am the right one to do this. Besides, you are mad if you think I will have Aubrienna return with no father waiting for her."

Harruq shoved Qurrah's hand away. His jaw clenched and he balled his fists together, as if he could punch his way through the entire universe and find an acceptable future on the other side. There wasn't one, though. Qurrah knew that. Strength and skill meant nothing here, not when the fallen held every possible advantage in this sick game.

"Damn it," Harruq finally muttered. "Gods and goddesses damn it, all of them. Why this? Why now? We were done, weren't we? Thulos is dead. Velixar is dead. We fought our wars, and we buried our loved ones. This was supposed to be our time of peace, wasn't it? When we got to be happy? What happened, Qurrah? Where did it all go wrong?"

It was weird seeing his brother cry. Weirder still to know it was because Qurrah chose the right course of action. A nice change of pace considering their sordid past.

"The world isn't ready for peace," he said. "Perhaps it never will be. But my mind is set, and when I go to Tarlak, we both know he'll accept my sacrifice over yours. Coming to you first was to make this easy for all of us."

"I could change Tarlak's mind," Harruq said, and he grinned despite his tears. "I'm quite bigger than that goofball in yellow, you know."

"Please spare us all that indignity."

After a brief pause, Harruq lurched toward Qurrah, wrapped him in his arms, and held him close. Qurrah accepted it despite how awkward it made him feel. Such contact was always strange to him, and never did he truly believe he deserved it. His sins were numerous, after all...

"All right, I'll go tell Aurry your plan," Harruq said as he pulled away. "Have you told Tess yet?"

Qurrah swallowed down a stone the size of the moon in his throat.

"No. Not yet."

A knowing look passed over his brother's face, but instead of acknowledging it he just lightly punched Qurrah on the shoulder.

"Good luck," he said. And with that, he sauntered off, still wiping tears off his face.

Qurrah lagged behind, needing a moment to recover. He wasn't crying, but he could tell he was close. There could be no weakness in him, not now. He looked to the blue sky and wondered if Karak and Ashhur were up there watching them right now. Priests often spoke of the gods as benevolent parents, yet after so many years of war and destruction, Qurrah was beginning to think the gods were more akin to children poking anthills with sticks so they might watch the little creatures scatter and run.

The King of the Fallen

Tess was not among the teeming swell of human soldiers. Not that Qurrah was surprised by that fact; it was rare for her to be anywhere near other people for more than fleeting moments. And he could not blame her for that, because he was the same way. They both were far more accustomed to silence and solitude than life among the masses.

He searched the perimeter of the encampment with only half-hearted urgency, pretending not to notice the occasional guard on patrol. Some glared, others tipped their heads in respect, but most just ignored him. His reputation among the people of Mordan was varied, and most often dreadful. By the Abyss, why shouldn't they be unsure of his motives? It's not like Qurrah didn't question them himself.

When he found her, it was an hour before sunset at most. The army had purposefully camped near the spring to resupply, and far upstream Tessanna sat in the fading grass with her feet dangling in the water. The shade of the trees hid her from the sun. How she wasn't cold from its icy flow, he couldn't begin to guess. Qurrah settled down beside her. He said not a word, merely taking her hand and enjoying the extended silence.

"You have something to say. Is it about Aubrienna and Gregory?"

"It is."

"You're scared to tell me. This isn't good, is it?" She leaned forward, hiding herself with her long hair. "Just tell me. I'll keep silent."

And so he explained to her his plan. She listened quietly. When he finished, he need not ask for her opinion. The tears running down her face were answer enough.

"And so you abandon me," she said.

"I'm not abandoning you."

"You are." Said with it no anger, no hatred, just a tired finality. "Why must it be you, Qurrah? I know the answer you will give, but I deny it already. I hate it. I know it and hate it."

"But you know it's true."

She turned her enormous black eyes his way. "The only true thing is that I lose you forever. Please, please, Qurrah, don't do this to me. I can't take this. I won't survive."

Qurrah told himself to be strong. He told himself he was doing the right thing. Every inner voice rang hollow, and so he spoke the only truth he knew.

"I cost my brother a daughter. The least I can do is save his other. A life for a life. Nothing in this world could be more fair."

"Fair? *Fair?*" She bolted to her feet, black fire swirling about her hands. "Fuck all that is *fair*. What of me, Qurrah? What of us? Must you carry guilt for Aullienna for the rest of your life? Are you never allowed to move on? Never allowed to pretend anything in this world, anything at all, is worth more than suffering under that burden?"

"Truly?" Qurrah asked. He tried to keep the bite from his words and failed. "The last time you told me to deny the guilt I felt for Aullienna's death, you put a knife in my hand and demanded I take Delysia's life. That's the cruel joke to this plight, Tess. I can't kill my way out of this. I won't make things equal with a lifetime of murders. Bloodshed leading to bloodshed leading to sorrow and yet even more bloodshed. Tonight I make it right. Tonight, at least I make it my own."

So often when Tessanna was overwhelmed she retreated into herself. She became a calm, hollow façade of a human being so that hurtful emotions did not break her. He thought she might do that now. Instead she laughed and cried simultaneously. Which was far worse.

"And so you die, I break, and all the world rejoices," she said. "Is that what happens? Shall that be how your brother tells the story? We'll be heroes. We'll be redeemed. We'll have found our salvation. I'd rather be damned, Qurrah. I'd rather be damned alongside you."

She took his hands and forced him to meet her gaze.

"Don't leave me," she whispered. "Please. Please, Qurrah. Don't leave me."

"It will be but a moment," he said, and kissed her forehead. "But a moment we are apart, the blink of an eye in the span of eternity."

He left her there, for to say any more, or hear another word, was to risk what little remained of his conviction.

***

Tarlak rubbed his hands together. "It's a good thing I've been practicing."

Qurrah stood before him at their camp, Harruq directly beside him. *For reference*, the yellow-garbed wizard had explained, as if he were painting a portrait...which he was, as a matter of fact.. The most accurate, realistic portrait imaginable.

"Many lives are at risk," Qurrah said. "Are you certain you are up to the task?"

"If I can recreate my devilishly handsome self, this giant hulk of half-orc muscle will be a piece of cake." Tarlak frowned, tilted his head to one side as he continued to analyze matters, then nodded happily. "Adjusting your height will be the most difficult part of all of this, plus adding in some additional mass. You two look similar enough that the real tricky stuff, the facial features, won't require too much work."

"Then get on with it," Qurrah said. "We do not have all night."

"More like an hour," Harruq chipped in helpfully.

"Yeah, yeah, I know." Tarlak clapped his hands together. "Let's do this."

So began a steady procession of spells from the wizard. Qurrah closed his eyes and endured, surprised by the bursts of pain he felt with each new spell. Multiple times Tarlak had to remind him to relax his jaw or pull back his shoulders. Everything had to be perfect. Azariah would see right through something as simple and obvious as an illusion spell, so there would be no illusions. There would be no false magic. Bit by bit, using the polymorphic magic that had allowed him to remake Cecil's body into his own, Tarlak crafted Qurrah into a perfect recreation of his brother.

"Look left," Tarlak said after half an hour. Sweat covered his brow and red veins marked his eyes. "Now right."

Qurrah did as he was told. He felt weirdly large and bloated. His every movement was clumsy. Despite looking like his brother, he certainly felt no stronger.

"All good?" Qurrah asked, and hearing the voice of his brother come out of his mouth instilled him with a sense of vertigo.

"All good," Tarlak said. "But you'll need to talk and act like Harruq to make this work. And whatever you do, don't get into any sort of real fight. Besides having exactly zero training, all that muscle I packed onto you is very much for show. Thank goodness we're doing this at night. I don't know if you'd hold up to close scrutiny during the day."

"We need only fool the fallen angel for a moment," Qurrah said. He grunted, then grinned at his brother. "Now get naked, dumb-ass, I need to look like ya."

Harruq started undoing the buckles of his leather armor. "I feel like I should be insulted."

"*I feel like I should be insulted,*" Qurrah imitated, doing his best to match the inflections. Weird as it was, it did feel nice having his voice deep and baritone compared to his usual rasp.

Harruq stripped down to his underclothes, and Qurrah did likewise. Aurelia helped them both, tweaking the buckles and shifting armor about to better hide the subtle differences between their bodies. The elf had remained oddly quiet during the entire process. Qurrah knew his brother's opinion on the matter, but what of hers? The same went for Jerico, who had been even quitter. His attention, however, was far from the matter at hand. The events at the Citadel had broken him, of that Qurrah was certain. The man's gaze was locked on the roaring campfire that gave them light, and they rarely left its flicker.

"Last, but not least," Aurelia said, taking Harruq's sword belt with Salvation and Condemnation still sheathed and holding it before her. "Whatever you do, don't draw them. Azariah's clever enough to notice the difference between a master wielding a blade and a novice."

"I'll keep it in mind," Qurrah said.

"Be gruffer," she continued as she tightened the buckle. "Especially right now. You're stressed and angry. Act like ripping

Azariah's head off is the only thing you want to do, and everything else is a maddening compromise."

"Not much of an act," Harruq grumbled, and Qurrah grumbled likewise.

When the sword was fully buckled, he expected Aurelia to pull away, but instead she leaned in, her face shockingly close. Her walnut-colored eyes bored into his, unblinking, unflinching. He felt the raw force of her personality, so similar to Tessanna's in that regard. It made her seem all that more beautiful, and all that more terrifying.

"The life of my daughter is in your hands," she said. "I give you my heart for this sacrifice, but do not falter, and do not lose confidence. This is your plan. Make it work."

Qurrah curled his lips into that very familiar, cocky grin of his brother.

"I got this," he said.

Aurelia wrapped her arms about him for one final embrace.

"I pray you do," she whispered.

There would be no goodbye hugs from Tarlak, not that Qurrah blamed him. Guilt for Delysia's death hung fresh in Qurrah's mind, and it wouldn't surprise him if the wizard held onto that bitterness forever. That was fine, and well-deserved. He had killed the man's sister, after all. Qurrah could only even so many different scales. If he tried to make up the grand weight of his sins upon the entire world, there would never be an end. He could spend an eternity performing good deeds and sacrifices and hardly make a dent compared to the destruction he helped unleash by bringing the war god Thulos into the land of Dezrel.

Instead, Qurrah turned his attention to Harruq and accepted the hug he knew would be coming.

"This is so damn weird," Harruq said. He laughed despite a fresh wave of tears beginning to flow. "Thank you, Qurrah, thanks a million. Now go get my daughter back."

They separated. Aurelia closed her eyes a moment to locate the angel Ezekai, then created rip a blue portal out of thin air. Jerico adjusted his sword and shield and stepped through, for they would not perform any trade until they knew for certain the fallen king would keep his word.

"Will Tessanna not come to say goodbye?" Aurelia asked as they waited.

Qurrah shook his head. "She's with me even now."

Jerico returned from the portal and crooked a thumb over his shoulder.

"The bastard is telling the truth," he said. "Harruq in exchange for the children."

"Then we best not delay," Aurelia said. She took Qurrah's hand, squeezed it tightly, and together they walked into the portal. Qurrah felt the now-familiar passage of distance despite seemingly covering only a single step. The world about him changed, and suddenly he stood in a scattered copse of trees. Fallen angels surrounded them, at least fifty in number. Qurrah fought off his initial response, instead hyper-focusing on how his brother might react. Disgust at the angels. Cocky confidence. And rage. So much rage.

"You fucking wretch," Qurrah said in Harruq's voice. "I'm here, now let the children go."

The king of the fallen's face lit up with obvious amusement, implying that Qurrah had nailed the intonation perfectly.

As the meeting progressed, Qurrah's confidence in his scheme grew. He endured the humiliations. He endured the scrutiny. When Azariah cast a spell to detect and banish illusions, he had to stop himself from grinning. Azaria relied too much on magic, not enough on common sense. The idea of asking Qurrah questions that only Harruq might know didn't even occur to him. Granted, given their lifetime spent mostly together, Qurrah expected he was one of very few alive who could manage such a test, hence why he had been adamant he take Harruq's spot. Still, he felt mild disappointment that he had not the chance to further outwit the arrogant bastard.

What he was not amused by was the sudden demand to kneel. The idea of dying on his knees, in worship of the fallen king, filled his stomach with bile. He felt confident his brother would act the same.

"I will not die kneeling," he said, and he meant it. Azariah's shock at being denied made it that much easier to stick to that conviction, and thankfully Aurelia backed him up when the fallen resorted to bluster. Qurrah stood tall, enduring the sickness and madness that was Azariah's mind. He cursed and swore when the fallen demanded Aubrienna watch her father's death.

She'll be fine, he told himself. *She'll go home through that portal, she'll see her real father, and she'll be comforted. She'll recover. She's strong, just like her parents.*

Even more darkly amusing was when Azariah tried to berate and belittle him. Qurrah held no delusions to his nobility. He was not the real Godslayer, but Azariah's claim that his act meant nothing, that it represented the failure of his life, only made him pity the wretch that this once noble Warden of humanity had become.

"The life I go to next is not the one I deserve," Qurrah softly whispered, and he spoke not with his brother's tone, nor his brashness; only his own pure honesty. "But of my life, and my many sins, I know this here and now is the one act which atones for it all."

He felt Tessanna's presence lurking like a shadow cast from a bird flying high above. She was watching and listening from afar with her magic. It was the best she could do, and it made him ache that he could not touch her one last time. He wanted to run his fingers along the scars on her arms. He wanted to feel her long dark hair settle across his chest. He wanted to hear her lovely voice sing a random song from her childhood. He wanted to embrace her, love her, convince her of how she was everything to him, and would always be.

The fallen angel's sword cut across his throat.

Qurrah, Tessanna's alarmed voice echoed in his mind. He felt her subdued panic, the overwhelming sorrow and defeat, and wished yet again he could embrace her. *Qurrah, I love you, I love you, I do, I swear...*

He collapsed to his knees, clutching his neck. Blood spurted between his fingers. His mind flashed to when he had died in such a similar way, his throat cut by Tessanna's hand, a hand forced into obedience by Karak's prophet. He'd bled out while his lover watched in horror, but this was different somehow. This wasn't a waste. It wasn't an end. Good would come of this, his darkening mind truly believed, and he clung to that thought as an airy lightness pushed away his pain.

"But a moment," he told Tess. "I leave...but a moment..."

It was not the first time Qurrah had felt his life leave him, his blood bleeding out, and his soul depart. He gasped, but air would not come. His hands sought movement, reaching for an image of Tessanna's face brightening the midnight sky. No movement followed.

Not the first.

Darkness now, faded light, but there shone a strange beacon high above. Eternity awaited.

Not the first.

But the last.

"**N**o!" Azariah screamed. He withdrew his hand from the lie that was Harruq Tun's body. He stood alone in the copse of trees, his every limb shaking. His jagged teeth clenched so tightly together the enamel cracked and blood poured from his mouth. A storm of emotions blasted through him. He'd been fooled. Lied to. Deceived.

The Godslayer lived.

"It doesn't matter," he said to the flames growing in his palms. "It doesn't matter! The goddess taunts me with deception. This world is mine. The souls of its denizens, they need us, need *me*. I will save Dezrel. Do you hear me, Karak? Do you hear me, Ashhur? These souls *will be saved.*"

He cast fire across the body, burning the manipulated mortal flesh of Qurrah Tun. He charred it to bone, and if he could shatter those bones to powder, he would have. Let nothing remain of the great betrayer. Scatter his every memory to the wind.

"Come tomorrow, we end this conflict," he raged. "We end the last war. We fight the last battle. Dezrel shall know peace, even if every last wretched, sinful life must be chained or slain."

He spread his wings and took flight, but he took no comfort in his proclamation. It was an empty promise. Nothing could shake the seed of doubt now embedded in his breast.

The King of the Fallen

Azariah's future was still uncertain. His life was once again in danger.

The Godslayer lived.

20

Harruq walked through the quiet forest. He had no sound nor light to guide him, but he found Tessanna easily. Her pain was a torch radiating heat, summoning him.

She sat on a log, knees curled up to her chest and face buried in her arms. Moonlight shone softly upon her, casting a beautiful reflection off her long dark hair, yet that same moonlight made the many crisscrossing scars upon her arms stand out in stark contrast.

"You shouldn't be alone," he said, and sat down beside her. She seemed tiny compared to him. He was a giant collection of muscle and armor, she a frail, bone-thin woman with pale skin and a doll's eyes. Yet this was a woman who could break the world if given the chance. He'd seen her wings. He'd felt her anger. And while he'd spent the past hour mourning with his wife, Tessanna had fled to the forest for solitude.

"Yet I am alone," she said, not looking at him when she spoke. "I'll forever be alone. It was my curse from the moment I was born. Even in birth, I slew the human mother who might have raised and loved me. It's all I'm to have, all Mother will grant me. No children of my own. No life to live. Only abuse, and slaughter, and a brief reprieve of love immediately taken because Qurrah was so damn stupid and foolish and wonderful."

"That's not true," Harruq said. He wished he was better at these sorts of things. Qurrah was always more…

Fuck. Harruq fought off a wave of sorrow. Qurrah wasn't anything anymore. He wasn't better or worse. So much of Harruq's identity had been formed in his own mind as a contrast to the faults and strengths of his twin brother. On his own, who was he? Could he be anything?

"I heard his final words," she said. "*But a moment,* he said. *I leave but a moment.* He knew. He remembered. When Velixar brought him back that first time, when he gave him a rotted, dead body he could safely command, I made Qurrah promise me. Never leave me, I begged him. Never leave me again. And then he…and then he…and then he did anyway. He's left me, and this time I have no body to bring back. But a moment, he says. But a moment, as if each and every one of these moments isn't a horrid lifetime."

By her words, by her tone, Harruq might have thought her sobbing. Yet she appeared cold and dead, as if she were but a talking statue.

"I'm sorry," Harruq said after an uncomfortable pause. "I wish I could offer you something better. We...we obviously didn't always get along, nor see things the same way, but I never stopped loving him. You'll never stop loving him either, I know that for sure. If it helps, I want you to know we're here if you need us. Or if you don't want to be alone. At the least, I bet Aubrienna would be happy for a visit with her aunt. She's always had a soft spot for you."

Tessanna gently bobbed her head up and down, but still wouldn't look at him. He couldn't begin to guess the thoughts running through that jumbled mind of hers. When she'd first entered their lives, she'd described her mind as a broken mirror, full of many jagged pieces, shards of identities. Over the years, she'd seemingly become better, more whole. Would she remain so? She had loved his brother so deeply. Qurrah and Tess had needed each other so much more desperately than he'd ever needed Aurelia.

The log groaned as Harruq started to stand.

"Why don't you hate me?" Tessanna asked. Her voice was so perfectly calm. She might as well have been asking why the night was dark or why a man wore a brown shirt instead of gray. "You have every reason, yet you don't. Why not? Why can't you?"

There was a time when he had hated her. A single, horrid moment when he'd lifted Aullienna's cold body from the stream. That tiny span of seconds, lasting no longer than a single heartbeat, had been permanently etched into his memories, forever defining him. The details still hadn't faded, and likely never would. He still remembered the sobbing, sputtering words he'd screamed. The sound Aully's wet hair made as it slapped across her back upon pulling her from the water. The feel of her clammy skin as he brushed her face. The blue of her lips. The lifeless, sightless gaze of her open eyes.

It took a monumental effort to pull his mind from those dark thoughts. "I can't be one to judge," he said. "I murdered children to aid my brother, after all."

"You don't hate me? Not even for Delysia? I demanded he take her life. I forced him to prove he was the monster I sought him to become. Surely that's enough?"

Harruq didn't understand her need for condemnation, but he wasn't about to give it.

"Qurrah may have asked me to bring him children, but the guilt was always mine," he said. "When it all comes tumbling down, we're responsible for our actions. I've always believed that. Qurrah was strong, so strong. His decisions were his own. I'd have had a better chance of convincing the sun to rise in the west and set in the east than make him change his mind once it was set. You and him, together, you were broken then. You were lost. I have to believe you both worked to make amends for your sins, because otherwise...otherwise, what salvation is there for mine?"

He hoped his words would give her comfort, but it seemed to have done the opposite. Tessanna crumpled in on herself and fresh tears slid down her cheeks. For a brief moment he thought sorrow had overtaken her, but when she spoke, he realized she wasn't despairing, but drowning in fury.

"You don't understand," Tessanna said. "I *need* you to hate me. I need you to tell me I'm a terrible person, because right now my only desire is to tear this whole damn world down to its roots. I want to bathe it all in fire. I want to slaughter everything and everyone until I create a land of corpses. If I'm not a horrible person, if what I want isn't horrible, and evil, and bad, then I should...I should...I will..."

Violet flame sprouted from her hands and wreathed her arms. Black light shone from her cavernous eyes. Anguish rolled out of her in waves, and Harruq felt it as if her sorrow was a physical force. Her control was a fraying thread growing ever thinner. Harruq wished he knew what to say, what to do, but he was the dumb idiot who hit things with swords. Where was Lathaar or Jerico with their fancy words? Where was Tarlak to crack a joke, or Haern to whisper a bit of wisdom taught to him in his childhood years?

But Harruq had to do something, for he truly believed her serious in her desire. So he did what he did best: be himself. Be honest and stupid and serious and nonsensical.

Harruq risked the fire. He endured the burn. His hands wrapped about her wrists, and he met her terrifying gaze.

"You're not evil. And you're not broken. You're hurt, and you want to spread that hurt so you don't feel alone. But you're *not* alone. I'm here. I'm no Qurrah, but I can try my best. Would a raspier voice work? Maybe mutter something about how big a buffoon that silly Harruq is? I'm not sure black is my best color, but I could give it a try…"

Amazingly, an uneven laugh broke through her rage. The fire faded, and though her tears still flowed she leaned into him, allowing her tiny little self to be buried in his muscles.

"Gods and goddesses above, you're such an oaf," she said. "Aurelia is lucky to have you."

"I'm pretty sure I'm the lucky one. Any sane elf would have looked at the complete disaster that I was and ran the piss away."

"The same could be said for all of us. Who among us isn't a complete wreck?"

"I don't know. Maybe Jerico?"

Tessanna nestled into him, her long black hair covering her face like a cocoon. "He has his own scars, I assure you. I even gave him some of them."

They fell silent, lost in their own memories. Harruq kept his hand gently on the small of Tessanna's back, and he let her spend the next few minutes silently weeping into his chest. It was controlled, though, as much control as could be expected. As for himself, he stared into the deep black of the forest, listening to the chirping of insects and remembering a thousand nights spent as children racing about the streets of Veldaren with his brother.

"Ahaesarus will move his army out tomorrow, won't he?" Tessanna finally said. Her tears had apparently run dry.

"It sounds like that's the plan. Now that Gregory and Aubrienna are safe, there isn't any reason to delay it further."

His sister-in-law slowly withdrew from his touch, wiping errant strands of hair from her face. She straightened up and met his gaze. A change came over her, and suddenly she was so calm it was disturbing.

"There will be no victors," she said. "No joyful outcome. Mother wakes, and she loathes what she sees."

"What does that mean?" Harruq asked, a chill coming over him.

"It means…it means…" She paused and looked to the grass. A deep frown crossed her face. "It means I have to do something I may not like. Something no one will like."

"Is it the right thing to do?"

She stood from the log. Moonlight shone off her cascading hair, and despite her scars, despite her sorrow, Harruq saw her as his brother no doubt saw her: stunningly beautiful, and overwhelmingly powerful.

"Right? Wrong? Does it matter when the gods who decree what is right and wrong are waging war against one another? I will do what must be done if Dezrel is to survive." She shuddered. One moment she was a living goddess, another a frail woman. Nothing seemed to mark the switch other than the raw strength of her personality. "What must be done if *any* of us are to live. Thank you, Harruq. For what it's worth, I'm…I'm glad you don't hate me. It will make what follows so much easier."

She slipped into the shadows of the trees, avoiding even the moonlight.

"I would like to be alone now," her voice spoke from the darkness. "But don't worry. This time, it is by choice."

Harruq trudged back to the army. He passed by human soldiers gathered around campfires. Fearful optimism shone on their faces, the stress of coming battle tempered by hope for a brighter future awaiting on the other side. Eyes lit up when they saw him, the mighty Godslayer, the unbeatable, undefeatable half-orc berserker with twin black blades and strength unmatched. His mere presence was apparently inspiring. Harruq stood tall, let them see the man who had slaughtered the world-conqueror, Thulos. He let them see grim determination and a will that would not break in the face of fallen angels seeking to conquer Dezrel.

He let them see it until he reached his tent, which he slipped inside to find Aurelia cuddled with a sleeping Aubrienna.

The King of the Fallen

Hidden from the world, and from fearful eyes needing his strength, Harruq broke. In the arms of his beloved, he said goodbye to his brother, and wept tears only his precious wife would ever see.

21

Should this be a happy moment? wondered Jessilynn.

She marched at the head of the beast-men divisions. Cheerful shouts rang out from the human encampment as the angels flew overhead, led by a proud Ahaesarus in shining armor. Two armies coming together in preparation for battle. There was hope in that. Yet none of that hope manifested in Jessilynn's own heart.

"Such grimness on the face of a human so young," said Dieredon. He marched beside her, leading Sonowin by the reins. The elf gestured to the humans following the boy king, all of whom lifted their arms and clapped at the sight of so many angels. "Do you not share their mirth?"

Jessilynn glanced over her shoulder at the wolf-men, hyena-men, and bird-men obediently marching under a vague promise of a new home.

"No. I share theirs."

The next hour was chaos. The human soldiers granted by Lord Eston were eager to make camp with their fellow refugees from Mordeina. The beast-men set up their section as always, which for many meant little more than setting fires and smoothing out dirt and grass.

Jessilynn separated from Dieredon and wandered throughout the beast-men factions, knowing she should return to the Mordan side but unable to force herself. There were people and faces there she felt nervous to meet. Would any ask about her failure at the Castle of the Yellow Rose? Would she be forced to relive her imprisonment at the hands of the wolf brothers? Her pulse quickened at the memory of Manfeaster and Moonslayer, and so she found every excuse to remain with the occasional grunts and unwelcome glares of the beast-men.

Hiding would not work forever, though. Sonowin's shadow flew overhead, followed by Dieredon landing lightly on his feet a moment later.

"There you are," the elf said. "Ahaesarus is already plotting tomorrow's battle with the boy king's retinue."

"His retinue?"

"The Godslayer and his little band of Eschaton, mostly," the elf admitted. "A friend of yours is there, too. Come with me, Jessilynn. You should be proud of all you have accomplished since becoming my ward."

"I killed hundreds of beast-men whose kin and friends now wage war under an angelic banner. I don't feel much pride in me."

It was a false complaint meant to hide her true fear. Her bow. Her arrows. Would any notice? And what would they say or do if they did? Her shaken faith in Ashhur embarrassed her deeply, and no matter how she tried to think matters through, she felt intense shame in her spiritual failure.

"I'm not asking you to brag," Dieredon said. "I'm asking you to come with me because Jerico specifically requested he see you. You're his student, and he worried greatly for your safety during our, shall we say, adventures in the north."

Hearing her teacher's name, and his desire to speak with her, only quadrupled her shame. Ashhur help her, must she confess her doubts and failures to one of her god's most accomplished heroes?

"If you insist," she said grudgingly.

The army's leadership were positioned atop the nearest hill, which wasn't much of a hill at all. To help cordon it off from the rest of the army, soldiers had pounded a half-dozen spikes at the hill's base and strung them with rope. A lone soldier guarded the 'entrance' gap, and he lifted a hand when he saw Jessilynn and Dieredon approaching.

"Hold up now," the soldier said. "Ahaesarus and the Godslayer are in a meeting."

"And I'm a friend of Ahaesarus," Jessilynn responded.

"Don't mean I should let you go through." The man dropped a hand to his sheathed sword. "Back off. I have my orders."

Jessilynn didn't acknowledge the threat. She barely felt anything more than mild annoyance. "I am a Paladin of Ashhur. And I shall pass."

She strode past him, practically daring the stunned man to strike at her. Dieredon grinned as he followed, and she heard him offer mild consolation.

"No hard feelings, human, but you truly don't scare her."

A large brown tent fluttered at the crest of the hill. Before its front flaps was a wooden table that looked comically small given how many leaned over it. Maps of Dezrel were stacked atop the table, along with tokens she assumed represented the various factions of Ahaesarus's forces, as well as those Azariah had at his disposal.

Jessilynn froze in place just outside their ring. Though her time with Dieredon had helped grow her confidence, she still felt overwhelmed by those present. Before her were legends of Dezrel, and though she had never met most of them, she knew them by reputation alone. Harruq Tun, a mountain of muscle and leather armor, towered over all but Ahaesarus. His elven wife Aurelia stood beside him, a stunning picture of beauty and elegance. Those two alone had been the stars of the many stories Jerico and Lathaar had told.

Speaking of Jerico, he too discussed preparations, looking infinitely more tired than he ever had during their lessons at the Citadel. A yellow-garbed wizard, most certainly Tarlak Eschaton, chatted beside him, gesticulating wildly with his hands as he argued. Even Tessanna Delone was there, standing quietly apart from the rest. At least that's who Jessilynn assumed the dark-eyed woman with black hair stretching down to her ankles must be.

"Forgive our intrusion," Dieredon said, loud enough to draw attention away from the discussion of troops and movements. Harruq was the first to notice, and the half-orc forced a smile.

"Hey, it's my favorite cranky and stubborn elf," he said, then winked at Aurelia. "At least, the most cranky and stubborn elf that I'm not married to."

"Yet," Dieredon said. "Give me time."

Jerico glanced up from the map, and upon seeing Jessilynn he jolted as if struck by a thunderbolt.

"Jessilynn," he said, stepping away from the table. She rooted in place, and it seemed time itself slowed to a crawl. Not that long ago, she'd have broken down in tears at seeing such a familiar face. Her memories of training and study threatened to overwhelm her, and she felt an intense desire to run to the older man and collapse into his arms, to receive his comfort, his reaffirmation. Instead, she thrust back her shoulders, refusing to flinch or succumb to her emotions. Let him see her stand tall. Let her bear with pride the scars the wolf-men had carved upon her face.

Yet it wasn't she who broke down, but Jerico. The older man laughed even as tears began to fall. He sprinted the distance between them.

"I know only pieces of your story," he said as he wrapped her in an embrace. "But praise Ashhur, you lived. You survived. I wasn't sure I could endure losing another."

"Another?" she asked, her entire body turning stiff.

Jerico glanced over her shoulder, and she heard a swish of leather as Dieredon bowed.

"I shall give you two your privacy," the elf said.

The paladin released his hold on her. He stared silently into the distance a moment before shaking his head and walking the other direction, away from those gathered around, discussing war over their table covered with maps and tokens.

"Come," he said. "I would not have others overhear."

Jessilynn followed him down the hill and past the barricade. For several minutes they walked with him in the lead, winding their way through the scattered encampment. Neither spoke. With each step, her dread grew. Questions she dared not ask pulsed through her mind, giving more fuel to her barely-controlled panic.

"I suppose I've stalled long enough," Jerico said once they were alone. He'd found a spot where two hills crested into one another, forming a gentle curvature lined with thorned bushes that might produce fruit come spring. Jerico stood before those bushes, armored hand gently brushing the thorns, and fell silent. Jessilynn gave him a chance to address her first, but when the normally boisterous man remained silent, she asked the question that had bothered her most.

"Jerico, why do you carry Lathaar's sword at your hip instead of Bonebreaker?"

Jerico snapped his fist shut, crushing the bush's thin little branches. "Because Lathaar no longer can. He's gone. The entire Citadel...it's collapsed. Fallen. And I think it's my fault that it did."

Whatever joy Jessilynn had felt at seeing Jerico alive and well shriveled and died. Again, she felt the need for tears, yet her insides were so deadened, so numb, she could only stare in shock.

"How?" she asked. That single word was all she could manage.

The other paladin crossed his arms and he closed his eyes. They remained closed when he spoke. Despair hung heavy on his every syllable.

"Betrayed. Stabbed in the back by our own students. When the fallen came for Aubrienna and Gregory, instead of fighting for them, instead of relying on Ashhur to protect those we loved, they..." He drew in a long breath and exhaled slowly. At last his eyes opened, and it seemed he'd gathered himself, if only for her sake. "I wasn't there, damn it. I confronted them afterwards. I demanded they show me their faith. They didn't. And every single one that couldn't, every single naked blade, I...I killed them, Jessilynn. My own students. All of them. Only Elrath and Mal survived, the only two willing to stand alongside Lathaar and insist the betrayal was wrong."

Jessilynn's dread turned to horror. These students he spoke of, they were her friends, the only family she'd ever known since she arrived at the Citadel as an orphan.

"You murdered them."

"I avenged my dearest friend and brother," Jerico insisted. "Would you judge me, too?"

Jessilynn pulled her bow off her shoulder and held it before her. Her fingers plucked the string. She showed the lack of light, the absence of her own faith.

"Am I next?" she asked. "Will you slay me for my own doubts?"

"You didn't betray Lathaar. You didn't hand two children over to murderers to use as hostages."

"Not those sins, no, but countless others. Answer me, Jerico. Is my life now forfeit?"

Jerico slowly drew his sword...or was it Lathaar's sword? She froze, for the first time in her life doubting the decision of a man she had idolized as a child. Jerico took the sword, flipped it in his grasp, and stabbed it into the soft earth. Next came his enormous shield, which he pulled off his back and held firmly tucked into his grasp so that she might look upon its surface.

His shield. His plain, light-less shield.

"No, Jessilynn," he said. "For I would have to take my own life first."

She stared at that slanted chunk of metal upon which she had witnessed bathed in holy light countless times before. Deep inside, she felt far too much of herself dying. The grief and shock and horror melded together into a cage locked about her heart. What did it mean? What did *any* of it mean?

"Have we abandoned Ashhur?" she asked. "Or are we the abandoned?"

The silence between them shouted an answer neither wished to accept.

Jessilynn met the tired gaze of her teacher. There was distance between them, a mutual understanding that went unspoken. All her childhood, she had prayed to be a hero like her cherished mentors. To become a legend of faith and power who stood against the forces of evil. Now she knew what it truly meant to be a hero. She had fought, and bled, and endured. Many lives had fallen to her bow, though that number paled in comparison to how many had been done in by Jerico's mace and shield. They recognized it in one another. They felt the weight of a thousand trials suffered, and it formed a gulf between them. It saddled them with exhaustion. It broke them with loss and sorrow.

Before her was the Jerico the stories never told. Victory and heroics didn't replace the dead. It didn't erase the pain or salve the hurt that came upon remembering the faces of those who were lost. She saw that now. She felt it in her bones. She knew it in the rubble of the Citadel, rebuilt no longer.

Knowing this, and accepting it, were still two different things.

"I saw Darius," she blurted out before her teacher could leave. "I know it sounds like I'm crazy, but I saw him. He spoke to me, and he helped me. He said to – to tell you to hurry up and die so he can show you a spot by a lake."

Jerico slung his shield over his back. He glanced aside, and a smile spread across his face despite his exhaustion and sorrow.

"Sitting around hoping I'll die? Some friend he is."

"I think it was a joke."

"I know it's a joke," Jerico said. He grabbed his sword, wiped it clean of dirt, and slammed it into its sheath. "He was just never good at them. Ashhur help me, I miss that idiot." The paladin chuckled, his laughter false, the sorrow in his eyes so very real. "It's a shame he's not with us, because I think we could all use the help of a real paladin tomorrow. At least there's a silver lining. If things go as it looks like, given how badly we're outnumbered, well...that bastard's about to get his wish."

22

Harruq checked the buckles of his armor one last time with Aurelia's help. They readied themselves at the rear of the army while soldiers scurried about the grassland like ants whose anthill had just been kicked.

"I should be able to protect you with my magic, so long as you don't do anything too stupid or reckless," his wife said, cinching the one of his pauldrons tighter.

"Have you ever seen me in a fight?" he asked.

She kissed his nose. "Yes. Hence my request."

The air was electric. Both armies marched toward one another, to collide on the chosen field of battle. The road leading between the Castle of Roses and Mordeina was flat and well-traveled, and it was in the surrounding meadow, on what Harruq had been told was known as Hemman Fields, that they would meet. The ground was firm and flat but for small little bumps of hills that would make perfect vantage points for each side's perspective leaders.

A good place to murder each other, thought Harruq. How grim was his life that he'd so calmly analyze a place where thousands were about to die and declare it 'good'?

The sound of wings was his only warning for Ahaesarus's arrival from the air. The angel landed beside him.

"Good, you appear ready," he said, looking Harruq over. "Come with me. So far as I am concerned, you are still steward for Gregory Copernus. You should bear witness to Azariah's answer."

"I'm not sure that's a good idea, me meeting him," Harruq said. "Not after what he did to Aubby, and to my brother."

"You'll keep your swords sheathed and your temper in check," the angel said, his tone brooking no argument. "Walk with me."

Harruq swallowed down the rest of his complaints. Just part of the joys of being the Godslayer. Still, he couldn't deny the potential pleasure in seeing Azariah's reaction. Whatever the reason, the angel had been obsessed with killing him. Reminding

Azariah he'd been outwitted could at least provide some measure of enjoyment.

"Stay safe," Aurelia said, and kissed his cheek.

"Not good enough," Harruq said. He swept her up and pulled her close for a kiss on the lips. He let the kiss linger, grinning when he heard a few of the nearby soldiers hoot and holler. He tipped his wife even further back. Might as well give them all a bit of a show.

At last she pulled away from him, playfully slapping his chest.

"Enough of that," she said. "Now go be a diplomat before you're forced to be a killer."

"Walk with me,' Ahaesarus had said, though that appeared to be a misnomer. The angel flew overhead, slowly keeping pace with Harruq, who crossed Hemman Field on foot. For him to be so low, and the angelic leader so high, felt a little too on the nose for Harruq's tastes.

Still, the walk gave him a chance to observe his opponents. Closest were the rows and rows of undead. They stood perfectly still, waiting for orders from their master. The sight gave Harruq a shiver. Armies of undead were tied to many of his memories, none of them good.

Behind the thousands of undead readied the smaller number of human soldiers. Harruq could only see bits and pieces of their formations, plus a few of their scattered banners, but he doubted any were eager for battle. Dozens of deserters had arrived at their camp overnight, seeking safety from their lords and pledging their swords to Gregory and his angels. If it ever appeared that Azariah would lose, he firmly believed those human lines would retreat, if not throw down their arms and surrender. In fact, much of Ahaesarus's strategy involved destroying the undead and the fallen angels in the hopes of stealing those human soldiers for their own ranks.

Last, and most frightening of all, were the hundreds of fallen circling the skies with their black wings. Harruq was glad they were not his primary foe. The thought of facing them tightened his already sour stomach. If all went as planned,

The King of the Fallen

Ahaesarus and the Eschaton spellcasters would handle that facet of their opponent's army.

As Harruq and Ahaesarus approached the center of the clearing, so too did a pair of fallen. Azariah and Judarius, as expected. A momentary spike of panic flicked across Harruq's heart at meeting them again. He clenched his fists, brushing aside his fear. He'd fought a god. Two bastard fallen angels meant nothing next to that.

Ahaesarus drifted to the ground and crossed his arms over his chest. Harruq halted beside him. Together they waited for the opposing party.

"I shall handle all negotiations," the angel said. "Not that I anticipate there to be many."

"If I'm to keep my mouth shut, then why am I here?"

"I never said to keep your mouth shut," Ahaesarus said, and he flashed a rare smile. "I said leave negotiations to me. You may threaten and insult as you wish. For whatever the reason, Azariah seems particularly frightened of you, so do your best to unnerve him."

The fallen brothers landed. Judarius glared openly, his fingers tapping the hilt of his enormous two-handed mace. Azariah at least pretended at diplomacy. He dipped his head in respect as his wings fluttered behind him.

"We need no introduction, but I, King Azariah the Wise, ruler of Paradise, greet you nonetheless. I see you were spared Ashhur's judgment." He flashed his jagged teeth. "We were not so lucky."

"Ashhur above, what happened to you, my friends, my kin?" Ahaesarus asked, and he looked genuinely disturbed by the sight of them.

He's never seen them, Harruq realized. *He wasn't there.*

When Ashhur used the mouth of a stranger to order the angels to fall, Ahaesarus was to the north, racing in vain to save the lives of those defending the Castle of the Yellow Rose. He'd not encountered any of Azariah's wretched, and there was no denying his shock at the sight. A crown of bone sprouted from Azariah's forehead, composed of what seemed to be interlocked horns connected to his skull. His feathers were dark as the night, his flesh a sickly gray, reminiscent of rot and decay. Eyes that once were as green and vibrant as a forest and speckled with gold were now dull, gray orbs spiderwebbed with angry red veins. His fingernails were black. His lips bled. His smile was rotten.

"We were abandoned by a god whom we faithfully served for hundreds of years," Azariah said. "But we have not abandoned Ashhur, nor the teachings he granted us when we walked Paradise as Wardens. It is not too late, Ahaesarus. I come to you now, before the clash of blades, to offer you a chance to surrender."

"Surrender?" Ahaesarus asked. "To one so clearly despised by my god?"

"Do not be deluded," Azariah insisted. "Your numbers pale compared to ours."

"The only person deluded about whose ass is about to get kicked is you," Harruq said. "We outsmarted you once, and it's gonna happen twice."

Azariah turned to him. Harruq couldn't help but be confused by the fallen's expression. Was he angry? Worried? Azariah obviously tried so hard to remain passive and give away nothing, but Harruq swore he sensed fear hidden behind that bloviated aura of indignation.

"Your trick may have worked, but the sparing of your life was a paltry reward," Azariah said. "The great betrayer is dead, denied a grave or funeral. It is the fate one such as he deserved. You will follow him, trampled on the field of battle, to die where you always belonged."

"You offered a king and my daughter in exchange for my life," Harruq said. "If you are so unafraid of my presence on the battlefield, you have a strange way of showing it." He smirked. "I'll be out there in the thick of it. If either of you have the stones, come say 'hello'. My twin blades will be waiting. At the least, you owe me a rematch, Judarius, since you fled like a coward the last time we fought."

Judarius took a menacing step forward before Azariah stopped him with his arm.

"Meager words," the fallen king said. "And they shall bring forth meager returns. My forces are greater. My cause is just. Die if you must, but Paradise shall be born anew under my reign."

The King of the Fallen

"The false hope of a fallen king," Ahaesarus said. "Farewell, strangers. I see my dearest friends died long before the sun rose this morn."

The angel turned to fly away. Harruq waited a half-second longer, to ensure their foes planned no cowardly betrayal. Judarius and Azariah rejoined the great cloud of black wings overhead their human and undead army. No betrayal. There was no need. Why risk battling two against two if they thought their army was the greater?

No stopping it now, thought Harruq as he returned to their own forces. The long walk gave him far too much time to be alone in his own head. In some ways, the beginning of a battle was so much worse than the battle itself. Sometimes, the imagined horror was worse than the actual blood.

Only sometimes.

A signal from Ahaesarus set the combined troops to marching. Harruq halted in place and let the army sweep him up in its flow. He scanned their ranks for a specific member, and he found him right at the front, where he and his shield belonged.

"Just like old times, eh?" Jerico said when the half-orc joined his side.

"At least we're not running for our lives like in Veldaren," Harruq said, laughing. "They've got a decent chunk of undead on their side. Think you and your shield can obliterate them?"

Jerico's confidence momentarily flickered.

"My faith, and the light of my shield, is not quite so strong as those early days," he admitted. "I do not know."

Harruq did his best to shrug away the man's concern. "The faith of the young burns hotter than the elderly, mostly because it's a whole lot easier to be stupid and eager when you're young. Don't start doubting yourself now, not when victory's almost at hand."

"Victory?" Jerico asked. He gestured to the sky full of black wings and dropped the volume of his voice by half so no one else would hear him over the rattle of armor and weaponry. "You expect us to find victory?"

"Come on now, Jerico. After fighting battles against the death prophet, the war god, the armies of orcs, undead, beast-men, assassins, demons, fallen angels, a shadow dragon, and my own crazy brother, do you really think this is the worst spot we've ever been in?"

That got a chuckle from the normally jovial paladin. "Not when you put it that way."

"Damn straight. Chin up, Paladin. I expect you to save my ass when I get in over my head, not sit back and mope about it. It's not a good look for you."

The pace of the march quickened. A glance overhead saw Ahaesarus's angels gathering into tight formations of five, each cluster flying in a V-shape akin to geese migrating south during winter. The howls and squawks from the beast-men to Harruq's left grew in intensity. His heart began to race. He looked across the empty field, to the approaching enemy. The foes he'd crush with his swords.

"I wish Lathaar was with us," Jerico said quietly as the undead let loose a synchronized moan, meaningless air pushed out through dry throats.

"Me too, friend. Me too."

They'd discussed the battle plan the night before. Despite being outnumbered two-to-one, Ahaesarus and his angels would engage Judarius in the skies. Tarlak, Aurelia, and Tessanna would remain just outside the battlefield, their magic countering any spells cast by Azariah and his fledgling wizards. Dieredon and Jessilynn would play the wild card, circling the air with their bows and targeting the various commanders in charge of the enemy regiments in order to sow chaos. The beast-men would form the left side of the ground engagement, the human soldiers the right. As for Harruq, he and Jerico were to be the bulwark in the center where the two sides met. Whether any of the beast-men would listen to his commands, he couldn't guess, but he suspected it would not be necessary. They were terrifying fighters, and would know best how to kill their foes.

A fine plan, but it relied heavily on their spellcasting trio to make up for inferior numbers, particularly in the air. Which made the sight of three robed members of the Council of Mages watching from one of the dotted hills quite worrisome. He'd take Aurelia over Azariah any day of the week, but those Council members? He'd heard more than enough stories from Tarlak. They were exceedingly dangerous, and could nullify their major advantage.

As if to test that theory, a trio of spells flew from the hands of the Council members. Two were enormous balls of flame, the third a chunk of stone that started out a pebble but grew as it flew until it was thrice the size of a human. Aurelia and Tarlak countered with spells of their own. Fire flew from their own hands, striking the balls of flame and detonating them harmlessly in the air. As for the boulder, a blast of lightning tore it asunder.

As magic crackled and pebbles rained harmlessly down upon the field, it seemed an unspoken understanding passed between both armies. This was it. War had come. Swords were lifted high. Shields clattered to the ready. What was a march became a charge, battle cries bellowing from the throats of soldiers.

"Side by side!" Harruq shouted as he burst into a sprint.

"Side by side!" Jerico shouted back, matching his stride with his shield leading.

The moaning of the undead may have been frightening, but that paled in comparison to the sudden cacophony unleashed by the combined races of beast-men. The shrieks from the bird-men, the howls of the wolf-men, and the yipping mockery of the hyena-men pulled Harruq back to dark memories of the fall of Veldaren.

Those inhuman sounds obviously had an effect on human soldiers sworn to fight for Azariah, for they sagged when confronted with the tide of feathers, fur, and claw. The undead, however, cared not, and such a discrepancy worked against Azariah's army. Instead of a solid line, it was two uneven waves that crashed against the united force Ahaesarus had brought.

The undead arrived, and Harruq could no longer focus on was happening in the battle at large. The fighting corpses were hardly a new foe for him, given his insane life. He fought using the same tactics he had taught the rest of the army over the last few days, when it was clear such a battle awaited. No shallow slashes.

No flesh wounds, and no thrusts meant to pierce internal organs that served no function. Every swing needed to cleave off limbs.

Hack them down. Break every bone.

Screams marked the true start of battle. The undead scraped and bit at their foes without hesitation or instinct for self-preservation. The clatter of snapping bones quickly followed. The line of undead, meant solely to focus on the beast-men, spilled over with the delayed march of the human army, granting Harruq and Jerico a chance to thin those numbers. Harruq paced himself, using methodical hits that relied on the powerful magic within Salvation and Condemnation to wreck his foes. The first minute passed, both impossibly fast and insanely slow. He lopped off a head, kicked back the still-writhing corpse, and then double-cut through another attempting to bite the face of the soldier beside him.

"Close one, eh buddy?" Harruq said, for he could see the man was an inch away from breaking down. "Fight with me, no surrender, no retreat!"

The soldier readied his sword, and Harruq made sure to cut down two more undead before they reached the man so he might gather himself.

The wave kept coming, packing in closer, closer, while behind them the opposing human army broke ranks ever further. Arrows sailed overhead. Thunder and crackling ice marked the battle of spellcasters, whose full fury he could only imagine. Howls and shrieks from the beast-men steadily grew in number. Whatever their own casualties, it sounded severe, so Harruq shifted his attention their way. His twin blades were less like a dancer and more like a lumberjack as he cut, chopped, and hacked at the stinking, rotting army forced to serve the fallen king.

He returned to Jerico's side right as the paladin lifted his shield and shouted out the name of his god. Light shone off his shield, and already it was brighter than when the battle had begun. Over a dozen undead collapsed, their pallid flesh withering beneath the holy light like paper tossed atop hot coals, granting the duo a moment to breathe before the next line of soldiers hit. Jerico jammed an elbow into Harruq's arm to gather his attention.

The King of the Fallen

"I go where I am needed," Jerico said, nodding toward the beast-men army to their left. While they were fearsome fighters, they wielded claws and teeth, which meant fighting at a much closer range than those with swords and spears. Against undead soldiers who felt no pain, and cared not if forced to bleed, their methods were proving ineffectual.

"You take left, I'll take right," Harruq said. "Meet in the middle upon victory."

He trusted Jerico to hold true as the paladin waded into the undead army. Jerico fought amidst the beast-men, and truth be told, he seemed much more comfortable among them. Perhaps it was because he fought an undead foe, whose lifeless rotting corpses he could crush without guilt or doubt compared to human soldiers conscripted by the fallen king.

Soldiers replaced Jerico in standing at Harruq's side. He lifted his swords high above his head so all could see their black blades and red aura. Those human soldiers forced to fight for Azariah neared, finally crossing the distance in the most heartless charge Harruq had ever seen. Breaking them would be child's play.

"We do not cower!" he shouted. "Stand with the Godslayer, and let's kick their asses!"

Wanting momentum on his side, he charged a half-second before the next wave hit. He lacked a shield, but his weapons might as well have been battering rams against these frightened adversaries. The human soldiers fighting for Azariah...they knew the stories. They'd heard how Harruq had fought one-on-one against the war god Thulos and emerged victorious. For every soldier that seemed eager for a chance at fame and victory, five more looked terrified to be anywhere in his vicinity. He could see it in their formations. He watched it in their movements. If they could fight anyone else, they did, turning to attack any up and down the line who weren't Harruq himself.

And so Harruq tore through them. He punished them for their cowardice. He *made* them turn their attention his way. Whatever guilt he felt for killing them, he buried beneath his rage. Memories of the Night of Black Wings pushed him deeper into the crowd. Aubrienna, crying in Azariah's arms. Qurrah, bleeding out

The battle was a bloody Abyss, the grass slick with gore, the footing uneven from all the corpses, but Harruq cared for none of it. Before him were a thousand enemies. At last, he could bring his swords to bear. He could strike at his foes instead of marching, or fleeing, or sitting silent and helpless as his own brother died. His swords could drink. His battle lust could be sated. These human soldiers, these young men fighting for the rule of a god-king they themselves did not worship, didn't stand a goddamn chance.

Harruq could not spare any attention toward the battle raging in the clouds, but that did not mean he was safe from it. The body of an angel fell to the earth a mere foot in front of him, broken limbs flailing, sword and armor cutting a groove into the dirt. Harruq stumbled over the corpse, blocked a chop while absorbing a second clumsy hit to his side, and then regained his footing. More bodies of angels plummeted like bloody heaps from the heavens, landing on, and felling, soldiers from both sides. Magic lit the sky in blinding flashes of lightning. Ice met fire. Translucent shields blocked beams of arcane magic. Eschaton versus the Council.

The powers wielded made Harruq's own swords feel small and insignificant, but he dared not dwell on such matters, not when the next wave of foes came crashing in. Unlike the leaderless undead, the second line of human soldiers were led by dark paladins. Harruq charged into the fray with a singular goal.

He may not be able to sunder mountains with his swords, but at least he could bring down a few stubborn bastards of Karak.

The clear lines of battle had grown wobbly. The beast-men cared not for careful formations, and there was no way to make sense of the war in the sky. As the casualties mounted and bodies soaked the grass with blood and gore, Harruq found himself with more and more space to duel. The shift benefited him. This was the type of battle Haern had prepared him for, not one of strict formations, but of reading opponents and controlling the chaos. When Harruq charged, a trio of fellow soldiers charged with him, and he appreciated their bravery.

The King of the Fallen

Together, the four of them hit the next wave of human soldiers. Alone, he doubted he could have withstood them. With the aid of allies, however, Harruq quickly cut down challengers, black blades chopping off limbs with remarkable ease. To be at the vanguard meant resistance, and though those with him fell one by one, Harruq soldiered on. He blocked blows with such force he often took the weapons out of his opponents' hands. He slammed enchanted swords through half-hearted attempts to parry. He felt like a god on the battlefield, and the hint of Ashhur's light shimmering amid the red glow of his swords made him wonder if there were a bit of truth to the feeling.

But there were other gods, and other followers, and at last Harruq crossed the distance to where the dark paladin Umber waited with his ax hoisted over his shoulder. If he was afraid of the half-orc, he didn't show it.

"An age of Karak shall follow," Umber shouted. He lifted his ax. "We'll sing our worship atop your graves, for I'll be a hero for taking your twice-condemned head."

Despite the blood, despite the sweat trickling into his eyes, the ache in his arms and the hitch in his left side, Harruq grinned. He clanged Salvation and Condemnation together, their metallic ring signaling his anticipation.

"Fucking try."

Black flames swirled about the ax head as Umber swung. Karak's anger and fury blessed the weapon, a power fueled by Umber's faith. Most weapons would shatter, but not Harruq's twin swords. They were the lone gift from Velixar that Harruq did not regret. With them, he had changed the world. With them, he could withstand the overhead chop, the ax's black fire meeting his swords' somber red glow.

Wisdom said to merely dodge the strike, but Harruq wasn't interested in fighting smart. He wanted Umber to realize he was outmatched. He wanted him to see how, when all his strength was brought down in a single, powerful strike, Harruq could meet it with a grin.

And so he did. The weapons crossed, Harruq's arms bulged, his legs braced, and then he slammed the ax aside. Fear replaced fanaticism in the paladin's eyes. He swept his ax back around, but the distance was too close. Harruq wedged Condemnation in the way, blade striking handle, and then slashed with Salvation. He meant to hit the neck, but his aim was slightly low. The sword struck Umber's pauldron, its enchanted edge cutting through metal and flesh and sunk into bone. Harruq ripped the blade free.

Umber screamed, grasped his wounded shoulder, and retreated a few steps. Harruq hesitated before chasing, the instinctual pause sparing him from the thrust of a spearhead. A second dark paladin intervened, this one wielding a shield and half-spear. He skirted back to position himself just in front of Umber, his shield protecting his injured fellow dark paladin and buying him a moment to lift his ax and push through the pain. Blood poured down Umber's arm, and by no means should he have been able to lift that ax, but wisps of violet flame flickered underneath his split pauldron, leading Harruq to suspect Karak's blessing was involved.

"Where is my grave, cowards?" Harruq roared. He smashed into the both of them, each of his swords shoving aside an attempted counter. Condemnation bashed a massive indent into the new paladin's shield. Harruq's shoulder collided with Umber's chest, flinging him several feet back. The dark paladin staggered, and he hollered mindless rage as he brought up his ax.

"Where is your song? Where is your dance?"

Harruq easily sidestepped a wild overhead chop. These men, they were so young. Karak's faithful had suffered horrible casualties during the Gods' War, no different than anyone else in Dezrel. These two were new to battle, just like the students Lathaar and Jerico had trained. They thought their faith would give them the strength to overcome. They thought Karak would bless them and lead them to victory.

Harruq quickly disabused Umber of that notion with a sword strike to his injured shoulder, and this time no unholy power would keep the arm moving. The paladin with the spear tried to stab Harruq through the back, but his attack was clumsy and not at all the surprise he believed it to be. Harruq sidestepped and locked the spear between his elbow and his side. A turn wrenched the weapon free of the suddenly mortified paladin's

The King of the Fallen

hand. Harruq looped his free arm, tearing open the man's throat with Salvation's tip. The paladin dropped in a shower of blood.

Harruq released the spear, twirled his swords, and turned back to Umber.

"Karak is with me!" the paladin shrieked. He lacked the strength to lift his ax, but neither did he run. The battle of panic against faith was obvious in his pained expression: how could he surrender or flee if his god was superior to the Ashhur the half-orc worshiped?

A single thrust to the throat ended Umber's torment. He dropped to his knees, gargling something unintelligible. Harruq cleaved his head off his shoulders for good measure.

"He's not with you," Harruq said. "But you're with him now. Enjoy the fire."

Somehow over the chaos of battle, over the screams of the dying, the clatter of steel, and the tearing of flesh, a soft whisper reached Harruq's ears. It was a tired proclamation, spoken by a broken woman, and he looked up to see black wings blotting out the war-torn sky. The sight filled him with far more fear than any opposing army ever could.

"Let it end," whispered the Daughter of Balance. "Let neither rule. Let the balance fall aside, and be judged not by brother gods."

She lifted her arms. The ground split. The sky roared, and it seemed all of Dezrel shook as Celestia unleashed centuries of fury upon the land.

23

The angels were mere nuisances to Tessanna. New to magic, they cast pitiful flames and thin shards of ice that she batted away with ease from her position on the tiny hill. Not even Azariah's impressive magic frightened her. It was masters from the Council of Mages that were truly dangerous, but Aurelia and Tarlak could handle them.

"Tess!" Tarlak screamed as a thunderbolt slammed down atop the three of them, only to break against a domed shield he summoned. "We need help, Tess! What are you waiting for?"

She stared at the battlefield, granting him no answer. What was she waiting for? She watched the bloodshed fill the sky. She watched the humans, beast-men, and undead crash against one another in a river of steel, flesh, and murder.

What was she waiting for? The truth ashamed her, and she dared not answer aloud.

She waited for courage.

The courage to do what must be done.

"Please, Tess, do not abandon us now," Aurelia said, flinging a massive boulder of ice directly into a ball of flame one of the Council members attempted to drop upon the battlefield. While Tarlak focused on protecting the three of them, Aurelia's attention was solely on protecting the field of battle. The outnumbered armies of Ahaesarus would be easily overrun without her aid, for even with Harruq and Jerico helming the front line, they were but two against far too many. Should a single magical attack sunder their ranks, their line would break. And no help would come to them from the skies, for Ahaesarus was hard pressed to take on the cloud of dark wings.

"Abandon?" Tessanna said.

She could delay no longer. To the Abyss with her fears. She walked toward the battlefield, but instead of grass, her feet touched air. Wispy illusions of wings sprouted from her back, so easily summoned. Had she not relied upon them her entire life? She hovered toward the battle, hands at her sides and head bowed. The sound of pain and death washed over her like a warm cocoon.

"Qurrah is gone," she whispered. "Are you with me, Mother? Is it too late to be what you've always asked me to be?"

Celestia's voice echoed within her mind. Though spoken softly, calmly, it still drowned out all other noises of the bloody battlefield.

The Balance must be preserved, my daughter.

"And if the Balance is broken beyond repair?"

Nothing is beyond repair. I lift you up, cherished one. I am with you, always.

Lightning crackled in the clear sky above, summoned by a trio of angels attempting to intercept her approach. Tessanna tilted her head to one side as the magic swarmed about her, brilliant and hot like the sun. She lifted two fingers, compressing the lightning down to a singular orb of blinding light. A flick of her wrist, and she unleashed it upon the angels. They screamed, power ripping through them, setting their insides aflame and dropping them dead. Their innards were so terribly charred, their skin parted from their bones as they fell.

Her ethereal wings spread wider. Tessanna felt more eyes upon her, but who would dare lay a hand upon her? Who could afford to turn their gaze her way when a war yet raged? In the sky, angel battled angel. On the ground, not even the dead were spared. Most terrifying, and heart-rending, were the beast-men diving upon their foes. She knew what they fought for. A promise. A lie.

"Karak or Ashhur," she said. "Two fates lie before Dezrel. Two kings, each determined to rule with a divine mandate. Each with their champions. Each with their angels and their avatars. Must it be so?"

It is a Balance I decreed when the world was young.

A beam of pure red magic shot from the open palm of a mage. Tessanna batted it aside with her bare hand. The beam careened upward, streaking toward whatever celestial object might one day intercept its path in the deep dark of the stars.

"You have loved Ashhur always," she whispered. "But I do not love him as you do. Will you aid me, even knowing this? Knowing the Balance must break?"

For what felt like an age, Mother remained silent. The goddess knew her plan, for how could she not? Even amid her broken mind, Mother had comfortably dwelt. There would be no secrets from her. Would she relent? Would she accept? Tessanna looked down to where Harruq battled like a monster. His black blades were like the claws of a dragon. They were the teeth of a beast drinking an ocean of blood. In so many ways, he was the purest of them all. Give him an enemy, and the half-orc would tear that enemy apart. Not even death could stop him.

But even Harruq represented one side of the balance. Karak and Ashhur, back and forth, a wobbling plate atop a gore-stained spike. Dezrel had suffered so greatly to keep it spinning.

May Dezrel forgive me. I abandoned hope at a lasting Balance, and gave my blessing to Ashhur. Death rewarded my selfishness. Take my gifts, daughter. Do what must be done.

It was the blessing she needed. The final confirmation that Mother would aid her in the path ahead.

"Let it end," Tessanna whispered. "Let neither rule. Let the balance fall aside, and be judged not by brother gods."

With a wave of her hand and twist of her fingers, the ground cracked. A chasm opened between the armies, forming into a slight 'v' so that the beast-men were separated from both friends and foes. Tessanna hovered above them all, the goddess whom all eyes must look upon. The air was electric, and the few who dared near her, be they angel or fallen, she cast aside with a mere glare that lit their wings aflame.

"Army of the Vile!" she bellowed. "Hear me!"

Whose words did she speak? She didn't know, but her heart ached for these poor creatures. Ahaesarus had dragged them here as slaves, forced them to fight a war they cared nothing about, for a reward they would never receive.

"For generations you have suffered, abandoned and unloved, for crimes committed by your forefathers," she told the beast-men. She cast her attention to the wolf-men, the bird-men, and the hyena-men. "You labored in the wretched wasteland of Kal'droth for siding with Karak in a war that ended centuries past. Let your curse be lifted. The North is yours. Live on lush soil, and hunt plentiful forests. The barren wasteland of the Vile Wedge is your cage no longer. Cast it aside. Make life anew, and be it one of peace, if you are to keep it."

Brief words of magic floated from her lips, tearing open a portal over fifty feet in diameter. It swirled with blue light, and white mist poured out of it as magic crackled across its surface. Through that dream-like haze, all could see the abandoned lands of the North. The races of the Vile hesitated only a moment before charging straight into its center. Tessanna felt a slight tug on her mind at their passage, but with them through, she banished the portal. It sealed with a roar of thunder.

All eyes were upon her now—angels and fallen, mages of the council and surviving members of the Eschaton, human soldiers from both sides, and even the remaining undead. It should have unnerved her. Instead it put a dark grin upon her face. She felt the first hint of happiness since watching her beloved Qurrah die in the form of another with his throat cut.

I want to bathe the land with fire, she'd told Harruq. Time had cooled her rage, but not her ambition. Perhaps not all the world, but those responsible for breaking it.

"Let there be no balance," she decreed. "Let there be no winner. I free Dezrel from your grasp. I free her from your war. Whatever remnants that endure, seek peace if you are wise, for conquest shall be beyond you."

Azariah and the council mages sought to bring her down, combining their attacks, a sudden barrage of fire, ice, and lightning, in an attempt to overwhelm her. Tessanna gritted her teeth and surrounded herself with a translucent shield. The assaulting magic burst across its surface, spreading thin cracks, but her resolve would not be broken, nor her shield. Deep clouds formed a halo in the sky above. The ground rumbled with anticipation.

There was a time she had screamed a similar demand. Now she whispered it.

"No more daughters. Let me be the last. Give me the power of the Weave, dearest Mother. Give me my birthright. Give me my wings."

From her shoulders burst her wings, her true wings, not the faint ethereal shadows she sometimes manifested. They were deep as midnight, without light or texture beyond the singular, infinite depth of the void. They stretched for hundreds of feet behind her, filling the entire sky. They flapped once, and a thousand feathers flew from them like leaves in an autumn wind. Tessanna lifted her arms and felt the power of creation swelling within her breast. She forced that magic to flow through her body, down her arms and out her fingertips to collect into a swirling orb of concentrated fury. It was a perfect sphere of elemental power. Fire swirled along its surface. Ice crackled in its depths. Lightning thundered within like an imprisoned storm. Deeper and deeper, the magic flowed. Deeper and deeper, it pooled. It built in her mind like a tangible manifestation of all her grief. Qurrah's face floated upon it. She imagined him watching her, and she wondered if he would praise her choice or condemn it.

  Another flap of her wings, whose lengths stretched across the entire horizon, whose darkness blotted out the sun and covered the entire battlefield in unnatural night. Her hands caressed the sphere. Her black eyes looked to Ahaesarus, to Azariah, and it was to both divine kings she offered a most deserving gift.

  "This day, I break your crowns."

  Tessanna opened her gift.

  The sky exploded. Lightning led the way, a thousand white-hot veins leaping from angel to angel. It cared not if they were those loyal to Ashhur or the fallen allies of Azariah. Both sides died, nearly half their number in an instant. Fire and ice followed, the fire unleashed in great plumes larger than buildings and billowing out as if belched from a legion of dragons. The ice intermixed with it, defying its heat, its razor-sharp edges sparkling as they slashed through the ground armies and undead without care for their armor. The torrent blasted outward, seemingly never ending. Tessanna fueled it with her hatred. She flooded it with her pain and sorrow. Her disgust would be made manifest for these soldiers of human gods that had twice destroyed the world and appeared all too eager for a third.

  Bolt after bolt slammed the battlefield, spreading further cracks beyond the chasm she had opened up for the beast-men. Angels fled in all directions, their wings flapping at their hardest to

The King of the Fallen

outrun the destruction. The three members of the Council collected their power together to form a shield, and it was only their combined might that allowed them to withstand the onslaught. The same could not be said for the undead, whom she crushed like the disgusting ants they were.

The sky darkened with smoke as the explosion continued onward, shadowing even that which her wings did not touch. The human soldiers of both armies tossed aside their weapons and fled, wanting nothing but to escape the frozen rain that slaughtered them with a million ice-tipped spears.

Tessanna guided the power with little mental nudges. The members of the Eschaton, she would spare. Ludicrous as it may seem given the context of her life, she viewed them as friends. The fire did not consume Tarlak Eschaton. The ice did not freeze Aurelia Thyne Tun. Lightning struck all around Harruq, but he himself was not brought low. It was a selfish act, she knew. But at the end of all things, after the misery she had suffered, she felt she deserved a bit of selfishness.

I want to slaughter everything and everyone until I create a land of corpses.

A land of corpses. It was within her reach. She need only continue to channel Celestia's power.

The explosion continued rolling outward in all directions. Fire licked from the sky into the nearby forests. Lightning gashed the grasslands. Deep cracks split the earth for miles in all directions, traveling on and on like the thinly frozen surface of a pond breaking beneath too much weight. Scream. All she had to do was scream. Let her mind blank. Let her hatred do the rest. Her whole life, she had been death and misfortune to those who knew her. Why not allow it to swallow all of Dezrel? Why not give the horrid, broken land some measure of peace, to become a place only the wild animals could claim?

But there were still a few she loved. She would not deny little Aubrienna Tun a world to live, even if it were a dark and troubled one. Nor would she take Aubby's parents from her. So let her have a world. Let her survive. With an unspoken command, Tessanna ensured the destruction would not swallow the world by instead allowing it to swallow herself. Magic tore through her own body. Fire burned across her flesh. Her wings shattered into long thin ribbons of darkness that dissolved like smoke upon the wind her own attack had unleashed. A scream escaped her, a banshee howl that somehow was silent to her own ears despite the raw pain it tore into her throat. Blood followed, lacerations opening across her arms and legs from shards of ice. Once again, she cut herself, and the grim realization would have made her laugh if not for the perpetual scream.

The fire faded. The storm abated. Tessanna fell, her body limp, her magic spent.

Anger and disbelief swarmed through the survivors of both forces, whose numbers marked perhaps a tenth of what they had begun their battle with. Soldiers below unleashed what few arrows they still possessed. The leaders of both sides flew toward her, Ahaesarus with his sword, Azariah with his magic.

Tessanna smiled as she plummeted, her long hair whipping across her face and neck. With their numbers so thoroughly decimated, they would hold humanity hostage no longer. Perhaps not immediately, not while humanity licked its wounds, but this was the first pangs of birth, the bloody, brutal labor of the world it would one day deliver. She would not see it. This fact did not sadden her. She had fulfilled whatever purpose had been destined to her. Only one person mattered now, and as her battered body fell, she spoke words that somehow pierced the chaos and the screams.

But a moment, her lover had said. He was so very right.

"I'm coming, Qurrah."

She glanced away from the sky long enough to see fire leap from Azariah's hands. Multiple arrows pierced her flesh. But it was the trio of Council mages that struck the killing blow, pooling their rage into a bolt of lightning from the sky that pierced straight through her forehead and into her heart. Ending the life of the final Daughter of Balance.

And sending her home.

24

Azariah paced before the dying fire. If given the choice, he'd have flown all the way back to Mordeina instead of resting for the night, but the earthbound humans and undead did not allow for that option. So they camped, and he brooded, the solitude of the open fields thoroughly unwelcome. He wanted to be in his tower, with his books and spells. He wanted to read Velixar's journal and prepare magical runes.

He wanted to escape this damn, wretched world of Dezrel once and for all.

Judarius landed before him. "The representatives of the Council wish to speak with you," the mighty angel said, crossing his arms and frowning. "I pray you have not separated yourself from our forces so you may sulk in private."

"Sulk? No, brother, I do not sulk. I rage. What should have been our triumph was instead turned into a farce."

"The goddess interfered," Judarius said. He seemed to be taking the defeat surprisingly well. "As she has always interfered. At some point we should stop being surprised by the interventions and instead anticipate them."

Azariah had not been able to banish the image of Tessanna Tun's power completely unleashed from his mind. To pretend they could have anticipated that was asinine, though he did not bother to argue so with his brother. The Daughter of Balance had unleashed the fury of the entire Weave upon that battlefield. The only glimmer of hope was that she had directed her ire upon both sides.

"Ahaesarus's forces were equally devastated," Azariah said. "They will not be able to give chase unless they wish to leave a trail of dead behind. While they lick their wounds, we will regroup. Victory is not lost."

"Don't tell that to me," Judarius said. "Tell that to them."

He gestured behind him, to the three approaching representatives of the Council of Mages. They walked proudly, but their faces were sunken, the tell-tale signs of exhaustion heavy on their mortal faces. Azariah crossed his arms and waited. What now?

The mage Anora stood front and center. Dark circles surrounded her, and her skin bore an unhealthy paleness that signified the tremendous effort she had exerted in the day's battle. One of her long, dangling silver earrings had melted and now hung from her earlobe in a misshapen blob. Tessanna's tremendous assault, perhaps? Azariah wondered if Anora had even noticed. Under different circumstances, they might have celebrated felling a daughter of balance, but tonight they looked beaten and cowed. Of the three members of the Council present, Anora was the highest-ranking, and it seemed she would be the one to do the talking.

"Greetings, King of the Fallen," said Anora. "I thank you for accepting a meeting at such a late hour."

He'd not exactly been given a choice, but Azariah didn't bother to argue that point. "Worry not about the time. Speak your mind, and without games or running round in circles. I am in no mood for pleasantries and hidden motives."

"Then I shall speak plainly," Anora said. "In my capacity as representative for the Council, I deem it no longer viable to continue supporting your kingdom in this war. My fellow mages and I shall return to our tower."

"You would betray me?"

"It is not a betrayal if one party in an agreement withdraws due to the other side no longer being able to fulfill its obligation. If it soothes your pride, we will not be siding with Ahaesarus, or bringing our magic to bear against you. We are simply withdrawing back to our towers."

This foul day was only getting fouler. Azariah tried to think through matters rationally, to conjure an appeal that would work on the notoriously fickle and reclusive mages, but he found himself grasping at air.

"Your leaders made a promise," he argued, and it sounded pitiful even to his own ears.

"And *your* promise, may I remind you, was that the nation of Ker would be handed over into our control once you overthrew the Henley family and conquered Angkar," Anora told him. "Pray tell me, angel, when do you believe your fallen will have the numbers to lay siege to Angkar? This year? This decade? This *century?*"

Azariah took a threatening step toward her. "You shall address me as king, not angel. You already insult me as you renege on promises made. Do not insult me further."

Anora's face remained passive as glass, yet he could sense the disdain bubbling just beneath her skin.

"Forgive me, your highness," she said. "I cannot in good conscience send more of my fellow Council members to their deaths for a promise I no longer believe you capable of fulfilling."

"That is preposterous," Azariah said. "You think there is nothing to gain by maintaining an alliance? That my fallen present no threat to your towers? Things are not so dire as you would paint them. Ahaesarus's forces suffered just as greatly under Tessanna's explosion of magic. I still have ears, and receive word from the south. Ker's forces are devastated, and by a priest of Ashhur no less. The beast-men who would fight for Ahaesarus are gone, presumably to a land they now believe their own. Victory remains before us, and grows with each day I perfect my magic. Reconsider, Anora. Do not give in to reactionary fear. Roand knew better. You would be wise to remember his decisions, and the logic behind them."

The argument crashed off her like water off a duck's back. "Roand the Flame made a deal with you to bring Avlimar crashing to the ground because he feared humanity would no longer have a voice in our own rule. It was never altruistic, for the daydreams of a hypothetical kingdom run by our Council have always lingered in our towers. Ruling Ker may no longer be an outcome available to us, but Roand's hope has already been realized. The daughter of balance forced it upon us with her fury. Karak? Ashhur? Neither of you possess the numbers and influence to conquer the world. And unless the sky splits open and the brother gods send another wave of angels and demons, humanity shall slowly retake control over our fates."

The rage Azariah felt must have been made plain on his face, for the woman took a careful step backward and narrowed her gaze.

"We would remain neutral in this fight, as we often do in political matters," she continued, smiling oh-so-pleasantly. "Unless you attempt to murder me here and now during a peaceful, diplomatic meeting. Your reign hangs by a thread, Azariah. How likely do you think you can hold on with the Council of Mages as your enemy?"

"Be gone," Azariah said, and spat a blob of bloody saliva at her feet. "Never sully my presence again. We walk a hard road, and we shall do it alone if we must to ensure Dezrel becomes the Paradise it was always envisioned to be."

The proud mage at least had the decency to bow before she turned, opened a swirling blue portal, and stepped through with her fellows. The portal swirled shut with a loud hiss of air, followed by stillness. Azariah glared at the empty space, his tired mind already scrambling to mitigate the disaster.

"As always, when we put our faith in human hands, we suffer," Judarius said. He'd watched the entire exchange in silence, and by his mild, bemused tone, it seemed he had been aware of the mages' intentions to withdraw beforehand. Azariah took in a long, deep breath. If his brother could be calm, then so could he.

"You expected this?" he asked.

"Expected?" the larger angel said. "Yes, though not by any understanding of their politics or inner squabbles. They're cowards at heart, Azariah. What the daughter of balance did, it shocked them to their core. They witnessed magic beyond any they've imagined. They thought themselves the pinnacle of spellcasting, and Tessanna revealed to them that they are little more than babes compared to the goddess and her chosen. Of course they've tucked their tails and fled."

Maddening as it was, could Azariah truly blame them? Memories of the explosion still echoed in his mind. It was as if the Weave itself had ripped into the material world. The elements had raged with such power it made a mockery of the swords and arrows of the mortal combatants. For one brief moment, when Tessanna's voice had thundered across the battlefield, Azariah had believed Celestia herself had arrived to condemn them all. He'd almost welcomed it. There would have been something honorable about the goddess abandoning her lying claims of neutrality and balance and instead outright admitted to take Ashhur's side, as she always had since the earliest days of Dezrel. At the very least, she could have stridden the battlefield herself instead of relying on her precious, long-suffering daughters.

"And so the cowards leave, and we must soldier on to make amends," Azariah said. He smirked at his brother. "You seem remarkably calm about all of this."

Judarius laughed, without mirth, without joy. "Never did I think this would be easy. We labor to succeed where gods and a goddess have failed. Do not all heroes stumble and encounter difficult times? I expect no differently for us, and we face a greater challenge than any who walked before. These stubborn children will bow before us, brother. We will succeed. It's just going to take more sweat, and more blood."

"And more killing."

"If that's what it takes," Judarius said, shrugging.

Azariah crossed his arms and overlooked the encampment of his survivors. After such a defeat, retreat to Mordeina was the only option. Ahaesarus would give chase, which meant another battle relatively soon. As the defender, he could decide the choice of battlefield.

"They won't lay siege to us," he said, thinking aloud. "They know we will not surrender, nor with our magic and wings can we be starved into submission. Devlimar was never built with war in mind. We should withdraw all our forces to the inner castle of Mordeina. My undead can guard the outer walls. We'll keep our wings close, and our human soldiers where they can best force our foes into choke points."

"I agree," said Judarius. He put a hand on Azariah's shoulder. "Let the humans and undead clash. It is wing against wing that will decide this war. Do not fret. Our numbers are still greater. This war will yet be ours."

Azariah wished he could share his brother's optimism. He pointed to the distant campfires, not of his own army, but the far specks of those belonging to Ahaesarus. A thought came to him, unwelcome but undeniable. To make his final stand at Mordeina…at the place of his visions…

"What if we do not retreat at all?" he asked. "What if we make a stand here?"

"And forfeit fortified defenses, walls, and ambush points of the city?" Judarius asked withdrew his hand. "Why would we do this voluntarily? And what of your fallback plan with the dragon?"

"Our ground forces may be weaker, but we could still control the skies," Azariah insisted. "There is some merit. We need not rely on the dark dragon."

His brother crossed his arms. What color remained in his ashen gray eyes smoldered in the moonlight.

"This is about the Godslayer, isn't it?"

Azariah almost denied it out of pride, but he would not stain himself with a lie.

"I saw a thousand fates," he said softly. "In all of them, I died at the hands of the half-orc. In all them, I died in the human city of Mordeina."

"So you'd throw our troops away, all because you never saw yourself dying on a grassy field?" Judarius asked. "You surprise me, brother. I thought you braver than that. I thought you one to spit in the eye of fate and create your own. Celestia deceives. She lies. Yet you would abandon all hope? Shall I order our brethren to surrender to execution, give up the hope of Paradise? I will not have us die for a future you yourself refuse to believe is possible. Fly high and fly proud, or I will not fly with you at all."

Yet again, Azariah felt the signs of a potential coup. Judarius commanded the loyalty and respect of all the fallen. Would they still honor Azariah if it came to blows between them? The warriors among their numbers, certainly, but what of the priest caste Azariah had begun training in magic?

No, it was foolish to think on such things. The moment they turned on themselves, the hope of Paradise died. Victory was already a terrible struggle, and they would never achieve it should they betray one another. Azariah smiled, and his hatred of Ashhur grew. He did not feel the joy he should feel. The curse upon him denied him the sensations of happiness and warmth that came with knowing he was trusted so greatly by his brother. This wasn't a threat of a coup. It was Judarius proclaiming to him he'd die believing in Azariah's dreams rather than submit to the cursed death Ashhur demanded of them.

"Even now, you believe in me?" he asked. A lone tear trickled down his face, and when he wiped it away, he saw it was red with blood. "Even now, you would join me in challenging a fate declared by the goddess?"

Judarius removed his mace from his back and held it before him while dropping to one knee. It was an act of honor, of servitude, and made Azariah's bloody tears fall all the faster.

"Hold faith," the fallen angel said. "Hold faith in us, faith in our cause, and for once, hold faith in me. The Godslayer's bones will break under my mace. Celestia believes the half-orc will take your life? Then let us prove her yet again a liar when I smash his skull flat upon the castle steps. Damn her fate, and damn her lies. This war is ours, my brother. No matter how many lives it takes, we shall bring peace to Paradise."

25

"It seems every day we suffer through another funeral," Aurelia said. She knelt before the freshly dug grave in which Tessanna's body had been buried, or at least what was left of it after she fell from the sky. Harruq had chosen the location, at the base of a tree growing atop a hill, positioned so that sunlight would shine directly on her tombstone only during sunset. If there was ever a time of day Tessanna associated with, it was most certainly twilight. Harruq knelt beside her, his right hand clutching her left, while Tarlak quietly leaned against the tree.

"She should have been buried with Qurrah," her husband said. "But Azariah left us no body to bury."

Aurelia leaned her head on his shoulder. Harruq had been uncharacteristically dour lately, not that she blamed him. Losing Qurrah had left a scar that would never heal. Tessanna, though? She was a far more complicated presence throughout their life. Even now, Aurelia struggled with how to feel. Not joy, certainly not joy. Pity? Sorrow? Dare she admit it, relief?

"For so long, she lived in isolation," Aurelia said. She pressed her free hand into the dirt. This would be the closest to a prayer she might offer the woman. Though human, Tessanna was most certainly a creation of the elven goddess...but Aurelia's connection to Celestia wasn't exactly on the greatest of terms, either. "Her mind broken. The world a constant betrayal. She lived with a burden knowing her divine mother sought her to destroy and break in a futile attempt to maintain a balance rapidly spiraling out of control. I pray...I pray Celestia now gives her the peace she was long denied."

"Peace," Tarlak said. He crossed his arms over his chest. "None of us get to have any peace. I almost envy her."

"It is a sad soul that envies the dead," Aurelia said, finding his mood in poor taste.

"Perhaps. Remind me to ask Delysia about that the next time I see her."

Harruq released Aurelia's hand as he stood. "I expect better of you," he snapped at the wizard. "Be respectful, or fuck off."

Tarlak looked away, his face flushed red. Odd as it sounded, the sight made Aurelia feel better. Even the brash, egotistical wizard knew his behavior was inappropriate. Tarlak muttered something to himself and then pushed off from the tree. He touched the gravestone, which to his credit he had carved with his magic, forming the stone into a pair of black wings bearing the name Tessanna Delone Tun in their center.

"Respectful," he said, shaking his head. "I don't know if I have it in me to be respectful. I'm tired. We're all tired. We...my Eschaton, we had a tradition for a while. If we lost a member, we burned something valuable of our own as a way to remind ourselves that whatever meager possession we lost, it was nothing compared to the loss of our friend. The loss of *family*. When Aullienna died I broke my staff and set it upon the pyre. A fine tradition, or so I thought. It helped keep me strong as I delivered the speech no one else had the strength to give."

Tarlak took a moment to gather himself. Aurelia trembled at her own remembrance of that solemn day.

"Could we even keep that tradition?" he asked when he continued. "We've been chased out of house and home so many times now. What possessions have we left? What objects have we to cling to that give us comfort? And what would I offer on a pyre for the terrifying, incredible woman that was Tessanna? She with magic that could shape the entire world?"

"You could offer her your pointy hat," Harruq said, slapping the morose wizard on the arm and chuckling despite the tears that ran down his cheeks. Tarlak stared at him, frozen in place with a mixture of sorrow and morbid humor etched on his face. At last he broke out into a laugh.

"Gods damn it," he said. "Tess was a daughter of balance, with power that rivaled the goddess herself. Her actions led to the deaths of so many. She ripped a hole in the world to let in Thulos's war demons. She demanded Delysia's death. And yet...and yet I feel no pleasure in her passing. Instead I look around, and my heart breaks. A woman whose decisions saved and destroyed cities, who unleashed armies, who made gods quake with fear...and now we stand at her funeral," he gestured about the barren hill, "with a mere three people come to mourn her.

"Is this the fate of us heroes and villains? To watch our friends and family fall one by one, with ever-dwindling survivors to mourn over us as the rest of the uncaring world moves on?" His lips quivered, and suddenly an entire dam of emotion broke free. He could barely manage the words fumbling from his mouth. "I shouldn't have to give a speech, damn it. I'm so tired of giving these speeches. I'm so tired of standing over these graves. Haern, Brug, Aully, Mira, Qurrah, Tess, Lathaar, Delysia...when does it stop? Damn it all. Gods damn it all."

Aurelia rose to her feet, slipped past her husband, and went to the sobbing wizard. She had known him for so long now, and she knew how much of his joyful persona was an act he put on for others. In his every joke, every laugh, he sought to improve the lives of those who knew him. It was a drain, of course, but his personality and strength were incredible, even for a human. He gave, and he gave, and now she saw him convinced he had nothing left to give. It wasn't true, of course, but it would *become* true if he believed it for long enough.

"I've never forgotten the words you spoke," she said. She recited them slowly, calmly, with none of his humor or cadence but all of his sincerity. "'My hurt, I'm sure it pales, but it's there, and Ashhur help me should such a day as this come to my heart.' But it did come to your heart, Tarlak. It came again and again, to you, and to all of us." She wrapped her arms around him, and he graciously accepted her embrace. She felt him trembling, some deep part of him long since broken now finally ripped open and exposed. "Tessanna is the reason some of that hurt befell us. Grieve not for her, if you must. But grieve for the hurt she felt, and the hurt she spread, and the life she might have lived if this world were not so cruel. Grieve for the guilt that broke her. Grieve for the hope that guided her to sacrifice everything. Her, and Qurrah, they've both given everything to make amends. I'll shed my tears, and I'll whisper my prayers, and I'll do my best to ensure their sacrifices were not offered in vain."

"And when it comes for us?" Tarlak asked. "When it's you I need to give a speech over? Or your husband? What then?"

"Well, if it's me, I'll get a damn parade," Harruq said. "I'm the Godslayer, after all."

Tarlak pulled away from Aurelia, shook his head, and laughed. "Harruq, you're lucky I don't turn you into a damn mudskipper for that. Leave the bad jokes to yours truly."

The wizard trudged down the hill. Aurelia and Harruq remained at Tessanna's grave, she with her arms tucked around his waist. Her gaze fell to the freshly dug soil. It felt wrong to leave so quickly despite having nothing else to say, so they lingered, solemn and silent. Honestly, it was likely all Tessanna would have wanted. What she would not have wanted, however, was the arrival of Ahaesarus from the sky.

"We move out with the dawn," the angel said after he gently touched down on the opposite side of the gravestone. "With Azariah's forces so decimated, we should have the advantage when we assault Mordeina."

"Interrupting a funeral to speak strategy is in ill taste," Aurelia couldn't help but snip.

"What I find in ill taste is your mourning of this woman. She struck down my angels as well as Azariah's, and her intrusion cost me the army of beast-men I labored to bring south. I know she was important to your history, but it was her hand that brought Thulos's war demons into this world. Her legacy is one of death and chaos."

"So was Qurrah's," Harruq said, a dangerous edge to his voice. "He was forgiven, and made amends. Is the same not allowed of her?"

"I speak of actions she wrought earlier today," Ahaesarus said. "Not atoned-for crimes made in years past."

"And now she lies within a grave, to be judged by the gods and goddess who lorded over her life," Aurelia said. "Do not come here and tell me how to grieve, angel. It will not end well for you."

Ahaesarus sighed over-dramatically and shrugged.

"If you so insist, elf. Her damage was great, but we shall prevail. In that, I promise."

He flew off, and Aurelia was glad to be free of his presence. She had never truly been comfortable around the angels, not because of their otherworldly nature, but of how similar they were to other humans despite their physical differences. It was unnerving, like wood dolls come to life with human souls.

"We should get back to Aubby," Harruq said after a time. They'd left Aubrienna in Jerico's care. The paladin had confessed himself too conflicted to attend the meager funeral. Aurelia, while disappointed, did not blame him. After Veldaren's fall, Jerico had been captured by Velixar, and been subjected to torture both physical and mental in an attempt to break his faith in Ashhur. The paladin never talked of it, but she knew Tessanna had played a key part in that suffering.

"I will follow later." She planted a kiss on Harruq's cheek. "Possibly several hours later. Do not worry."

"All right, I won't," he said, despite him obviously starting to worry immediately. "Stay safe."

He left, following the same path Tarlak had taken, back toward the army encampment. Finally alone, Aurelia knelt above the grave and dipped her hands into the dark earth. She let the soil cake across her hands, let it prepare her mind in a way she knew she needed. Tonight would be difficult, but it was an act she had put off long enough. She was the daughter of Kindren and Aullienna Thyne, and arguably the strongest elf left alive carrying the gift of magic within her blood. She would not be ignored. Her prayer would not go unheeded.

Tessanna, like Mira before her, had been a daughter of balance. In Aurelia's heart, she knew it was time to speak with their Mother.

To travel the distance took a few portals cast in succession, but having to transport solely herself made the burden an easy one for her to bear. Aurelia crossed hundreds of miles within minutes. She passed the grasslands south of Mordeina with a single step. Another portal took her to the edge of Lake Cor. The final portal was the hardest, but not due to the magical effort required. It was the memories that held her back. It'd been so long since she'd been there. So long, but return she would. If there was any one place Celestia would hear her prayer, it would be in the ruins of the fallen elven city of Dezerea.

The world shifted as she exited, the sparkling lake replaced with towering trees.

"I'm home," Aurelia whispered.

In the earliest days of her childhood, Dezerea had been a wondrous city. The trees that grew in its forest were the tallest in all the world, and from those branches the elves had built interlocking homes and a dizzying array of bridges. It wasn't only trees, though, for all of nature had been used with reverence. Stone towers had been pulled from the earth and carved with magic into edifices far more flowing and delicate than any human construction. The grandest of all had been the emerald tower, Palace Thyne, in the very heart of the city.

Then came the fires. King Baedan's campaign had been one of complete and utter cruelty, harnessing the prejudices of his people to blame the elves for every single ill that befell the kingdom of man. He didn't send his soldiers, not at first. He sent the poor, the desperate, even prisoners from his jails. He armed them with oil, torches, and a simple command to burn. And burn they did, from every possible edge of the forest, without ceasing. The elves posted guards, but how did one protect miles of forest from something as simple as a torch? Aurelia's parents had conjured rainstorms to combat the spread. They'd opened chasms in the ground to form control lines. It was never enough.

Aurelia knelt in a patch of tall grass, and a sparkling glint reflecting the setting sun caught her eye. A necklace of elven construction, the gold molded not by hands but by the touch of magic, the sapphires between the chains each carved into crescent moons. Aurelia held the necklace in hand, wondering at the fate of its former owner. Had they died in the fires? Beneath the cavalry that chased after them? Perhaps this had been dropped by one of the ten spellcasters who made their final stand at the Corinth Bridge, whose destruction and slaughter had led to its renaming as the Bloodbrick.

"So much hatred," Aurelia whispered. "So much suffering and death. Will you answer for none of it, Celestia?"

She walked what had once been the road through the heart of the city. The smooth stone was cracked throughout, grass and weeds occupying each and every exposed crevice. Most of the trees were still barren, their lives claimed by the fire even if they still towered overhead. The buildings and bridges were long gone but for a few scattered remnants clinging on with stubborn nails and weathered ropes. The stone structures remained, albeit blackened from the tremendous fire and stripped of any former decorations. Still, there were signs of life returning. New trees grew about the old, and the forest floor was as lush with life as ever.

Aurelia tried to take hope from the regrowth as she approached the emerald palace which bore her family name. Within its shadow she knelt, and waited as the sun set. She held the necklace in her hands, twirling Celestia's symbol of the moon slowly as she pondered what to pray. Even for an elf, she had witnessed far too much death and destruction. While most of her kin had avoided humanity, and been dragged into the second Gods' War reluctantly, she had witnessed it at its very beginnings when Karak's prophet, Velixar, recruited the two half-orc brothers to aid him in sparking the battle at Woodhaven. It was appropriate, she thought, so very appropriate.

Elves suffered so the human gods could fight their war. Was that not the way of Dezrel?

Night fell, and the moon rose. Aurelia felt a change come over her, like a gust of cool night air chasing away a hot summer day. The hooting and chirps of the night birds that sang for her during her wait suddenly ceased. No wolf or coyote dared howl. She closed her eyes and stood. Despite all her preparation, she knew not what to say, so she spoke her heart's most painful truth.

"I know you awaken, Celestia. And I know you watch with keen eyes. Speak with me, goddess. I demand that right."

"Demand?" asked a soft, feminine voice. "Who are you to make demands?"

Aurelia opened her eyes to witness the presence of her goddess. She was beautiful, with features as delicate as crystal. Divine radiance shimmered about her form in tiny twinkling lights like fireflies. Her dress, while smooth as silk, looked as if carved from the moon itself. Yes the most striking thing about her was how *familiar* she appeared. Her eyes were pools of night. Her skin was pale as moonlight. Her long dark hair trailed all the way to her ankles, bound with silver thread every two feet. If Tessanna or Mira had been born of elven blood, this was the form Aurelia would have imagined.

"The child of Kindren and Aullienna Thyne," Aurelia said. She pulled back her shoulders and stood to her full height, needing the pause to gather her strength. To stand before Celestia took an incredible force of will. Even now, the urge to kneel and avert her eyes was extreme.

"And your birthright guarantees presence with a goddess?" Celestia asked.

"Not my birthright, but the deeds I have accomplished, in both my name and yours. With each passing day our world slides closer toward a nameless destruction. Is it wrong of me to speak with the goddess who raised the mountains, planted the forests, and crafted the sand-swept shores?"

Celestia crossed her arms. Her moon-dress rippled like calm water now disturbed.

"Your demand may be prideful and lacking, but I grace you with my presence nonetheless. What do you seek, child? What need brings you here, to these ruins?"

"What need?" Aurelia thought of the tremendous bolt of lightning that crashed down upon Tessanna, the retribution brought against her for banishing the beast-men and tearing apart angels both loyal and fallen. "The last of your daughters of balance, Tessanna Delone Tun, lies in a grave. You ask what need brings me here? I come to see if you watch us, my goddess. I come to see if you still cast your eyes upon our meager souls, or if you have abandoned us completely."

Celestia stepped closer. Her feet hovered an inch above the ground, yet the grass buckled as if crushed underneath a tremendous weight.

"Abandoned?" she asked. "How have I abandoned you? Do I not send my own flesh and blood to guide the balance?"

Aurelia knew she walked a dangerous road, but she would not temper her words with caution. That just wasn't her. She was the rebellious elf who lived among the humans and married a half-orc. She would not hold her tongue, not even to a goddess.

"That balance you so preciously guard? That is *their* balance, between their gods, and their war. What of *your* children? Where were you when Dezerea burned and her people were chased east? Where were you when my mother and father sacrificed their lives upon the Bloodbrick? What balance do you cherish when you watch our numbers dwindle, our cities fall to ruin, and our people hide in forests watching humanity steadily destroy all that was once majestic and grand?"

If Celestia struck her dead right then and there, Aurelia would not have been surprised, so great was the anger upon the goddess's face.

"My heart has wept for you with every step you take," Celestia said. "But I made a promise to the human gods, and I shall keep it until the sun rises in the west and sets in the east."

"Damn your promises," Aurelia seethed. "Your eyes and heart should have been upon *us,* but they are not, and have not been since you first laid with Ashhur in the earliest days of creation. The brother gods and their human children would break the world you built. The balance you strove to maintain is beyond repair, and the daughters you birthed to save it are dead. Give me their gift. Let me at least complete one facet of their impossible task."

"And what would you do with that gift?" Celestia asked. Strangely, the divine being seemed curious. At this, Aurelia smiled darkly.

"I would slay her murderers, my goddess. The edifices of power throughout Dezrel are crumbling. Jerico tells me the Citadel has fallen. Veldaren is in ruins. Avlimar crashed to the dirt, and tomorrow we march upon Devlimar. Yet a pillar of human arrogance remains. This may not be our final war, but I would still rid us of a sickness that has infected Dezrel for far too many centuries."

She'd been afraid to voice her concern since the battle, for to give it words risked confessing to Harruq her plan to solve it. But the members of the Council of Mages proved themselves too dangerous to allow to go on unchecked. They had aided Azariah

The King of the Fallen

in bringing Avlimar down, destroyed Antonil's army, and sent assassins to kill Aubrienna and Gregory. All the power in the world to do good, and they sought only to lurk safely away from the people of Dezrel in their twin towers, secretly manipulating events as they saw fit.

And then when Tessanna sought to do the most good she could for all of Dezrel, to throw the course of fate back into the hands of humans...the members of that council had taken her life with a bolt of lightning from the heavens.

"For whose benefit do you ask this gift?" Celestia asked after a moment of silence. "Is it for elven-kind? Or is it your own revenge?"

There was no lying to a goddess, so she admitted the truth.

"Not so long ago, Tessanna told me husband that she wished nothing more than to tear the world down to its foundation. I would honor her memory. Let it be revenge. Let it be for a better world. Let it be many things that fate may one day decide. I do not care. My course is set. My path is chosen. All that matters is if I walk it alone, or with your blessing."

Aurelia bowed her head, closed her eyes, and waited. This was it. The final judgment. Would her goddess uplift her, or condemn her? Seconds dragged long, and it seemed a great debate raged within Celestia. At last she spoke, and though Aurelia braced herself for pain and thunder, she received only tired words.

"I cherish all life, Aurelia, daughter of Kindren and Aullienna. Yet I have watched the slaughter go unabated since the very first grains of sand fell through Dezrel's hourglass. You bear our lessons. You know our teachings. Our wisdom has been passed down through stories and scripture, yet do we witness its fruition? No, meager elf, we do not. We watch as brother murders brother. We watch as mankind labels a stranger inhuman, and sacrifices him upon twin altars of greed and power. Elf, orc, human, and beast, all murdering one another without ceasing. And as you stand in pools of blood you yourselves have spilled, you scream up at us in the heavens that same maddening question: *why?*"

Celestia rose higher off the ground. The leaves of the trees about her withered, the trunks blackened and burst into flame. The moon in the sky melted as the stars streaked by like comets. Aurelia stood within an indescribable maelstrom of magic and creation and felt the very rules of existence start to tremble, yet she knew this was but a fraction of the power that once founded Dezrel.

Aurelia fell to her knees and bowed her head to the divine being who had blessed their world with life.

"Am I cruel to let humanity suffer the fruits of its own labors?" said the goddess. "Am I cruel to diminish slaughter and bloodshed, and seek to guide with the softest hand through my chosen daughters instead of the great floods and fires you mortals so richly deserve? What path do I take when all lead to death, despite my heart's desire being nothing more than to create life and happiness? I *tire* of this, little elf. The prayers of joy, and the laughter of my children, pales in comparison to the suffering I am expected to excise. Days pass, each an eternity to one of my nature, and throughout every sprawling century these nails pound into my flesh, these selfish wants masquerading as heartfelt prayers poison my blood. I tire, Aurelia. I tire, so greatly I tire, yet to slumber while Dezrel languishes would be an even greater crime."

The maelstrom ceased. Celestia's light dimmed. She suddenly looked so mortal, so very elvish. She bent down, her hands gently cupping Aurelia's face, and she whispered now instead of roaring. Her eyes, solid black windows into an infinite void, locked her in their gaze.

"If you would have my power, then take it. I am here as always, my child. Do not blame the river for your thirst if you are not willing to walk the harsh road to its banks. Do you desire the wings of my daughters? Scream that desire. Bellow to the heavens your rage. Make me believe, and I shall reward you with a gift to make the mortal realms tremble."

The physical manifestation of the goddess vanished, but her presence remained. Aurelia felt it in the air. She heard it in the rustle of leaves and grass. Chills coursed up and down her spine. Her heart felt ready to explode out from her chest, for she felt herself standing on a precipice. One more step and the fury of a goddess would be hers.

"Not yet," she whispered. "Do not give it to me yet."

Destination firmly in mind, she opened another portal. Aurelia left the ruins of Dezerea behind and crossed many more miles to the waters of the Rigon.

26

Two grand towers loomed before Aurelia Tun. On the eastern side of the river was the crimson tower of the apprentices. On the western side, darker than the night itself, the black spire belonging to the masters. The single bridge linking them rose high above the rivers, the red and black bricks interlocking in a checkered pattern. From within these two buildings the Council of Mages taught, trained, and plotted.

Aurelia strode deliberately toward the towers, her feet sinking into the muddy soil of the Rigon's banks. Wind blew about her, and only her. The magical wards defending the twin towers were visible to her eyes, and they were innumerable. They would turn aside all teleportation magic, reflect all elemental attacks, and render useless attempts to manipulate the earth or warp the stone. But Celestia was the source of all magic, the birthing river of its power, and it cared not for even the most intricately carved rune. Those within did not realize her presence, not yet.

But they would.

"The elite of humanity," she whispered into the night. "Can you withstand the disdain of a god?"

The maelstrom of the goddess returned to her. Aurelia reached deep within herself, drawing in power for her spells. She would not assault the towers themselves. She would rip them apart at their very foundations. Within her mind's eye she saw the twin buildings' foundations, dug deep into the soil and protected with arcane wards. Ancient words rolled off her tongue, and she knew only half of what came out of her mouth. The rest sprang from her soul itself, from a knowledge that seemed to belong only to her.

The words ended, the first wave of spells flowing out of her to assault those protective runes. Dozens shattered, the writing upon the stone melting away like wax in a kiln.

Lamps and candles lit throughout many of the towers' windows. "Do you feel the world tremble beneath your feet?"

The King of the Fallen

Aurelia asked the unseen mages. "Do you hear the stone crack, and the muddy earth groan?"

They knew her presence now, and they were not amused. Multiple balls of flame burst from the windows, accompanied by ice lances that were nearly invisible as they streaked through the night sky. Aurelia crossed her arms and summoned a magical shield about her body. Fire and ice thundered against the magical dome she'd crated, and upon that impact, lightning unleashed from the sky. The elements swirled about her, seeming so quaint to her eyes. Celestia's presence overwhelmed her now, almost impatient for its use. Aurelia dared tap into but a tiny sliver.

"Do you seek fire?" she asked, and from her palms burst a stream to make a dragon jealous. The flames spread higher, higher, so grand it rivaled the height of the towers themselves. The night sky became bright as day as the flames washed over the crimson side of the apprentice's tower. Faint white light burst and popped all along the windows, the people within enacting spells to aid the runes carved into the tower. After a moment the fire ceased; the silence following its roar felt deeply unnerving.

Such a display should have left Aurelia drained and unable to stand. Instead her hands shook, not from exhaustion, but from the struggle to contain the rising tide of power within her.

Limitless, Tessanna had once declared. *The well is limitless.*

For the first time in her life, Aurelia understood, truly understood, and it humbled her knowing that the daughter of balance had held together for so long despite her traumatic life. Another barrage of spells lashed out at her, trying to crush her with an overwhelming display. Aurelia crossed her arms and summoned her shield. Cities might have crumbled, but she withstood, with such ease that it excited and frightened her in equal measure.

When the attack passed, she looked to the towers and saw pitiful human playthings, no more special or imposing than Aubrienna's and Gregory's playthings. The comparison put a grim smile to her face, and she half-sung a song as she cast her next spell. That Tessanna often behaved similarly did not go unnoticed to her.

"And all the castles and all the keeps came tumbling, tumbling, tumbling *down*..."

Aurelia dropped to her knees and slammed her palms to the damp earth. Magic flowed through her fingers, intense enough to steal the words from her mouth. The land split. Cracks veered in all directions like a great spiderweb. The towers might have seemed impervious to magic, but she would tear them out at the roots, excising them from Dezrel like a stubborn weed. She did not embrace Celestia's gift, not completely, but she felt it hovering about her, strengthening her. The remaining wards protecting the stones of the towers' foundations popped and sparked. The paint burned to ash. Her fingers hooked. Her grin spread.

"Down, down, down."

She rose to her feet, and the towers began to fall. Their bases cracked. It started slowly at first, just the slightest wobble. The Apprentices' Tower toppled first, its red stones splashing into the Rigon as the bridge linking the two towers snapped like a twig, raining bricks both red and black. Aurelia expected the same of the Masters' Tower, but the mages within were more resourceful than she anticipated. Jagged lances of stone ripped free of the earth and slammed into the base of the massive structure. The largest halted the initial fall, and then several more poked out like gargantuan fingers to steady the sides and support each and every direction. It soon became a tremendous web, crisscrossing pillars of brown earth locking the tower in place.

Aurelia grinned. It seemed the masters would not give up their home so easily. The fools. If they wanted to survive, they should have fled.

"Bellow to the heavens your rage," Aurelia said, echoing the words of her goddess. "Do your ears detect my cry now, Celestia? Do you sense my anger amongst the stars?"

Her body felt weightless. Her mind ached with understanding. Though the night was dark now that her fire was gone, her eyes saw every little wisp of the ethereal essence of magic, and it was blinding. The surviving masters gathered another barrage, and they unleashed it all at once, in a display to make Dezrel tremble. Fire, ice, lightning, even stone and pure magical essence: it all flew toward her, but she felt not afraid. She remembered the assassins who had come to kill her daughter in Mordeina. She remembered Avlimar's fall. She remembered the final moments of Tessanna's life, when she lowered her hands and smiled to the heavens, relinquishing her tormented soul so that she might be with the only one she ever loved.

"Give them to me," she whispered, her calm voice belying her infinite ferocity. "Give me my wings."

Aurelia's feet lifted from the ground, the earth holding no sway upon her any longer. She drifted as if amid ocean waves, her hair floating, her clothes billowing in unseen, unfelt winds. Though they bore no physical connection to her flesh, she gasped as two ethereal wings burst from between her shoulders. They shimmered and swirled with smoke and light. The left wing, brilliant white, brighter than the sun, purer than the moon. The right wing darker than midnight, its feathers glimmering shards of the infinite space beyond the stars. Those wings stretched out behind her as she rose, twenty feet in wingspan, forty, one hundred, until it felt like all the world would be swallowed, the wing tips reaching the very ends of the horizon.

Fire and lightning shattered against a barrier she summoned with but a thought. She saw the ice and stone flying toward her with intent to kill, and she broke it all as easily as she might pull a blade of grass up from dry soil. The magic seemed so childish to her now, so inconsequential.

"*You slew a daughter,*" she spoke, but the words, the voice, did not feel like they belonged to her. "*Face a mother's wrath.*"

She lifted her hands to the heavens, the great distance seeming inconsequential now. Size, space, time; it all crumbled and broke loose. Far, far away, she clutched a chunk of stone flinging through the cosmos within her grasp. Her fingers curled as if she held it in her actual flesh and bone hands. Power flowed from her, but it was an inconsequential speck. With each steady beat of her wings she felt renewed. One pull, and she tore the celestial stone from its path. She guided it home.

A star shimmered in the sky above.

"Send your spells," she laughed as another barrage launched from the windows of the tower. This time they did not strike her invisible barrier. They merely faded away, absorbed into the swirling light and shadow that her wings had flooded the surrounding landscape with. The very rules of magic were breaking, she their new master. The elf envisioned the stars, and the chunk of ore she'd grabbed, and pulled harder. Her teeth clenched and her back arched from a sudden spike of pain. The effort only angered her, and she shrieked out her furious denial.

"END. IT. ALL."

One moment, it was a distant, sparkling star. The next, the meteor lit the sky with fire as it came crashing down. It struck the Masters' Tower, the burning chunk of stone thrice its size. It made a mockery of their wards and protections as it blasted their foundations to rubble and carved a mile-long gash across the earth. The waters of the Rigon churned and spilled eastward as it attempted to follow the meteor's wake. The land roiled, a shockwave blasting out in all directions, but Aurelia was high above it. Dirt and stone shifted, the rubble soon hidden by a cloud that hung in the air like smoke over a forest fire. The sound, at first deafening from the cracking earth, breaking stone, and swirling waters, slowly eased as the destruction ceased.

Amid that silence, Aurelia's wings faded away. Her sight shifted, her awareness shrinking, her mental grasp of the world returning to that of a mere mortal. The elf slowly drifted until her feet touched down on cool grass. Aurelia looked upon the destruction she had wrought and felt complete and total horror—not at her own actions, but the future they had all narrowly avoided. Her husband had told her of Tessanna's pain, of her quiet confession in the awful night following her beloved Qurrah's death.

I want to slaughter everything and everyone until I create a land of corpses, Tessanna had said. It wasn't folly, or beyond her reach. The end of all Dezrel had truly been within her grasp, and yet she had chosen a different path. She had given up her life, perhaps because the last reason she had to live it had left her.

I'm coming home, she had whispered before the Councils' spells had torn her apart.

Home. To where her beloved Qurrah waited.

"Home," Aurelia echoed. The elf looked to the stars, and she no longer saw the infinite space beyond them, nor felt control over those celestial bodies. Somewhere up there, she knew Celestia watched, and listened.

"Thank you," she whispered, shivering. "But never again. Not to me. Not to anyone."

Her fingers waggled, and she ripped open a portal to Ahaesarus's camp, where Harruq and Aubrienna waited. To step through felt akin to escaping a dream. The heavy aura of magic that had enveloped her slipped away, removed like an unneeded suit of armor. The portal took her to the army's encampment, just outside the rows of tents. A dizzy spell overcame her when she exited, but it quickly passed. Once recovered, she re-orientated herself and headed for her family's tent. Despite the late hour, it seemed something were amiss, given how many soldiers were awake and softly murmuring among themselves.

Harruq was not asleep when she returned, nor was she surprised by this fact. Instead, her husband waited at the entrance to their tent, one of his swords laid out across his lap as he steadily sharpened it with a whetstone. Upon her arrival, he rose to his feet and smiled with relief.

"You had me worried," he said, sheathing the blade.

"I thought I told you *not* to worry."

He slid an arm around her waist and kissed her lips. "Yes, but then the hours kept on passing without you. That, and the earthquake that just hit the camp. Felt like all of Dezrel was suddenly pissed."

"Did it now?" Despite her exhaustion, she could not keep a hint of amusement and playfulness from her voice. Harruq detected it immediately, and his eyes narrowed.

"That...that wasn't you, was it?" he asked.

Aurelia smiled, kissed his cheek, and entered the tent without saying a word.

27

Deathmask perched along the same southern edge of Mordeina's outer wall from which he and Veliana had watched the fallen army march out to face Ahaesarus's angels. The same place where they had observed Azariah's army come limping back several days ago, signs of defeat upon every flutter of every black wing. The fallen's' return had only heightened Deathmask's excitement. An assault upon the city would follow. Ahaesarus would absolutely give chase after a victory, and the sight of an army marching over the grasslands confirmed his belief.

"Hardly the numbers I was expecting," Veliana said beside him. They didn't bother to hide themselves in shadow this time. With how few Azariah had left to defend the city—the bulk of them being undead—the King of the Fallen had seemingly abandoned the outer wall entirely. Mordeina was guarded by two walls, the narrow space between them meant to be a killing lane should the city ever be invaded. The wings of angels nullified much of those defenses, so Azariah was keeping his forces bunched together at the entrance to the interior wall. That was same reason Deathmask suspected Azariah had forfeited Devlimar entirely. Too open. Too difficult to defend.

As for Ahaesarus, it seemed the angel cared not for the golden city either, not even to take it as a symbolic victory. They marched straight for Mordeina, eager to fight.

"That is a far cry from the army Thulos brought against this city years ago," Deathmask said.

Veliana glanced to the perfectly still rows and rows of undead. "It is the same for the defenders. Last time, the defense bore a bit more a pulse."

"The angels appear evenly matched," Deathmask muttered. He rubbed his chin and squinted against the midday sun, whose light made it difficult to count the winged figures flying amid the clear sky. "Ground forces appear even as well. If anything, Azariah has more undead. Not exactly the numbers advantage you would expect from a besieging force."

The King of the Fallen

"They won't lay siege, though. They're going to assault immediately. These angels have the patience of children."

"Either that, or a traditional siege means nothing when the besieged can fly out at night for clean water and smuggled food. Plus, most of Azariah's army doesn't need to eat. How do you starve out the dead? The only ones who would suffer are Mordeina's citizens...and they'd only join the army upon their deaths."

It was a grim thought, but it mirrored what they had seen nonstop since Azariah's return. The king of the fallen had begun pillaging every single graveyard in both the city and the surrounding villages to supplement his undead army. The Night of Black Wings had perversely aided him in this regard. The fallen angel's forces were more skeleton than rotted flesh, but that wouldn't be all of it. Oh no. Azariah had his surprise ready for the defenders, which meant Deathmask's own additional surprise awaited. Truth be told, Deathmask was giddy as a school child about it.

The human army marched toward the outer gate of Mordeina. No beast-men among them, Deathmask noted, which ran counter to the rumors he'd heard describing the make-up of Ahaesarus's army. Had they fled? Been killed in the battle reportedly fought at Hemman Field? Getting information about that fight had proven maddeningly difficult, and what few human soldiers he'd questioned in taverns after returning from defeat had been spotty and nonsensical. Supposedly, the goddess Celestia herself had come to condemn *both* armies.

"No siege weaponry," Veliana remarked. She casually leaned over the battlement wall, her chin resting on her fist as if observing a play in a park.

"I suspect their spellcasters *are* their siege weaponry. That, or they expect the angels to open the gates for them."

Veliana glanced to the sky full of black wings and the undead army gathered near the entrance, no doubt ready to bury any angel who attempted to land.

"Good luck with that, I suppose."

A sudden roar shook the city. Deathmask grinned behind the cloud of ash hovering about his face.

"There it is," he said, turning to gaze at the distant castle. He felt a pull on his mind as the runes he'd modified flared to life. "Come grace us with your presence, Rakkar."

Though it'd only been five years since its last summoning, it seemed a beast of a different lifetime burst forth from the royal gardens. Deathmask could not see it, but he could imagine it. Had he not witnessed its birth once before, when the priest-king Melorak had ruled over this very city? A creature of pure shadow, so deep it seemed to swallow all light. Its wings were like a bat's, its face reptilian and full of obsidian teeth. It was foul magic given life, and it reeked of Karak.

Veliana heard the roar and turned from the city wall. Her eyes widened.

"Azariah didn't," she said.

Deathmask grinned. "He did. He begged to Karak, and Karak answered."

Rakkar took to the air, flying out from the castle garden to the outer wall, the same exact spot where it had first been summoned by Melorak years before. The dragon looked like an obsidian knife cutting across the blue sky, leaving behind a thick trail of smoke that stubbornly refused to dissipate in the soft wind. It roared again, a gargantuan creature of myth that soared on black wings, with violet eyes and claws the size of a man.

The creature looped once overhead, then dove for the inner wall, landing with a tremendous rumble of earth. Its third roar tightened Deathmask's stomach and gave him a vague need to kneel and confess obedience. It was nothing like that first imposing moment when confronted by the dragon. Was it because he was farther away? Or did Azariah's faith in Karak pale compared to Melorak's when summoning the otherworldly creature?

"I suspect you have a plan to kill it?" Veliana asked. She crossed her arms and glared. "Ahaesarus can't possibly win against that, not when their forces are mirrored."

"Kill it?" Deathmask lifted his hands. His mind receded into itself, into the realm of runes and magic. "No, Vel. I have something far more amusing in mind. I'm going to *steal* it."

The King of the Fallen

Words of magic slipped off his tongue. He closed his eyes. All was pitch black save the form of Rakkar, a half-mile away. A violet outline, seen only due to Deathmask's attunement to the realm of magic, shimmered about the dragon like a glowing fire. That fire originated not from Rakkar, but from a distant source: Azariah, exerting his control. Even now the angel flew from the royal gardens where he'd performed the summoning ritual, connected to the dragon by a glowing tether. Through that magic he gave the dragon his commands, as well as gave of his own strength to keep it upon the land of Dezrel.

But Deathmask had tweaked the summoning runes. He had, in a sense, carved a secret password that only he knew. Letter by letter, rune by rune, he'd inscribed his true name. Azariah might be the anchor holding Rakkar to Dezrel, but he was not its final master. He was a prince. Deathmask was king.

Do you hear me, Rakkar? he cried out with his mind. *Do you sense the words of your true master?* An invisible fire gathered about his hands, though in his mind's eye it was the same violet color as that which flowed from Azariah.

The dragon roared. Ahaesarus's angels backed away from the wall, and the encroaching human army halted its approach. They had not anticipated such a foe. No doubt they scrambled to discuss its arrival. Deathmask laughed. Such reactions were unnecessary, as he would soon show them.

The violet fire about his hands shot across the void to Rakkar, swarming along its form, wrestling control away from a stunned and clueless Azariah. The dragon was his now, and it would obey.

We have guests coming to our fair city, he told the dragon. *Open them a door.*

Rakkar bellowed out its acceptance. Dark fire grew within its gullet, which it then unleashed in a tremendous burst. The several dozen undead soldiers standing between the dragon and the inner wood gate were charred within seconds.

The fire shattered the gate as if it were made of twigs and mud instead of aged oak and iron supports. Azariah's fallen angels, at first hovering in steady formations above Rakkar in a show of strength, suddenly panicked like bees from a knocked beehive.

Not that there was anything they could do. Only one fallen angel mattered...

Deathmask screamed as pain spiked in his forehead, like a terrible migraine sprung to life in the blink of an eye.

Azariah, fighting for control.

"He's strong," Deathmask muttered, dropping to his knees. "Holy shit, Vel, he's so strong."

Rakkar howled in confusion. Its scaled body swayed side to side, like a bull trying to toss an unwelcome rider. Deathmask clenched his jaw and bared his teeth.

No you don't, he thought. *That shadowy fucker is mine.*

Deathmask rose to his feet and reached out a hand, imagining his own tether into the dragon's mind solidifying. Azariah would not outmatch him, not in this. He was a child new to magic. He was a divine brat convinced of his kingliness. Deathmask was a former member of the Council of Mages. Before Veldaren fell to the orcs, he'd been a master. A goddamn legend.

"A door," he hissed. "Do not keep our guests waiting."

Rakkar snapped its reptilian head up and about, its long neck undulating like a pinned snake in a state of panic. Deathmask spared not a fraction of his concentration. He curled his fingers and poured his reservoir of magic deep into the spell. The distant garden runes flared, and somehow he knew they were wreathed in flame. The limits of the magic were starting to break. The summoning spell had never been meant for this type of dual control.

"A door!" he screamed. "Give our guests a door!"

Rakkar barreled forward with a terrifying roar. It smashed stones free as it passed through the first gate, then charged straight for the outer wall. It did not make the turn for the other, distant gate to the outside. Instead it charged straight ahead, fire belching from its mouth as if it could burn away the stone. Another spike of pain pierced Deathmask's temple as a panicked Azariah used every bit of his own magical influence to order the dragon to halt.

It's too late, he thought. *The beast is mine, angel. You failed.*

Rakkar slammed into the wall, dug its enormous claws into the earth, and pushed. The crack that followed was like an earthquake. The ground shuddered. Stones broke and fell, sending dust and debris into the air, mixing with the dark smoke that seemed to leak off the dragon's scales. Larger chunks of stone toppled moments later as hidden supports broke and gravity took its toll. Meanwhile, Ahaesarus's army, seeing the dragon's arrival, pivoted to greet it. Did they think it enemy?

Perhaps, but Deathmask would quickly disabuse them of that notion.

The way in now open, he turned the creature back to the numerous undead who waited oh-so-patiently for orders. More fire belched from the belly of the wounded dragon. Sadly, he was too far away to see clearly, but Deathmask estimated at least fifty to one hundred of the dead fell beneath the first wave of flame that scorched through the heart of the undead formation. Fire swelled in Rakkar's throat for a second blast, this one much longer and wider. Dozens upon dozens of rotting, skeletal slaves collapsed against its raw power. They knew no fear. They had no instinct to flee. Only Azariah could command them, and he was locked in a losing battle with Deathmask for control of the dragon.

Burn them all, he thought. *Roast every last rotten body forced into servitude.*

Azariah had only one recourse. Unable to take back control of the dragon, he banished it entirely. The anchor holding the magical creation released. The modified runes Deathmask used to control it faded, their magic ended. Rakkar had time for one last mournful roar before its body dissolved into smoke. It didn't matter now, Deathmask told himself. The damage was done. The defensive walls were nullified, and the fallen angel's undead forces were cut in half.

Deathmask's legs wobbled, and he collapsed to one knee. His dark hair clung to his face and neck from sweat. Had he really used up so much of himself to keep control? He hadn't noticed, not in the thick of the mental battle, but now he felt like he had run a dozen miles. His breathing was labored, shallow. Abyss take him, maybe he was just starting to get old?

When he glanced up, he found Veliana standing above him offering a hand.

"I hope you weren't planning to sit this out," she said, hooking the thumb of her other hand over her shoulder. Deathmask leaned to the side to see Ahaesarus's army sprint full-speed toward the double openings in Mordeina's walls. His angels soared above, providing cover against the fallen that flew to intercept.

Veliana smirked. "I believe we have some fallen angels to decapitate."

Despite every bone in his body demanding he rest, Deathmask laughed. He would push through. He would endure. Vengeance waits for no man, be they mortal or divine. He took her hand and accepted her help.

"You're goddamn right we do."

28

"What is *that?*" Jessilynn asked. She need not point or clarify, for all eyes were upon the creature of darkness flying to the outer walls.

"Karak's dragon," Dieredon answered, needing to shout to be heard over the rush of the wind as they flew. "Celestia have mercy."

Jessilynn rocked backward, remembering the stories she'd heard of the creature known as Rakkar, the otherworldly dragon used to keep Mordeina in line during its brief occupancy by the priest-king Melorak. Dieredon had modified Sonowin's saddle so that it also seated Jessilynn with her legs wrapped tightly into stirrups. This allowed her to remain steady atop the winged horse's back while still wielding her bow. Together, their arrows had claimed dozens of lives during the battle at Hemman Field, and the plan had been for them to do the same here at Mordeina...at least until this terrifying dragon appeared.

Her elven teacher leaned closer to Sonowin's ear to give an order, and then the winged horse banked hard to the left. Their path veered to the many angels flying over what was ostensibly King Gregory's army, though in truth all saw it as Ahaesarus's. It was to him they flew, Dieredon calling to the angel a question.

"What now?" the elf asked.

Ahaesarus watched the dragon's approach with a grim smile on his face.

"We kill it," he said, as if it would be so easy.

Dieredon banked Sonowin back around to face the city. Jessilynn could tell the elf wanted to argue, but it seemed he knew it would be futile. Instead they watched the dragon approach, heard it roar out its supernatural fury.

Watched it drop down behind the city walls and tear a hole straight through while slaughtering Azariah's undead forces.

"It's on our side," Dieredon said incredulously.

Jessilynn's mind mirrored his shock. It had certainly looked to be a creation of Azariah's, and wasn't Rakkar a beast solely loyal to Karak? But no, it thrashed through the fallen angel's troops, until with little fanfare it broke apart, the shadow that made up its body melting away like snow before a warm spring sun. Far below, she saw the ants that were Ahaesarus's ground troops lift their arms to hoot and holler. What had been fear quickly turned to elation. The way was open. They wouldn't even need to rely on Tarlak and Aurelia to make them a door.

Dieredon gently tugged the reins, guiding them back down. They flew over the human army, Sonowin's white wings spread out to their full length. More cheers, and Jessilynn allowed herself to smile and wave at the soldiers. The upcoming battle would be vicious, and they would need their morale at its highest to endure. The elf guided Sonowin to the very front of the attacking force, and instead of banking upward like she expected, he lowered them to the ground. When she saw Harruq Tun marching at the front of the human forces across the grasslands, she quickly understood.

"Yet again you lead an army to Mordeina," Dieredon shouted to the half-orc.

"Better be the last time, too!" Harruq shouted back, a wild grin on his face. "Getting damn tired of evil bastards taking this city from us."

Jessilynn understood that the two of them were keenly aware others listened to the conversation, and that these soldiers would remember their words as they charged the walls of the city. She kept her head high, doing her best to look stately and impressive, as no doubt Jerico would prefer.

"We will aid you as best we can with our arrows," Dieredon said, hoisting his wicked-looking bow high above his head. Jessilynn almost joined him, but decided to let the elf have his moment. He was a legend to these humans, a hero of the second Gods' War whose name was whispered among Harruq's and Aurelia's.

"Just leave a few for us to kill!" Harruq requested. Dieredon slung his bow back over his shoulder and smiled, so light-hearted, so jovial, that Jessilynn thought it might actually be real.

His next shout didn't bother to address Harruq alone, but all those with him. "I shall leave you plenty, so long as you promise to do your job, half-orc! Cut them down, and leave them bloody. Dezrel needs its heroes."

"Heroes?" Harruq bellowed. "I have a thousand heroes with me, don't I?"

Sonowin returned to the air, a rousing chorus of cheers and swords slamming against shields chasing after their flight. Jessilynn leaned closer to Dieredon so she wouldn't have to shout.

"You're charismatic when you try to be."

"You sound surprised."

"You don't try very often."

He laughed, and it warmed her heart. She clutched to that warmth to fight her own nerves as they flew toward the walls to join Ahaesarus and his angels. The battle was near. They would focus solely on the aerial fight. Silence fell over her, and she closed her eyes to silently pray to her god.

Are you with us still, Ashhur? Are you with me? Forgive my lack of faith. Forgive my doubt. Be with me, please, as we try yet again to do what is right.

Perhaps there were better final prayers to offer before potentially meeting her maker, but she could only offer what was truthful to her heart. Eyes snapping open, she pulled her bow off her back, gripped it tightly, and drew an arrow from her quiver. Her pulse quickened. This was it.

Sonowin joined the initial charge of angels, Ahaesarus himself not far to her left. Black wings filled the sky. Bone-metal rattled. Weapons ready. Spears up. Azariah's magic, and those of a few spellcasters with him, crossed the gaps between armies. Tarlak and Aurelia immediately countered, and it was through that explosion of fire and ice the angelic forces crashed.

The few seconds were but a blur. She did not behold a battlefield, but individual snippets of combat. There was too much to see, too much to understand. Ahaesarus, slamming aside an attempt to block with Darius's enormous blade, and then ramming the sword all the way to its hilt into his foe's stomach so that it pierced out his back in an explosion of gore. A ball of fire from a spellcaster detonating to her left, consuming angels from both sides. Charred corpses fell, feathers still burning, some angels screaming in pain. Jessilynn released arrow after arrow, but she did not aim, not really. All around her were black wings, and so she sent her arrows in their vague direction as her mind struggled to make sense of the chaos.

One of Azariah's angels flew overhead, his sword swipe barely failing to cleave off her head. She spun on instinct to track the fallen, only to see him be chopped in half by an angel. Sonowin dipped, Jessilynn's stomach lurched, and she clung to Dieredon as they weaved through a trio of attempts to spear the winged horse. Enemies surrounded them all on sides. She fought her fear, telling herself to ready another arrow, but this was so much worse than Hemman Field. They had kept their attacks focused on the ground forces during that battle. To be amid the aerial war? To fly through a rain of blood as bodies collapsed and wings snapped? Too much, it was too much.

And then they burst through the opposite side of Azariah's soldiers. The sudden emptiness was like a breath of fresh air. Jessilynn drank it in and used it to gather herself. There would be time to suffer through the mental scars later, if she survived. Her friends needed her. Humanity needed her. The fallen angel's rule must end this day. She believed that with all her heart.

Sonowin's path shifted, and she followed the trajectory with her eyes to realize why Dieredon had led them on such a dangerous path directly through the heart of the aerial battle. Azariah's spellcasters were their target, what few yet remained after Hemman Field hovering in the relatively calm airspace between the walls and Mordeina's castle. Sonowin's approach did not go unnoticed. Spells screamed their way. Sonowin banked left, then rotated ninety degrees the other direction. Jessilynn gripped her bow in one hand and clutched Dieredon's waist with the other. No chance to loose an arrow, not during this. A chunk of ice swooshed over their heads. A single bolt of lightning flashed to her right, leaving a blinding afterimage in that eye. Dieredon leaned over, every muscle in his body tense. He trusted his steed, and he merely watched. Waited.

For one brief moment Sonowin pulled up and spread her wings. Their flight leveled out, and in that half-second Dieredon lifted his bow. His hands were a blur. Four arrows flew through the air, though she saw him pull the string only twice. His aim was impeccable. Four arrows, two shots, and just like that, the few spellcasters Azariah had left fell from the sky, arrows jutting from their faces and throats.

Dieredon slung his bow over his back with one hand and clutched Sonowin's neck with the other. "Away!" he commanded. Sonowin folded her wings into a dive in a desperate attempt to gain speed. Only two fallen gave chase, for Ahaesarus's angels had locked nearly every one of them in a savage battle. White and black wings slammed into each other, chased, and looped. The entire sky was filled with blood. Jessilynn trusted the stirrups holding her in place as they dove, and she twisted around to fire behind her. The first shot struck flesh, sending the fallen careening away. Realizing he was in danger, the other attempted to dodge, but he could only move so much if he wished to maintain proximity.

She let off two more arrows, and the fallen shifted too much to his left. Sonowin's wings carried them the opposite direction. When the fallen tried to change his angle and regain speed, one of Ahaesarus's angels slammed into him from above. The distance was great, but she swore she saw the fallen's head separate from his shoulders.

We fly through the Abyss, she thought darkly during the momentary reprieve.

Jessilynn could only spare an occasional glance to the battle below. With their numbers already thinned by Rakkar's betrayal, the undead struggled against the human army. She could not see Harruq amid the chaos, but Jerico's shield shone like a beacon. Blue-white flashes of light sparked across the battlefield, spiritual replicas of his shield slamming outward like divine battering rams to crumple tens of undead at a time. Jessilynn felt pride at the sight. Diminished they may be, but Ashhur's paladins would still make their mark upon the battle.

If only her own arrows would shine with that holy glow. She missed far more than she hit with regular bolts, for not only must she anticipate her target's moves but Sonowin's own shifts and turns. Worse was the fear that she might accidentally injure one of Ahaesarus's angels. She suspected Dieredon shared the same fear, for his path was a wide loop around the bloody chaos that was the aerial conflict, hunting isolated fallen and any injured who attempted to flee. She put an arrow through the head of one such angel with black wings, who flew with the nub of his left elbow clutched to his side, blood pouring from the stump where his arm had once been.

They were nothing of the beautiful, majestic creatures they had once been, Jessilynn told herself. They had chosen their path. They had abandoned their protection of humanity.

Those justifications helped a little, but only a little.

A flash of light turned her gaze downward, to where Aurelia was bathing rows of undead with fire. Tarlak stood beside her, blasting lightning into the human formations with bolt after bolt. Jessilynn wished she could have more time to watch the two spellcasters work their magic. At the start of the battle, they had fought in similar fashion as at Hemman Field. Their spells focused on the defensive, protecting the ground troops from elemental fire and ice unleashed by their aerial foes. But as there were no mages from the Council to keep the pair on the defensive, and Ahaesarus's angels had locked Azariah's fallen in bloody swordplay, they could unleash their full wrath. It was terrifying.

Thank Ashhur they're on our side, she thought as Aurelia vanished momentarily through a blue portal she tore open before her. The elf reappeared atop the unmanned inner wall, granting her a tactical vantage point over the army. Jessilynn wondered if Azariah regretted leaving the walls unmanned now that Aurelia launched fireball after fireball from her fingertips, the spells exploding into rings of flame that consumed dozens with each detonation. She was savage in her efficiency, and showed not a hint of fear to the fallen angels high above her.

Dieredon obviously saw the same display, because Sonowin's course deviated into an intercept path between Aurelia and the few fallen who noticed her destruction and dove to stop it.

"Give her time!" he shouted.

Jessilynn was all too happy to oblige. Their curved path gave her a clean shot. Her first thudded arrow into the side of a fallen, and it looked like the shaft snapped in half upon striking

The King of the Fallen

bone-plate armor. Dieredon's, to no surprise, sliced right through the fallen's neck. The angel's flight slowed, wings fluttering limply as blood spurted heavenward in a wide spray. Jessilynn released two more arrows, but the fallen were aware of their approach now, and they twisted and weaved to avoid the attacks. Her next three missed entirely, the closest being her second, which sliced through a few feathers on the fallen's left wing. To her perverse relief, Dieredon missed his next two as well, the combination of a distance, an aerial dive, and enemies who dodged too much for even the otherworldly-skilled elf to overcome.

The distance between them quickly shrank. Of the four fallen diving for Aurelia, Dieredon scored another shot straight through the eye, and Jessilynn managed to chase off a second with a hit to the stomach. The other two continued unabated, and Jessilynn braced for the worst as she readied yet another arrow.

But Aurelia wasn't oblivious to her own danger. She suddenly dropped to her knees and pressed her fists to the top of the wall. Arcs of ice sprang up around her, sliding upward with jagged edges to slam into one another to form an uneven dome. The diving fallen quickly veered to either side lest they smash themselves against the ice. Suddenly alone and slowing from an attempted climb back into the air, they were both easy pickings as Sonowin looped between them. Two shots from Jessilynn, one from Dieredon, and they both dropped, dead or dying.

Jessilynn turned back for Aurelia. Through the top of the crystalline clear dome, she saw a hint of the elf within. The telltale blue of a portal appeared, and just like that she was gone to some other part of the city.

"Eyes up, Jessilynn!" Dieredon shouted. She brought her attention back around to find him offering her a handful of arrows to replace the ones she'd used.

"How many arrows can that magic quiver of yours make?" she asked.

"As many as I need. Or at least five hundred."

"Ever run out?"

"My aim is too good. My foes are dead before that happens."

Jessilynn laughed. The jokes helped blunt the trauma she knew lurked at the edges of her mind.

There was so much death around her, it didn't seem real. Angels fell from the sky, some beautiful with white feathers and golden skin, others dark-winged and with sickly, pale flesh and bone-thatched armor. Even the size of the city was overwhelming, for she had spent her life mostly isolated in the rebuilt Citadel. Thousands upon thousands of homes, stretching out for miles, and yet the city felt empty. The streets were barren.

They fought over a lifeless husk.

Once more into the fray they flew, Sonowin's speed plus the range of their arrows keeping them just outside danger. From what Jessilynn could tell, Azariah's ground forces had completely collapsed. Ahaesarus's soldiers marched into the city, overwhelming the undead who only now began to scatter. The battle in the sky appeared much closer, but neither Aurelia nor Tarlak had begun directing their spells heavenward.

A sudden burst of light at the far end of the aerial battle seemed to mock her conclusion. It didn't come from the elf or wizard, but from Azariah, who lingered near the outer edge of combat. The spell was flashy but without any harm or danger, just a bright red and yellow spark lighting up the air space between Azariah's angels and the castle. The reaction of the armies immediately revealed its purpose. It was a signal to retreat. The surviving fallen angels immediately abandoned their engagement, turned their wings, and flew for Mordeina's castle.

"Celestia have mercy," Dieredon muttered.

Jessilynn realized their error a moment after the elf. They had skirted the outer edges of the battle, picking off stragglers, but that had put the duo directly in the path of the entire fallen forces as they fled to the castle. They might be fleeing, but as the black wings raced toward them, it was clear they'd be happy to take a few more lives with them along the way.

"Hang on!" the elf screamed. Jessilynn slipped her bow over her back, securing it just before Sonowin dedicated herself fully to evasive maneuvers. The wrath of the fallen was brought upon them. There would be no time or chance to retaliate. The winged horse banked hard right, avoiding a gigantic icicle that looked large enough to knock down a house. Swords swung at their sides, missing by several feet as the speedy mount weaved this way and that. Jessilynn clung tight to Dieredon as Sonowin's actions grew more desperate. A spear shot above her shoulder, and she winced when her mind cruelly imagined what might have happened if its aim were true.

A second spear, followed by a hit with a shield that thumped off Sonowin's front hooves. The attacks lessened, for Sonowin was faster than the fallen angels once she reached full speed. Jessilynn dared believe they would escape untouched. It was a fool's hope; she realized that a half-second before an angel whose trajectory she'd not once witnessed barreled into them.

The collision rocked Jessilynn backwards, and her rear lifted off the saddle. Her arms slipped free from Dieredon, and she collided with the fallen, crying out in pain as the angel's armor left a dozen bruises across her arm and chest. The angel twisted as he fell, lashing out with his sword. Sonowin banked into a spin immediately, throwing off his aim, but his jagged blade hooked the right stirrup securing Jessilynn. The leather was nearly sliced in half. Latching onto the winged horse's back with all her might was all she could do to keep from falling.

Sonowin's bank revolved into a full corkscrew. Dieredon, showing the reflexes that made him one of Dezrel's most fearsome killers, had already abandoned his bow and drawn one of the long knives he kept sheathed at his hip. Sunlight flashed off the blade's edge as their corkscrew path brought them up and around to make contact yet again with the fallen. Blood followed in a great crimson shower. The motion had him momentarily standing atop the winged horse, and try as she might, Jessilynn could not reach him, nor was she adequately prepared for the sudden head-over-head spin.

Her heart leaped into her throat. She felt herself slipping.

The stirrup fully separated from the saddle. Sonowin's spin continued amid the frantic dive, and Jessilynn reached out for Dieredon, to hold onto him as she fell. Her fingers touched the leather of his armor, a brush of green cloth, and then she was drifting away. The other stirrup tightened around her leg, she screamed as it wrenched her body sideways. The spin continued.

The stirrup, never meant to handle such strain, twisted once and then snapped free of the saddle.

She fell.

Sky rotated over ground over sky. Her arms flailed, and she kicked as if she were swimming and not plummeting to her death. She saw Sonowin briefly, her wings flaring outward to slow her dive. Jessilynn was so disoriented, she didn't even know if the winged horse was above her or below her. Dieredon remained so close, diving she saw, diving for her. He crouched atop the saddle, one hand clutching the reins, the other outstretched. She reached, but too far, he was too far above her, the ground too close. Panic threatened to take her, but she refused it. Think. Move. Act.

Jessilynn gave up reaching, and instead she pulled her arm back, drew her knees to her chest, and then kicked so that her feet pointed toward the elf instead. Dieredon could not reach her legs, just as he could not reach her arm...but he could reach the dangling stirrup still wrapped tightly about her leg. He grabbed the leather and pulled with all his strength. She floated closer, closer. His hand was on her ankle. His other hand took her waist. He pulled her close, she felt his arms around him, and then Sonowin's wings filled her vision as they banked hard.

The streets of Mordeina flashed underneath her, so close they were a blur. She held onto the elf for a second longer, needing to feel his proximity, needing the comfort of his arms about her, before she pulled free of him. She returned to her seat behind him, only now without stirrups, she needed to wrap her hands about his waist to keep herself steady. Dieredon craned his head around to address her over his shoulder.

"Never do that again," he said. A smile was on his face.

He wasn't watching Sonowin's flight path. He never saw the spear. Jessilynn did. Her eyes widened and she went to screech a warning, but it was too late.

The spear did not pierce his chest so much as scrape across it. The sharp end, twisted and curved by Ashhur's curse into a strange, cruel shape no mortal blacksmith would ever recreate, tore apart his leather armor. It gashed open his chest, and by the terrible snapping noise that haunted Jessilynn's mind, it no doubt broke several ribs. Dieredon immediately went limp, his

The King of the Fallen

hands releasing the reins. There were no stirrups to catch him, and Jessilynn's mind was but a blank white slate incapable of giving her body movement. They were too close to the castle. Sonowin veered to the right to avoid colliding with the castle wall. Dieredon fell, hit the hard ground below, and then rolled.

She screamed. Wordless horror. A meaningless protest. Perhaps it had words, maybe the word 'no', maybe the elf's name. None of it registered in her mind.

Jessilynn didn't need to give a single order. Sonowin turned immediately, circling back to retrieve her master. The bastard who threw the spear had the same idea. His black wings beat with frantic strength as he flew to finish off the injured elf. Panic tried, and failed, to overcome Jessilynn. Instinct took over. No thinking. No doubt. She pulled the bow from her back, withdrew one of her last few arrows, and nocked it. She didn't calculate the wind, the speed they traveled, or the path of her target. She didn't need to. She would never allow him to reach the elf, never allow him to hurt her dear friend further. She aimed the arrow to where it felt *right,* and then released.

The arrow pierced one side of the fallen angel's neck and out the other. He dropped instantly. She hoped it hurt. She hoped it hurt like the Abyss.

"Go to him," she pleaded into Sonowin's ear, a thoroughly unnecessary command.

Together they dove for Mordeina's castle, to the body bleeding out upon the steps, and she prayed to a god she feared no longer listened to her that the elf would survive.

29

Azariah dashed through his tower like a madman, scattering books and tossing aside tables as he rambled the same phrase over and over. The city had fallen, his undead army crushed, his fallen forces decimated. The battle still raged, but it was scattered and wild, less a war between armies and more a hundred skirmishes, of which his loyal subjects were losing far too many.

"Not enough time, not enough time, damn it all, not enough *time*."

It seemed Dezrel, and all three of her gods, conspired against him. Never before had the need to escape shown so clearly. But the runes, the gateway...he failed once. Could he manage it now?

"Have I even a choice?" he asked, now standing before the gateway in the heart of the tower chamber. His wings folded behind his back. He withdrew Velixar's journal, his skin shivering at its touch. There was so much power within those pages, so much wisdom for him to gain. Perhaps he had been too hasty in his plans to throw Avlimar to the ground, too confident in the righteousness of his cause. Better now to escape it all. Dezrel was a sinful, wretched mess. Any other world surely had to be better.

"As many worlds as there are stars, and each with its own creators, its own gods, and its own people living lives as best they know how before their souls depart their meager flesh," he read aloud, a bit of wisdom Ashhur himself had shared explicitly with the first man, Jacob Eveningstar. And if Azariah could harness the necessary power within him, he could open a gateway to one of those worlds, just like the daughter of balance, Tessanna, had granted the war god Thulos entrance six years hence.

Azariah started the necessary chant. Words of power flowed out of him, and he felt the strain on his mind grow at a frightening pace. Light gathered in the center of the ring of thirteen stones, swirling together to form an ethereal doorway. It was so faint, the translucent blue not yet leading anywhere. He needed to connect it to a destination, but where, and did he have the strength?

The King of the Fallen

The door to his tower opened. Azariah turned, and his stomach clenched at the sight of his visitor.

"Here you are," Aurelia Tun said. She stepped inside, and the door closed behind her. Sparks of flame flew from the top of the staff she held. Her beautiful dress was stained with ash and smeared with blood, yet none of it appeared to be hers.

"Are you hunting me, elf?" he asked, stalling for time. There was no chance for him to finish the spell in her presence. The elf's magical prowess was legendary, as he had seen for himself during the second Gods' War. Panic fueled his thoughts while he pondered a solution. He couldn't open a portal, not to any world beyond Dezrel, so what options were left to him?

"Hunting?" she asked, her footfalls echoed upon stone as she approached. "No, angel, not hunting. I am no hunter, and you no fleeing prey. You are snake curled in a robin's nest, having already devoured all the eggs. Consider me the one who has come to rip off your scales."

Azariah prepared to release his hold on the portal so he might battle, but then paused. A thought occurred to him. No, he could not open a doorway to another world beyond Dezrel, not one watched over by other gods. There was one world, though, that was far closer, and whose walls had grown dangerously thin.

"No, I dare say you won't," Azariah said. He took a careful step back as the elf neared. He feared she'd clobber him with her staff before he might speak his proposal. "What you will do is create for me a portal to some far distant land on Dezrel, and claim you took my life and reduced my body to ashes, thus allowing me to live the rest of my days in peace."

"Will I?" she asked. "Why is that?"

"Because of what I can give you in return."

The anger in her walnut-colored eyes would be impressive if it weren't so dangerous.

"There is nothing you can offer me I would care to accept, angel," she said.

Azariah grinned despite the blood it spread across his teeth. "Oh, I think there is." He clenched his hands into fists and poured more of his power into the shimmering gate. It quadrupled in size, its surface shimmering with newfound color. Ripples washed over it, and as they calmed more colors hardened into view. The green of a rolling field. A lighter blue, of a calm, peaceful sky. Aurelia watched, her obvious curiosity getting the best of her.

Sweat beaded Azariah's forehead, but he dared not break his concentration. He focused on a singular entity in his mind, a being whom he had personally met prior to the sky splitting open and Ashhur sending them to wage war in his name.

One last gasp, and the door ripped open completely, revealing an image otherworldly stark and bright. Azariah's entire body shuddered, his wings fluttering with his every breath, as he maintained control.

"It can't be," Aurelia whispered.

On the other side of the portal was a young girl with auburn hair that hung down to her waist. Her chestnut eyes sparkled, her smile without a care in the world. Her dress was a pristine white with green trim. Flowers bloomed within her hair. She lay in a field of grass, singing a song neither could hear, as she splashed her free hand in a shallow stream that flowed beside her. Though she last drew breath at the age of two, she was older now, yet not quite as old as she would be upon Dezrel. Time moved in strange patterns in the Golden Eternity.

"I can bring her to you," Azariah said. He gestured to the girl oblivious to the tear in the fabric of reality mere feet away. "I can pull Aullienna through this gate, returning her to Dezrel not unlike what Ashhur did to us Wardens. Do you still believe I have nothing to offer? Or would you deny yourself the dream of every grieving parent that lived before you?"

The elf froze, her grip upon the staff so tight her fingers had turned white. She stared at her deceased daughter, a wave of tears beginning their descent down her slender cheeks. Azariah stepped closer, and he softened his voice. He had once been a comforting presence to the suffering. He could be so again, if it suited his needs.

"You could play with her again," he whispered. "Watch her grow as she was meant to grow. Think of it, Aurelia. She could meet her sister. She could cuddle in the arms of her father. The trauma of exiting the eternal lands will fade from her mind, I assure you, the comforts of the Golden Eternity drifting from her like a pleasant dream. All you must do is give me your promise that you will let me escape. My life, for the return of hers. It is more than a fair trade, given that I offer you the impossible, and you offer me only what would take the snap of your elven fingers and a few deceitful words in the right ears."

Aurelia stood before the portal, openly weeping. Her hand hovered in front of the entrance, fearful to touch it as if it were made of fire. Stroking the cheek of her daughter, Azariah realized. Wishing her fingers touched warm skin instead of air.

"I've missed you," the elf whispered. Haunting sorrow clung to her every word. "You're just as beautiful as I always imagined you'd be."

So close, Azariah knew, she was so close. She just needed one last gentle push.

"How could you turn down such a gift?" he asked. "I give you the opportunity to see your daughter again. Do not forfeit this over misguided pride or a faulty sense of justice."

Aullienna looked to some unseen thing in the distance, and the sight of it stirred a joyful laugh. This was it, Azariah felt certain. She would accept. The laughter broke her. The elf's entire body shivered as if stricken by a fever. Her tears fell without ceasing, that childish laugh unsealing a thousand memories Aurelia had long buried beneath grief and time. No matter how strong her resolve, Azariah knew his temptation was successful. How could anyone choose to willingly endure such sorrow when given a chance to rectify it?

Yet Aurelia somehow turned away. It looked as if it caused her physical pain, but she put her back to the image of eternal calm. The staff shook in her grasp. The change that came over her was like watching water turn to stone. It was like watching humanity created from clay in the time of Paradise.

"To think you would ever believe me so selfish," she said. "Velixar would be proud of your honeyed words. I have prayed over her pyre, Azariah. I have mourned, and given her my sorrow. I would not return her so she might suffer anew. I would not ask her to feel death's sting twice. In this second life you promise her, I see ashen skin, jagged teeth, and withered wings. I deny you,

Azariah. I deny your gift, for it is no gift at all. You offer me nothing I shall not one day already have. Without you, I shall meet my daughter again, only it will be on verdant fields that stretch beyond the horizon, in a land without anguish, hunger, sorrow, or loss."

"Don't be a fool," Azariah said, vainly trying to salvage the situation. "After all the sacrifices your family has made, is it not fair that you be rewarded in kind? Will you not heed my promise?"

"You once promised you would conquer Dezrel with Ashhur's grace," she said. "You indeed brought conquest, but there is no grace here, only a cruel mockery meant to save your own life. I will have none of it, fallen one."

She slammed the butt of her staff against the tower floor. A shockwave rolled with it, so heavy it flung Azariah to his knees and toppled reams of books from the bookshelves. The thirteen runes surrounding the portal exploded into chalk. The image of the Golden Eternity flickered once and then faded, the portal sealed away with a loud, shrieking hiss.

In the sudden silence, the sound of steel drawn from scabbards was deafening.

"You're a real bastard, Azariah," Harruq Tun said. He stood at the doorway, having entered at some point when both Azariah's and Aurelia's attention were focused on the portal. "And just when I think you can't sink any lower, you find a way to fall so deep into the dirt you should be popping out through the roof of the Abyss."

"You would refuse it too?" Azariah asked, scrambling back to his feet. "You, who has carried Aullienna's name like chains across your neck every day since her death? You, who used her very memory to split the sky and bring us rushing forth to Dezrel's salvation?"

The half-orc twirled Salvation and Condemnation in his hands and joined his wife's side.

"Stop talking, angel," he said. "She made the right choice. She always does."

Azariah summoned fire and ice about his hands as he steeled himself for battle. Taking on either foe would be a challenge, but it appeared he need not do so alone. The glass panes above him shattered, and amid their colorful shower his Executor descended. Judarius's enormous mace slammed downward to obliterate the half-orc. Harruq blocked the blow, his reflexes ever-perfectly honed. The entire tower seemed to rock from the collision of their weapons, but Harruq did not relent. His legs tensed, and he shoved Judarius back.

"Need to try better than that," the half-orc said.

Judarius hovered beside Azariah, and he cast an unpleasant look to his brother.

"I pray you weren't seeking to abandon me here on Dezrel."

"We are all abandoned," Azariah said. "You were meant to prevent them from reaching the castle."

"Our foes are ever the slippery ones." Judarius glared at Harruq. "You've been lucky before, half-orc, but your good fortune ends this day. Dezrel will not fall into mortal hands."

Aurelia's magic gathered atop her staff in the form of brilliant golden fire. Beside her, Harruq grinned for the first time since entering the tower.

"You know what, Azariah?" He clanged his swords together, the red aura about them shimmering with bloodlust. "I'm going to kill you both, and when I do, I promise you, it's going to fucking hurt."

"No, Harruq, not both," Aurelia said, as much savagery showing in her eyes as her husband's. She grinned a devilish grin as orbs of fire swirled about her, summoned by a mere twitch of her fingers. "Azariah asked that I deceive the world by claiming I charred his corpse to ash, and with all gods and goddesses as my witnesses, I shall make a truth out of his desired lie."

30

Jessilynn sprinted up the steps to Mordeina's castle, her bow and quiver thudding against her back. Her eyes locked on Dieredon, who had landed near the cast entrance and rolled halfway down the steps. The panic threatening her mind was so overwhelming she refused to acknowledge it. Every thought ceased to be as she ran to him. All other distractions, she denied. No noticing the way his legs were bent entirely wrong from his fall. No looking at the blood pouring from the savage gash across his chest. No dwelling on if the wound and fall had been fatal. Just run. Just close the distance.

She arrived at his side and dropped to her knees. Her hands pressed against the wound. Warm blood flowed beneath her palms. "You...you'll be fine," she pleaded. "My prayers, they'll—they'll heal you."

"No, don't," Dieredon sputtered, blood coming out along with his words. He tried to push her aside. She refused him, pushing back when he went to remove her hands.

"I can," she said. "I will!"

He lay still beneath her, though if he was accepting of her help or simply lacked the strength to fight, she did not know. No time to find out. Her eyes closed and she bowed her head, begging to her god for aid. All her life, she had trusted Ashhur to be with her, to watch out for her, but now more than ever she needed him. He'd been there for her when she was trapped with the wolfmen. He'd been there with her throughout her childhood, during those difficult early years at the rebuilt Citadel. He'd be with her now. He had to. *He had to.*

"Please, Ashhur, I beg you," she whispered, keeping her hands pressed to the wound. She dared not watch. She dared not look for the holy glow. "Heal this wound, my god, please. Mend the flesh. Make right the body, so the soul might remain."

There should have been a soft, gentle ringing in her ears, or the distant ringing of bells. Jessilynn lifted her gaze. She still saw the blood. The wound remained. The only distant sound she heard was the clash of swords and the cries of the dead as the fallen fought their war against Ashhur's remaining loyal angels.

"It's not your fault," Dieredon said. He grabbed her elbow and clung to her with the last of his strength. "I didn't...I didn't want you to blame...yourself."

The color drained from his body faster than the blood pouring down the steps. Tears blurred Jessilynn's vision, and she angrily wiped them away with her sleeve. The blood was cloying to the touch. The smell of it overwhelmed her senses. Sonowin's hoofbeats clopped upon the stone behind her, the faithful steed coming to inspect her master, but Jessilynn could not spare the horse any attention.

"No," she said. "No, these prayers, I–I–I just need to try to—harder."

She pressed her hands to the wound and pleaded for Ashhur to hear her once more. She begged for healing magic. Deep down, she refused to believe herself abandoned here and now. Not when victory was so near. But the words she spoke, they remained just words, just air. No light. No power. As the elf grew more and more still, his breathing shallow, she couldn't even form the words anymore. She sobbed over him, trying not to hate herself, and failing.

"Don't," Dieredon said. He put a trembling hand to her chin and slowly lifted her head so she would cease the prayer. "You were ever...a perfect student."

Sonowin leaned down over the elf, her wings folded in against her sides. Her nose brushed his face, and he patted her jowl, smearing the white of her hair with his blood.

"I'll miss you, too," said the elf. Despite it all, he coughed out a weak laugh. "It's...it's funny. These steps...I belong here. Foolish Haern. Took my place for...for nothing."

His hand went limp and fell to the stone. The elf breathed his last on the steps of Mordeina's castle. Jessilynn collapsed, her strength completely gone. The months of travel, of fighting, of bleeding to save innocents only to watch them slaughtered by beast-men or fallen angels, broke her completely. She wept over Dieredon's body, but her tears and sorrow could not overcome the rage that swallowed her. Her hands clutched Dieredon's shoulders as she looked to the war-torn sky.

"Are you there, Ashhur?" she asked the raging battle. "Are you with us? Or must we suffer alone?"

Angels and fallen clashed, fought, bled, died. Was Ashhur with them?

"Will you not let me save even those I love?"

Fury brought her to her feet. She could not see Ashhur in the sky, but she could imagine him up there. Had the sky not split? Did the Golden Eternity not lurk behind the blue curtain? All her rage, all her broken fury, she projected to the unseen father she had envisioned guiding her throughout her life. Her voice might mean nothing against the cacophony of war, but she offered it anyway.

"Are you even listening!" she screamed.

"No," said Darius. "He is not."

Jessilynn spun around. The dead paladin stood at the base of the steps, his form faintly illuminated with the same blue-white glow that had once shone from her holy arrows. His long blond hair waved in an unseen wind. His dark armor was gleaming, his face handsome and without a scar or blemish. All the world dimmed at his presence, and it seemed time itself slowed to a crawl. Darius pressed a hand to Sonowin's neck, comforting the grieving animal. What joy Jessilynn might have felt at his presence was muted by the body at her side and the battle overwhelming the human capital.

"Is that possible?" she asked, suddenly regretting her outburst. "He's...he's a god. He's *our* god."

Darius pressed his forehead to Sonowin's, then left the horse's side to climb several steps to where Dieredon lay. He looked upon the body with a mixture of sadness and pity.

"Because his eyes are fixed," he said, and he pointed up the castle tower. "In there. Upon the battle he eagerly awaits."

"I...I don't understand."

Darius put a hand on her shoulder. His gaze never left the elf's body. "He and Karak were once one, and will always seek to be one. This was destined from the very first moment they set foot upon the world of Dezrel. They have fought this battle, not

The King of the Fallen

once, not twice, but a hundred times. Karak and Ashhur, Bardaya and Velixar, Bernard and Melorak, Harruq and Qurrah, Cyric and myself, and now Ahaesarus and Azariah. Over and over, they dance. Over and over, they war. It has changed him, Jessilynn."

"A god can't change," Jessilynn insisted. "Ashhur is the same as he has always been."

"And yet we preach that Karak changed once he was given the sinful and traitorous to rule amidst his fire."

"This...you can't be right. Ashhur hasn't changed. He watches over us. He loves us."

Darius smiled, and she wished she could have known him in life. She wished she could have walked alongside him, learned from him, and known him as something more than the stories her mentor had told.

"Jessilynn," he said. "If that were true, that Ashhur's eye never strayed...do you think I could be speaking with you? Could I, a soul of the dead who should be in the Golden Eternity, instead linger here on Dezrel?"

It was an argument she could not defeat. Long had the teachings of Ashhur insisted there were no such things as ghosts and hauntings, for such implied that Ashhur was not master of the afterlife, or that Celestia could somehow lose track of something so divine and important as a soul. Yet here Darius stood, and if he were not a gift from Ashhur...what else might he be? What else could it mean?

"I still don't understand," she said. "How is Ashhur different? Do we not still feel his blessing? Has he not given us strength and guidance?"

"Means to an end," Darius said. He looked to the sky, and when she followed his gaze, she saw Ahaesarus flying through the air wielding the paladin's former blade in warfare against the fallen. "Strength, so we may find victory. Guidance, so our light outshines that of Karak's darkness. That's all that matters now to him. Not salvation. Not the love of his children. Only victory in his name. So long as we believe our righteousness is defined by our victories, we will ever confuse the two."

The paladin shook his head. He looked so divine, and yet so broken.

"It will continue," he said. "Again and again, this cycle never-ending. And I fear that when Ahaesarus strikes Azariah down, it will only be yet another stepping stone in their war. Ahaesarus will become king, and the newfound power will corrupt him as it always corrupts. Once he has become what he hated, another loyal follower of Ashhur will rise up to prove his faith is stronger. Dezrel will never move on. Karak's followers will stir, and then two more champions shall clash. This dance, this cycle, this war, however you wish to name it, has refused to cease even at the end of the world. The splitting of the sky did not end it. What now shall be the cause?"

Jessilynn trembled. Such confessions from a loyal paladin, whose faith she had never doubted, filled her with a fear that ran deep down into her bones.

"If you're right, then Ashhur did not used to be as he is now. There was a time he meant what he preached of forgiveness. He sought peace on Dezrel, did he not?"

"Despite the perversion of facts the fallen have told you, yes. There was once a peaceful Paradise."

"And Ahaesarus himself once walked this Paradise, this land without war, at his god's side?"

"He did."

Jessilynn took Darius's hands into hers. So many times in her life, this specter of a man had come to her when she needed support most, but for once, she felt it right to give something back.

"Then Ahaesarus knows that was ever the goal. He knows the gods sought to grant us happiness, life, and love. There's still a chance to end this, Darius! Ahaesarus isn't too far gone, I know it! Caught up in this war, he's only forgotten."

A faint smile tugged at the sides of Darius's mouth. He leaned down to kiss her forehead. The touch of his lips was like fire to her skin. He whispered to her, his words so powerful it seemed the entire world quaked along with them.

"Beloved child, if that is true, then *remind him.*"

The paladin disappeared. The muted colors of the world returned to their painful, stark vibrancy. Jessilynn lifted her bow, and she looked to the nearby tower. It was that tower Darius said Ashhur's eyes were fixed upon, so that would be where she went.

"I am a poor replacement," she told Sonowin, who stood protectively over the body of her slain master. "But will you give me one last flight?"

The majestic beast clomped her hoof and nodded. Jessilynn had always wondered how much the winged horse understood. Perhaps it was far more than she first guessed. Jessilynn climbed atop her back, wrapped her hands about her neck, and held on as Sonowin's wings spread wide. They took to the air, only this time she did not try to fire her bow. She had her destination, and nothing could stop her.

There was no space for Sonowin at the top of the curling steps winding their way outside the tower, so she slowed to a hover just beside the enormous door. Jessilynn hopped off and turned to face the beast. Sonowin neighed twice and wiggled her head. Somehow Jessilynn felt certain she knew exactly what she wanted.

"Thank you," she said. "Return to him if you must. I'm...I'm sure he'd be honored."

Sonowin neighed one final time and then curled back around toward the steps far below. She would watch over her master, even in death. Perhaps it was the only way the winged horse knew how to grieve. Jessilynn envied her. She wanted nothing more than to collapse and weep over the dead, but there was no time. The door was already cracked open an inch. The sounds booming from within were of battle, and a moment of caution had her peek inside instead of entering.

Of course Jessilynn had heard stories of the Godslayer. Everyone had. He had accepted a sword through his own chest so he might slay the war god Thulos. When pressed, Lathaar would also share tales of Aurelia Tun's magic, of the overwhelming power she commanded, and he was always quick to credit her for saving thousands of lives after Veldaren's fall. Legendary figures, fateful heroes whom the entire world of Dezrel shifted and tilted by their actions.

All those stories, all those daydreams while listening beside a fire, paled in comparison to witnessing firsthand the fury of the husband and wife when fully unleashed.

Harruq and the fallen Judarius slammed into one another like two boulders crashing together during a tumble down a mountainside. Their weapons were blurs weaving through the air, occasionally marked by the sparks of their contact. Judarius attempted multiple times to slide past the Godslayer to strike Aurelia, but the half-orc never gave him an inch. Harruq's feet were always moving, his stance shifting so that Salvation and Condemnation could strike at the angel with maximum power with every swing.

And he needed to protect Aurelia, for she was the shield saving him from the words of magic flowing unceasingly from Azariah's lips. The self-proclaimed king hovered above the battle in the tower room's high ceiling. Fire and lightning flew from his hands, and if he feared harming Judarius, he showed no sign of it. Aurelia countered each and every attack. White shields pulsed from her staff to absorb the lightning. Stone boulders ripped from the tower walls to smash aside spears of ice hurtled from the fallen angel's palms. How Azariah could even keep aloft stunned her, for wind howled within the chamber, the very air crackling with immeasurable magical energy.

And yet, despite it all, Jessilynn saw that the half-orc was laughing. That image, of Harruq parrying aside Judarius's enormous mace while sporting a dire grin on his face, was all Jessilynn needed to know who would achieve victory.

A flutter of wings sounded behind her, accompanied by the rattle of armor. At last, the visitor she awaited had arrived.

"Do not be afraid, Jessilynn," Ahaesarus said as she slowly turned to face him. "I come to end what fight yet rages within."

She looked to the commander of Ashhur's faithful, truly looked at him for the first time since he had arrived too late at the carnage of the Castle of the Yellow Rose. His skin had lost its golden luster. His wings were pale, and much of them covered with blood. Most damning of all was the sword he held in his hand. Darius's sword. The weapon of a man who would now denounce him. The weapon Ahaesarus had once claimed himself unworthy to wield.

"The fallen are routed," the angel continued. "Victory is ours. All that matters now is putting an end to the traitor hiding within this tower. I will make an example of Azariah. Of that, I assure you."

It was exactly what she was afraid of, and the worst possible assurance he could have given.

"Harruq and Aurelia will defeat him," Jessilynn said, and she stood before the door, blocking his way. "Do not interfere."

Ahaesarus's expression darkened, his eyes narrowing as he towered over her.

"I would prove Ashhur the true god of Dezrel," he said. "Not the heresy Azariah preached of Karak and Paradise. Why do you deny me, Jessilynn?"

"Because Dezrel never belonged to us! This was Celestia's land, to which our gods came as refugees." She tilted her head toward the door she guarded. "A land of elves, or even orcs. Her beloved, and her cursed. That's who is in there now, Ahaesarus. I hold faith in them. Don't you?"

Ahaesarus stood to his full height and spread out his wings so that he seemed ever grander. "Azariah is everything I am sworn to break. He betrayed our kind, and he brought our home crashing down to this wretched earth. I will not have my vengeance denied, not even by one of Ashhur's most faithful. Step aside, Jessilynn. I shall not ask again."

She could hardly believe her own actions, but she kept Darius's words close to her heart. *Remind him,* the paladin had demanded, and so she would. Slowly she lifted her bow, pulled an arrow from her quiver, and closed her fingers about the well-worn string.

"I hold faith," she said, drawing the bowstring taut. "And I will not move."

Ahaesarus's eyes bulged with fury. "You would threaten me?"

"If I must to end this dance."

The angel slammed Darius's sword into the steps so it remained upright and then crossed his arms over his chest.

"Then do it, child. One arrow. One meager bit of iron and wood, and without the light of Ashhur's blessing. Tell me more of your faith, Jessilynn, even as my god reveals its hollowness."

Her arm began to shake from the strength needed to hold back the bowstring. She met the angel's gaze, saw both bloodlust and desperation within them. Did he even understand his own part to play in this? Or was slaying Azariah all that mattered to him? But this refusal, this act, this sacred time…in all the stories she listened to while growing up, stories forever etched upon her heart, it was moments like these that decided Dezrel's fate.

Jessilynn slowly lowered her bow, the tension of her bowstring easing. She cast aside her arrow. Ahaesarus let out a sigh of relief and pulled Darius's sword free of the stone.

"A wise decision," he said.

"I know," Jessilynn said. She lifted the bow, this time empty handed. Her fingers closed about the drawstring. There was no doubt left within her. Remind him. *Remind him.* She had thought Darius meant Ahaesarus, but now she understood. Ashhur's eyes were upon this city, upon this tower, upon *her*. She straightened her spine and lifted her chin. Before this towering presence of the divine, she once more readied her bow.

"I hold faith," she said, and pulled back the string. A shimmering blue-white arrow materialized, its light intense and blinding. "And I will not move."

Ahaesarus saw that light, saw that holy glow, and he knew not what to say. Anger replaced argument. Panic replaced words. He lunged toward her, his free hand closing about the upper half of her bow even as she released the string. The arrow punched through his shoulder, his fanciful armor be damned. It blasted out his back, taking cloth and feathers with it. The angel screamed and staggered backward. His hand closed on reflex, cracking the bow with his inhuman strength. Still Jessilynn did not release her hold.

At last his hand went limp, and he collapsed to one knee while clutching his wound. Shock overwhelmed his anger. His mouth opened and closed, unable or unwilling to muster any argument. Though her bow was broken, Jessilynn drew back the string. Another arrow appeared, and she aimed it straight for his forehead.

"This war was not fought for your vengeance and pride, angel. Dezrel has suffered enough. Let Celestia's children end it as they must."

Ahaesarus's wings flared wide, and he more fell than flew off the side of the stairs. He settled into a glide, his blood dripping like rain across the far distant steps below as he circled downward. Jessilynn watched him go, then looked to the skies. With neither Azariah nor Judarius to lead them, the surviving fallen had fled the city. To Devlimar, no doubt, to make it their last holdout. From what Jessilynn could tell, the angels did not give chase, perhaps because their own leaders were occupied.

Setting aside her broken bow, she looked to the tower door and the raging battle within. Harruq and Aurelia Tun, once more fighting with the fate of worlds on their shoulders. Dieredon's words echoed in her mind, and finally allowed herself to grieve his loss while whispering them. The emotions she had held at bay came roaring to the surface, and only now did she let them overwhelm her.

"Cut them down, and leave them bloody," she said, tears starting to flow. "Dezrel needs its heroes."

She sobbed, for despite her every attempt, her every prayer, Dezrel had lost one such hero upon the steps of the castle below.

31

Harruq dared not focus on the magic unleashed by the king of the fallen. Judarius was his foe, his only foe. The gigantic warrior and his mace were all that mattered. Aurelia would keep him safe. In that, he held faith.

"Come now, try harder!" the half-orc bellowed, slamming Salvation and Condemnation into Judarius's warped mace. "I thought you were angry. I thought you wanted revenge!"

"I want your sinful, wretched people wiped from the face of Dezrel," the warrior angel roared back. "I am done with your failures. I am sick of your excuses."

Once, twice, the mace pounded down at Harruq as if it were a hammer and he the nail. He quickly disabused the angel of that notion. Nothing would break him, not here, not now, at the very end of a long, horrid road. The people of Dezrel would be free. The rule of the angels, the rule of the fallen, it ended here. It ended now. Spells exploded about him, lightning meeting lightning, pure beams of magic striking shields that enveloped the dueling pair like a dome.

"Do you ever shut up?" Harruq said as he batted aside another blow from Judarius's mace. "Asking for a friend."

He met the angel strength for strength and showed him whose rage was greater. Every swing, he remembered the fields of the dead. The slaughter of the Night of Black Wings. The chaos and devastation of Hemman Field. The warm embrace of battle enveloped him. This was where he belonged, where he would always belong, and no longer did Harruq fear or reject it. His swords, his skill, it was everything Dezrel needed. A gift of peace, granted to a beleaguered people. Let the fallen angel make his bitter proclamations. Death stalked him in the form of black steel with a crimson glow.

"Bugs beneath our heels," Judarius said, as if speaking these words would give him strength, would make it true. "Mortal creatures, propped up by your betters. You are worthless, half-orc. You are a wretch elevated by Ashhur. Blessed by Velixar. You are nothing on your own, and I shall prove it!"

The King of the Fallen

Down came the mace with the strength to break boulders. Harruq crossed his swords into an 'x' and intercepted the hit. A groan slipped through his clenched teeth at the impact. Gods above and below, the angel was strong! He tried shoving both weapons to his right, but Judarius resisted. Their weapons only interlocked further. Harruq braced his left leg and shifted his body while suddenly pulling away his right sword. The mace pushed through at the sudden drop in resistance. A guiding shove kept its path from angling inward, so instead of taking out Harruq's leg, it smashed into the stone floor.

Judarius, sensing his vulnerability, released his mace with one hand to slam a fist into Harruq's face. The pain rattled his vision, and he feared he would lose a tooth, but he need not see to react. He swung his closest sword, hitting the long handle of the mace. Another blow to his jaw. Harruq abandoned subtlety. Their bodies rammed together. His forehead struck Judarius's nose; blood splattered from his nostrils. Weapons entangled, they struck with elbows, fists, whatever was available.

It was the angel who retreated, panicked and bloody. Harruq twirled his swords, eager to give chase.

A spell sneaked through Aurelia's protection, a jagged lance of ice meant to further separate the combatants. Harruq dodged back half a step as it smashed between them, its upper half remaining embedded within the groove Judarius's mace had gouged into the floor. Harruq never hesitated. Coiled legs exploded him into movement. Instead of preventing an attack, he would use it to his advantage. His foot kicked off the ice. His body twisted as he vaulted higher, spinning to give Salvation and Condemnation speed when his hands linked together for a dual slash. Judarius's panicked swing passed beneath him, hitting only air. A single, ludicrous thought entered Harruq's head as his massive, muscular form spun like an acrobat.

Haern would be so damn proud.

The twin swords smashed down upon Judarius's left shoulder and collarbone. Their magic made a mockery of his armor. The black blades separated bone. They tore apart ribs. They cut, and cut, until bursting out near the fallen angel's hip. Harruq landed with a loud thud, his body tense, his weapons out in yet another stance. His head ached and blood dribbled down his chin, but nothing stopped his smile.

"Fucking angels."

Judarius split in half, two piles of gore dropping lifeless to the tower floor. Aurelia halted her attacks on Azariah for a split second to hit the body with a ball of flame for good measure, burning away the flesh so that only broken bones remained.

"Come play," the elf said, wisps of flame dancing about her eyes. Frost wafted from her fingertips. "We'll have such fun now that my husband is no longer distracted."

Harruq watched the hovering angel lock in place for a single heartbeat. Azariah's magic was great, but Aurelia had years of experience and study over him. With his brother slain, he couldn't hope to endure her assault as well as his swords. The fallen angel's wings spread wide, and he flew toward the shattered windows of the ceiling, attempting to use the same entrance Judarius made as an exit.

Aurelia gave him no reprieve. Her fingers hooked. Ice slid along the floor to either side of her, curling like vines growing at unreal speed. The ice clawed up the walls to meet over the broken windows, jagged edges slamming into each other to seal the barrier. Azariah spun about, and Harruq saw the confusion lock him in place. The fallen angel clutched Velixar's spellbook to his chest as if it might give him some sort of comfort or guidance. He could stay and fight, or he could attempt to flee.

He chose flee. Fire bathed his free hand, and he poured it into the ice to burn himself a path. It was exactly as Aurelia anticipated. High above the tower, the sky darkened. A bolt of lightning dropped from the heavens, streaking through the opening Azariah had created. It tore him asunder. His wings shriveled. His body went rigid. Stunned and helpless, he fell to the tower floor, where Harruq waited to catch him with his swords.

Salvation pierced his chest, tearing into his left lung. Condemnation punched right through his gut. Azariah's body collapsed into Harruq's arms, as if for one final embrace. Warm black blood flowed across them both with both swords buried all the way to the hilt in pallid flesh. Harruq wanted to say something, anything, but what words were there even to offer?

"Qurrah deserved a better death than what you gave him," he said. He twisted the hilts of his swords. "But he is free now, saved by the grace you rejected."

Harruq jerked his arms forward, tearing his weapons free and dropping Azariah to his knees. Blood and gore sprayed. The spellbook fell from Azariah's limp fingers and tumbled in front of him before resting half-open. Harruq clenched his jaw tightly and he told himself to feel nothing. To weep for no loss. No death.

The fallen angel gasped, clutching at his spilled innards as he collapsed onto his stomach. Words scraped out of his throat in a voice rapidly losing strength. Harruq stood over him, watching, listening, as his blood cooled and his swords shook within his grasp from the withdrawal of battle.

"So we suffer," Azariah groaned, his voice wet and weak. He crawled bleeding across the floor. "So we die for your sins."

"This was on you," Harruq said. He pointed Condemnation's gore-coated tip in his direction. "No one made you declare yourself king. Ashhur may have given you a crown of bone, but you put a gold one on first. The Night of Black Wings? That slaughter? That sickness? That was your failure. Those were your sins."

"Didn't...want this," Azariah gasped. Blood pooled beneath him as he dragged himself another inch. Several times he coughed for air that would not properly fill his damaged lungs. "Your prayer...brought us here. Your fault. This is...your fault."

Harruq lowered his swords. On one quiet morning, at the insistence of both Celestia and Ashhur, he had sneaked outside the city of Mordeina. He had crossed the empty grasslands and knelt before an approaching army of war demons and undead. His failures had brought that war upon them. His personal struggle with Qurrah had led to hundreds of thousands of lives lost. In that moment, he had bowed his head and trusted the gods to save Dezrel from total destruction. He had offered himself, for what more could he give? At worst, he thought Qurrah might see and be moved. He had hoped to show his brother the lengths he would go to make amends.

And then the sky had split, and a piece of eternity had come forth, along with Ashhur's Wardens, now blessed with wings, having become angels to fight the forces of Thulos's war demons. His friends had raced to his aid. Jerico had protected him with a divine shield as large as the battlefield itself. Harruq had never felt more loved, nor more certain that Ashhur would do everything in his power to protect his home and his people. It was a feeling the subsequent years had slowly cut out of him.

Azariah's fingers curled about the yellowed pages of Velixar's spellbook.

"We were home," the fallen angel said. "Safe. In peace. You took us out. Brought us here, among the sin. Made us see."

Harruq stared at the bleeding, dying king with a crown of bone. Now he knew the lengths to which all the gods would go. Thulos was slain, but others remained, still plotting, still warring, still treating mortal lives like pieces of a game instead of cherished, beloved children. None seemed immune, and he feared the same rot would claim Ahaesarus if given time.

"You never should have stayed," Harruq said softly. "You never should have been left to rule. Perfection cannot last, not in this world, yet it was expected of you. It broke you. I don't know what god shall take you when your eyes close, Azariah, but I pray they show you mercy."

"Mercy?" Azariah gasped. He slid another bloody foot along the floor. He turned a single page, his fingers leaving bloody smears upon the parchment. "I don't want...mercy. Don't want justice. Emptiness, Harruq. Give me *emptiness*."

Words of magic passed through bloody lips. The dying angel should have lacked the energy for a meager cantrip, let alone a spell, but his proximity to death was exactly the power he needed. Harruq's eyes widened, and he realized too late his foolishness.

"No, don't!" Harruq screamed. Azariah's blood bled upon the pages. A specific page, used for a specific purpose.

Azariah reached to Karak, and the Lion answered.

The words ignited in violet fire upon the page. Aurelia flicked her hand, blasting lightning into the fallen angel, but a cocoon of magic already surrounded him. Fire burned across his body. What was flesh was consumed. What was living, died. Shadows crawled about his body. An unholy blessing, once given to Karak's most cherished and devoted prophet, flowed into a former Warden of Ashhur. The demanded power blasted outward in a shockwave. Harruq crossed his arms before him to protect against its power, choking down a cry of pain as it lifted him into the air and dropped him on his back.

Another roar of the Lion. Books were lifted off their shelves and sent careening through the air when a funnel of magic formed around Azariah's body, raising it off the ground as with invisible strings. His robes darkened. His body changed. When his feet touched down, it seemed the very stone were scorched black from an unseen fire.

"What have you done?" Harruq whispered.

Despite his exhaustion, despite the ache in his limbs and the collected bruises from hours of battle, he stood and readied his swords before the recreation of an entity long dead. Azariah's hands were exposed bone held together with an inky, tar-like substance. His eyes glowed red. His face...his face was not his, nor that of any other single living being. Its features shifted and changed. Not quickly, only a gradual, subtle change so that nothing ever seemed quite right. A thousand faces, but yet Harruq saw but a single one.

The face of Velixar.

"I thought you had fallen," the half-orc said. "I thought you at your worst. I was wrong."

No longer did Azariah wield the divine magics drawn from Celestia's Weave. His heart was fully committed to Karak, and he drew power from the Abyss. He garbed himself in shadow. He wreathed himself in dark flame. Judarius's bones animated, and they circled around Azariah's body, collecting together to form a clacking cloak that hung about his neck as a most morbid ornamentation.

Aurelia had slammed her staff upon the stone. Her slender hands gripped its wood in a white-knuckle grip.

"I don't know how much longer I can withstand," she told Harruq as bolts of shadow collected within Azariah's tightly clenched fists. "Make haste, and cut him down. He cannot live. Whatever the evils of Paradise, the new kingdom he would create is a thousand times more wretched."

"A kingdom?" Azariah said. He pressed his wrists together, and from their contact burst a tremendous deluge of black fire. Aurelia braced her entire body, and a shimmering, partly-translucent shield bathed her and Harruq to protect them from its heat. If the undead monstrosity cared, he did not let it show.

"I will create no kingdom. I am done with the humans of Dezrel. I care not for your wretched race. Let the doors be opened. A million other worlds await me, and I would go to them instead."

Harruq lifted Salvation and Condemnation. He thought of Azariah arriving at some unsuspecting world. What destruction might he unleash with his foul magic? When he summoned his armies of the dead, would there be heroes ready to rise up and face him? He didn't know, but it wouldn't matter. He would not let it happen. This monster was his responsibility. His blades would end it.

A shadowy door opened halfway up the wall, but it was no spell from Azariah. Deathmask emerged from within like some nightmare specter, Veliana right behind him. Violet flame burst from his palms, taking the shape of razor-sharp daggers. Nine of them slashed across Azariah's face and neck, tearing into his robes, opening his throat, and clacking off his bones. Deathmask landed, but Veliana's momentum continued, her heels colliding with the fallen angel's stomach. Her knees curled with the impact, and her daggers lashed out, scoring several more cuts across Azariah's already mutilated throat. She kicked, and up and away she soared to land beside Deathmask. The pair stood together, smug grins on their faces that rapidly vanished when Azariah not only remained alive, but responded with heightened fury.

"Maybe I am a fool, but I feel like that should have killed him," Deathmask said.

Azariah's wings became liquid shadow, their edges elongating while also sharpening along one edge. The two surviving members of the Ash Guild dodged as the wings tried to slice them in twain. Harruq burst into motion, his twin swords striking the wings to beat them back. He did not cut through them as if they were bone and feather. Instead, the pieces he hacked free

The King of the Fallen

twisted and squirmed like serpents before dissolving into nothing. The sight sent shivers up his spine and made his stomach tighten from a nameless, unwelcome fear.

Aurelia assaulted Azariah with multiple lances of ice and fire, forcing Karak's newfound champion to defend himself. The reprieve allowed Harruq to retreat and for Deathmask and Veliana to regain their bearings. Once back with Aurelia, Harruq stared at the rotting entity with the ever-changing face. Just like Velixar...

There had once been a pendant that belonged to Velixar, a pendant Azariah himself had requested permission to study rather than having Judarius destroy it with his mace. The Prophet had bound his soul to the object, denying any true death from taking him. There could be only one potential choice for Azariah during his own transformation, given its hasty and desperate nature.

"The book!" Harruq screamed. "Destroy the spellbook!"

"Why does the fucker need a spellbook?" Veliana asked, dodging another half-dozen spikes of shadow that embedded into the wall upon missing.

"It has his soul in it!"

Aurelia launched a fireball the fallen angel's way. A dismissive wave of Azariah's hand detonated it early. Harruq charged through the dissipating heat and smoke. The fallen angel's hands danced, forming a great shield of darkness. Despite the powerful magic within Harruq's weapons, he could not break through. Sparks flew as he battered the shield, which rippled on impact like some strange, floating liquid. At last, he was forced into a retreat from shadows that sprung from the floor like vipers, seven of them with three fangs that tried to bite at his wrists and ankles. He not once reached the spellbook, never scored a hit with his swords, but that had never been his intention.

As was often the case, Harruq was a loud, furious, muscle-bound distraction from the true threat.

Veliana sprinted to the nearby wall, leaped off it, and soared upside-down as if gravity held no sway over her body. Her twin daggers lashed out, the violet flame wrapped about their blades flaring with power and rage. They sliced off three of Azariah's fingers. Her body rotated further, and just before landing she kicked the spellbook with her heel and sent it flying. The assassin landed on her back, gasping as the wind was knocked from her lungs.

"You wretch!" Azariah bellowed. He slammed his foot into her side, lifting her off the ground and bashing her body against the tower wall. She lay still when she landed, a soft moan escaping her lips. Azariah's attention turned to the book, which had landed right in Deathmask's waiting arms.

A single whispered word, and the spellbook burst into flames so hot that every page was consumed within moments. The remains floated upward to join that cloud that hovered about Deathmask's head.

"You have a bad habit of not holding onto things that are yours," he said, and no cloud of ash was thick enough to hide his amused grin. "First Rakkar, now your soul. Tsk tsk, angel."

Deathmask's magic was advanced, but even he could not withstand the barrage sent his way. A dozen bolts of shadow slammed into a shield he frantically summoned to protect himself. Aurelia struck the floor with her staff, a second shield growing upon impact to wrap about the beleaguered man. It was enough, but only barely. Both shields broke, the energy of their explosion flinging all within the tower backward.

"Enough with your prattle!" Azariah howled. "Never ending, never quieting. Enough, all of you, I say enough!"

Dark magic exploded out of him, taking the form of rolling shadow. Aurelia protected Harruq against the brunt of it, but the same could not be said for Deathmask. The magic slammed into him like a solid wave, and flattening him against the wall. He slid down until his rear hit the floor, looking dazed and confused. His head whipped toward Veliana, whose unconscious body had suffered a similar fate as his own.

Harruq sprinted toward the fallen angel, determined to steal his attention before he might finish the two of them off. Azariah flapped his wings once, unleashing a gust of wind so powerful it lifted Harruq off his feet. He flailed, helpless to control himself in such a state. Another flap, and he somersaulted head over feet back toward Aurelia. He was upside-down when he saw her smack her staff against an overturned bookshelf, transmuting it into an overstuffed pillow full of goose feathers. He landed atop it and rolled off with a groan. His wife clutched his arm to steady him.

"This is bad," he muttered. Aurelia said nothing, but the worry in her eyes was clear as day.

"Stubbornness was always your finest trait, half-orc," Azariah said, more magic gathering about his body as Karak's power filled him. "It shall make breaking you all the more satisfying."

The shadowy hands of ethereal giants emerged from the walls, passing through the stone as if it were but a mirage. Six fingers closed around Harruq, and from the corner of his eye he saw six more clutch his wife. Though the hands lacked any physical substance, they were cold like ice to his exposed skin. Harruq tensed his every muscle, his face flushing with heat and his body quivering from the strain.

He couldn't break free. He could barely even breathe.

"Always so clever," Azariah said, the fallen angel suddenly whirling in place. He caught a newly-awakened Veliana in mid-lunge, twisted so he guided her momentum instead of slowing her, and then flung her into one of the toppled bookshelves.

"Vel!" Deathmask cried pitifully with his hoarse voice. He pushed to his feet, but his reward was a lash of black lightning that sent him dropping back to his knees. Blood poured down both his nostrils and ears. Harruq dug his feet into the ground and pushed, pushed, but he could not break the grip. The lightning continued. It would be fatal. There was too much shock. Too much blood.

An arrow of pure light sliced through the room, connecting with the arc of lightning, which then exploded in brilliant blue-white mist. The lightning ceased, and Azariah howled as he rocked back several feet on his heels. Pieces of his illusory flesh peeled away from his face and neck, only to be immediately replaced. Deathmask collapsed at the reprieve, coughing and hacking to clear away the blood that had gathered in his lungs. Both Harruq and Azariah turned to the entrance, to witness their interloper.

Jessilynn stood at the tower door, a broken bow held in hand. That single arrow appeared to be the only one she had to offer. She stood there, a look of shock and horror upon her young face. Velixar was before her time, Harruq knew. She'd not seen the true face of Karak, and the horrid future he'd inflict upon Dezrel. Azariah snarled at her like an angered beast, hands lifting to assault her with Karak's magic, but she was not alone.

Jerico entered the tower, sword drawn, shield at ready.

"Must I slay all of Ashhur's pets this day?" Azariah asked. Dark magic swirled around his fingers, the beginnings of a great beam of shadow. The red-haired paladin dug in his heels, lifted his shield, and pulled back his sword as if for a thrust.

"I made a promise," he said. "And I shall keep it."

The roar of a lion marked the beam's tide. It slammed into a glowing shield half its size. Harruq cried out in worry, what little noise he could make given the force constricting his chest and lungs. Normally he would believe the paladin able to withstand any blow, no matter the source, but Karak had poured every shred of his lingering power upon Dezrel into this wretched recreation of the Prophet.

Jerico dropped to one knee, but his resolve never shook. He screamed, the act strengthening him, but his resolve was not the steel of his shield bowing inward. Already the light around it flickered. The metal cracked. Splintered.

Shattered into shards.

"Elholad!"

No metal touched his arm but for broken remnants of the metal grip. There was no need of it A shield of pure light swirled beside him, despite no physical substance to hold it firm. The blast of Karak's magic broke against it, making not a dent. It could not even dim its light.

"A promise made," Jerico repeated. A flick of his arm, and the beam of magic ricocheted aside. Two bounding steps, and the distance between them vanished. Lathaar's sword buried deep into Azariah's heart. The fallen angel might have survived the touch of plain steel, but Jerico was not alone. An after-image of an armored man shimmered into view like a wraith to stand with him side-by-side. His hands closed about the sword hilt.

"A promise kept," said the soul of Lathaar. Holy light swirled about his former blade. It blasted apart undead flesh. It turned bone to chalk. The red of Azariah's eyes burst like glass smashed beneath a soldier's boot. Shadows crawled in thousands of directions as the unholy power dissolved into nothingness. The image of Lathaar vanished with the explosion, but the holy light wreathing the blade remained until the last of Azariah's screams faded into nothingness. The mutilated corpse collapsed, and with it the dark hands that held Harruq and Aurelia imprisoned. Harruq dropped to his knees and coughed, beyond thrilled to have clean air flow into his lungs.

"Cutting it close there, bud," he spat out.

The light of both shield and sword faded, and a very tired Jerico turned his way. A loose smile pulled at his lips despite the tears running down his face.

"Sorry about that," he said. Jessilynn came running into the room and flung her arms around his waist. "I guess I still needed some help."

Harruq pushed to his feet and went over to help Aurelia to hers. His worry diminished a hundredfold when he saw she was likewise unharmed. She sank against him, and he wrapped her in his arms and kissed the top of her head.

"We did it," she whispered. Her forehead pressed to his chest. "Did I decide right?"

He held back a shiver.

"We'll see her again, Aurry. Never question that, or yourself."

Whether she believed him or not, he couldn't tell, but it seemed his words soothed her nonetheless. Her eyes closed, the tenseness of her muscles faded, and he held her tightly as his own exhausted fears drained from his body.

"Good, you left some for me," Deathmask said. Without even asking, he grabbed Lathaar's sword from Jerico's hand, limped over to Azariah's corpse, and knelt. Two quick cuts, and he tossed the sword to clatter on the floor. Deathmask stood, Azariah's head dangling from his grip, held by its pale, colorless hair. It no longer shifted and changed with magic, instead having reverted back to the angel's original features.

"Something the matter?" Harruq asked the enigmatic assassin, who stopped before the tower entrance.

"I also made a promise." Deathmask flung the fallen angel's head out the door. It bounced down the tower's winding outside steps and out of view. The man laughed despite his obvious pain and injury. "And damn it all, did that feel good."

32

Jessilynn climbed the steps of the tower through sheer force of will. The hour was late and her body begged for sleep. Her legs felt like wood. She cradled her bow to her chest, unable to feel her fingers. Every step up was accompanied by a wobble in her knees and the fear that she'd topple backwards. She never did, though, so slowly she ascended until arriving at the tower's very top.

"It's not enough, is it?" she asked the wind as she crossed the small flat balcony jutting from the tower's side. This tower was the highest of Mordeina's castle, and its view was spectacular, if not a bit intimidating. She leaned her hips against the crenelated wall and stared at the muted gold image of Devlimar, reflecting the moonlight in the distance. "Will it ever be enough?"

For all her bluster, her turning away Ahaesarus so elves and orcs might decide the fate of Dezrel, she had failed. Jerico had arrived. A paladin of Ashhur, come to slaughter a newborn prophet of Karak. Her attempt to break the constant cycle of Dezrel had been thwarted.

She tried to tell herself it was necessary. How could it not be, given the horrific power unleashed by that rotting, ever-changing body Azariah occupied? But knowing that and believing it were two different things. The brother gods had their battle, and as it had been since the dawn of humanity's creation, Ashhur had prevailed through the friendship and the aid of others. There was solace to find in that knowledge, she knew. Had it not been lectured so to her by her teachers? Karak was lonely and hateful. Ashhur welcomed all. His love of others was his strength.

Yet today, that gave her no comfort. She tried to convince herself that justice had been met and order restored. Proper order, not the nightmare Karak would build. Yet she could not shake the image of Ahaesarus with a crown...or would it be Jerico who accepted that new role?

There was no guarantee this would happen in her lifetime, of course. What of Jerico's children? What of her own? Might those of her blood one day attempt to claim the throne from Gregory? Absurd thoughts, she told herself, but could she deny them given Dezrel's long history? The Stronghold yet remained within Ker's lands. Who was to say they wouldn't one day convert the heart of a king?

Footsteps echoed behind her. She turned, and it seemed her own thoughts of him had summoned the red-haired paladin to join her upon the high balcony.

"Forgive me if I intrude," Jerico said. "I thought it best you weren't alone."

"Why's that?" she asked.

He joined her in looking out across the city to the distant Devlimar.

"I lied. I don't want to be alone, is all. There are few who might understand why, and I suspect you are one of them."

Jessilynn glanced at him, envisioning a golden crown upon his head. Dezrel could do far worse than Jerico as its new ruler…but then, no doubt many had thought the same of Azariah.

"Gregory will be king still, won't he?" she asked, unable to shake her fears and hoping that perhaps the other paladin might put them at ease.

"That so far seems the consensus," Jerico told her. "With Harruq returning to his role as regent until he comes of age. Not everyone is happy with this arrangement, of course. Some blame a lack of leadership for allowing Azariah to consolidate his power so quickly and easily. They prefer Ahaesarus to rule as regent over Harruq. Given how badly angelic rule devastated Mordan, I doubt that plan will gain much momentum."

Jerico cleared his throat, attempting to address something he knew would be awkward.

"I heard about what you did to Ahaesarus, by the way. He's fine, just a little worse for wear. It'll take a lot more than a holy arrow through the shoulder to bring a monument like him down."

Heat flushed up her neck. "Should I be ashamed or proud of what I did?" she asked, earning herself a laugh.

"Perhaps a little bit of both? Though from what I heard about how Ahaesarus had begun behaving, I think you saved him from walking down a path similar to Azariah. Perhaps a little bit of humbling was exactly what the big oaf needed."

"Is that what this oaf needed?"

They turned to find a very solemn Ahaesarus climbing the stairs behind them. He sported a cloth bandage tied around his bare left arm and side.

"I'm surprised you didn't fly up here," Jessilynn said, turning back to the balcony and fighting off a fresh wave of embarrassment.

"The movement of my wings angers my side," the angel said as he exited onto the tower balcony. "Not to say I don't deserve it, but I'd prefer not to seize up and plummet to my death when I try to join you."

She glanced over her shoulder. "Join me? Or kill me?"

"I do not bring my sword, Jessilynn. And if we are to judge by recent events, my life is more in danger of you than yours is of me."

Jessilynn laughed despite her exhaustion and heartache. Whatever pleasure she felt, it was short-lived when staring at Devlimar. The surviving fallen had fled Mordeina upon Azariah's death, and they holed up in rooms and mansions scattered throughout that beautiful city. That they still lived robbed whatever joy she should feel. Not that she wanted them slain, whether or not they deserved it or not. No, what bothered her was knowing that the war wasn't over yet. More bloodshed lurked upon the horizon.

"I hear we're to attack Devlimar tomorrow morning," she said.

"That was my plan, yes. Do you disagree?"

"Do you care what I think?"

His enormous hand settled upon her shoulder. She flinched. She shouldn't be afraid, she *knew* she shouldn't be afraid, but it didn't change her instinctual reaction. She grimaced, but when she glanced his way, it was clear that Ahaesarus saw her fear, and it was *him* who felt ashamed.

"I believe you are a voice I should have listened to from the very beginning," he said. "Yes, Jessilynn, I do care what you think. I care greatly to hear it, because right now I fear I am in danger of becoming my brother. I do not seek to use humans to wage my war, nor their bloodshed to prove my own righteousness.

So speak your heart, young paladin. I believe I am finally ready to hear it."

Jessilynn looked to Devlimar. Her mind swam through a dozen different memories. Darius's words echoed in her ears. *That's all that matters now to him. Not salvation. Not the love of his children. Only victory in his name.* She remembered the dead paladin's fears, his beliefs, even as he sat beside her as no more than a shimmering soul. Against those memories she cast the sight of Ahaesarus lording over his army of beast-men, angels, and soldiers. The sight of him threatening to kill her if she did not step aside so he might slay Azariah. Of the two, she knew who to trust, and who to believe.

She turned to Jerico, who crossed his arms and nodded to her.

"Speak freely. Neither of us are here to judge you."

Jessilynn's attention returned to Devlimar. *Speak freely*, he tells her, as if it would be so easy. As if she herself fully understood her heart.

"I don't know what I believe," she said. "I know only how I feel. I see Devlimar, and my heart breaks. We fight, and we die, and it seems to never end. The war is won. Karak has been defeated. Azariah is dead, his undead army broken, and his few surviving fallen retreated into hiding. And still it isn't enough. Come the morning, we march again to bleed and die for Ashhur. We'll cover the streets of Devlimar with blood, and to prove what? That Ashhur is better? That Ashhur is stronger?"

Jessilynn clutched her bow tightly to her chest and closed her eyes. Tears threatened to overwhelm her.

"I have always believed Ashhur cared for us. I have always believed that our god—our kind, forgiving god—*loved* us. Yet now it seems we do nothing but battle for his amusement. We suffer so he might be proven superior. We wage war. We kill. Tomorrow we march into Devlimar with banners held high and our swords sparkling as we commit yet another slaughter. Does Ashhur love us, Ahaesarus? Does he truly? Because he abandoned us when we needed him five years ago. He abandoned us on the Night of Black Wings. Yet again, Karak's followers rise up. Yet again, we fight a Gods' War. I don't feel loved. I don't feel cherished. I feel used. I feel like a weapon."

"You would blame Ashhur for the actions of his fallen?" Ahaesarus carefully asked. She could sense his stubbornness surfacing, his refusal for Ashhur to accept any blame.

"Look at what he did to them," she said, fighting off a fresh wave of tears. "Look at what monsters he made Azariah and his angels when he commanded them to fall. But only to fall, damn it, only fall. Why not kill them if such a curse is within his power, Ahaesarus? Why leave them so wounded and furious? To teach them a lesson? To make them suffer? But while they suffered, *we* suffered! *We*, the children he professes to love above all else. I grew up listening to stories of the sky splitting, and angels flying forth from the Golden Eternity to protect us. How do I put that side by side with a god that cast down his fallen, and then did nothing as those fallen took out their hatred and fury on the innocent? As tens of thousands needlessly died in a slaughter that will haunt us for generations? I see no answer that does not horrify me. We are all dying, and for what? Games, Ahaesarus, all I see are games and wars and chances to prove Ashhur is better. But he's not better than Karak, not if that's all we are to him. Not if he stops caring for us."

She gestured to Devlimar and the waiting fallen.

"Is Ashhur master of this world, or are we? Because all I see is us dying to prove him its master. It's a cruel joke. It's everything backwards. And tomorrow morning, we will suffer it all over again."

The angel fell silent. She could not read the expression on his pristine face. What she said, it teetered close to blasphemy, at least in how she understood it. But was she wrong? She didn't think so. She wished she were, so deeply that it made her heart ache. That she might believe Ashhur's grace surrounded her, protected her, and held her as if she were the most important thing in all the world. A wounded part inside her still believed. Another part believed the power of her shining arrows, and the destruction they caused, was more important to her god than any forgiveness or wisdom that might pass through her lips.

"Heavy words," Jerico said quietly to break the silence. "But are you willing to listen, angel?"

Ahaesarus stepped closer. Something about his demeanor changed. His voice softened. His eyes flickered, and they suddenly shimmered gold.

"Jessilynn," he said. "Take up your bow."

The air thickened about her. The hairs on her arms and neck stood on end.

"It's broken," she said.

"Take up your bow, Jessilynn, and ready an arrow for flight."

Jessilynn lifted her bow in her left hand and grabbed the string with the right. A deep crack ran along the wood just above the grip, and it split open as she pulled the string. Not much, but just enough so that she could withdraw the string even farther than normal before the resistance heightened. At the touch of her fingers, an arrow of light materialized, soft blue wisps of what seemed like smoke rising off its arrowhead. Jessilynn held the arrow at ready, pointed toward Devlimar, but she did not release. It wasn't time. She felt it in her bones.

"Death was never my intention, yet it always seemed my path," Ahaesarus said. "Tonight, let me make amends. I leave this world to you. I leave it to my children, whom I still love."

The arrow on Jessilynn's bow flared with light. A distant song rang in her ears, the words indistinguishable but their meaning crystalline. Hope. Change. Determination. Wind blew across her, as if a thunderstorm were brewing about their tower. The walls between the worlds were thinning.

"What's happening?" she whispered, for she was no longer alone. Two women hovered to either side of her, mirrored reflections of one another. One she recognized, the woman named Tessanna, her billowing dress blacker than the night, matched in hue only by the hair that flowed behind her with such length it rivaled a floor-length cloak. The other woman appeared the same in face and hair, though her dress was white, and her skin a healthy gold compared to the pale, almost porcelain hue of Tessanna.

The two most recent daughters of balance, Jessilynn realized. This was Mira, whom Lathaar had told her stories of during her childhood. The woman who gave her life fighting Thulos.

Both daughters extended their hands. Orbs grew from their fingertips, one black, the other white. They crackled with lightning. They shimmered with power so deep the heavens rumbled. When they spoke, their voices carried undeniable authority.

"Let the unending war see its end," said Mira.

"Let my proclamation be unmade," said Tessanna.

Then, in unison, "Mother has seen enough."

Jessilynn felt the arrow threatening to slip from her fingers. The ringing in her ears reached its crescendo. The tower shook beneath her feet. She caught sight of movement from the corner of her eye, and she glanced over to see Darius standing nearby with his arms crossed and a smile on his face. Blue light shone about his body, and upon his arrival, Jerico staggered in surprise.

"Cast down the golden city," spoke Darius. "Let this war end, and Dezrel belong to the mortals who walk its lands."

The moment had come. Jessilynn looked to Devlimar, and within its extravagant halls she saw every horrid sin Azariah had wrought. She saw his need to rule. She saw his ambition to be a king, if not a god. Above all, she saw his aching desire to be superior to those he was meant to serve. When the armies of the beast-men were devouring the north, too many angels had remained behind to build their monument to their flying city, as if the marble and gold were more important than the lives they were sworn to protect. Now the survivors hid within it, and they would kill any who came for them. Even in defeat, they would kill. They would spread more suffering.

But no more. Cast down the golden city. If it must be done, then let it be done.

Jessilynn let fly her arrow.

It streaked across the night sky, and it did not travel alone. Mira and Tessanna unleashed their own tremendous blasts of energy, twin beams of darkness and light that made a mockery of mortal limits. The night sky did not split, not like the stories Jessilynn had listened to all her life, but it did crack in a long spiderweb of light. Angels hovered in the air above her, first dozens, then hundreds, then thousands. They all held golden bows in their hands, and they pulled back their strings to manifest holy arrows so very familiar to her.

Jessilynn's arrow was not the greatest, but it was the first of a thousand that followed. The earthbound city of angels collapsed under the assault. The ground roiled as if Dezrel itself were enraged. The twin beams of Celestia's daughters shattered buildings. Arrows of light battered down rooftops and walls. The gold withered and broke. The city twisted and tumbled. The assault was mercilessly complete. Jessilynn watched it with her broken bow in hand, tears streaming down her face as the stone beneath her trembled. Her ears ached from the depth of noise, greater than any storm, louder than any thunder.

Arrow after arrow, swirling around the twin blasts of the daughters. Nothing halted its flow. They carved deep grooves into the soil. They collapsed the city's great spires. She saw faint black-winged dots scurrying like ants, but there was no escape from the arrows that fell like rain. What remained of the fallen were buried with the rubble, the twisted wreckage of Devlimar forever their tomb.

Mere seconds passed, but witnessing the destruction felt like it took an entire age. Part of Jessilynn wished to break down sobbing. Part of her was too empty and drained to offer anything for the lost city but a weary sigh.

When it ended, the silence was frightening to her ringing ears.

"No more false balance," Tessanna and Mira said in perfect unison. "No more wars. Peace, if humanity may keep it."

Jessilynn dropped her bow and looked behind her. Ahaesarus was gone. So too were the daughters of balance. Darius remained, and he stood there grinning at a stone-faced Jerico, saying nothing, only waiting.

"Shouldn't you be busy being dead?" Jerico asked.

"I made a promise," Darius answered, and he laughed. "I'm still waiting for you, Jerico. It's not my fault you're too stubborn to die."

The men embraced, yet even as they held one another, Darius faded into mist and memory. Jerico dropped to a knee on the balcony floor, and only then did he let his emotions break. He bowed his head low, tears starting to fall, and wept in prayer to his god.

"Jessilynn?" cried a familiar voice. She looked to the eastern side of the tower to see Ahaesarus flying up to join her. Despite his injured side, he seemed quite capable of flight. There was no hiding the shock and surprise on his face. "Jessilynn, what have you done?"

I fear I am in danger of becoming my brother.

Jessilynn looked to the stars, and the fading silver lines that had broken the heavens. The angelic brigade of archers had long since faded, and they left behind only a peaceful, twinkling night sky. Nothing remained of Devlimar. It was a brutal crater, a smote land of upturned earth, broken marble, and buried gold. She trembled at the realization that swept over her, of a truth she should have realized sooner.

Ahaesarus had no brother.

"Peace," she whispered, and she bowed her head in prayer to the god that watched over her, the god who had stood at her side in the guise of a loyal angel. "Yes, Ashhur, we will keep it, and cherish it. We have no choice, lest we be buried with the city of your fallen."

33

Tarlak stood at the cusp of the crater that now marked the burial grounds of what had been Devlimar. It was the morning after the victorious siege of Mordeina and the defeat of Azariah's fallen angels. Tarlak looked upon the ruins for the first time in the morning light and shook his head in awe.

"Makes one feel quite small, doesn't it?" he said.

Harruq stood beside him, hands resting comfortably on his sword hilts. "It's definitely a lot more than I could ever do with Salvation and Condemnation."

Nothing remained of the city. It was as if the fields of Dezrel were a mouth, and they had opened up to swallow the gold, silver, and pearls of the tiny shard of the Golden Eternity. No grass remained, only upturned earth. If it had been flat, it might have resembled a recently plowed field in preparation for planting. Instead, it was drastically uneven, with jagged hills rising up to cover crumbled spires and deep pits marking where chasms had swallowed entire buildings. The very tips of various spires poked through in places, like faint landmarks of a bygone age. Despite their presumed value, no citizen of Mordeina had dared venture forth in an attempt to pillage its wealth. Maybe one day, Tarlak presumed, but not yet. Everyone alive was deathly, and rightfully, afraid of these ruins.

"Why not do this from the start?" Tarlak wondered. He gestured to the complete and total devastation. "Why have us bleed and die in warfare? Was it really so important we meet on the battlefield?"

"Why did Ashhur wait until I knelt alone to send us his angels?" Harruq asked in a somber tone. "Why did Celestia grant Tessanna her power if she'd use it to let in the war demons at Veldaren? Why let us live our lives at all, since we're certain to fuck it up and make a mess of things?"

"And so the alternative is a painted, static world with no changes or decisions of any kind," Tarlak said, following the thread of logic. "Huh. Sounds like something Karak would be proud of."

The half-orc's mouth crooked into a half-smile.

"I don't think these questions have answers we'd like, Tar. Certainly not if you want to keep wearing that pendant of Ashhur around your neck."

In response, Tarlak pulled out the golden mountain looped by a chain he kept with him at all times. The wizard held it up, letting the morning light reflect off the gold.

"Did you see it, when it happened?" he asked, referring to Devlimar's destruction.

"Not well," Harruq admitted. "I was down by the castle, so I only saw everything that happened above the city walls."

"I opened a portal to outside the city the moment it started." He shuddered at the memory. "I had to witness it for myself. It was terrifying, Harruq. The wrath of god and goddess, unleashed upon a city. They could break us in moments, if they so desired. With a wave of her hand, Celestia could unleash both Karak and Ashhur from their prisons, and all we'd know is endless warfare. Even the line between life and death feels so loose. So *arbitrary*. This world of Dezrel they created, and all of us saps that fill its cities and rivers and valleys...we're just playthings. Do our decisions even matter? What importance do our lives hold against such cosmic significance?"

"Well...we're important enough to be playthings of gods. That means something, right?"

Tarlak returned the pendant to its rightful place underneath his robe and over his heart.

"I try to be serious, and you respond by being glib."

Harruq elbowed him in the side. "I *was* being serious. We *do* matter to them. How else can you interpret Dezrel's history? The question is, *why* do we matter to them? Do they love us? Hate us? Wish for us to do better? Or are we mere pieces in a game they're pushing around a board, eager to see which of the brother gods can pull off a win?"

They both fell silent as they overlooked the broken hills marked by jagged tips of golden spires.

"I don't think we're pieces anymore," Tarlak said. "Nor part of a game. Do you know what I see before me? Celestia has flipped the table. The board is upside down. The pieces are scattered and gone, those that survived being crushed underneath said table."

"Which means...?"

The wizard laughed. "You need ask a scholar of religious studies. Maybe find a priest or three. As for myself? It gives me hope. If Ashhur is willing to focus on us becoming our better selves, and less on defeating Karak, then maybe Dezrel will see a few years of peace."

A shadow passed overhead, and they looked up to see a familiar winged horse slowly curling down from the clouds to join them. Tarlak lifted his hat in greeting. Sonowin landed, stamped her hoof twice, and then lowered her neck so Jessilynn could dismount.

"Come to admire your handiwork, Arrow of Ashhur?" Harruq asked with a shit-eating grin. 'Arrow of Ashhur' was the title clumsily given to her by some of the first people who heard of her involvement in the destruction of Devlimar, as well as in reference to the initial, leading arrow that had soared across the night sky to mark the start of the ensuing heavenly barrage.

"Please don't refer to me as such," she responded. A bit of red crept up her neck to her cheeks and she looked aside. "It makes me deeply uncomfortable hearing people give me credit for something so far beyond my power. This was hardly my doing. I was merely the catalyst."

"You're talking to the Godslayer," said Harruq. "And the reason the angels arrived on Dezrel in the first place. I'm one of very few people alive who knows what you're going through."

Tarlak smacked the half-orc in the chest. "Relying on this big idiot for sympathy? You poor girl. But duly noted, paladin. We'll spare you further compliments, and instead I'll ask why you're out here with us."

Strangely enough, the red in her cheeks refused to go away.

"I plan to fly with Sonowin back to the Dezren elves and inform them of Dieredon's...passing," she said. "I was hoping to say goodbye to Jerico before I left, but I cannot find him. I thought perhaps he was out here with you."

The King of the Fallen

Tarlak flinched despite efforts to the contrary. He'd long considered Dieredon a friend, and hearing of his death during the battle had added yet another stone of sorrow onto the mountain already lodged atop his back. No funeral would be held for him in Mordeina. Harruq, acting as little King Gregory's steward, had ordered the body wrapped and preserved in preparation for travel to the Quellan elves. Scoutmaster Dieredon was a hero of Dezrel, and he deserved to be honored by his people. Tarlak wondered if he might be allowed to attend the ceremony, or if the elves would deny him a presence.

He shook his head, forcing away the depressing thoughts. He'd have more time to dwell on politics later, as well as mourn in private the loss of a friend.

"I can open you a portal to him, if you'd like," Tarlak said instead.

Jessilynn thought a moment, then shook her head.

"I think we both need some time alone to dwell on everything Ashhur has said and done. We will speak when I return. When you do see him, tell him..." She paused a moment, her eyes far away. "Tell him we need no Citadel to have a place in this world, and when I return, I hope together we may find it."

"Of course," Harruq said. His demeanor turned somber enough to ensure Jessilynn knew he was serious. "I'll tell him. And if you'll listen to any advice this dumb half-orc has to offer, it would be to focus on yourself for now, paladin. A lot's happened, and you'll bear the shame and honor of your role for the rest of your life. Find a way to make peace with it."

"Is that what you did, Godslayer?"

"He sure did," Tarlak answered for him. "Over the course of five years, while kicking and screaming the entire time. I pray you do better than he did."

She laughed, and it was so light, so soft; a reminder to Tarlak of how young the woman still was, especially compared to old war heroes like he and Harruq. He sincerely hoped a better future awaited her than the past that left her face scarred and her faith horribly tested.

"Thank you," she said. "Good day to the both of you, and good luck in your work with King Gregory."

She returned to Sonowin's back. The horse dipped her head and neighed, which Tarlak safely assumed was the loyal beast saying goodbye in her own way. Tarlak bowed as if accepting the gratitude of a noble lord. As far as he was concerned, Sonowin was better and more useful than most human lords, anyway.

"Safe travels," he said.

Sonowin's wings spread wide, and she took to the air with a sudden gust of wind. The two watched her fly, the winged horse rapidly becoming a distant white speck amongst the clouds.

"Even Ashhur's paladins are shook," Harruq said after a time.

"Good," Tarlak said. "After the gods ravage the world in war three damn times, you'd think everyone involved would need some time to reassess."

"Even you?"

He smiled. "Of all us Eschaton, my sister was the best of us. If Delysia's faith in Ashhur never wavered, then neither will mine. At the very least, I'll keep her in my heart, and trust that when my time finally comes, it'll be her face I first see when I step into the Golden Eternity."

"Hopefully," Harruq said with a grin. "What if it's that Cecil person whose body you stole, there to demand it back?"

"Fuck that guy. He's rotting in the Abyss, I'm sure of it."

They both laughed, Harruq at the joke, Tarlak at the sheer absurdity of his entire life. The weight of the world lessened, and when he looked once more to Devlimar's ruins, lit by warm morning light, he decided that perhaps his initial view of the land was accurate. It was a field recently plowed and prepared for harvest. Tarlak was starting to get on in years, but he had the entire second half of his life ahead of him as far as he was concerned. Perhaps he might help grow a new world in it, one with a lot less death and destruction.

Suddenly tired of looking upon Dezrel's largest grave, Tarlak looped his fingers together and stretched out until his knuckles popped.

"Well, Jessilynn might not want a portal, but I sure as the Abyss don't feel like walking back to the city. Where to next, half-orc? The castle, and young Gregory? Maybe to Ahaesarus so we can find out what he and the rest of his angels plan on doing now that Azariah's been defeated? I don't think anyone will be too happy for a return to angelic rule, but we'll likely need their help to ensure what lords are left alive properly bend the knee and swear allegiance."

Harruq laughed, easily dismissing all of Tarlak's suggestions.

"Nah, piss on all of that," he said. "Take me to Aurelia. I want nothing more than to spend time with my wife and daughter."

"Request granted," Tarlak said. A snap of his fingers ripped open a swirling blue tear in reality. "And honestly, right now, that sounds like the absolute best place to be."

34

Harruq scratched at a bite on his neck, once again grumbling at Ahaesarus's need to meet him so many miles north of Mordeina in some bug-infested forest.

"If you're going to trudge me through the wilderness, you could at least give me a reason," he said. "Or have let Tarlak open us up a portal instead of making me walk."

The angel pressed on, unbothered by the low-hanging branches and the occasional thorny bush he had to shove aside.

"You whine like a child. More so, perhaps, for during my time with children I do not remember them being so full of complaints. Is that your nature, or the nature of all half-orcs?"

"Nah, that's just me, but I wouldn't call it whining. 'Stating the obvious truth' sounds a whole lot better."

"Well, then I shall tell you an obvious truth, and that is we are almost there."

It had been two weeks since Azariah's death and the complete obliteration of Devlimar. Treasure hunters had attempted to excavate the ruins, as Tarlak had predicted, but what little they found was withered and rotten. There would be no salvaging it. Ashhur's and Celestia's condemnation was complete. With the fallen angels' deaths, and Ahaesarus's guidance, young Gregory had been reappointed to the throne in a modest ceremony. And of course, as much as he grumbled about it, Harruq had been declared his regent. All the duties Harruq loathed resumed immediately, including more long meetings and constant complaints from those in power. So when Ahaesarus had asked Harruq to accompany him on a trip north of the city, to some secret place in a forest, he had been all too eager to accept the diversion.

"So should I be worried?" he asked as the trees started to thin. "I feel like you're plotting something, and I doubt I need to remind you how well things went the last time angels were secretly plotting behind all our backs."

"No," Ahaesarus said, flinching as if he'd been kicked. "You need not."

The King of the Fallen

The trees suddenly halted and the ground became uneven. Enormous slates of stone rose up to form caves and shelters, and only the occasional skinny tree managed to find a home amid the turmoil. Before one such cave swirled a tremendous golden portal. Harruq stared at it, certain he could see images on the other side, but they were hazy and unsteady, like reflections atop a pool of water. Within them he saw hints of green hills, a blue sky, and a distant palace of gold. Several dozen angels stood before the portal, and upon Harruq's arrival, they bowed low.

"To the Godslayer," they said in unison. A chill ran up Harruq's spine.

"This is far too much," he said, but he could not help but grin. "But it's nice to get *some* recognition, finally."

The angels began filing into the portal, whose surface shimmered like a melting mirror.

"I feel like I owe you, of all people, an explanation," Ahaesarus said. "For it was your heartfelt prayer that split the skies and brought us to Dezrel. If we are to leave, then let you be the one given our reason, and left to share the news with others."

Harruq crossed his arms and grunted. That the angels were eager to leave didn't surprise him, not after all that had happened. He stared at the swirling golden gate, wondering just what lay on the other side. Wondering if his little girl was in there. If she watched. If she waited.

"I'm listening," he said.

Ahaesarus removed his sword from his back and jammed it deep into the earth. His hands clutched the hilt and he leaned his weight upon it.

"It is only after much thought and prayer that I came upon this realization," he said. "One I wish my friend Azariah had reached himself before he...crossed lines that must never be crossed." The angel paused momentarily, then shook his head as if to clear away a fog. "Once the first Gods' War ended, and we joined Ashhur in the Golden Eternity, we believed we were made perfect. We were granted our wings, with our status as Wardens elevated to a truly divine nature. Living in a land without sin, without darkness, for so many centuries seemed to prove us correct. This was the fate of all things, was it not? To be made good, and perfect, once the turmoil of this mortal life reached its end."

Ahaesarus closed his eyes, apparently needing another moment to gather himself before continuing with his shame.

"I see now that we were are not perfect, Harruq. How could any of us think so, after witnessing the destruction Azariah wrought? But that was not our belief when we first returned. The Golden Eternity changed us, blessed us, made us perfect…or so we thought. Except in that divine land, we suffered no hunger. We felt no thirst. We encountered no temptation. Free of every burden, surrounded only by love and friendship, what darkness were we to find?"

The angel ripped his sword free of the earth and held it before him.

"Then we returned, and we were as foolish, prideful, and fallible as we had always been. Nothing about us had changed, yet now we walked Dezrel with a certainty of our own perfection. If anything, we were weaker to the temptations, for we were no longer willing to accept our positions as Wardens. We saw humanity as being beneath us, for had we not watched over them for centuries from on high? Had we not been free of the sins you committed daily? And so came our pride. So came our fall."

Harruq put a hand on the giant angel's shoulder. "You did your best. I've always thought that of you. But you were given a tremendous burden, Ahaesarus. Try not to blame yourselves for sometimes failing. We've all had our share of fuck-ups. But for most people, an occasional stumble means breaking a chair or hurting a friend's feelings. With you, and us, it meant the fate of kingdoms."

A faint smile crossed Ahaesarus's golden face.

"A comforting thought," he said, "but I need not pity or comforting. Our time on this land will only wear us down. We who have tasted the peace of eternity no longer know how to endure the stings of mortal life. To remain your guardians will lead to yet another fall, of that I am certain. It is time we return. It is time we leave Dezrel in human hands."

"And elvish hands," Aurelia added, emerging from the woods behind them. "Don't forget, we lived here first."

The giant angel crossed his arms and grinned at the elf.

"Did you follow us?" he asked.

"I did, and it wasn't hard. You two leave a trail wide enough for wagons to rumble through. I'd apologize for following you, but I decided it not worth the risk that my lunk of a husband here might make important decisions without me."

Harruq took his wife into his arms and squeezed her against his side.

"I'm glad you're here," he whispered.

"Need the emotional support?" she whispered back.

"I was more thinking a portal home. I've been dreading the walk out through that forest, and you can spare me the hassle."

The little elf kissed the tip of his nose. "Just for that, I'm tempted to make you walk anyway."

She pulled away from him and addressed Ahaesarus like the elven representative she truly was. Her hands swayed out as if in a dance as she curtseyed before him. Her green and gold dress fluttered in the wind billowing forth from the divine portal.

"All of Dezrel owes you a great debt for the sacrifices you have made," she said. "Defeating the war god Thulos spared us all from his tyranny. Despite the failures that followed, and the great fall of many of your brethren, I pray you accept the good you did upon this world, and know we will cherish your memories with fondness and joy."

Ahaesarus laughed and used his sword to salute her.

"You possess a far more silver tongue than your husband," he said. "But thank you, Aurelia Thyne Tun. I will try to keep your words close as the days of eternity pass."

Ahaesarus bowed once more, and then approached the golden portal. Harruq felt a spike of panic flow through him despite it being thoroughly irrational. He wasn't ready to let go, not yet, so he stalled with a question that honestly did worry him.

"What of Ashhur?" Harruq asked. "And what about Karak? Are they truly done with this world? It's...it's a little hard to believe that."

The angel paused. He tilted his head to the side and closed his eyes for a moment, as if listening to a distant voice.

"The brother gods will never truly be done with this world," he said. "I will not speak for Karak, but Ashhur will always love his children. He will always grant them mercy, and he will keep his eyes upon Dezrel so his followers may wield his power. But this is the end of the wars. This is the end of the dance of brother against brother, each determined to prove superiority over the other. Karak may still try, but he will dance alone."

Ahaesarus lifted his sword, staring at it as if seeing the blade for the first time.

"Ashhur is a god of forgiveness and love, and there is neither in warfare. I pray Dezrel remembers this lesson, and takes it to heart. As for myself..." He gestured with the sword. "I have no need of this where I go. Might you one day give it to someone deserving?"

"If we're lucky, no one will have need of it here, either," Harruq said. "But yeah, I'll keep an eye on it if it'll make you feel better."

Ahaesarus jammed the sword back into the dirt, and without another word, he walked into the portal with his head held high. The divine gateway sealed with a loud crack, the sound of stone sliding over stone, and then it was gone. The clearing dimmed. The sounds of nature resumed with birdsongs and the occasional buzz of insects. Aurelia slid her hand into Harruq's and leaned against his arm.

"Are you all right?" she asked

He stood there, staring at the cave entrance where the portal had once been. He couldn't bring himself to leave. It felt like his feet were rooted to the ground.

"I will be," he said. "I was just realizing this was it. We're alone. For five years we've relied on the angels to keep us safe, and it was their presence that ensured Antonil, and then Gregory, could hold Mordan's throne. Now they're gone. It'll be up to us."

"But not only us," Aurelia said. "And I hope it will never be just us anymore. We've done our part for peace, wouldn't you say?"

Harruq laughed. "I'm not sure either of us has the heart to retire to some forgotten village and wile away our days in quiet solitude. That was more of a Qurrah thing to do, anyway. If people need help, I'm going to help. If having a big scary half-orc at the boy king's side prevents anyone from acting stupid and trying to shove this country into another goddamn war, well...I'm willing to make that sacrifice."

"I'd say 'never change,' Har, but you've actually changed a lot since we first met." She squeezed his hand.

"For the better, I hope?"

She stood on her tip-toes so she might kiss his lips. When she finally pulled back, she stared up with those walnut-colored eyes of hers that were, in Harruq's modest opinion, the most beautiful sight in all creation.

"I wouldn't still be with you if it wasn't." She flicked a hand behind her back, opening up a blue portal into the forest air. "Are you ready to go home?"

"Home," he said, and gave a crooked smile. "Gods, yes, I'm ready."

Epilogue

Young Mathis knelt behind the crate, his hands over his nose to block the stink of fish from the surrounding docks. He peered around the crate's edge, trying to catch sight of the enormous trade ship that harbored several docks over. The entire city of Angkar was abuzz with the news, so much that Mathis had to see if he could spot the newcomers.

"Whatcha' doin'?"

Mathis jumped as if caught with his hand down his pants. He angrily spun to face the newcomer, then calmed upon seeing it was only a rather pretty girl a few years older than him. Her hair was dirty blond and cut short at the ears, and she wore dark gray trousers and a pretty blue shirt of a style that Mathis didn't quite recognize. Her eyes were such a deep brown that they almost faded into the black of her pupils.

"Didn't you hear?" he said, choking down his initial frustration and hoping she wouldn't notice how he'd been staring. "Boats from Angelport arrived, the first in years!"

The girl knelt beside him, her shoulder brushing his as she peered around the barrel. He couldn't decide if she were teasing him or not, and that made him feel all the more awkward.

"Is that so?" she asked. "What's so special about Angelport?"

"Are you stupid?" he asked. Mathis didn't know much in his nine years of life, but he sure knew more than this older girl. "No one has sailed here from Angelport because the orcs have been holding Angelport under siege for like...ever. It's the only place that's somehow survived in the east."

"That sure sounds impressive," the girl said. "Do you know how they do it?"

"I heard it's with dark magic."

"Dark magic?" she asked incredulously.

"Yeah, dark magic. How else do you think they lived so long as they have? They sacrifice their babies, that's what my friend Willa says."

The King of the Fallen

Willa was one year Mathis's junior, and had never been outside the walls of Angkar, but his father was a sailor and that made the claim seem trustworthy enough to him. This strange girl, however, was far from convinced.

"No, I don't think that's it," she said. "It's a lot simpler than that. A lot of hard fighting, and a lot of dead soldiers who deserved better. Now shush. Look. There they are."

Mathis knew men and women had disembarked from the giant boat all throughout the day, but he assumed something was special about this group. A squad of four men armed with swords escorted the man and woman down the gangplank. They were distant, so Mathis could see only a bit of them, but what he noticed immediately was how the young man's fancy blue coat ended at the elbow for his right arm.

"That's Nathaniel Gemcroft," he said, proud of his knowledge. He'd picked the name up from various conversations he'd been eavesdropping on all morning. "He used to be rich, and like, super rich, but now he isn't anymore. I bet he's come here to beg for money. Rich people don't like it when they're not rich anymore."

"You're right about that," the girl said. The way she stared at the distant couple made Mathis feel uncomfortable. This girl, she only seemed maybe two years old than him, three at most. Yet her focus reminded him of an adult. Too calm. Too sad. "But do you know of the woman with him?"

Her clothes were expensive, that much he could tell. Her dress was a vibrant purple mixed with some sort of white silk wrap. Most her face was hidden underneath a wide-brimmed white hat meant to block out the sun.

"I don't know," he said. "But I bet she's important."

"Oh, very important. Don't you know? I thought you were smart and knew everything."

His neck flushed. So she *was* making fun of him.

"Stop being mean," he said with a frown. "I didn't do nothing to you."

The girl dipped her head in a bow that was strangely formal.

"Forgive me," she said. "I'll make it up to you, how about that? I know that woman. Her name is Zusa Gemcroft. Have you heard of her?"

The name was less common among the rumors, but not unknown.

"Um, a family friend, I think," he said. "Someone real important to Alyssa Gemcroft before she died."

The girl slowly nodded, and yet again it felt like she was suddenly sizing Mathis up.

"Close, but not quite. Zusa was her lover, Mathis, and her appointed godmother for Nathaniel."

"How do you know that?" he asked, her matter-of-fact statement making him blush. Just who was this girl? At first he thought her mocking him, or at the least just having fun, but there was an aura about her that was distinctly dark and serious. It triggered his instinct to run away, even as her beauty drew him in. Their eyes met, and he again realized he was staring. He quickly looked to the ground, hoping she wouldn't notice. Only then did he see the twin pair of daggers hanging comfortably from her belt.

"There you are," said a new voice.

Mathis looked up, and he nearly shit his britches. The woman named Zusa, she was there, right there, along with her escort of soldiers. Nathaniel was by her side, and he looked even more like a young prince up close, what with his fancy clothes and ornate rapier strapped to his thigh.

"You shouldn't be running off on your own," Nathaniel said. "You'll make us worry."

"Make *you* worry," the girl said, grinning. "I think my mother would call it 'good practice'."

"I'd still prefer some warning before you vanish into a foreign city," Zusa said. She glanced Mathis's way, and one of her dark eyebrows crooked upward. "Have you made a friend?"

Mathis immediately wanted to deny even knowing her, but the girl just smiled sweetly and put her hand on his sleeveless shoulder. Her fingers felt like fire to his skin.

"Just a boy with ears listening everywhere he shouldn't be," she said, and apparently that was good enough for Zusa.

One of the soldiers quietly whispered something to Nathaniel, who nodded when the man finished.

"I thought so," he said, turning to Zusa. "Our home is ready, but not without incident. It seems the guilds here are already making sure we feel...welcome."

The smile that crossed Zusa's face was colder than the ocean in the deep of winter.

"To be expected," she said, and turned to the girl beside Mathis. "Come home before dark. I'd like us both to have at least one worry-free night of sleep before you resume your training."

The squad left the docks for the city proper of Angkar. Mathis watched them go, his mind struggling to piece together everything that just happened. Home? This girl with him, did she...did she live with the Gemcrofts?

"I should be going," she said, and she blew Mathis a kiss. "I'll see you around."

"But, um, where will you be staying?" he asked.

"My mother bought us a mansion," she said. "I'm sure you've heard, what with all that eavesdropping you've been doing. Come knocking. Maybe we can play sometime."

Mansion? Come knocking? What was this absolute nonsense? Mathis's father was a fisherman. He shared a home with two other families, for they could afford no better. The idea of playing in a mansion, and enjoying oneself among that level of wealth, was so beyond his understanding it frightened him with the mere attempt to imagine it.

"Wait," he called. His feet weighed a thousand stone. His tongue was lead in his mouth. "Who...um, what's your name? You never introduced yourself!"

She gave him a sweet smile eerily similar to her mother's, and it was equally cold.

"Erin," she said.

"Erin Gemcroft?" he asked. Did that mean she was related to Nathaniel? An unheard-of sister?

"No, not Gemcroft," she said. Her hands fell to the daggers at her sides as she calmly walked into the crowd, and she called out over her shoulder, "Erin Felhorn."

David Dalglish

A Note from the Author

Five years. It's been five years since I wrote one of these end notes for a Half-Orc novel. I don't know how to truly convey the difficulty in returning to a world after such a long gap (though hopefully you didn't notice that while reading it, or I performed my job poorly). I'm a lot better about taking notes and outlining storylines now, but it's a fairly recent change for me. For this book, I had nothing but what lingered in my head for where I 'thought' the story was going. So when I came back, finally ready to get this story put to paper, I decided to toss everything out the window. I re-read the Prison of Angels and King of the Vile, and decided to let the story go where it wanted to go.

And it so very much did not go where I originally intended it to go all those years ago.

Before I ramble more, I do want to thank everyone who has patiently—or even semi-patiently—waited for me to get back to this series. I may joke about "when's the next Half-Orcs" on Twitter or Facebook, but I assure you, I do understand how blessed I am to have so many eager to return to this world I created and the characters who inhabit it. I've written a lot of different series at this point, what with the Half-Orcs, Shadowdance, the Paladins, and Breaking World. I've also steadily branched out beyond my world of Dezrel (the Seraphim Trilogy, and now recently the Keepers Trilogy). But the Half-Orcs has always been special. It's dear to me in a way none of the others are, because the characters themselves are closer to me than any that populate my other set of books are, and perhaps will be for the rest of my life.

If you'll permit me a moment to demonstrate, be it in a fairly grim manner.

Before I tell this story, let me assure you Alyssa is fine and healthy. Got that? No panicking, ok? But two years ago, my two-year-old daughter Alyssa snuck outside into the backyard. A plastic truck of hers was floating in the pool, and she tried to grab it. She fell in. We don't know how long. What I do know is my wife was

The King of the Fallen

in the kitchen, I heard her scream, and I ran from the living room to the backyard.

There I saw my baby girl floating face-down in the pool. I screamed. I jumped in and lifted her out of the water. What you read in this novel, in that memory of Harruq, at this point I don't know which is based on Cost of Betrayal, and which was my own life. Her eyes were open and glassy. Her lips were blue. She wasn't breathing. While my wife called 911, I performed mouth-to-mouth while standing knee-deep in water, all while convinced I was wasting my time. She wasn't breathing. She wasn't breathing. She wouldn't start breathing, not now, not ever. I still, to this day, remember my frantic pleading, to her, to God, to anyone listening, not to take my precious baby away. I could recite it word for word, if I wished, but I don't. Not even here. Never again.

While I sobbed and held Alyssa to my chest, quite literally a heartbeat after I decided to abandon continuing mouth-to-mouth, she took a breath.

As I said, she's fine now. Healthy, no permanent damage whatsoever (the same can't be said for the psyches of her parents, though…). Every single second of that incident is permanently burned into my memory. And readers, something sticks out. In that moment, that godawful horrendous span of a minute that is the worst of my entire life, I remember the first thought I had when I saw her floating in the pool.

Just like Aullienna.

I don't know how to explain how fucking ridiculous it is to think something like that, in a frozen moment of horror so awful it didn't even seem real. But Harruq *is* me. There's no separating that, not if I want to be honest with myself. Not with how raw and charged this whole series is, and how young I was at the time of writing those early Half-Orc novels. To say they're *real*, even if only to me, doesn't quite convey how personal and dear those stories and characters are. So as you finish this novel, I hope you understand that no decision was made carelessly or without emotion.

Younger me enjoyed killing characters with a vicious glee. That'll make the readers cry. That'll shock them and show how fearless I am! That ain't me, not anymore, and certainly not with this Half-Orc series that has grown so personal. Hell, one of the earliest stories I ever wrote was in high school, featuring Lathaar meeting Mira. If you go by that metric, I have known Lathaar for over eighteen years. Yet no matter how precious, how dear, I knew it was time to say goodbye to a lot of these characters, and I did it in ways that I hope honored them, or at the very least, broke a few hearts.

Rereading HO6 and HO7 years later had me asking questions. They are the questions some of the characters themselves voiced. Reasons for decisions, questions over the limitations of the gods, what the purpose of Karak, Ashhur, and Celestia even serve for Dezrel. Some I had seeded years and years ago, such as with the fall of the angels when Azariah proudly proclaims he will conquer Dezrel with Ashhur's grace not a day after setting foot upon the land. Some, though, particularly with Jessilynn, came unplanned. Unwilling. I have done my best to honor those as well, and let someone like Darius speak the needed truth when necessary.

So I guess now we reach the end, and the arrival of a storyline that's been lingering since...hell, 2015? What happened to Zusa/Alyssa/Haern's Kid is easily the most common question I get. I plan on answering that, in HO9. I make no promises when, not after dropping the ball so thoroughly between HO7 and HO8. I hope to write it soon, but that is all I feel confident in saying anymore. Soon. Eventually. I have one last novel in store. One last part of Dezrel that I need to reckon with, and it's the legacy of the Watcher.

That's the new title, by the way. The Legacy of the Watcher.

See you then, dear readers.

David Dalglish
August 3rd, 2020

Printed in Great Britain
by Amazon